Percy Hetherington Fitzgerald

The Life and Times of William IV.

Including a view of social life and manners during his reign. Vol. 2

Percy Hetherington Fitzgerald

The Life and Times of William IV.
Including a view of social life and manners during his reign. Vol. 2

ISBN/EAN: 9783337424275

Printed in Europe, USA, Canada, Australia, Japan

Cover: Foto ©Raphael Reischuk / pixelio.de

More available books at **www.hansebooks.com**

THE LIFE AND TIMES OF WILLIAM IV.

THE LIFE AND TIMES OF

WILLIAM IV.

INCLUDING A VIEW OF SOCIAL LIFE AND MANNERS DURING HIS REIGN.

By PERCY FITZGERALD, M.A., F.S.A.,

AUTHOR OF "THE LIFE OF GEORGE THE FOURTH,"
"THE LIFE OF GARRICK," "A NEW HISTORY OF THE ENGLISH STAGE,"
"KINGS AND QUEENS OF AN HOUR," ETC. ETC.

IN TWO VOLUMES.
VOL. II.

LONDON:
TINSLEY BROTHERS, 8, CATHERINE STREET, STRAND, W.C.
1884.

THE LIFE AND TIMES

OF

WILLIAM IV.

CHAPTER I.

Duɪɪɴɢ this interval it may be conceived that nothing
was omitted to work up the feelings of the populace, so
as to furnish support to the ministry in the struggle.
The populace had long been ripe for tumult and agitation under the instruction of proficient agitators of a
curiously coarse but vigorous type, conspicuous specimens of which were Mr. Cobbett and Mr. "Orator" Hunt.

To analyse the character of the lower *couches sociales*,
which were now germinating, would require a deeper
philosophy ; but one is struck by the greater earnestness
and violence which marked their conduct whenever a
political question was concerned. Whether this was
owing to the absence of efficient police control, the
difficulty of communication, or to the pressure of
political grievances it is hard to say ; but it at least
contrasts curiously with the quiet indifference or
moderation with which the same classes regard a question of Reform nowadays. Much of this violence was,
of course, owing to personal oppression and the injudicious tyranny of the officials, like Lord Sidmouth,

whose arbitrary arrests, use of informers, pillory, etc.,
excited deserved odium.

One of the humbler Radicals of the time, a well-
meaning, earnest fellow, who was sincerely devoted to
his party, has left us an interesting account of the mode
in which the hopeless cause, as it then appeared to be,
was followed. This was Samuel Bamford, a worthy
man in a poor struggling way, but whose honest faith
contrasted curiously with the flashy and selfish conduct
of certain of the leaders of the party. In a scarce little
book, this Bamford has left an interesting account of
his faith and trials. For in these days the cause was
to be fought at serious and certain risk of the dungeon
and long imprisonment—of, at least, street-fighting, or
of being ridden down by the soldiers—a contrast to the
present safe propagation of opinions of a still more
advanced kind. Bamford was a Methodist weaver in
Lancashire, and early joined one of the numerous provincial clubs for spreading and organising Radical opinions.
There was a desperation among many of their plans and
proceedings, which were clearly inspired by recollections
of the Revolution, and the bolder spirits felt that
without due intimidation and some deeds of violence it
was hopeless to think of making any impression. The
dangers incurred by persons living in remote and
solitary districts was really serious, and justified some,
at least, of the harsh severities of the Government.
Attending a meeting at the notorious "Crown and
Anchor," in 1816, Bamford sketches with a native
vigour the leading figures of his party.

"Henry Hunt was gentlemanly in his manner and
attire; six feet and better in height, and extremely well
formed. He was dressed in a blue lapelled coat, light
waistcoat and kerseys, and topped boots; his leg and foot

were about the firmest and neatest I ever saw. He wore his own hair ; it grew in moderate quantity, and a little gray. His features were regular, and there was a kind of youthful blandness about them which, in amicable discussion, gave his face a most agreeable expression. His lips were delicately thin, and receding ; but there was a dumb utterance about them, which in all the portraits I have seen of him was never truly copied. His eyes were blue or light gray—not very clear, nor quick, but rather heavy ; except, as I afterwards had opportunities for observing, when he was excited in speaking, at which times they seemed to distend and protrude ; and if he worked himself furious, as he sometimes would, they became blood-streaked, and almost started from their sockets. Then it was that the expression of his lips was to be observed—the kind smile was exchanged for the curl of scorn, or the curse of indignation. His voice was bellowing ; his face swollen and flushed ; his griped hand beat as if it were to pulverize ; and his whole manner gave token of a painful energy, struggling for utterance."

Thus Henry Brougham appeared to him : " I soon understood that he had let go the Ministry, and now unaccountably, as it seemed to me, had made a dead set at the Reformers. Oh ! how he did scowl towards us— contemn and disparage our best actions, and wound our dearest feelings ! Now stealing near our hearts with words of wonderful power, flashing with bright wit and happy thought ; anon, like a reckless wizard changing pleasant sunbeams into clouds, ' rough with black winds and storms,' and vivid with the cruellest shafts. Then was he listened to as if not a pulse moved—then was he applauded to the very welkin. And he stood in the pride of his power, his foes before him subdued but spared—his friends derided and disclaimed—and his former principles sacrificed to 'low ambition,' and the vanity of such a display as this."

Sir Francis Burdett was another of the popular leaders, though he later fell away from the party in disgust.

"He came to us in a loose gray vest coat, which reached far towards his ankles. He had not a cravat on his neck; his feet were in slippers; and a pair of wide cotton stockings hung in wrinkles on his long spare legs, which he kept alternately throwing across his knees, and rubbing down with his hands, as if he suffered, or recently had, some pain in those limbs. He was a fine-looking man on the whole, of lofty stature, with a proud but not forbidding carriage of the head. His manner was dignified and civilly familiar; submitting to, rather than seeking conversation with men of our class. He, however, discussed with us some points of the intended Bill for Reform, candidly and freely; and concluded with promising to support universal suffrage, though he was not sanguine of much co-operation in the House. Under these circumstances we left Sir Francis; approving of much that we found in and about him, and excusing much of what we could not approve. He was one of our idols, and we were loath to give him up.

"Still I could not help my thoughts from reverting to the simple and homely welcome we received at Lord Cochrane's, and contrasting it with the kind of dreary stateliness of this great mansion and its rich owner. At the former place we had a brief refection, bestowed with a grace which captivated our respect; and no health was ever drunk with more sincere goodwill than was Lord Cochrane's; the little dark-haired and bright-eyed lady seemed to know it, and to be delighted that it was so. But here scarcely a servant appeared, and nothing in the shape of refreshment was seen, a lesson surely for those who would cultivate the affections of the 'many headed.'

"These plain-speaking and plain-dealing men 'meant business,' as it is called, and were prepared to fight for their opinions." Thus in March, 1816, we hear of "the blanketers'" meeting, where two hundred women, each armed with a stout cudgel and a blanket strapped on her back, seriously prepared to march on London. This was a ludicrous failure. Then followed the well-known "Peterloo Massacre," so nicknamed because it was held at Peter Street. Bamford, whose whole heart was in the cause, describes bitterly the behaviour of the "ornamental" Radicals of the upper classes— Sir Charles Wolseley and others, as though he resented not being treated on a footing of equality. Thus with Peter Finnerty he presented himself at the baronet's castle.

"I went over to the hall, and found Finnerty quite comfortably domiciled. Lady Wolseley was in the straw upstairs, so that Sir Charles had much of his own way below. Friend Finnerty, now that he had the run of a splendid suite of apartments, attendance of servants, and all hospitalities, was also somewhat changed in his manner. His place was in the parlour with Sir Charles; mine in the housekeeper's room, with the occasional company of that amiable, respectable, and well-informed lady. Finnerty had become quite *condescending*, for which I could not prevail on myself to feel thankful. Sir Charles was always kind and affable, without pretension; but still I could not but feel that in his house I was only a very humble guest. I had read how 'an Ayrshire ploughman' had once been deemed good company for a Scottish duchess; but I found that the barriers of English rank were not to be moved by 'a Lancashire weaver,' though he could say, 'I also am a poet,' and, quite as much as the Scottish bard, a patriot also. I lodged at the inn ; and often on mornings would I stroll out solitarily to look at the deer on the moorlands. Those majestic and beautiful animals would toss their proud antlers—gaze a moment in surprise, as if they also knew I was a stranger.

"At length the glad morning came, when an end was to be put to this. I was to go with Finnerty to London, with a gig and horse which Charles Pearson had left at Stafford, I think, on his way down to Lancashire. Sir Charles made me a present of two pounds ; Finnerty took the whip, and, bidding good morn to our worthy host, we drove slowly from Wolseley Hall."

The proceedings at his trial, for his share in the insurrection at Peterloo, are still more instructive. There "Orator" Hunt was to be the chief performer, and this patriot required his follower to sacrifice his interest to his theatrical glories.

"It became apparent towards the noon of Monday, the fourth day of the trial, that the prosecutors were about to close their case, and that the defence must be commenced on the afternoon of that day. Whilst we were talking of the matter, Hunt said :

"'Bamford, you will be called on to address the Court the first of all the defendants.'

"I said I thought that scarcely probable, as we should most likely be called in the order in which our names stood in the indictment. Hunt said he knew that was contemplated by the opposing counsel, and particularly by Mr. Scarlet, who wanted to bring him out in the evening when he was exhausted, the Court wearied, and the public satiated and listless. But, with an oath, he said he was not to be taken aback that way; he was too old a bird to be caught by such a manœuvre.

"'Now, Bamford, by ——,' he said, 'I'll tell you what you must do if called this afternoon.'

"'Well, what should I do?' I inquired.

"'You must talk against time.'

"'Talk against time—what's that?'

"'You must keep possession of the Court an hour and a half,' he said. 'You must talk to put on time, in order to prevent them from calling on me, under any circumstances, to-night. I know well that is what Scarlett is aiming at, and we must play our game so as to put it beyond his power.'

"'But I am not prepared with matter for an hour and a half's speech. I should break down if I attempted it.'

"'Don't mind that—don't mind anything—only keep on.'

"'I should make myself look like a fool; and they would be laughing at me, and stopping me.'

"'Pshaw! and suppose they did, you could listen, and, when they had done, begin again.'

"'But I should not know what to say.'

"'Say! say anything—the d——est nonsense in the world. Never mind what you say, only keep on until they cannot call me to-day.'

"Something like a glimmer of the naked truth flashed across my reluctant mind, and I replied:

"'No, Mr. Hunt, I will not do as you desire; I will not exhibit myself before this Court as a fool. I will speak as long as I can speak to the purpose, and with common sense. I would speak until dark, if that would serve you—and I was prepared for the task; but I am not, and I won't make myself ridiculous.'

" 'Very well,' said Hunt, and looked another way, quite cool and distant."

Bamford, after many trials and imprisonments, at last had his eyes opened to the little profit he was making out of the cause, and retired to his village, to devote himself to the support of his family, leaving the care of the nation to persons with more leisure and fortune, though not of more sincerity.

The life and career of his two conspicuous leaders— Henry Hunt " the orator," and William Cobbett—offers nothing so agreeable as that of the simple Lancashire mechanic. The whole course of Hunt's life was one of blatant selfishness and coarse violence. Inheriting a handsome fortune, he wasted it in extravagance, while he abandoned an amiable and interesting wife, whom he had married in defiance of his father's wishes, and rather scandalised his admirers by his open adoption of another companion. Cobbett will ever command admiration for his vigorous English, his masterly powers of controversy, and, strange to say, his charming descriptive powers of scenery and the beauties of nature. But his uncontrolled violence and vindictive spirit embroiled him with everyone with whom he worked. Orator Hunt and he soon quarrelled, owing to the workings of jealousy. These men had nothing of the Washington spirit and of pure love of country; and it is remarkable into what utter insignificance they fell when the great end was gained, and more genuine patriots came upon the scene.

The character of Hunt is a disagreeable one, and he seems to have been a thoroughly selfish, extravagant man, fond of pleasure and indulgence, dissipation and licentiousness. Cobbett, long after, attracted Macaulay's attention as a good subject for literary treatment.

The result of the elections was truly disastrous to the Tories. Old occupants of safe seats and rotten boroughs were all swept away as if by a torrent. "The Duke of Newcastle lost his; two Reformers are returned for Newark; and in both Bassetlaw and the county of Notts at large, His Grace, who returned two members last autumn, now returns no more. The Duke of Beaufort's own brother, and his eldest son, justly popular noblemen, and highly distinguished in the career of arms, are both flung out, because they stand against Reform. Their kinsman of Rutland loses both his county seats, and his relative loses both his also at Grantham.

"The Percy of Northumberland is signally overthrown by the Prime Minister's son, who, last autumn, had not ventured into the field; and, above all, the Lowther influence was destroyed for ever."

It is curious to read how the news of these things affected the veteran Lord Grenville.

"How can I talk or think," he wrote, "of anything but the fearful news I this morning receive of the dissolution? I most deeply pity the poor King, to whom, if I myself had the fearful duty of advising him (God be thanked that I had not!), I really do not see what other course I could have suggested. It would have been quite as impossible for Peel as for the present men to carry on any Government in such a body. Will this step bring together a better, either now or hereafter, when they shall have passed, or attempted again without success to pass, their Reform Bill?*

* It was in the discussion on the Reform Bill that the famous Mrs. Partington and her mop made their first appearance, introduced by the facetious Rev. Sidney Smith. "In the midst of this sublime and terrible storm, Dame Partington, who lived upon the beach, was

" I know not, and my mind and body are no longer strong enough to look calmly at such dangers as now threaten us on every side.

" God bless and preserve you and yours ! "

These were surely the tremors and apprehensions of old age. Nor was the Duke of Wellington less absurd in his gruesome forebodings.

" It appears true," he wrote, " that we are in a bad way. I don't believe that the King of England has taken a step so fatal to his monarchy since the day that Charles I. passed the Act to deprive himself of the power of proroguing or dissolving the Long Parliament, as King William IV. did on the 22nd of April last. My mind is travelling in the same direction as yours. We must make a noise in the House of Lords, I believe ! I don't think that we shall be able to do more, as I understand that the Government are about to create numerous peers. They say as many as thirty or forty ; and I should not be surprised at this or any other act after what I have seen. The dismay of all reasonable men upon what is going on is beyond description. It is impossible that there should not be a reaction. I am only afraid that it will not be in time or sufficiently strong to influence the decision of Parliament."

The dissolution having taken place, the usual reaction occurred in His Majesty's feelings. He was first of all deeply offended by the behaviour of the Lord Mayor, and with the illuminations in honour of the dissolution, and positively declined to visit the City as he had

seen at the door of her house with mop and pattens, trundling her mop, squeezing out the sea water, and vigorously pushing away the Atlantic Ocean. The Atlantic was roused. Mrs. Partington's spirit was up ; but I need not tell you that the conflict was unequal. The Atlantic Ocean beat Mrs. Partington."

intended. Sir H. Taylor had to write privately to the minister : "Independently of other reasons which certainly have influenced the King to decline the visit to the Lord Mayor, His Majesty is by no means well. This is the season at which his health is in general more or less affected ; and he is suffering from gouty symptoms, which affect his whole frame and his nerves and spirits, which is in almost all cases the effect of the disorder when it does not fairly show itself. Mr. Davis also tells me, that there is a little return of the swelling in the neck, but he attaches no consequence to it ; still, all this together gives to him an appearance of weakness and helplessness and of dejection, which renders it desirable that he should not go to any public show if it can possibly be avoided ; indeed it is with great difficulty that he gets in and out of the carriage, and he requires considerable assistance. His Majesty will probably, on the same account, give up the intention of going to Portsmouth. I shall be obliged to your lordship not to answer this letter, or notice it in any shape."

The rejection of the Bill was attended by startling excesses on the part of the mob ; attacks on obnoxious opponents of the Bill and the Houses being now common. Such things, however much deprecated by a Government in the position of Lord Grey's, are, perhaps, viewed with a secret satisfaction as an additional "motor" to the cause ; and in our day it has been matter of accusation against a popular Ministry, that it actually permitted disorders in order to supply leverage for a Bill quite as obnoxious to the Upper House as was the Reform Bill of 1832.

To the day of the Duke of Wellington's death one of the most puzzling sights in London for the country

visitor was the spectacle of the "mailed" windows at
Apsley House, the iron blinds facing Piccadilly drawn
down and never raised. This inflexible custom was
only abolished by his successor, the present Duke, who
admitted daylight to the principal chambers of the
mansion. This, as is well known, was in consequence
of the behaviour of the London mob.*

"He had witnessed," said a member in the House
of Commons, "a procession that day in Piccadilly, in
which he had seen the coach of a member of that
House. It was preceded by a standard-bearer with a
white flag, on which were inscribed the words, 'The
King, Commons, and People.' He followed the procession along Piccadilly, and wished to go to the Duke of
Wellington's, but he was not then able to effect that

---

* One of his most characteristic letters, impossible to read without
a smile from its pleasantly sarcastic tone, is his answer to a gentleman
who made a claim for protecting him in a crowd, and who had been
robbed of his seals.

"London, Feb., 1821.

"The Duke of Wellington recollects perfectly having met a
gentleman in the crowd at the door of Drury Lane Theatre on the
6th instant, who, having recognised the Duke, mentioned his name,
turned about, and walked before him through the crowd to the door
of the house. This service, if it can be so called, was purely voluntary on the part of this gentleman. The Duke is as well able as any
other man to make his way through a crowd, even if there existed
any disposition to impede his progress, which did not appear, and
therefore the assistance of this gentleman was not necessary; and,
moreover, the Duke's footman attended him.

"In stating this, however, the Duke does not deny that he considered this gentleman's conduct as very polite towards him; and he
was flattered by it, and returned his thanks for it.

"It appears that this gentleman is Mr. ——, who states he lost
his seals, not in returning through the crowd after having walked
before the Duke, but in returning through the crowd some time afterwards, after having walked through it to the door of the theatre before

purpose. When he got near the house of the Duke of Wellington he saw a number of respectable persons, and very well dressed, walking four and four, with ribands tied round their arms; he saw those people leave the main body, while those who followed them rushed into the gate. Those well-dressed persons made room for the individuals whom they headed, and who immediately began breaking the windows."

"I was," says Mr. Raikes, "at a ball given by him at Apsley House to King William IV. and his Queen, when the mob were very unruly and indecent in their conduct at the gate; and on the following days they proceeded to such excesses, that they broke the windows of Apsley House, and did much injury to his property. It was then that he caused to be put up those iron blinds to his windows, which remain to this day as a record of the people's ingratitude. Some time afterwards, when he had regained all his popularity, and began to enjoy that great and high reputation which he

Lord Palmerston; and he desires to have compensation from the Duke for this loss.

"Upon this statement, and in order to avoid making this case a precedent for others of the same kind, the Duke, however flattered by Mr. ——'s politeness, must positively deny that he has any claim upon him for compensation for his loss. The Duke does not consider that Mr. —— rendered him any service whatever, and on the ground of service he must refuse to give him compensation for his loss, even if it had occurred in returning from the door of the theatre after having walked to it before the Duke.

"But as Mr. —— may be a gentleman in circumstances not able to bear the expense of such a loss, and as the Duke certainly considered his conduct towards him as very polite, the Duke feels no objection to assist him to replace the loss he has sustained; at the same time taking the liberty to recommend to Mr. —— in future to omit to render these acts of unsolicited and unnecessary politeness unless he should be in a situation to bear the probable or possible consequences."

now, it is to be hoped, will carry to the grave, he
was riding up Constitution Hill, in the park, followed
by an immense mob, who were cheering him in every
direction ; he heard it all with the most stoical indifference, never putting his horse out of a walk, or
seeming to regard them, till he leisurely arrived at
Apsley House, when he stopped at the gate, turned
round to the rabble, and then pointing with his finger
to the iron blinds which still closed the windows, he
made them a sarcastic bow, and entered the court
without saying a word.

" That night the Queen went to the Ancient Concert,
and on her return the mob surrounded the carriage; she
had no guards, and the footmen were obliged to beat
the people off with their canes to prevent their thrust-
ing their heads into the coach. She was frightened and
the King very much annoyed. He heard the noise and
tumult, and paced backwards and forwards in his room
waiting for her return. When she came back Lord
Howe, her chamberlain, as usual preceded her, when
the King said, ' How is the Queen ?' and went down
to meet her. Howe, who is an eager anti-Reformer, said,
' Very much frightened, sir,' and made the worst of it.
She was in fact terrified, and as she detests the whole of
these proceedings, the more distressed and disgusted.
The King was very angry, and immediately declared
he would not go to the City at all."

We also find the King forwarding marked passages in
seditious newspapers, which contain a direct recommendation to the Poles, individually and collectively, to *assas-
sinate* the Emperor of Russia. He, however, gratified
himself by presenting to the 2nd Life Guards, on May 6th,
the handsome silver kettle-drums, which excited the
admiration of the crowd on military festivals.

Lord Grey, for political reasons, pressed that the visit to the City should take place. He heard that "the news had excited the greatest dismay." The Lord Mayor felt himself peculiarly aggrieved, and was preparing a manifesto. "It is my duty not to conceal from the King what is passing. The truth is that, notwithstanding all that can be said to the contrary, the *conduct of persons supposed to be in His Majesty's favour, like that of* —— *at* ——, *the known opinion of persons composing Her Majesty's household,* ——, *and the declared hostility of the Princesses,* have produced suspicions which every endeavour is used to propagate, that the King is in reality adverse to the measure of Reform." This was speaking out very boldly.

At this time this interesting character was recovering from an attack of sickness, and contemplating the certain destruction of his country; and must have been surprised at a well-meant but awkward appeal made to him by the obstreperous Dr. Philpotts, Bishop of Exeter. This prelate, after reminding him of all the glory he had enjoyed, began a sort of homily : "Need I say that this is nothing if it makes its possessor forget how utterly helpless and worthless he is in the sight of God." With this frank consideration the Duke was familiar; but he might win a greater grace "by casting down all high imaginations, and humbling yourself," etc. Then he beseeched him to do honour to God and men by *regularly attending his public service,* "by showing the world that you *glory* in being the servant of God, by setting an example." The Duke's reply is characteristic and in a vein of pleasant irony. After assuring the Bishop that his letter was highly creditable to him, he first said he had been altogether misled by newspaper reports as to his sickness—as though it had not been of such a serious nature as to invite spiritual aid *—"but that which I am particularly anxious to remove from your mind is the impression that I am a person without any sense of religion. I don't make much show or boast upon any subject. Then in private life I have been accused of every vice and enormity; and when those who live with me testify that such charges are groundless, then the charge is brought, ' Oh, he is a man without religion !' I am not a Bible Society man. I make no ostentatious display of charity or other Christian virtues."

He then explained that he was deaf, and could not hear sermons; but wherever his example was useful, as at Walmer, he always went to church.

The Bishop replied in an unctuous strain, thanking the Duke for bearing with his intrusion. He never believed those stories of the "*tales of libertinism,*" which a licentious press," etc. ; but still, being fearful "of a too great complacency in his great services," he could not but feel an apprehension of his being betrayed into a too great confidence in your own state before God. Should he not urge reliance on the Saviour, "frequent heart-searchings," askings for grace ? Mr. Pitt owned he had too long neglected prayer. I am sure I need not apply the lesson.

One of the plotters who were thus working to compass the destruction of the Bill was the Duke of Cumberland, who now reappears, though he had not regained the favour of the King. He was getting ready to give the measure a proper reception in the House of Lords.

---

* As in his story of the reprieved convict, who politely restored the Bible to the chaplain, saying he hoped he'd never have occasion to use it again. '

One of his schemes seems to have been to work on His Majesty by getting Tory Peers to ask an audience. This device he tried during the struggle against emancipation, and with some success. Some of these schemes were opened to the Duke of Wellington, and it was suggested that there should be a *rapprochement* between him and H.R.H. In a characteristic and contemptuous letter he seemed to put the proposal aside :

"The more I consider of the Bill, the more convinced I am of its disastrous consequences to the country ; but it is not easy to defeat it. I have never offended the D. of Cumberland. After the settlement of the R. C. question, H.R.H. did me the honour of noticing me, and of speaking to me more than once. H.R.H. afterwards, that is to say, from the 12th August, 1829, thought proper to discontinue to do me that honour. When H.R.H. or any of the royal family notices me, I consider that an honour is done me ; I regret much when that honour is withheld from me ; but I have done nothing to deserve the deprival of it. On the contrary, I believe that it is known to H.R.H. that I did my duty by him in a case in which he was personally interested. I never have failed, nor ever will fail, in respect for His Royal Highness or his family, and I must wait with patience till the moment will arrive when H.R.H. will think proper to notice me."

This was accordingly shown to the Duke of Cumberland, who, in a letter equally scornful, exhibited his puerile temper in this awkward controversy.

THE DUKE OF CUMBERLAND TO THE DUKE OF BUCKINGHAM.

"St. James's Palace, April 8, 1831.

"My DEAR DUKE,

"I have just received your Grace's letter of yesterday's date, for which I beg your acceptance of my

best thanks, as well as for the extract of the Duke of
Wellington's letter, upon which I cannot refrain from
stating that when his Grace says 'that I had spoken to
him more than once after the settlement of the R. C.
question, and that it was only since the 12th of
August, 1829, that I had ceased doing so,' his Grace's
recollection and mine do not concur.   According to my
recollection, since a very long, and I may say very unpleasant conversation that I had with the Duke at
Windsor, the latter part of February, 1829, I have not
had any conversation with him ; and according to that
recollection have not exchanged a word with his Grace
since once in the Park when he met with an accident at
the review.

"What the Duke can mean by saying 'that I knew
he did his duty in a case in which I was personally
interested,' I am really at a loss to make out, not knowing what circumstance he can allude to, unless it be
respecting a diabolical threat of murder by a person
named *Ash ;* with regard to which I considered his
Grace as acting as H.M. Minister.   I merely make these
remarks, however, to your Grace in order that my conduct
may not appear to you capricious or inconsistent.

"However, now I am sure I am, under present circumstances, the last person to touch upon these past
events, and as the Duke of W. called on me, I thought
it right immediately in return to call on him at Apsley
House, and shall feel no difficulty in conversing with
him whenever I may meet him.   I certainly lament
very much having been from home when he called at
St. James's ; and though I called on him the next day
at twelve o'clock, I was told he had left town that
morning.   It appears to me that, in times such as these,
it is necessary for every well-wisher to his country, who

is attached to the monarchy and the constitution, to meet and resist the revolutionary Bill now pending in Parliament; which, if carried, must, according to my humble opinion, annihilate all our institutions both in Church and State, and, sooner or later, lead to the repeal of the Union.

" Ministers, I understand, boldly affirm they will carry the Bill by a majority of twenty-five to thirty; but I believe this is a mere *ruse de guerre*, for I am told of no diminution in our ranks by those who I believe are pretty well informed.

" I am ashamed at the length of my letter; but I felt it necessary, after the confidential manner in which your Grace has entrusted me with the D. of W.'s reply, to say what I have done.

" When you return to town I hope to see you.

" Believe me, my Lord Duke,

" Yours very sincerely,

" ERNEST."

It certainly seems hard that the King should have been harassed in this fashion. It was evidence of the aggressive character of the new Radicalism that so moderate a character as Lord Grey should not have been content with the King's acceptance of his programme, but that he must be forced to take active steps in support of it.

Lord Brougham tells us that his ill-humour was increased by the successes of the Reform party at the elections, by the strength the minority had gained, which, he adds, is never a very acceptable thing to a sovereign. The King discharged his feelings by a homily to Lord Grey, in which, among other curious passages, will be found the following:

" His Majesty admits that the expressions of loyalty and attachment to his person have been very general during the late elections ; but he cannot help ascribing these effusions of loyalty to the gratification of popular clamour by his sanction of a popular measure, rather than to any feeling upon which much reliance could be placed ; and he cannot but apprehend that, if he had not yielded to this popular clamour, the most merito-rious discharge of his duty, in other respects, would not have secured him from the fate of Sir Robert Wilson and Mr. Hunt. This may appear to Earl Grey a strong expression of the King's opinion of popular feeling and favour; but it will also serve to show the degree of value which he is disposed to attach to it *in these times.*"

He noticed with alarm, "in the course of the elections and the popular demonstrations, the seeds of revolution, a disposition generally hostile to the aristocracy of the country, a strong inclination to introduce a form of government purely democratical, and other symptoms.

" It is impossible that His Majesty should not have noticed with regret that there has, upon this occasion, been in many instances no real freedom of election ; that violence and intimidation have had the effect of excluding it, that pledges have been called for and given by the candidates for popular favour to an extent which may be productive of extreme inconvenience to the Government hereafter, as those pledges have not been confined to the measure of Reform. The King thoroughly agrees with Earl Grey in his view of the extreme importance of carrying through this measure of Reform, and in deprecating the endeavours of the opposers of the measure to place the House of Lords in opposition to the House of Commons and to the strong opinion of the public."

He concluded with a sort of naval metaphor, highly characteristic of the old seaman : " His Majesty fears that, in the anxiety to collect ample materials for the repair and amendment of the foundation of the building, some timbers may have been introduced and substituted for others of sounder quality, which may prove defective at the core, and may, with the active aid of that dry rot, the press, endanger the safety of other essential parts of the fabric."

In another appeal, dated May 28, he says : " He is grieved to find that the House of Lords will not accept the Bill—that he dreaded a collision. He wished," he said, " not to detach himself from the great badge of the aristocracy, and therefore urged his favourite modification." Lord Grey, in reply, assured him " that they meant to use the interest for removing defects and obviating objections, so far as it could be done. But he declared frankly that no alterations that would satisfy enemies could be allowed. The King explained that he did not mean anything that would touch the principles of the Bill. The persons he thus hoped might be conciliated by such fair concessions were not irreconcilable opponents—were the moderate—that portion who might be disposed to sacrifice their objections so as to avoid a collision between the Houses."

All these letters were laid before the Cabinet. A fortnight later Lord Grey renewed his complaints of influences working against him.

" I learnt with great regret that Lord —— as well as Lord —— are decidedly against the Government. I had hoped that, with respect to the former at least, it might have been otherwise. I feel that it would be

improper for me to urge His Majesty more on this head
than I have already done, but I must also feel the
greatest regret in contemplating the embarrassments
which the conduct of these persons may produce, not
only to the Ministers, but to the King himself. In
truth the Government is, at this moment, deprived of a
great part of the support which it ought to command,
or rather finds a considerable portion of what may be
considered as its natural strength turned against it."

This was certainly plain speaking, and seemed to
pass the limits of due respect. The King wrote a
dignified and not ineffective defence.

" The King cannot help noticing these remarks, as
they would seem to imply that the Government is
exposed to difficulty, is deprived of much of the support
it ought to receive, and may be placed under serious
embarrassment in consequence of His Majesty's con-
tinuing to admit to his private circles individuals with
whom, or their families, he has been, during great part
of his life, on habits of friendship and the most familiar
intercourse, though never politically connected with
them, His Majesty having ever avoided to attach himself
exclusively to any party, or to yield to the influence of
political opinion or feeling in the selection of his friends
and associates. The King is perfectly sensible of the
necessity of giving a positive and unequivocal support
to his Government, and he had flattered himself that
the whole of his conduct had been calculated to satisfy
his Government and the country, that it had been fairly
and honestly directed towards the establishment and
the maintenance of this principle. He had not hesitated
to discard from his household any individual, whether
holding a superior or an inferior situation, who, being a
member of either House, had withheld or stated his

intention of withholding his support from the Government upon the question of Reform."

Lord Grey felt he owed an apology for "what he wrote with too much haste and freedom." He also wrote privately to the secretary.

"The truth is, that a most unfair use is made of His Majesty's kindness to those who, either by themselves or their connexions, hold places in the Court; and it was under the impression of the effect produced by this that I wrote perhaps too hastily and unguardedly. But having said what I have now said in the enclosed letter, I shall never revert to the subject."

Lord Howe, the Queen's Chamberlain, was a young nobleman, then thirty-four years old, who was said to nourish a romantic attachment to his royal mistress. He took up the side of the Court with extraordinary vehemence and some indiscretion. But it was certainly irritating to Lord Grey to find the enemies of their Bill using the King's influence—which the King himself did not use—to plot against his ministers. An excited letter of Lord Howe's, gives us a glimpse of what was going on in this "back-stairs" direction, the beginning, as the reader will see later, of a long train of plots and intrigues.

LORD HOWE TO THE DUKE OF WELLINGTON.

"It was not quite fair in me to write so chatty as I did; but really to find my sovereign weeping with me over the state of affairs, and lamenting the wonderful imprudence of his confidential servants, and actually advising his private friend to consult the political enemy of his Ministers, was so new a situation for a quiet country gentleman, that I hardly knew what I did from shame and vexation at the deplorable state in which I saw my beloved master, whose kindness and liberality are beyond all praise. Would to God I could say as much for his morals.

"I certainly was very angry when I went to him. I said, here are circumstances only known to yourself, Taylor, and myself, and yet published in a few hours. Lord Grey comes and asks if the King had written to me on my resigning. Sir H. T. said he had seen this in the papers. It *must* open the King's eyes to the firm purpose of Ministers to *force* from him every soul who does not agree with him. But nothing shall now induce me to resign. I have the King's leave to vote as I like. My Lord Brougham may yet find me a thorn in his side, more annoying than he is now aware of."

CHAPTER II.

During the interval, before the question was again brought on, the grave business of the Coronation engrossed attention. The Duke of Cumberland began to put questions on the matter, making the characteristic objection that His Majesty had not yet taken the oath to maintain a Protestant religion. The King seems to have thought of doing without the old-fashioned ceremony, and with much good sense discussed this matter, urging "the useless and ill-timed expense attending such a public ceremony and exhibition; next, the excitement and agitation which must attend and arise from that ceremony, at a period when it is so desirable to avoid all that can promote popular effervescence. It has occurred to His Majesty that he might take the prescribed oath in the House of Lords before the Lords and Commons assembled, and that this might satisfy all legal and conscientious scruples."

It was expected to take place by September, and Mr. Greville went to Windsor to settle with the Queen what sort of a crown she would wear. The scene shows in what a thoroughly *bourgeois* spirit the royal pair regarded the business. "I was ushered into the

King's presence, who was sitting at a red table in the
sitting-room of George IV., looking over the flower-
garden. He sent for the Queen. She looked at the
drawings, meant apparently to be civil to me in her
ungracious way, and said she would have none of our
crowns, that she did not like to wear a hired crown, and
asked me if I thought it was right that she should. I
said, 'Madam, I can only say that the late King wore
one at his coronation.' However she said, 'I do not
like it, and I have got jewels enough, so I will have
them made up myself.' The King said to me, 'Very
well; then *you* will have to pay for the setting.' 'Oh,
no,' she said; 'I shall pay for it all myself.' The King
looked well, but seemed infirm."

It was indeed extraordinary to contrast this homely
view with the enthusiastic magnificence of the late King.
£240,000 represented his outlay on the gorgeous ceremony, while on this occasion the Council, by laborious
economy, reduced the estimate to something under
£30,000.

As the prospects of the Bill became more certain
the vaticinations became gloomy. Again, it will be noted,
however, in every possible way the unhappy King was
worked upon by those who felt they were powerless
themselves.

"We hear," wrote the Duke of Wellington to the
Duke of Buckingham on July 22nd, 1831, "every day
of Peers to be created, and I confess, that I concur with
you in thinking that Lord Grey will stick at nothing.
There can scarcely be a question about the King, considering what he has done by *dissolution*.

"I asked the question about the coronation, because
I really thought that it was not fit that the second

summer should be allowed to elapse without this ceremony, without any cause whatever for the delay : considering the nature of the obligations imposed upon the
King by the oath, and considering that H.M. had crowned
himself on the 22nd of April, the day of the dissolution
of Parliament.

"The coronation will afford a pretence for creating
some Peers. But it is a pretence only. They will
be created for the purpose of the destruction of the
monarchy.

"In respect to attendance, I have to observe that
the Peers each of them take a very important oath in
the ceremonial in the Church. In conversation with the
King, I urged the importance to him of this oath ; and
I would not absent myself. I don't think that you would
like to be absent either."

In the last reign it was found a useful topic to press
on the King *his* coronation oath, but in this jaundiced
effusion His Majesty is pressed with the coronation
oath of the Peers. A week later he wrote in stronger
terms :

"The King has brought upon himself the existing
state of things by the dissolution of Parliament. He
says that nobody is disposed to make an effort to extricate
him.

"Did he listen to the advice given to him not to
dissolve his Parliament ? Did he believe those who told
him that the circumstances which had broken up the
former Government no longer existed on the 21st of
April ? Did he then make an effort, or manifest a wish
to make an effort, to extricate himself ?

"How do we stand now ? The King and his
Ministers, and a settled majority of the House of Com-

mons, allied with the mob, the Radicals, the Dissenters
of all persuasions, against the gentlemen of property of
the country, the Church, and all the establishments,
religious, commercial, banking, political, etc. etc.
If the King, who says that nobody will extricate
him, was to quarrel with Lord Grey to-morrow about
coronation robes or any other such material point in
discussion, and to wish to change his Ministry, the
monarchy might be overturned. I feel that we have
done a great deal to open the eyes of the country. We
may and we shall do more. But we must proceed with
caution and circumspection ; and be prepared, and prepare the public mind, for events which must occur,
rather than prematurely create them.

"I cannot advise you to come to town. Indeed, I
would go out of town myself if I was not afraid that my
absence might lead to a belief that I gave up the question of Reform as lost."

The 8th of September was the day of the great
solemnity. On that morning labourers in scarlet
jackets and white trousers were actively employed in
completing the arrangements. Some forty private
gentlemen acted as pages of the Earl Marshal, attired
in a costume, devised for the occasion, of blue frock
coats, white breeches and stockings, a crimson silk sash,
and a small ill-shaped hat with a black ostrich feather.
Each was provided with a gilt staff, bearing the arms of
the Earl Marshal, and his duty was to conduct persons
provided with tickets to their proper seats.

Shortly after five o'clock in the morning a royal
salute was fired, which was taken as a signal for everyone interested in the proceedings of the day to be on the
move. Company soon began to arrive at the ancient
minster, the different doors of which were appropriated

to different classes of visitors. At six the household troops arrived in St. James's Park, and were distributed along the thoroughfares through which the procession was to pass. The members of the House of Commons —three-fourths of whom were in military uniform, and a few in Highland costumes—took their accustomed route by Parliament Street; but having arrived at the door of Westminster Hall, found a covered platform raised for their accommodation across to Poets' Corner.

The equipages produced for the occasion added greatly to the splendour of the preliminary portion of the pageant—the Lord Chancellor rivalling the Lord Mayor in this display—and the Austrian Ambassador, Prince Esterhazy, excelling both. Many having to make a long round before they could fall into line, formed a source of attraction to the thousands of spectators of a humbler class that filled the streets from every available point of view.

The usual processions, etc., and precedents were followed; but the effect was poor, compared with the grand Exhibition of the late King. It was all over by three o'clock. No banquet in Westminster Hall followed—suppressed from a taste for economy.

"The Queen," says Lord Macaulay, "behaved admirably, with wonderful grace and dignity; the King very awkwardly. The Duke of Devonshire looked as if he came to be crowned instead of his master. I never saw so princely a manner and air. The Chancellor looked like Mephistopheles behind Margaret in the church. The ceremony was much too long, and some parts of it were carelessly performed. The Archbishop mumbled. The Bishop of London preached, well enough indeed, but not so effectively as the occasion required; and, above all, the bearing of the King made the foolish parts of the ritual appear monstrously ridiculous, and deprived many of the better parts of their proper effect. Persons who were at a distance perhaps did not feel this ; but I was near enough to see every turn of his finger and every glance of his eye. The moment of the crowning was extremely fine.*

There were two circumstances, however, which attracted public attention. The first, the absence of the Duchess of Kent and the young Princess Victoria, the excuse being indisposition. The other was the extraordinary creation of peers, no less than twenty-two ministerialists being added to the House of Lords ; while twenty-eight baronetcies and as many knighthoods were bestowed.

The debate on the second reading of the Reform Bill was distinguished by a great speech from Lord Brougham, five hours long, of which his colleague gives this malignant sketch :

" Without a note to refer to he went through all the speeches of his opponents delivered during the five nights' debate, analysing them successively, and, *with a little aid from perversion*, giving them all *a seemingly* triumphant answer. The peroration was partly inspired by draughts of mulled port, imbibed by him very

* The Royal plate made a splendid show at the Coronation banquet. It is now stated, according to inventory made on the departure of Her Majesty for Italy, to be of the value of £1,800,000. It includes a gold service, ordered by George IV., which will dine one hundred and forty persons, and one of the finest wine-coolers in the world, added to the collection by the same monarch ; a shield formed of snuff-boxes, worth £9000, and thirty dozen plates, worth £10,000. There are also a variety of pieces brought from abroad and India. The latter include a peacock of precious stones of finest description, worth £30,000, and Tippoo's footstool. The extravagance of the last Coronation may be conceived from the fact that £16,000 was charged for the *hire* of jewels for the Crown.

copiously towards the conclusion of the four hours
during which he was on his legs or on his knees :

"'Therefore I pray and I exhort you not to reject
this measure. By all you hold most dear—by all the
ties that bind every one of us to our common order and
our common country, I solemnly adjure you—I warn
you—I implore you—yea, on my bended knees (*he
kneels*) I supplicate you—reject not this Bill !'

"He continued for some time as if in prayer; but
his friends, alarmed for him lest he should be suffering
from the effects of the mulled port, picked him up and
placed him safely on the woolsack.

"Like Burke's famous dagger scene in the House of
Commons, this prostration was a failure. So unsuited
was it to the spectators and to the actor, that it produced a sensation of ridicule, and considerably impaired
the effect."

Lord Grey's speech in reply closed with a handsome
compliment to the King, for his patience and anxiety
to do his duty. "I certainly will not abandon the
King as long as I can be of use to him. I am bound
to the King by obligations of gratitude, greater, perhaps,
than subject ever owed to a sovereign, for the kind
manner in which he has extended to me his confidence
and support, and for the indulgence with which he
has accepted my humble but zealous exertions in his
service."

Jeffrey describes the scene, which has a lurid air :

"Lord Grey's reply on the whole admirable ; in
tone and spirit perfect, and, considering his age and
the time, really astonishing. He spoke near one hour
and a half, after five o'clock, from the kindling dawn
into full sunlight, and I think with great effect. The
aspect of the House was very striking through the

whole night, very full, and, on the whole, still and solemn. The whole throne and the space around it clustered over with 100 members of our House, and the space below the bar nearly filled with 200 more, ranged in a standing row of three deep along the bar, another sitting on the ground against the wall, and the space between covered with moving and sitting figures in all directions, with twenty or thirty clamber-ing on the railings and perched up by the doorways. Between four and five, when the daylight began to shed its blue beams across the red candle-light, the scene was very picturesque, from the singular grouping of forty or fifty of us sprawling on the floor, awake and asleep, in all imaginable attitudes, and with all sorts of expressions and wrappings . . . The candles had been renewed before dawn, and blazed on after the sun came fairly in at the high windows, and pro-duced a strange but rather grand effect on the red draperies and furniture and dusky tapestry on the walls."

When the Reform Bill was rejected on October 8, by a majority of forty-one, news of which defeat was sent express to Windsor, with a despatch of Lord Grey's, written at six o'clock in the morning, His Majesty said he, though disappointed at the result, could not but indulge in some mild reproaches; he had warned Lord Grey; "his advice had not been taken," etc. His Majesty would deceive Earl Grey if he were to say that the result is not such as he had long expected; that even the majority is not larger than he had expected, notwith-standing the accession of strength by the new creation of peers at the Coronation; and it would be idle, after all His Majesty has said and written on the subject, more especially after the urgent representation contained in his letter of the 24th of April, written immediately after he had consented to a dissolution of Parliament, to admit now that he had not anticipated such a result, if the Bill should be carried to the House of Lords *without such essential modifications* as should render it more palatable to its opponents, or to admit that he had not then, or had not ever since, ceased to apprehend this result, and the consequent collision between the two Houses of Parliament."

He went on to say he trusted the dangerous suggestion of creating peers would not be thought of, nor resignation.

His Majesty again gave his ministers a lecture on the severe lesson they had received. " It should show them how wrong they were in thinking that the Bill must pass; and generally he has felt (and has, indeed, had occasion to satisfy himself from *personal* observation), how necessary it had become, upon this occasion, to make allowance for the excitement and irritation produced by the agitation of a question on which the opinions of those who had been in the habit of legislating for the country appear to be so much divided.

" But a respite has been obtained; time is given for consideration and for revision; the Bill has been withdrawn. It may be remodelled, and advantage may be taken, in this interval, of all that has been said and written, to correct whatever may have been shown to be objectionable, to amend the details without abandoning the principle of the Bill."

Lord Grey wrote to Sir H. Taylor to say that they did not intend to resign, and thus emphasised his declaration as to the creation of peers : " The amount of the majority puts all notion of an attempt to counteract it by a further creation of Peers quite out of the question. Indeed, I should not have been willing, under any circumstances, to resort to such a measure, and certainly not unless a very small addition would have been effectual for the purpose." Then followed further warnings, faint protests, etc., on the part of the King, but in the end he agreed that a measure substantially the same should be introduced. But there was certainly an *aigre* tone, and Lord Grey seemed inclined to be stiff and even captious. Thus the King urged his favourite nostrum, *moderation*, while they should abandon the obnoxious portions of the Bill, adding the rebuke that he "does believe, and has always believed, that this calm and dispassionate consideration, free from 'the warmth and hurry, and rashness of party conduct,' would be most likely to be obtained from the *opponents* of the Bill, and would thus ensure in future 'proceedings more orderly and more deliberate,' by carefully abstaining from all that can provoke warmth and irritate feeling. The King has already said that he does justice to the feeling and to the course pursued by Earl Grey in this respect; but Earl Grey cannot be surprised that his attention should have been called to the importance of inculcating this advice on others, and of preventing a reaction which might prove fatal to the measure, by the perusal of a public letter from one of His Majesty's confidential servants (Lord John Russell), in which the opposition of a large body of the aristocracy of the country, and of a majority of the House of Lords upon a great constitutional question, which had been gravely and unreservedly discussed in that House, is called 'the whisper of a faction,' and by observing the irritation thus produced at the very moment when His

Majesty had been so earnestly urging the necessity of conciliation."

The King had shown himself very impracticable in minor matters, especially in the distribution of honours to the services. The claims of Sir James Saumarez were pressed on him, but he positively and in a sort of mulish fashion declined.

"The King spoke to me about the Naval Peers, but did not mention Sir J. Saumarez," writes the secretary. "His silence gave me the impression which your letter confirms. I regret it, but there is nothing more to be said."

He was further irritated by several incidents that affected him in his private capacity—one, a radical and revolutionary speech of Colonel Napier, "that factious individual," as he styled him. His Majesty was so disturbed that he proposed that he should be dismissed the army.*

* A few years later His Majesty was equally displeased with the behaviour of Admiral Napier, who was in the Portuguese service. "Mrs. D.," writes Mr. Raikes, "showed me a letter from ——, which says : ' I went, yesterday, with their Majesties to the private exhibition at Somerset House. We were received by the president of the Royal Society, who, among other portraits, pointed out to the King that of Admiral Napier, who has been commanding the fleet for Don Pedro. His Majesty did not hesitate to show his *political* bias on this occasion by exclaiming immediately, 'Captain Napier may be d——d, sir, and you may be d——d, sir ; and if the Queen was not here, sir, I would kick you downstairs, sir !'"

There were plenty of strange speeches of this kind reported. "The talk of the town," says Mr. Greville, " has been about the King and a toast he gave at a great dinner at St. James's the other day. He had ninety guests—all his Ministers, all the great people, and all the foreign Ambassadors. After dinner he made a long rambling speech in French, and ended by giving as ' a sentiment,' as he called it, ' The land we live in.' This was before the ladies left the room. After they were gone he made another speech in French, in the course

These things sounded strangely, but a more serious matter, connected with the Household, irritated the Court still more. This was the renewed business of "influence behind the throne," of Lord Howe, whose romantic personal devotion to Her Majesty excited the ridicule and suspicions of all.

This nobleman was conspicuous for his open partisanship, and in the late division had actually voted against Ministers. The latter, who had long been complaining of this evidence of the bad feeling of the Court, now insisted that an example should be made. The King had to yield to his secretary, and wrote on October 10 : "The King has honoured me with his commands to acquaint your lordship, that Lord Howe has, in consequence of the communication with His Majesty agreed to make to him, resigned the office of Lord Chamberlain to the Queen, and that Her Majesty has accepted his resignation."* But *en revanche,*

of which he travelled over every variety of topic that suggested itself to his excursive mind, and ended with a very coarse toast. Sefton, who told it me, said he never felt so ashamed ; Lord Grey was ready to sink into the earth ; everybody laughed of course, and Sefton, who sat next to Talleyrand, said to him, 'Eh bien, que pensez-vous de cela ?' With his unmoved, immovable face he answered only, 'C'est bien remarquable.' On another occasion he attacked the officer of the Guards for not having his cap on his head, and sent for the officer on guard, who was not arrived, at which he expressed great ire. It is supposed that the peerages have put him out of temper. His Majesty did a very strange thing about them. Though their patents are not made out, and the new Peers are no more Peers than I am, he desired them to appear as such in Westminster Abbey and do homage."†

* The dismissed Chamberlain, whose position seemed to be not in the least altered, attended the Queen as usual, " never taking his eyes

† It was at this time that the Wellington Barracks were built. Not before they were needed, as it was the practice to billet the privates of the Guards about the district in public-houses.

they were informed that " His Majesty has further ordered me to say, that he forgot to mention to your lordship that it is not his intention to prorogue Parliament in person."

In reply, Lord Grey, after dwelling on the " distressing occasions " and " the pain," etc., which he felt in requiring so " disagreeable " a sacrifice, took up the point of the prorogation, and was " impelled, by an imperious sense of duty, humbly to express to your Majesty his anxious hope that your Majesty may be induced to reconsider your determination not to prorogue Parliament in person, which at this moment would be too likely to excite a feeling of distrust injurious in the highest degree to the interests of your Majesty's Government."

off her," and plotted and worked unceasingly to counteract the plans of her ministers. It is extraordinary to find him acting as the agent or emissary between Her Majesty and the Duke of Wellington.

The Queen, as Lady Howe told Mr. Greville, was specially indignant at the underhand mode in which her chamberlain had been dealt with; neither the King nor Lord Grey had told her a word about it.

CHAPTER III.

IT will be seen that a serious attempt was now about to be made to influence the King, a little plot being formed in which the Duke of Wellington, the Queen and the Chamberlain, seemed to be concerned. This may appear to be rather a strong phrase, but it will be supported by the revelations of the parties, and the curious coincidence of their exertions with the King's sudden resistance. It began with a movement of the Duke, who in a rather unconstitutional or unusual fashion uttered his well-known warning regarding the political unions. It might be said there was nothing very unreasonable in this course of the Duke's, considering the alarming state of disorder that reigned —the famous Bristol riots, in which buildings were sacked and destroyed, the military firing on the people, the alarming Birmingham and other Unions. It might seem a patriotic course enough, but the ministers scented hostility in this attempt.

Accordingly, on November 5th, the Duke had addressed a memorandum to the King on this subject, in which he gave warning of the dangerous spirit of these associations. The King acknowledged this paper in a long answer of his own, and forwarded the Duke's paper to his ministers. Lord Grey took it in high dudgeon, and actually addressed a thinly veiled rebuke to the Duke, in which, referring to this charge of arms having been largely bought by the Birmingham Union, he tells him that, "no such information having reached any department of the King's Government, I think it my duty to request that your Grace will have the goodness, if it is in your power, and if you see no objection, to furnish me with the means of ascertaining the accuracy of a fact, which is certainly of a nature to call for the most careful attention on the part of His Majesty's Ministers."

The Duke, thus called on to give some proofs, now mentioned a gunmaker in Oxford Street who had sold the Birmingham Union 6000 stand of arms. The man, however, said there was no ground for this assertion, and, indeed, the whole case seems to have been a weak one. But the curious part is this, that we find the Duke later revealing to his friend, the Duke of Buckingham, the motive of his interference:

"When I wrote to the King in November, on the armament of the political associations, I had in hand a case on which I was certain that nineteen-twentieths of the whole country would concur with me. I did it likewise at a period of the year at which I knew that if the King wished to get rid of the bonds in which he is held, I could assist him in doing so. There was time to call a new Parliament, and the sense of the country would have been taken on a question on which there would be no doubt. What did the King do? He concurred in (I may say without exaggeration) every opinion which I gave him.* His Ministers saw their scrape, and pre-

* Yet, when lectured by Lord Grey on the subject, the King through his secretary, told quite another story:

"I can easily conceive that you would be surprised at the Duke

vailed upon the Press and the political associations to
alter their course; they issued a mock proclamation,
and promised the King a Bill to repress the associations,
which promise they never performed, and the King is
quite satisfied and goes on with them as well as ever."

This is candour, indeed. But it is also much to the
credit of the King that he remained staunch.

They so far succeeded in awing His Majesty, that
in another communication he assured them that "any
further communication from his Grace would be confined to a simple acknowledgment." They thus made
His Majesty very amenable for the future.

The real "burning question" that now came to be
considered was the remedy of "creating peers" to force
the measure through the House. That this was a violent,
even unconstitutional, step in its *spirit*, the smallest
consideration will show. It seems akin to "packing a
jury." A tribunal, supposed to be independent, decides
against you, and it is transformed into a favourable
tribunal by adding additional members to those whose
interest it is to have a decision in their favour.

Lord Brougham had a long conversation at Brighton
with the King. The reports of various interviews of
this kind are not nearly so interesting as those of
George IV. with his ministers; the latter generally
giving more expression to his feelings, and emotions
and contends with more spirit. But the remarks
of King William on the whole show good sense and

of Wellington's communications, which the King has, I think,
correctly described as *unnecessary*. I hope you were satisfied with
His Majesty's reply to them, and that you will be so with his letter of
this date to yourself. His Majesty observed, when he read the Duke's
letter, that, as a Peer and a Privy Councillor, he had a right to
address to him by letter that which he might have communicated in a
private audience if he had thought fit to ask for it."

moderation. The conversation took place on the 28th of November, at the Pavilion.

THE KING'S CONVERSATION WITH LORD BROUGHAM.

"I was at the Pavilion from half-past eleven till two, and about two hours of that time with the King. I found him extremely well, and in peculiarly good spirits. He sat opposite to the light, as he generally does, and I opposite to him. After a few words, His Majesty himself began upon the Reform Bill, a thing I have hardly ever, perhaps not ever, known him do before. Indeed he has often avoided the subject, and never more than when I passed two days at Windsor on the eve of its coming on in the Lords. To-day he was very desirous to discuss everything relating to it, and the whole conversation was occupied with it.

"He repeatedly expressed his great regret and astonishment (strongly marked) at the conduct of those who had prevented it from going to a committee. He said there was nothing they might not have debated there—even Schedule A ; (qualifying this remark by saying ; ' Suppose I agreed with them—as I certainly do not—in regard to Schedule A, even that question might have been raised in the committee.') He asked me how I could account for such a proceeding, which seemed so great an error even upon their own views, and supposing they only wanted, most safely for themselves, to alter the Bill. I said I always looked to an adversary as acting upon some views of his own advantage which might be more or less judicious, but seldom supposed any gross blunder ; and that I imagined they had reckoned upon a better division with proxies, and were distrustful of their forces attending, especially should there be any excitement in the people as the committee went on. He said, still he thought this a blunder, for they could, after being beaten in the way alluded to in committee, throw it out on the third reading. He had alluded to Lords Wharncliffe and Harrowby, and I set him right as to the former's degree of influence, drawing a distinction between the two; and I also endeavoured to prevent any idea of negotiation with Wharncliffe so as to modify the Bill, representing his communications with Lord Grey in their real light (which he seemed to have understood). He expressed his wonder at Lord Harrowby's opposing the second reading, and asked how I explained it. I said that he had certainly either changed his intention within a week before the debate began, or at least had become fixed in his latter resolution, which I accounted for by the irresolution of their party, and their various opinions, all ending in referring the matter to the decision of a firm man, namely, the Duke of Wellington —who had insisted on the step being taken, and they complied. He said, still he could not account for the Duke of Wellington doing so, for it seemed unaccountable in any view of his policy. (This introduced the former part of the conversation, which I have transposed.)

" We conversed on various parts of the Bill—and he dwelt on the London districts—the qualification varying in different places, and the want of seats for Ministers and Crown lawyers. I alluded to the change of my own opinion as to the qualification, and explained about the state of the small and even many large towns (as Leeds) in respect of [*illegible*] houses, and the difficulties at all times, and impossibility now, of having the varied qualification.

" Upon the seats for Government I also referred to my speech, where I had confessed this difficulty ; but I said that though I should be well pleased the other parties, either Tory or doctrinaire broached it, we never could ; indeed, he had agreed that it was a far more violent innovation than anything we had ever been charged with. When I said that I understood the doctrinaire party were not at all averse to it, he inquired all about Bentham and others, which I explained. But I showed how little risk there was of *no* places being accessible, and explained as to several of the boroughs being sure to be in whole or part in the hands of powerful proprietors. I said I was persuaded the evils of the London districts were greatly exaggerated, and that good members were sure to be returned by most of them.

" He very distinctly said that *he* was quite clear the shock of the change was much overrated, and that when once the Bill was passed, things would slide into an easy and quiet posture as before, but that there was no quieting the alarm of the Tories as to this, and that the great matter was to prevent the certain shock which would result from the Bill being thrown out again. He dwelt on this, and I stated all that occurred to me of its mischiefs. (I think this introduced the last head of conversation, which I have again transposed.)

" I more than once referred to the loss of the Bill as synonymous with the breaking up of the Government, and the signal for every kind of evil—but not in this part of the conversation.

" Peel's name being mentioned, he said he could not comprehend him at all, and that, except the Duke of Wellington, every one of the last Government, when he saw them on their resigning, had stated their belief of some reform being necessary. On my saying I had always given them credit for rather going out on the Civil List division than on my Reform motion, he asked if I thought that would have been carried. I said I knew it as certainly as one could know anything of the kind, and by twenty-seven majority, according to my calculation. A good deal of conversation ensued as to the plans, and what they could be, of the Duke of Wellington and Peel. I said, after a good many observations both from His Majesty and myself, that I really thought it a plain case enough ; that though some, even a considerable number, of the anti-reformers were otherwise, yet they (the Tory leaders) were *politicians;* and that the Duke of Wellington and Peel no doubt wanted to throw out the Ministry, that they might come in and propose the Bill themselves, which, after what we had seen, was quite on the cards. He almost anticipated this topic (of the Catholic question), and had it out, before I named it; but said, even supposing that to be their object, it was to be so considered that they might have tried it in a safe way, by letting the Bill pass, resisting it all the while, and then endeavouring to get into power and carry on the Government upon the ground of the Reform when carried. This began to be a somewhat delicate and difficult speculation (viz., what was to happen after I was myself officially defunct), so I only observed, that I supposed they thought that plan would have many fewer facilities. He conversed a good deal about Peel, and his conduct on the Catholic question. I gave Peel all manner of credit for it, and said he had really made a very great sacrifice, but that he could not both be praised for that and expect to retain what he lost; and that it was quite clear he had entirely lost all influence in the country, both with Church and Tories.

"He repeatedly expressed his surprise at the ultra Tories taking the line they did; and I showed him how they were actually joining the Hunt and rabble party as far as they could, in order to spite the Government and oppose the Bill. I dwelt on many other topics connected with the subject, and among others on the importance of His Majesty using his influence with those about him, such as Lord M. ; and stating that the Tories were still as busy as ever representing him (the King) as unfriendly to the Bill. He seemed aware of this, and only spoke of Lord M. as under the Duke of Cumberland's influence, from old anti-Catholic connection. There was a good deal said by His Majesty about the late King changing his opinion on the Catholic question, on which subject he (present King) and Lord Donoughmore, in 1806, used to be quite anxious about his committing himself so far and so indiscriminately. He said the late King had quite forgotten it before he died. I saw Sir Herbert Taylor for about half-an-hour, and dwelt with him on the chief of the above topics, such as the impossibility of any change of the franchise. I also saw some of the females of the family of both sides, and intimated the risk they were in of having the public feeling directed towards them, were they to persist against the Bill.

"Of course abundance of denial here, as far as overt acts went, but candid avowals of direct enmity to the Bill.

"I forgot to mention that the King, on my speaking of the Archbishop of York's strong opinion that, *as a bishop*, he was bound to look with dismay at another

rejection, he dwelt much on this and on the duty of
bishops to prevent such horrors as might ensue. I
repeated much of what I had represented the last
audience I had, on the state of the country, about the
universality of the feeling for the Bill; that its enemies
were either a few of Hunt's mob, or people small in
number, though important in point of property. He
said the only person he could find who was against *all*
change, was Lord Mansfield; and *he* had held a different
language to him in April, saying he was not against
Reform, but the Bill. He said the Duke of Wellington
himself had changed. I observed that he certainly had,
late in the day, made a most surprising declaration on
the subject. He desired me (when I said I would send
him a corrected copy of my speech, which he received
very kindly) to send him Lord Harrowby's, and any
others that had been *corrected.* I don't distinctly
recollect if it was to His Majesty or to Sir Herbert
Taylor, or both, that I explained the degree in which
newspapers *influence,* and the degree in which they
only *indicate* the public opinion; and the difference
between the London and provincial papers in this
respect (the latter being found to follow the opinions
of their readers much more closely).

" One of the females (hostile) came upon this part of
the subject, and said *The Times* was well known to
change about, if ten less were sold. I said that might
be an exaggeration, but that undoubtedly they generally
followed the *City* opinion—and gave the remarkable
instance of the Princess of Wales's case, in May, 1813.

" I also omitted what he said of an idea having got
abroad of divisions among us, to which I gave the most
positive contradiction, and expressed my surprise how
those stories could have originated. He said that Lord

Durham was thought to keep himself aloof, but he did not seem himself at all to think this owing to any difference; and when I spoke of the state of his family in the distress his loss had occasioned to them, he spoke with the greatest feeling and kindness, and inquired about his regaining his spirits by the excursion to Brussels."*

It has always seemed astonishing that such a device as the "creation of peers" should have been suggested by Liberals; nothing more autocratic could have been conceived even in Star Chamber times. It was virtually destroying free debate, setting aside the power of the genuine majority, and taking away all power from the House of Peers. No wonder that true Liberal, Lord Grey, set his face against it; while it was equally natural that the advanced Radicals of the Cabinet hailed this violent measure with delight. This it was that determined them to send Lord Brougham to the King, at Brighton. The Cabinet, moreover, was divided in opinion on such a question. Those who came at last to call for this step being taken did so against their convictions, and on the ground of avoiding a revolution. The turbulent Brougham was prepared for it, though he later owned his mistake; the intemperate Lord Durham and Sir J. Graham were for it on principle. Oddly, though many disapproved, the whole Cabinet came round; and they were willing to approve of it to a certain extent, to the making of twenty peers or so, but not to the vast amount of sixty or eighty. A characteristic letter of a Member of the Cabinet, Lord Althorp, shows the embarrassment which must always arise from considering a great question on the low ground of expediency, instead of on principle.

* Lord Durham's elder son had died on 24th September.

On November 23rd, 1831, thus wrote Lord Althorp to his chief.

"MY DEAR LORD GREY,

"I wish to prepare you for a conversation which you will have to-morrow. After the Cabinet, Graham came to me, and said he felt himself very much embarrassed by being convinced that if the Bill was rejected a second time by the House of Lords, the most disastrous consequences would follow; he, therefore, thinks we are not justified in running any hazard of such an event. He has no hopes that the Peers who formed the majority will be converted in such numbers as to give anything like a certainty of success. His idea, therefore, is that we should immediately secure to ourselves the consent of the King to make the requisite number of Peers, whatever that number may be, pledging ourselves that we will not act upon such consent without an established necessity, or beyond the extent of that necessity; if the King refuses his consent, that we ought immediately to resign. I told him that I felt a very decided objection to making any great number, and that I was convinced the Cabinet would not agree to make this application to the King. His answer was, that if this was the case he had made up his mind to resign. I advised him to speak to you about this to-morrow. I confess I have had my misgivings upon this subject, and that was the reason I mentioned it to you this morning. I feel what I believe to be an insurmountable objection to overwhelming the House of Lords by a large creation of Peers; but still I must admit that if it was clearly proved to me that a revolution would be the consequence of not taking this step, and that not only the House of Lords, but every other thing of value in the country would be overturned, it would be a very strong thing to say that it ought not to be taken.

"The reasons for making up our minds to take some decisive steps to secure our success are undoubtedly very strong. We are supposed by the Reformers to have the full support of the King to the utmost extent of his prerogative ; and the example set by Casimir Perrier in France, though in reality by no means analogous, tends to make them expect this from us. I should not, I think, be able to make up my mind to follow it; but I do not feel so much objection to requiring of the King that he should put this power in our hands—the possession of it would render the use of it unnecessary. If the King refused to give it to us, and we resigned now, our measure is carried ; for no other Ministry could be formed, and we should come back with such an overwhelming strength that the House of Lords must give way at once. These are my views at present ; you perceive they are not very steady or fixed, and I shall be very glad to be guided by you.

"Yours most truly,
"ALTHORP."

The difficulty indeed was to get Lord Grey to adopt a decided course as the crisis drew on. Brougham was eager that in good time this weapon, the power to make peers, should be obtained in advance and not when the crisis came. The fact of *having* the weapon might prevent the necessity for its use. At the end of December, Lord Grey was induced to go to Brighton to get the King's consent ; and the unwearied Chancellor again and again "primed" him with arguments and kept him up to the mark.

LORD GREY'S CONVERSATION WITH THE KING.

"Having prepared the King to expect a communication on the means of providing against the danger of a second defeat of the measure of Reform in the House of Lords, both by previous correspondence and a preliminary conversation yesterday evening, I had the honour of a long interview with His Majesty this morning on the subject."

After stating the danger the Bill was in, and that on calculation there was likely to be a majority of twenty votes against it, he said : "It was impossible, therefore, to delay looking to the fearful alternative which was thus forced upon our consideration, of either incurring all the danger attending the loss of the Bill in one or other of these modes, or of preventing it by the use of the means which the prerogative of the Crown afforded for meeting such an exigency.

"To look first at the danger of losing the Bill : it appeared to me of the most formidable nature ; that the country was at present in a state of comparative repose, from a confident expectation that the Bill would be carried; that the consequence of a disappointment would be fatal to the peace of the country ; that the House of Lords, already a good deal injured in public opinion, would incur a danger threatening its very existence ; and that the administration, and perhaps the King himself, exposed to a degree of odium proportioned to the confidence which they at present enjoy, would be involved in the common danger. I saw nothing, therefore, left, but a creation of peers ; that I considered this in itself as a great evil, exposed to great and weighty objections, and which nothing could have induced me to think of resorting to, except the danger, or I should rather say the certainty, of incurring one infinitely greater ; that it was painful to me to propose to His Majesty a measure to which I knew that His Majesty objected, and to which I myself had originally had the greatest objections ; that I still saw them in their full force ; but that, in looking at the alternative with which we were threatened, the danger of adopting such a measure seemed to me so infinitely less in the comparison, that I could no longer hesitate in stating my deliberate conviction, that it was become necessary for the safety of the country ; that I had stated this view of our present situation to the Cabinet ; that several of my colleagues concurred with me, and perhaps went farther than me, in this opinion, and that others still appeared to entertain a strong sense of the objections which they had felt from the beginning, to a measure which they considered as so injurious to the character and independence of the House of Lords, as not to be thought of whilst there remained any hope of averting the danger, by other measures ; but the result, however, of our deliberation had been to authorise me to submit the whole matter to His Majesty's consideration, on the ground of making a partial addition to the House of Lords as at present, to repel the notion, which had been assiduously promulgated, that any new creations were positively precluded ; and of our being allowed to propose a further addition hereafter, if it should be found necessary.

" To all this the King listened with the greatest attention and with evident anxiety. He stated that he had long foreseen that such a proposition would eventually be made to him, and that he had given it his most serious consideration ; that his objections to the creation of Peers for such a purpose had already been stated to

his Ministers; that I myself had acknowledged their
validity; and that he still contemplated, with un-
diminished anxiety, the danger of such a precedent; that
he was prepared, however, to listen to the advice which
his Ministers might think it their duty to offer to him,
but that he wished it should be in writing; that his
answer would be given in the same manner; and that if
it should ultimately be determined to make an addition
to the Peerage, for the purpose of increasing the strength
of the Government on the question of Reform, he
trusted that it would be so managed as to affect the
permanent character of the House of Lords as little as
possible, and asked what were my views on this part of
the question.

"I stated that it was unquestionably my wish to
limit any new creations in the manner to which His
Majesty seemed to allude, as it had been my anxious
desire to avoid it altogether; that in any new creations,
therefore, I should look to such as would produce the
least possible permanent addition to the numbers of the
Peerage; that there were two which I had formerly
mentioned as having been promised, and suspended only
on account of temporary circumstances at the period of
the coronation—Lord F. Osborne and Mr. Dundas.
These, His Majesty observed, stood on separate grounds,
and that he had no objection to them. That, in addition
to these, I thought it would be desirable to seek for the
additional strength that would be required by calling up
eldest sons; that a considerable number might thus be
obtained; and that, in the first instance, I would propose calling up those who were not in Parliament, which
would furnish enough for the partial creation tȯ which I
had alluded as advisable at present (say in all eight or
ten), and would afford the best indication of the possi-

bility of a further addition from those who had seats in
the House of Commons, if it should be wanted; that,
next to these, collateral heirs to peerages, where no
direct heirs were likely to succeed, should be resorted to;
and that, in this manner, any permanent addition to the
peerage of any consequence might be avoided; that I
did not say, however, that some creation of Commoners
of high character and great property might not be
advisable, but that I certainly thought it most desirable
that such creations should be as much limited as possible, both for the purpose of avoiding a permanent
increase of the Peerage, and the subtraction of more
property from the House of Commons, too much having
already been withdrawn from that assembly.

"I added that, by a first partial creation, such as I
had recommended, I had great hopes that an effect
might be produced, which would in a great degree,
if not entirely, obviate the necessity of a subsequent
addition.

"To all this His Majesty most graciously listened,
and stated his decided opinion, that if an addition was
to be made, it should be regulated in this manner; in a
word, that the addition should be made, first, by calling
up eldest sons; next, collateral heirs; and, thirdly,
Scotch and Irish Peers; so that the whole Peerage of
the United Kingdom should not be augmented.

"His Majesty added that he trusted it would not be
proposed to raise to the Peerage any of those who had
been forward in agitating the country, as nothing could
induce him to consent to the advancement of persons of
that description. His Majesty also, after expressing the
greatest anxiety as to the present state of the country,
stated his confident expectation that his Ministers, after
the settlement of this question, should it be happily

effected, would make their stand against any further encroachments tending to a dangerous diminution of the necessary power of the Government.

" To this I gave a ready assent; and the conversation, in which much more passed, but nothing material has been omitted, ended by His Majesty again desiring that the advice of his confidential servants on this important question should be submitted to him in writing."

This Report of the conversation was submitted to the King, who seized the opportunity to make more precise what he had expressed, and perhaps to add certain additions and qualifications. I give it at length.

" The King has read with attention the Minute which Earl Grey has made of what passed in his interview with His Majesty yesterday, and he acknowledges its perfect accuracy in all points.

" His Majesty will proceed to make some remarks upon the questions submitted by Earl Grey for his consideration, with the understanding, however, that he shall not be thereby considered as pledging himself to the adoption of any proposal or suggestion, and that he reserves his decision, until his pleasure shall have been taken in the more formal shape of a Minute of Cabinet.

" Earl Grey has most correctly admitted his sense of the strong objections entertained by His Majesty to any addition to the Peerage for the purpose of carrying the Reform Bill, or any other measure; and he has, with similar justice, taken credit to himself for having originally, and indeed at all times when the subject has been touched upon, expressed his own objections to a creation of Peers upon such an occasion. Earl Grey has added that he still sees these objections in their full force. The King is, therefore, satisfied that nothing but the appre-

hension of a second rejection of the Reform Bill in the
House of Lords, and a conviction of the danger of incurring a greater evil, and all the lamentable consequences which have been so forcibly stated by him,
could have induced Earl Grey to yield to the advice of
those who have urged a resort to this alternative, and to
have proposed it to His Majesty.

"The King is naturally confirmed in this opinion by
Earl Grey's verbal communication of the sentiments of
some of his colleagues (recorded also in his Minute) as
being still strongly opposed to this measure, whilst
there remained any hope of averting the danger by
other means.

"Strong as is and as ought to be the King's feeling
on this subject, he is, on the other hand, sensible that
circumstances must occur, as indeed they have occurred,
in which it becomes a duty to sacrifice feeling to
necessity. It has always been his desire to remove
difficulties rather than to raise them; and he therefore
will not add to those which have now arisen by
hesitation, or by keeping those who are entrusted with
the administration of the affairs of this country at this
critical period in suspense, as to the view which he may
be disposed to take of circumstances which call for his
decision.

"As matters now stand, His Majesty is assured, and
he believes, that the peace and the tranquillity of the
country depend upon an early settlement of the question
which so intensely agitates it. He has reason to know
that Earl Grey and the other members of his Government consider the success of the measure as identified
with their continuance in office. He has no wish for
any change of his Ministers, as he is satisfied with the
manner in which they discharge the duties of their

arduous and laborious offices ; and as he is equally satisfied of the serious injury which the country must sustain
from frequent changes of men and measures, more
especially from such change at the present period, when
the state of its domestic and foreign concerns and
relations so imperiously calls for stability of authority
and consistency of purpose so essential to the establishment of confidence.

"But even if such were not His Majesty's sentiments,
and it should be his desire to escape from the measure
which is so repugnant to his feelings, by risking the
alternative of the loss of the Reform Bill, or the dissolution of the present Administration, a doubt would occur,
whether there be in the country any individuals of
respectability and capacity willing to undertake the
task he would impose upon them, by calling them to
his councils ; or whether, if these could be found, they
would be able to maintain themselves in office and to
carry on the government of the country ; and His
Majesty believes that this doubt would be solved in the
negative.

"If, however, all these considerations should appear
to the King sufficient to justify his consenting to an
addition to the House of Lords, for the purpose of
giving to his Government such a preponderance of
influence and votes as shall enable it to carry the
Reform Bill, he cannot lose sight of the objections
which he entertains to this measure, so far as not to
feel it to be his duty to cause his assent to rest upon
a principle which shall, as far as possible, maintain the
respectability of the House of Lords as it is now constituted, as shall preserve to the Peerage of this
country the *hereditary* distinction which it has not yet
ceased to enjoy, and shall secure the character and the

independence of this high and important branch of the
State from any permanent consequences of an act
resorted to with a view to a present emergency.

" His Majesty therefore must establish, as a condition
inseparable from the possibility of his assenting to the
proposal which may be submitted to him by his Cabinet,
that, with the exception solely of Lord Francis Osborne
and Mr. Dundas, to whose elevation to the Peerage he
had already consented, and which had indeed, as
observed by Earl Grey, been merely suspended, and
possibly of Sir John Leach, which would stand on
distinct ground, although taking place upon this
occasion, the addition to be made to the House of
Lords, whatever may be the numbers, may be effected
exclusively by calling up eldest sons, or collateral
heirs to Peerages, where no direct heirs are likely to
succeed.

" His Majesty is satisfied, from the inspection of the
lists which Earl Grey put into his hands, that enough
could be obtained from this source, without resorting
to Scotch and Irish Peers, to whose transfer to the
English Peerage he, however, would not have objected,
if it had been shown to him to be indispensable towards
making up the number required.

" But His Majesty does not think it would, in any
view of the question, be wise to limit the selection to those
not in Parliament, even in the first instance, it appearing
to him that the objections to the exclusion of those
holding seats in the House of Commons are greater and
more deserving of consideration than any that may
attach to opening the representation of counties, or
other seats for which contests would arise. Besides
which the course and results of these contests may
serve the purpose of the Government, by affording a

good criterion of the feeling of the country in favour of the measure of Reform, a contradiction to the assertion that a strong reaction in it has taken place, and therefore an additional ground of justification for so strong an exercise of the prerogative as that which is now recommended.

" His Majesty is further of opinion that, upon these occasions, when once the decision is made, the measure should be effectual and conclusive, and taken without the *appearance* of doubt or hesitation, not subject to contingencies which might defeat its object, to the risk of erroneous estimates of comparative strength, or to the possible necessity of a *second edition*, in consequence of the insufficiency of the first. If Earl Grey considers that twenty-one may be required *eventually*, and is satisfied that his data are correct, that number should be added at once in the manner proposed, instead of feeling the pulse, and beating about the bush, by adding eight or ten, at the risk of a failure, which would betray the absence of due calculation and discrimination, and of a fixed determination, and might possibly increase the difficulty and the objection, so as to render the propriety or policy of a renewal of the attempt very questionable.

" The King, having declared that his acquiescence in the proposed measure must be subject to the exclusion of all *creations*, excepting the three specially named, it becomes unnecessary that he should repeat his caution as to raising to the Peerage any individuals who have been forward in agitating the country.

" But His Majesty cannot close this communication without again stating to Earl Grey and to his other confidential servants, the extreme importance, which, in times of great peril, when the overthrow of all legitimate authority, the destruction of ancient institutions, of social order, and of every gradation and link of society are threatened, when a revolutionary and demoralising spirit is making frightful strides, when a poisonous press, almost unchecked, guides, excites, and at the same time controls public opinion, His Majesty must attach to their assurance, that, after the settlement of this all-engrossing question of Parliamentary Reform shall have been happily settled, they will strenuously exert themselves to resist and repress further encroachments tending to a dangerous diminution of the necessary power of the Government, and to a systematic reduction of the authority, influence, and dignity of the Crown. It is impossible His Majesty should view otherwise than with serious apprehension the preponderance of the House of Commons in the direction of the affairs of this country, if it be applied, as it has been occasionally applied, and more frequently attempted to be applied, to the prejudice of the Monarchy and the degradation of its attributes. He is not conscious of having betrayed any disposition to an extravagant display of dignity and splendour, or to the exercise of despotic and arbitrary power. He is therefore warranted in ascribing the propensity for encroachment, which has been shown by the House of Commons, to that growing fancy for *Liberalism* which, however fair its appearance, is by many assumed to cover democratic and levelling purposes, and may mislead others to the encouragement and support of schemes fatal to the existence of the Constitution and the form of Government under which this country has so long prospered.

"It is His Majesty's duty, it must be his anxious wish, to endeavour to preserve to his dominions the

blessings which a bountiful Providence has bestowed
upon them, and to transmit them to his posterity as
little impaired as the spirit of these times will allow ;
and he appeals earnestly to his Ministers for their
utmost aid towards this object, and for their strenuous
support of his endeavour to stem the torrent."

Such was this lengthy exposition. But now, after
these deliverances, we find the Duke " in privity " with
the plot that was going on within the Palace to shake
the King's purpose. This, it will be seen, was but the
beginning of a long discussion or contest ; for Lord Grey,
it must be remembered, had merely accepted the principle,
but was determined not to put it in practice till the
last extremity. The more serious point, of the extent
to which it was to be carried, had next to be considered.

Lord Lyndhurst, presently to take so important a
share in the oversetting the Government, was watching
carefully what was going on, and, curiously enough,
found himself at Brighton, when the ministers arrived
to put pressure on the King. It may be fanciful to say
so, but there seems a tone of petty intrigue about the
following letter, which Lord Lyndhurst wrote to the
Duke of Wellington from Brighton :

" I hope you continue to gain health and strength. . .
I hope it for the country, for there never was a period
when intelligent and active exertions was more requisite.
Lord Grey is here to-day, rumour says, to make thirty-
six peers ; but you know how to value the rumours of
Brighton. Rumour also says that *les batards* are *all* to
be included. Sir T. Kempe is to succeed Lord Hill, that
Brereton is to be upheld for his moderation, and the
activity of Digby Mackworth to be made, in some shape,
the subject of complaint. The party at the Pavilion, to

meet Grey, consists of the Bristols, the Wharncliffes, and the Beverleys !!!! A very happy arrangement."

From the privately - printed memoirs of Lord Broughton, who was in office at this moment, we learn how critical was the situation, and how distracted was the ministry. The thorough-going Radicals of the Cabinet —Lord Durham and Hobhouse—were almost on the verge of frenzy from the critical nature of their position. They had joined on the terms of the Bill being carried, and of everything being done to carry it. Now matters were to be left to the chance of events, to the chance of returning sense in the House of Peers, instead of making it certain. They were ruined and disgraced for ever, with their party, if a failure occurred. Much agitated by such doubts, Hobhouse sought an interview with Lord Howick, the present Earl Grey, not wishing to add to the Premier's other annoyances. A curious scene followed, Lord Howick telling him frankly that his father would never have taken up the Bill had he foreseen all the confusion that was to ensue. He explained how, up to a certain time, all the Cabinet were for "making peers;" but Brougham fell sick, and then took fright; then Lord Grey had his doubts; Lord Durham had determined to resign if the Bill were not thus made safe. The others, who were now against making the peers, were the Duke of Richmond, Lords Melbourne, Palmerston, and John Russell.*

After this, the plan was set on foot of collecting signatures to addresses, with which Lord Salisbury repaired to Brighton, and, obtaining an "audience,"

---

* Fragments only are given in the *Edinburgh Review.* Lord Grey, then Lord Howick, declares he does not recall this conversation at all ; but it must be said, Lord Grey has denied the accuracy of many incidents connected with the Reform Bill.

tried to "work" on His Majesty. He describes his attempt to the Duke of Wellington :

"After some remarks, the King saying that, 'before he was King, he had seen a great deal of the world,' he was reminded by his visitor that the nation was not so unanimous as was supposed on the Reform Bill. On which he interrupted, and said 'he believed that a Reform, and a considerable Reform, must take place, but it was another question *whether it ought ever to have gone so far.*' He listened with great good humour to the objections to adding to the Peerage, saying that he never was a violent man, and met him half way."

Lord Camden also had an audience, on the 27th of January, and spoke very firmly on the Peers question, but the King was very cautious in his replies. Meanwhile, the usual incident of the interposition of moderate men from the ranks of the opponents, represented by Lords Wharncliffe and Harrowby, "the waverers" as they were styled, offered a chance of compromise. For this the King was most eager, and indeed rested all his hopes. He wished the ministers to yield to the wishes of this party, and gave his support. The ministers argued truly that their force was overrated —that they had only a small following, and that any concessions to them would entail a fresh hostility. With Lord Wharncliffe the King had an interview, which is thus reported.*

"His Majesty has ordered me to acquaint your lordship that Lord Wharncliffe has been with him nearly an hour, during which His Majesty said little himself, and

---

* Mr. Charles Greville is stated to have been the originator of this scheme ; and it will be seen from his own account that he found it already in hand, though he himself worked at it.

was extremely cautious of betraying any sentiment,
feeling, or opinion he might entertain upon any pro-
vision or feature of the Reform Bill, or the possibility of
resorting to the exercise of his prerogative towards
enabling his Government to carry it.

"Lord Wharncliffe repeated much of what he said
to me. He assured His Majesty that he had never been
opposed to a measure of moderate Reform; on the
contrary, that he had supported the partial arrangements which had been proposed during former Administrations, and resisted by them. He also stated, as a
proof of his disposition to facilitate, rather than to
impede, the settlement of this anxious question, that he
had earnestly promoted the meeting in the City, and
the object for which it was called, and which was
defeated by the violence of —— on the one side, and
the folly of —— on the other. He expressed, in the
strongest terms, his unwillingness to abandon the hope
of an accommodation while it seemed to exist in the
slightest degree; and offered this and the urgency of
many others who shared that feeling as his excuse for
the liberty he had taken, of which he stated that he had
apprised your lordship by last night's post.

"The points of objection to the Bill which he urged
were, the representation of the metropolitan districts;
the non-exclusion of the influence of represented towns
from county elections; the representation of any towns
by single members, the £10 householders not being
effectual.

"These are given as stated to me by the King, who
observed that the last item had, he believed, been already
set right.

"His Majesty gave no opinion upon any of these
points, or upon any part of the Bill, principle or detail,

observing that he could not commit himself in the discussion of a measure upon which he would have to decide, on the best advice which could be submitted to him by those who were officially responsible for giving it : that he had come to the throne at a period of great difficulty, but with his judgment happily unfettered by party prejudice : that he had continued the Duke of Wellington and his colleagues in the situations in which he found them, had been satisfied with their proceedings, and had regretted their retirement, which could not be ascribed to any absence or diminution of his support : that he had invariably acted upon the same principle towards your lordship, who had been called to his councils at a most critical period, and whose conduct had fully justified the confidence he reposed in you and the support he had given you, and which would be continued to you.

"His Majesty further assured Lord Wharncliffe, that the manly and straightforward character of his proceedings had been duly appreciated by him, as it must be by the country at large."

On January 13th, a Minute of Cabinet was drawn up making fresh demands on His Majesty, growing out of his concession. In this they set out precisely what they required as to the time, mode, and extent of the application of the principle. They knew how "slippery" sovereigns are likely to be on such points. "The extent should be *adequate* to the necessity of securing the object in view. To make a new creation of peers, which should prove *ultimately ineffectual* for its purpose would obviously be productive of the most unfortunate consequence. The rejection of the Bill after such an attempt would be even more calamitous than if no new creation had taken place ; and your Majesty's servants, in return for the generous confidence with which your Majesty has honoured them, are bound to state, without reserve or concealment, their deliberate conviction, that any augmentation of the numbers of the House of Lords, with the avowed intention of influencing its decision, would be unadvisable, unless your Majesty is prepared to carry it to the full extent.

"If it is considered that twenty-one new creations might be eventually required, that number should be added at once." To the soundness of this opinion your Majesty's servants have no hesitation in subscribing, subject to the following observations:

"In the present uncertain state of their information, they cannot take upon themselves to say whether the addition of any given number of Peers would be sufficient, or whether it might not be more than the object in view would eventually demand.

"Unwilling, therefore, to overstep the necessity of the case, they would humbly suggest the expediency of postponing any new creations till they shall have more accurate means, which, during the progress of the Bill through the House of Commons, they may hope to obtain, of judging to what extent they should be carried. In offering this advice, however, they beg further to represent to your Majesty, that they do so in full confidence that, when the time shall come, your Majesty will allow them the power of acting at once up to the exigency of the case."

They agreed with him as to the *mode*, namely, calling up elder sons, and adding Scotch and Irish Peers. As to the amount or extent, they appeared to accept the King's suggestion.

The King sent his answer on January 15th, beginning by laying down that he did not "dispute the correctness of the reasoning, or the soundness of the argument by which this advice is supported, always, however, with the reserve that it is applicable to the *existing* contingencies, and that the decision must be made upon due consideration of present circumstances, and of the necessity of incurring a serious evil in order to avert one which may prove yet more serious. This, therefore, is the ground to be taken."

He then added that, "however desirable it is, in his opinion, to put an end to such collision, His Majesty cannot, under any circumstances, consent to undervalue the importance of the House of Lords as a separate and independent branch of the Legislature, nor lose sight of the high functions which it has to perform, and of the power with which it is invested for the preservation of the Constitution ; and he declares that he looks to that House principally, and to its high, honourable, and loyal elements for the support of the monarchy, and for the exertion of due vigour in resisting popular clamour and in opposing a barrier to popular encroachments.

" It is now stated, ' that the expediency of making an addition to the Peerage must depend upon His Majesty's *being prepared to allow to his servants the power of carrying it to the full extent which may be necessary to secure the success of the Bill, with which view it cannot be limited to any precise number at present.'*

" In other words, the King is required to surrender into the hands of his Ministers this important prerogative, to be exercised and applied without any other reserve or limit than that which their calculation or anticipation of the difficulties or opposition they may have to encounter shall produce ; nor does the unrestricted surrender of this prerogative derive security from the character of those to whose honour and discretion His Majesty would not hesitate to confide it, inasmuch as the limits of its exercise must be dependent on circumstances, on contingencies of which the estimate may be precarious and uncertain, and which may therefore lead to an extension of the evil, far greater than His Majesty or his responsible advisers could ever have contemplated.

"The King has stated freely his view of the question as now submitted to him, and has done so because he conceives that he owes it to himself and to his confidential servants not to shrink from the avowal of his sentiments ; but, having done so, he will not, after having allowed that the resource should be effectual, and having, indeed, insisted upon the absurdity of incurring any risk by an insufficient addition to the House of Lords, if resorted to at all, deny to his Ministers the power ' of acting at once up to the full exigency of the case ; ' it being understood that the contemplated addition shall be deferred till it may appear certain that, without such addition, the strength of the Government would be insufficient to bring the measure of Parliamentary Reform to a successful issue.

"But His Majesty cannot give this pledge, nor consent to this surrender of the exercise of his prerogative, without attaching to it the positive and irrevocable condition that the *creations of new Peers* shall, under no circumstances, exceed the three to which he has already agreed, namely of Lord Francis Osborne, Mr. Dundas, and Sir John Leach ; that the other additions shall be made by calling up eldest sons, or collateral heirs of Peerages where no direct heirs are likely to succeed, without reference to the objection which has been made of throwing open the representation of

F 2

counties or boroughs, which, if suffered to prevail, would have the effect of excluding many of those whom His Majesty considers the most eligible; that if these sources should prove insufficient (which, however, His Majesty can hardly conceive possible), recourse may be had to the Scotch and Irish Peerage for promotion to the English Peerage on this occasion, but that the selection shall be made from the oldest and most distinguished houses, so as not to detract from the value of the translation.

" It has always appeared to His Majesty that the creation of Peers under the direct influence of the Crown and the Government, for the avowed purpose of obtaining a majority in the House of Lords, is altogether inconsistent with the principle on which the measure of Reform is professed to be introduced, and with its main feature, the abolition of nomination, or, as vulgarly called, rotten boroughs, inasmuch as nomination votes are created and introduced into the House of Lords, etc."

This last was not a bad thrust, and must surely have been suggested by an adviser.

All this time, however, the topic of Court influence, and what was termed "backstair" influence, was revived, and in January Lord Grey had again to lecture His Majesty on this and other matters:

" It is with great pain that Earl Grey observes the increased apprehensions of your Majesty from the effect of the Reform Bill. He will not revert to the circumstances under which he proposed the introduction of the measure. He feels deeply all the difficulties with which it is now surrounded; and if he could have foreseen, or contemplated, the persevering and irreconcilable opposition which is given to it in the House of Lords, and which he begs your Majesty will excuse his saying that he believes, however conscientious on the part of some, to be chiefly directed to the overthrow of your Majesty's present Ministers, he would have humbly declined the trust with which your Majesty was pleased to honour him. In the situation to which things are now brought, there appears to Earl Grey to be no safe course but that of using every exertion to carry the measure safely through Parliament; and he cannot help humbly stating to your Majesty his sincere conviction that if the efforts of those who are urging the House of Lords again to defeat it should prove successful, the total destruction of the power of that House (to the importance of which Earl Grey is not less alive than your Majesty) to maintain itself as an institution placed between the Crown and the people, for their mutual defence and security, would be immutable."

Again Lord Grey renewed the attack upon the secret advisers behind the throne. He had doubtless learned the efforts that were making to sway the King —the "audiences" and the letters. As he found they were growing bolder, and likely to prove successful, he spoke with greater force and vehemence.

"I fully appreciate," he wrote, "all the generous and amiable feelings which have induced His Majesty to banish all party distinctions from his society, and to receive with the graciousness which belongs to him, and with hospitality and kindness, those who are in the most bitter opposition to his Government. But a very unfair advantage has been taken of this condescension. His Majesty's feelings have been most industriously misrepresented; the falsest accounts of the impression made upon him by those who have been admitted to his presence have been circulated; feeling that they are equally well received has encouraged those who vote in opposition; and the result has been, most indisputably, very injurious to the strength of the Government. His Majesty will, I am sure, do me the justice to acknowledge that I have never presumed to interfere with the rule which he has adopted for his private society. I admire the benevolence which in this, and every other instance, marks his conduct; but I should have much to answer for, when the stability of his Government is at stake, if I were to disguise any of the circumstances by which it is affected."

It must be said that both the King and his ministers used every exertion to dispense with "the dreaded measure," the King canvassing the Archbishop of Canterbury and seeing the "waverers." But Lord Grey was all the time being more and more pressed to make the second reading "safe," by pressing the peers' creation on the King. On February 10th, he addressed a desponding letter to the King's secretary, deploring the way in which he was pressed.

"Nothing but absolute necessity shall ever induce me to press this measure upon the King; but unless I can be justified by a satisfactory assurance that, on the second reading at least, a majority is certain, what am I to do, what answer am I to give to those who urge me to take a step which they represent, I fear too truly, is absolutely necessary for the security of the throne and for the peace of the country, if the passing of the Bill cannot otherwise be secured ? "

In answer to which question came a long and not by any means reassuring manifesto from the King, recapitulating His Majesty's opinions, taking part with those who wished to amend the Bill in Committee.

"His Majesty was assured by your lordship on the 4th of January that many of your colleagues felt the

strongest objections to this step, although they afterwards joined in the *unanimous* recommendation to His
Majesty, that it should be resorted to, if it should become absolutely indispensable.   His Majesty cannot
imagine that they should have so far abandoned their
original sentiments, as to be among those who are now
hourly and daily urging you to take the step, etc.

"But supposing even that your lordship should
yield to this urgency, or allow yourself to be influenced
by the impatience which is felt and expressed with regard
to the creation of Peers, His Majesty wishes to know,
what security you have that this step, whether resorted
to at present or hereafter, or at any time, will have the
effect for which it is intended.   The number of Peers
to be added was at first estimated at twenty-one : it was
afterwards stated that more might be required, but that
it was impossible to fix any number ; and His Majesty
consented that it should be indefinite.   Yet there must
be some limit ; and it cannot be supposed by those who
urge your lordship, that His Majesty would agree to
exceed certain bounds.   Should forty or fifty be required
(and His Majesty trusts he shall never be called upon to
consider of an addition to that extent), the King wishes
to know, whether there be any security that such number will suffice.   It may, indeed, prove equivalent, and
more than equivalent to the number by which the last
Bill was rejected ; but may not that number be increased by many of those who then voted for it, who
are still friendly to the measure, but who feel and are
known to have expressed the strongest dislike of an
addition to the Peerage for the purpose of carrying the
Bill ?   Your lordship has admitted the objection to a
second addition, if the first should prove insufficient; nor
is it likely that it would answer the purpose, as there

might be a corresponding falling off in the previous support. The step might, therefore, have been resorted to, twenty-five or thirty Peers added, and the Bill might still be lost (whether by one vote or more would matter little), after incurring the odium of the objectionable step, and the apparent ridicule of having miscalculated that which, in His Majesty's view of the subject, is not susceptible of calculation, and leaving His Majesty saddled with a large share of both."

Lord Grey answered this in a letter full of vexation, saying that the communication " had made a very painful impression on me,' as it conveyed an expression of the King's regret ' in tones amounting almost to disapprobation,' of his viewing with little satisfaction the disposition of the opposite party to support the second reading, there being little more than a hope to support such an idea. He was probably nettled by the charge that he had changed his views on the question of the Peers, ' a change, owing to conviction, he would never be ashamed to make ;' but it was the peace of the country that was involved. He would, however, make a further attempt to see Lord Harrowby, and make out the real data and some assured facts on which it may be safe to act as to the Tory support they would get for the second reading. If this should prove satisfactory, much embarrassment and distress may be avoided ; if otherwise, it will be for His Majesty's servants carefully to consider at their meeting on Wednesday, what advice they should give him. For myself, the decision is easy. There is nothing I would not do to give ease or comfort to His Majesty's mind ; and if by doing so I could give hope to produce this effect, I would to-morrow humbly tender to His Majesty the resignation of my office, with no other

regret than that which would accompany my separation
from so kind and indulgent a master."

The secretary replied for the King in the sense
of approval, that he believed things would turn out
better. He dwelt on the necessity of not leaving things
dans le vague, and ascertaining beforehand the support
to be given. If, however, these attempts should fail,
" the difficulty must be provided for ; *and your lordship
will not find the King fail you in the hour of need, being
satisfied that every attempt will have been made to avert
the necessity of the dreaded alternative.*"

This was an important promise, and Lord Grey
wrote gratefully to him : "Nothing can be more satisfactory to me than your letter is in every respect ; and
I shall go with a new heart to the further consideration
of this difficult and complicated business."

The interview with the "waverers," Lords Harrowby
and Wharncliffe, took place ; but, as might be expected,
nothing very accurate or certain could result.

" I confess I have been disappointed at not finding
Lords Harrowby and Wharncliffe enabled to state anything more specific as to the persons whom they consider
as pledged to the second reading ; they expressly stated
that they could give no such pledge, and even admitted
that many of those on whom they now count might
change their opinions."

However, towards the end of February, when the
Bishops presented an address to the Queen, her answer
was taken by ministers to be in some degree hostile or unfavourable to them, and gave Lord Grey fresh ground for
dissatisfaction. " The Archbishop of Canterbury spoke
to him on the subject of the answer of the Queen which
has appeared in the papers. He showed me his address,

in which there certainly was no political allusion ; and
he thought there was none in the answer, which, he
stated most truly, would have been exceedingly improper. The answer in the papers, however, is very
differently interpreted ; and I regret, most deeply regret,
the effect this and other circumstances are producing
with respect to Her Majesty."

On this fresh "grumble," the poor harassed King
endeavoured to vindicate his Queen.

"The Queen's answer was verbal, and His Majesty
verily believes as unexceptionable in all respects, and
as free from political allusion as possible. Nothing can,
in His Majesty's opinion, have been more cautious and
guarded than the Queen's conduct for months past ;
and His Majesty is persuaded that you are too well
aware of the manner in which the newspapers distort
words and misrepresent facts, as well as of their predilection for any invention that can serve their purpose and
make mischief, to suffer their reports to weigh with you."

The truth was, all this time Lord Grey was being
pressed on all sides by friends, acquaintances, and
partisans to strike at once ; even the Rev. Sydney
Smith ventured to remonstrate with him, on his hesitation. Lord Grey now found it necessary to have a
long conversation with the King. This took place at
Windsor Castle, on April 1st, 1832.

"His Majesty honoured me with a long conversation
this morning, in consequence of the Cabinet Minute
which had been addressed to His Majesty on March 27th,
and His Majesty's answer thereto.

"He began by stating the deep anxiety he felt upon
this subject, and his desire to hear from me, without
further delay, the observations which I had given His
Majesty reason to expect I should have to submit to

him on the subject of His Majesty's answer to the Cabinet Minute.

"Thus called upon I stated to His Majesty the grateful sense with which those of his Ministers who were in town had received the renewed expression of His Majesty's confidence and approbation, but that there were some points in His Majesty's answer which had also produced considerable anxiety in their view of it.

"That they had thought it their duty humbly to submit to him the various contingencies in which they might be called upon to act, and on which it was necessary for them to be prepared to act at once and without hesitation.

"That, the first, viz. the Bill being carried by a satisfactory majority, left little for consideration at this moment; that it must then go to the Committee, where both its main principles and its subordinate details would be to be considered.

"That with respect to the first, I could only repeat what I had frequently submitted to His Majesty, that there were certain provisions of the Bill which I must consider as fundamental, viz. Schedule A, the enfranchisement of the great towns, and the £10 franchise.

"With respect to the first (Schedule A) His Majesty said, and frequently repeated during the conversation, that being satisfied that a Reform is now necessary, he considered Schedule A, with the exception, perhaps, of one or two particular boroughs (and His Majesty particularly specified Amersham) [His Majesty observed and meant Amersham only] as essential indeed, that he now considered it as a matter of State necessity; and on my observing upon this that His Majesty would therefore consider his Government as being placed in the same situation by the rejection of Schedule A as they would be by a negative of the second reading, His Majesty at once assented to this view of the case [completely.] The enfranchisement of the great towns His Majesty considered as the necessary consequence of the disfranchisement of the boroughs in Schedule A; and on the £10 franchise His Majesty said he would not give an opinion on a question which he imperfectly understood, but that he had been informed that the chief objection to this extension of the elective franchise arose from its operation in the metropolitan districts." [Precisely; the King thus endorses the accuracy of the paragraph.]

"The second point to be considered was, the necessity of a creation of Peers, if the Bill should be carried by a small majority only, on the second reading. I stated to His Majesty the obvious inducements to such a measure, but that, perhaps, this question might be left open to future consideration, by our acquiescing in the proposition which we have reason to expect will be made, for postponing the Committee. This interval might give him time to consider to what extent the creation should be carried, if His Majesty did not object to it. His Majesty stated that he did not mean to say that he would not consent to it, but seemed to wish that it should be reserved for consideration in the way that I had stated." [Correct.]

"The third and last, but most material, point, viz. the rejection of the Bill on the second reading, came then to be considered. I stated to His Majesty my sanguine hope that an event, which I must consider as so calamitous, would not happen; but that if it did, the consequences which I contemplated were of so serious a nature, that, as was stated in the Cabinet Minute, it was absolutely necessary to be prepared for

them : That, after much anxious consideration, His
Majesty's Ministers were convinced that only one of
two courses remained, as had already been pointed out
to His Majesty, viz. either the immediate resignation
of His Majesty's present servants or the prompt and
decisive adoption of the measures which had been
submitted to His Majesty's consideration : That the
first would be a most painful alternative to persons
who had received so many marks of favour and confidence from His Majesty ; and that, if compelled to
resort to it, it would be their first wish to render
it as little embarrassing to His Majesty as possible ;
but that there was no other alternative but that of
proroguing Parliament and creating Peers : That this
must be done, if His Majesty should be pleased to
assent to it, so immediately, that the country should
receive, at the same time with the news of the rejection of the Bill, evidence of the determination to
carry through a measure on which the hopes of the
public were so intently fixed, by the only means
which would then be left for the attainment of that
object : That I did not conceal the difficulties which
would attend this course ; that of having to renew
the measure, subject to another long struggle in
Parliament, was amongst the first of these ; but that,
in a choice of evils, we must take the least ; and that
this might be lessened by introducing the Bill in the
House of Lords, and after having been enabled to
carry it by an addition of Peers, we might hope to
encounter less difficulty than had obstructed the former
discussions in the House of Commons : That by such
means the effect of the disappointment which was
to be apprehended, might, it was to be hoped, be
obviated ; but that there appeared to be no other

chance : That the irritation of the public mind would
be very great ; that it would be directed against me
personally, more than against any other member of the
Government ; that, if the public saw any negotiation
going on, such as His Majesty had suggested, for alter-
ing the provisions of the Bill, so as to make it more
acceptable to the moderate opposers of Reform, this
irritation would be still more excited ; that the public
impatience would neither wait for such a negotiation
nor accept from the present Ministers, and probably not
from any other, what would bear the character of a
mutilated measure ; and that I could not, without
entirely disqualifying myself from acting usefully for
His Majesty's service, propose anything which would be
so entirely at variance with all the declarations which I
had made on the subject. That I was afraid the evil
would not stop here ; and that, if there should be any
delay in taking the measures which appeared to be
necessary, to obviate the effects of the general disappointment, the consequence would be, that instead of
waiting with a disposition to accept a modified plan of
Reform, there would be a renewed cry for Universal
Suffrage and the vote by Ballot, which had ceased since
the present measure was proposed. I, therefore, repeated
that there seemed to be no alternative but that which
had been submitted to His Majesty.

" His Majesty listened to all this with the kindest
attention. He stated that he felt all the difficulties of
the situation in which the Government was placed, and
of his own ; that what he had suggested (and he wished
it to be considered as a suggestion, and not as a negative
on the proposition of the Cabinet) was to facilitate
matters, and assist in the maintenance of the present
Administration, which His Majesty was pleased more

than once to say it was his anxious wish should remain. His Majesty further asked if it might not be possible to go through the remainder of the Session, and defer the introduction of a new Bill till the next, which would afford a favourable interval for considering carefully both what should be done and the best way of doing it. These suggestions, His Majesty stated, were made with the view of removing, as much as possible, both the difficulties of the Government and his own ; but he did not decide positively on the adoption or rejection of the course of proceeding which had been submitted to him ; and expressed his satisfaction that the interval of another week before the second reading would afford opportunity for further consideration." [All correct.]

" His Majesty then asked what number of Peers would, in my opinion, be required, if he were brought to consent to a further creation. I answered that I should be deceiving His Majesty if I stated that I thought a less number than fifty or sixty would be sufficient to insure success. This, he said, was a fearful number, and how was it to be made up ? that he must have information before him to enable him to make up his mind, both as to the number of new creations and the persons of whom that number was to be composed. I answered that, undoubtedly, this was a matter which must be brought fully under His Majesty's consideration, before His Majesty could be expected to decide." [Correct.]

" His Majesty then asked, Whether it was intended to send any answer to his letter ? I stated that it was in contemplation to do so, but that it was deferred till the whole Cabinet could be assembled. He then desired that the matter should remain on this footing for the present, till he should receive the answer of the Cabinet,

and should see me again on Wednesday, when His
Majesty proposes being in town for the levee."
[Correct.]

"The result then is, that there is no positive rejection, on the part of His Majesty, of the advice tendered to
him by his servants, and that the matter still remains
open for His Majesty's decision." [Certainly.]

This, I think, is the substance and the result of what
passed on this interesting occasion, and the conversation
was marked throughout by the graciousness and kindness of His Majesty's manner, and by repeated expressions of the confidence which he places in his present
Ministers.

"In the course of it I stated my views of the present
state of the House of Lords, which had given to a party
in it, which had possessed the Government for the last
seventy years, a power which enabled them to resist the
united wishes of the House of Commons and the people ;
that this made a large creation of Peers, the general
objections to which were forcibly stated by His Majesty,
and the strength of which I acknowledged, bear a very
different character from that which would have belonged
to it under different circumstances ; and that this was so
strongly felt as to induce many reasonable men to urge
the necessity of an addition to the House of Lords, to
counteract the predominance of this party, independently
of the present question." [Perfectly correctly stated.]

"There was also some discussion as to the probable
majority, and the Peers, and particularly the Bishops,
who are now likely to vote for the second reading. But
I have not adverted to these more particularly, as not
being of such immediate importance to the chief and
very interesting object of this conversation.

After this conversation, further "Minutes of Cabinet"

were submitted to the King, fixing definitely the course they were determined to take in case of defeat, or of a small majority, and all laying stress on the purpose to create peers. This led the King to send them a very lengthy document recapitulating all his opinions, letters, etc. ; and in his turn finally laying down what he would do under the supposed conditions. The concluding passages, however, are remarkable as showing a serious limitation of his general promise to create peers.

"It has been the object of the King to show, by reference to previous correspondence, that he has not, at any time, withheld from his confidential servants the option of availing themselves of the permission to propose an addition to the House of Lords whenever circumstances should appear to them to impose the necessity of so doing. But he has not at any time withdrawn the consent to which he had pledged himself, nor attached any restriction to the period at which it should be taken advantage of.

"His Majesty has, however, strongly objected to the *growing* extent of the measure, which he had certainly not contemplated when it was first proposed, and upon which he would have placed a *positive* restriction if he had considered it possible that an addition of fifty or sixty Peers could ever be suggested to him ; and yet that is the number which was recently mentioned to him by Earl Grey. With regard to the other restrictions, those which he declared to be '*inseparable*' from his consent '*and irrevocable,*' he is induced now to advert to them only as conditions to which he is determined, under any circumstances, to adhere.

"Subject to these conditions, and to that consideration which the King is bound to give to the propriety of

limiting the extent of any proposed addition to the
House of Lords to a *reasonable* number, His Majesty
is prepared to exercise that prerogative when circumstances shall call for it, and he shall be advised to do
so ; but he deems it to be his duty to call the serious
attention of his confidential servants to the observations
which he made in his letter of the 30th ult., and to the
embarrassment under which they would be placed by
resorting to this measure, if the second reading should
be carried and the Bill should be in Committee.

"Nor can the King omit to point out to them the
apparent inconsistency of the intended course, namely,
the re-introduction of the Bill in the House of Lords in
the first instance, and the animadversion to which it
may be liable, inasmuch as hitherto the discussion of
the measure in *the House of Commons and its decision
there have been considered and declared to be of almost
paramount importance, and the voice of the House of
Lords has been held out as of very secondary moment ;
such, indeed, as might without objection be obtained and
secured by the nomination of additional members. Yet
it is now proposed that the House of Lords should take
the lead in this momentous question, and should legislate
for the House of Commons.*

"The King cannot also but doubt the expediency of a
prorogation of Parliament upon this occasion. But this
is a question which must be decided by circumstances ;
and, indeed, what His Majesty cannot help feeling is,
that all that is now connected with this question and
with the measure submitted for his consideration and
decision is *speculative, and calculated to engage him
and commit him in that which is uncertain in its nature,
its extent, and its issue.*

"WILLIAM R."

It will be seen at once that this was almost a new attitude, and very different from the accommodating consent he had given at the private conversation. There can be no doubt the reason of this caprice was his being worked upon privately by his secret advisers.

The creation of forty peers would thus appear to have been the amount the King would agree to, "if the dreaded necessity should arise." It might be thought that this was precise enough, but it will be seen what casuistical device he was to find to help him to elude his engagement.

But now a fresh subject of the King's irritation came to inflame matters still more. He called Lord Grey's attention to the state of foreign politics—to his own views on the topics of Poland and the Papal States, as expressed in letters to Lord Palmerston, especially in reference to the behaviour of France : " His Majesty *does not trust France*. Their treachery (*i.e.*, of certain French officers) and their attempts to promote war or revolution have been too gross to escape detection."

After dwelling on this grasping policy and the necessity for watching them, he abruptly requested that no communication be sent in future "to his Ministers abroad without obtaining his previous concurrence." This serious rebuke alarmed Sir H. Taylor, who, in a private letter, explains matters to Lord Grey, informing him that "the questions appear to have agitated him a good deal. Your lordship remarked to me on Saturday, after you left His Majesty, that his manner and conversation had not on that day, or in the preceding interview, been so cordial or easy as usual ; and I assured you, with truth, that he had said nothing to me which could justify the impression that there had been any change. I did not see the King after you left St.

James's, nor until yesterday morning, as I dined with Lady Taylor's sisters at Kensington, and arrived here late on Saturday. Yesterday, however, His Majesty began at once, and very eagerly, upon what had dropped from your lordship respecting Poland, and of the insidious views of the French, which he owned were a source of constant uneasiness to him, as was the disposition shown by his Government to unite with France in support of the introduction of *liberal* opinions and measures agreeably to 'the spirit of the times.' His Majesty added that he should, therefore, require that no instruction should be sent to his ministers abroad until it had been submitted to and sanctioned by him.

Lord Grey wrote warmly and almost angrily on the subject. But to the King he entered into a defence of this policy, and then proceeded:

"And here he would abstain from trespassing farther on your Majesty's time at present, had it not been for the concluding passage in your Majesty's letter, which is so painful that he cannot help adverting to it.

"Your Majesty is pleased to order that no instruction should be sent to your Majesty's Ministers abroad, which has not obtained your Majesty's previous concurrence. Earl Grey might have hoped that such an injunction could not have appeared to your Majesty to be required. Your Majesty's Ministers, he trusted, would have had credit with your Majesty for too just a sense of their duty, to allow of any communication with your Ministers abroad, which might commit your Majesty to a line of policy which had not previously received your Majesty's sanction. He trusted, at the same time, that the concurrence in views and sentiments between your Majesty and your servants might have allowed them in any case of urgency, without waiting for a previous communication with your Majesty, to convey to your Majesty's Ministers abroad such directions as they might justly presume to be in accordance with your Majesty's opinions.

"Earl Grey is, therefore, most painfully compelled to consider this restriction as showing that your Majesty no longer reposes in your Majesty's Ministers the confidence by which alone they can be enabled to act, either usefully for your Majesty's service, or honourably for themselves. If that confidence is withdrawn, Earl Grey has no alternative left but that of humbly tendering to your Majesty his resignation of the office which he received from your Majesty's goodness, and in which he has been hitherto supported by your Majesty's approbation."

To Sir H. Taylor he wrote privately:

"My dear Sir Herbert,

"When, in my letter to you yesterday, I stated that our prospects appeared to be improved, I little expected that, before I could close it, I should receive such a communication as that to which I have replied in the enclosed letter. The pain it has given me is hardly to be expressed, and it was impossible for me to delay conveying to His Majesty the impression it had made upon me. It was, too, as unexpected as it was painful; and I cannot help fearing that His Majesty may have been influenced by representations made to him with respect to the conduct of the Government in matters of Foreign Policy, which have given an unfavourable bias to His Majesty's mind.

"That His Majesty's confidence is diminished is too apparent, from the whole tenor of His Majesty's letter. It expresses not only a want of confidence, but even

suspicion and distrust. If such are His Majesty's feelings, the only course consistent either with his own
comfort, or the safety of his present advisers, is to
resume a trust of which they can no longer discharge
the duties, either usefully to His Majesty or honourably
to themselves."

Thus the rather undignified controversy went on. Lord
Grey's letter to Taylor, marked " private," was shown to
His Majesty, who vindicated himself in this style :

" His Majesty assures Earl Grey that he is greatly
mistaken in the inference he appears to have drawn from
His Majesty's manner and communications on recent
occasions, that there is any diminution of his confidence,
or the least desire to withdraw it from himself or from
his colleagues, who have proved themselves so well
deserving of it under very serious trial.

" Above all the King owes it to himself, and to the
honest principle which has guided his conduct, on all
occasions, to declare that there is not the *slightest*
ground for the impression which his recent communications may have produced upon Earl Grey, as would
appear from his letter to Sir Herbert Taylor, that ' His
Majesty has been influenced by representations made to
him with respect to the conduct of the Government in
matters of Foreign Policy, which have given an unfavourable bias to his mind.' He assures Earl Grey that
he has not conversed, nor otherwise communicated, with
anyone, except his Ministers, upon this subject ; and
that the immediate occasion of his communication of
yesterday was, as therein stated, connected of course
with those which had passed with Viscount Palmerston
on previous occasions."

The friendly Sir Herbert did his best to soothe the
Premier. He pleaded that allowance should be made

for the effects of the continued agitation of a question "which had been the cause of almost uninterrupted worry, uneasiness, and embarrassment." It was natural that all this should have produced some irritability and impatience, "and during His Majesty's last visit to London, and since his return here, there has been a good deal of nervous excitement, such as I had not observed before, and which I ascribe to the above causes. It is now subsiding, and His Majesty is resuming his usual calmness."

These excuses are painful to read; but again comes the natural objection that anything a private secretary urged could not be the official act of his master, who himself did not excuse his demeanour. Lord Grey seems to have taken this view, and replied rather stiffly that, "I perceived, with considerable pain, both in His Majesty's letter and in what passed in the interview with which he honoured me, symptoms of feelings which it must be to me a cause of deep regret that His Majesty should continue in any degree to entertain."

"In stating to me that he had not withdrawn his confidence, His Majesty at the same time expressed, with some warmth, the necessity under which he felt himself of insisting that no instructions relating to Foreign Policy should be sent without his previous concurrence; the repetition of this, after what I had said in my letter to His Majesty on this point, gave me, I confess, considerable pain. I ventured to remind His Majesty that, in no case, had any instructions of importance been sent without their having been previously submitted to His Majesty, etc. His Majesty did not dissent from this, and expressed himself as well satisfied with the conduct, not only of Lord Palmerston but of the other two Secretaries of State; but neither in saying this, nor in the long conversation that followed, was there that expression of cordial feeling which I have heretofore experienced in my communications with His Majesty.

"I have served His Majesty to the best of my ability, and it will be my pride and my duty to do so as long as my services are agreeable to His Majesty; but the moment His Majesty ceases to regard them with a favourable eye, I trust that he will, with the frankness which has always marked His Majesty's conduct, signify to me the change which may have taken place in his opinion."

Having thus established his position, he proceeded once more to attack His Majesty on a favourite topic:

"The assiduity with which reports of such a change are circulated is really surprising, partly from things caught from conversation, but still more from invention. I cannot help suspecting that some of those who have access to His Majesty's society assist in propagating these reports. I desired Wood to send you an extract from *The Standard*, in which His Majesty's altered feelings are alluded to; and for the last two days I have heard nothing but stories of expressions used by His Majesty in his conversations with the Princesses and others, of his being pledged to nothing beyond the second reading of the Bill, and of his being entirely indifferent as to any alterations which may be made in the Committee. It cannot be necessary for me to say that I know all such statements not only to be untrue but to be impossible; but they show the necessity of guarding against even a casual expression, which may be perverted by persons always on the watch for anything that might be represented unfavourably to His Majesty's Government."

The unhappy monarch, thus put on his trial, again defended himself, and with some effect ; saying that what appeared in the papers was too absurd to merit notice. " But His Majesty cannot prevent this, and he believes this evil to have prevailed at all times and under all circumstances, more or less. He thinks it more than probable, also, that some of these reports might be traced to individuals occasionally admitted to his society, and that feelings are often expressed by these and even by members of his own families (which your lordship knows to be much split in opinion and feeling with regard to public men and public questions), which are calculated to produce and encourage the reports to which you allude."

But the real meaning of this treatment of Lord Grey was no doubt to prepare the way for the open breach in their relations that was now to take place.

A crisis for both the Court and the Ministry was fast hurrying on. Both sides were indeed in desperate straits. If the Bill failed to pass, through lack of generalship or courage, or compromise with the Court, the Radical section of the Cabinet was undone. In this view, the fury with which, as described by Mr. Greville, Lord Durham attacked his father-in-law at the Cabinet was hardly the wanton, indecent exhibition the diarist makes it out to be. From Lord Broughton's account of his interview with him it is clear that the advanced Reformers felt themselves to be in a most perilous position if the Bill did not pass. Lord Althorp talked of shooting himself, and seriously said he had his pistols put out of his way ; Sir J. Cam Hobhouse (Lord Broughton) declared he would be ruined for life, and his honour lost. It was not unnatural, therefore, that when

Lord Grey's weakness was visible, they should have spoken vehemently and without ceremony. It was odd, however, that three at least of the Ministry were thought to be verging on madness from this excitement, or despondency, or fury—Lord Althorp, Lord Durham, and Lord Brougham.

The Duke himself was urged forward by his indiscreet friend the Duke of Buckingham.

"Every nerve," wrote that nobleman on 1st January, 1832, "must be strained, and that in the course of the next twenty-four hours, to save the country. You have often perilled your life for that country. Thank God you are sufficiently recovered from your late illness to enable me to *urge* you by every feeling of patriotism to put yourself in your carriage and go to Brighton ; then to throw yourself at the King's feet, speak in your own name and that of your friends. Tell him you are ready to save him from the task of putting his sign-manual to the downfall of his country. Fail to do this, and you will have on your mind, to the last minute of your life, that you have missed taking a step which, at least, might have had the effect of saving us from a revolution. I can add no more. Your own good mind must fill up imperfections."

This melodramatic appeal, it may be imagined, had little effect on the Duke, who wrote that he was not well enough to undertake such an expedition, and that, if he did, it would be of no use. He had lost all confidence in the King.

"Observe what is to be done. I am to see the King, to advise him to refuse to create peers, to tell him that I will form a Government and protect him from that demand ; to convince him that I can so protect him. I must then form this Government and dissolve the Parliament, which, with all haste, could not be effected in ten days; which would bring the opening of the new Parliament to the 18th March.

"But it may be supposed that we can do without a new Parliament. That appears to me to be absolutely impossible. This House of Commons is formed purposely to carry parliamentary reform. It is a part of the conspiracy against the House of Lords; it would not hear of a Minister who should found his authority on the basis of protection of the independence of the House of Lords. If I should go to the King, therefore, I must answer the first question which he would put to me, by telling him that I could not look for the support of the present House of Commons to any ministry formed on the principle of supporting the independence of the House of Lords, and that I could not at this moment advise him to dissolve his Parliament.

"But would the King embark with me in a new course? He would just talk enough to discover whether I had myself any confidence in the course which I should recommend to him. If he should find that I saw the risks and dangers, which as an honest and experienced man I could not avoid seeing, he would shake me off, and would found his compliance with the recommendations of his Ministers even upon what should have passed with me.

"Believe me, my dear Duke, that no man feels more strongly than I do the dangers of our situation. The great mischief of all is the weakness of our poor King, who cannot or will not see his danger, or the road out of it when it is pointed out to him; and he allows himself to be deceived and trifled with by his Ministers.

"I know that the times are approaching, if not come,

when men must consider themselves as on a field of battle, and must sacrifice themselves for the public interests. But it behoves a man like me to look around him and consider the consequences, not to himself alone, but what is more important to the public interests, of every step he takes ; and I must say, that in that view of this case, I differ in opinion with you, and am convinced that I should do harm rather than good by interference."

It is curious that, not so long after, the Duke should have completely forgotten all these excellent salutary arguments ; and when the opening came should have greedily seized on a precarious chance of power. The letter is indeed extraordinary, and written under a bitter sense of failure.

But a crisis was now at hand, when all these shifts and precautions would be brought to the test, and Lord Grey's serious forebodings justified.

CHAPTER IV.

On May 7th, when the Bill was in Committee in the House of Lords, the King received the following, through Sir H. Taylor:

EARL GREY TO SIR H. TAYLOR.

"[PRIVATE.]

"Downing Street, May 7, 1832.

"MY DEAR SIR,

"This accompanies the very painful communication which I have to make to His Majesty of the result of to-night's debate and division. The whole plan was evidently concocted by Lords Harrowby and Wharncliffe, with Lords Lyndhurst and Ellenborough, and I have no doubt sanctioned by the Duke of Wellington, though I do not see how it is possible for his Grace to consent to the plan of Reform announced to the House after the division by Lord Ellenborough.

"He took care not to let his plan be known to the House before the division, which would, I believe, have been very different if it had been previously announced. I make no remark on this proceeding, or on the conduct of Lords Harrowby and Wharncliffe in concerting it after their communication with me, and without giving me any notice of it.

"The only point we shall have to consider to-morrow would be whether we should propose a creation of Peers, or at once tender our resignations to His Majesty. I will send a messenger as soon as the Cabinet breaks up, and perhaps His Majesty will allow me the honour of a personal communication with him as soon afterwards as may be convenient to His Majesty.

"I am, etc.,

"GREY."

In answer, the King addressed to him a long defence of his behaviour.

"Earl Grey will recollect that he told His Majesty that they contemplated not less a number than fifty; that he admitted that even this number might prove insufficient; that he and Lord Brougham agreed that His Majesty had *never* encouraged them to expect that he would consent to so extensive a creation. His Majesty has been induced to make this reference to some of the past transactions, because he is aware that gross misrepresentations of his conduct have gone abroad, that he has been accused of having betrayed his Ministers, and these calumnies have not as yet received any due contradiction."

He then proceeded to reproach him.

"He could not but regret that Earl Grey and his colleagues should, at this period, and circumstanced as is His Majesty, have connected with the expressions of their readiness to continue to him the benefit of their services, the call upon him for the surrender of a pledge that they shall receive his consent to a creation of Peers, if it should be required to give additional strength to His Majesty's Government in the House of

Lords. Had the King forfeited any pledge given to them, had he withheld his support, had he hesitated to place at their disposal all that could be useful to them, had he pursued a course calculated to raise doubt or suspicion of his honesty, he must have been prepared for the imposition of conditions at such a period."

The following day a Cabinet was held, when they felt bound humbly to suggest the advancing to the peerage such a number of persons as might secure the success of the Bill; resignation was the alternative. Lord Grey and the Chancellor went down to Windsor with this disagreeable alternative.

"We went to Windsor together, as the King had always required we should on any great emergency, and with the intention of asking for an unlimited creation of peers as the only means of carrying the Bill. We discussed on the way the names of those whom I had set down in my list, formed upon the principle of making the smallest possible permanent addition to the Peerage. As soon as Grey had stated that we came humbly to advise His Majesty that he should accede to our prayer of having the means of carrying the Bill, the King said: 'What means?' I said: 'Sir, the only means—an addition to the House of Lords.' He said: 'That is a very serious matter;' and we both admitted that it was, and that unless quite convinced of its necessity, we never should think of recommending it. He then asked: 'What number would be required?' and I said: 'Sixty, or perhaps even eighty, for it must be done effectually, if at all.' He said 'that was a very large number indeed; was there ever such a thing done before?' I said: 'Never to that extent, or near it; Pitt had at different times made creations and promotions of much above one hundred, and Lord Oxford, in Queen Anne's time, had

created twelve in order to pass one Bill.' But I admitted these cases did not afford a precedent which went
so far as this proposed creation. He said : 'Certainly
nothing like it.' We continued to dwell on the necessity
of the case, and our great reluctance to make such a
request and tender such advice to His Majesty. He
said he must take time to consider well what we had
laid before him ; and when we saw Sir Herbert Taylor
in the anteroom, while waiting for the carriage, and had
some conversation with him, he said we were sure to have
the King's answer to-morrow. Grey and I then set
out, and on our way home had a wretched dinner at
Hounslow, where he ate mutton-chops, and I insisted
upon a broiled kidney being added to the poor repast.
He laughed at me for being so easy and indifferent ;
and said 'he cared not for kidneys.' Nevertheless he
ate them when they came. And we were in all the
print-shops in a few days."

Lord Brougham had other interviews with the King,
who pressed his Chancellor to continue in office with the
new ministers, when he would have the cordial support
of "*my friend Richmond*," as His Majesty styled him.
He was much agitated, and spoke of "the desperate
situation in which we had placed him." Lord Campbell,
in this, as on other occasions, was led away by his
malignant dislike of his "friend." He says that "a
stratagem resorted to for the purpose of enhancing his
popularity" was to spread a report that he had been
strongly solicited to retain his office under a new government, "but it is quite certain *such a preposterous
conception* never entered the royal mind." It seems,
however, certain that the offer was made. The fact
was known at the time to Sir D. Le Marchant ; it was so
stated in *The Times*, and he himself gave it out publicly.

"The Lord Chancellor," Sir D. Le Marchant heard on good authority, "had a private audience of more than half-an-hour, in which the King pressed him most urgently not to give up the Great Seal. The King also reminded him of what had passed when he came into office. 'I told you then,' he said, 'that you were *my* Chancellor—besides, after all, the office is a civil and not a political one.' The King wept, but the Chancellor was firm and withdrew. The day after he wrote to the King, thanking him for his kindness, and regretting his inability to avail himself of it. The King repeated his previous protestations of regard, and there the matter ended."*

"The Lord Chancellor," says Sir D. Le Marchant, "showed throughout these transactions the most firm allegiance to Lord Grey. When he returned from his mission with Lord Grey to Windsor, he found a note waiting for him from Lord Devon, in these terms: 'I am in the greatest suspense; tell me, I entreat, is all right?' He at once replied: 'To be sure it is all right, you blockhead. How can it be otherwise, when we have done what is right?'

"I was with him at half-past eleven, when a note was brought to him which he read out; it was very short: 'Our resignations are accepted.—GREY.' He

---

* Lord Brougham gives this account: "He was affected to tears, and asked if I too abandoned him. I said that most certainly, had I even a desire to accept his gracious offer, I should be wholly unable to render him the least service, or to assist him in his difficulties, for that I should only injure myself irretrievably without being able to form a Government which could carry the Bill. He argued to show what materials there were in the present Government and in some parts of the Opposition, and I showed him how hopeless such an attempt would be, even if I had not the most insuperable objection to making it."

observed that this was only what he expected, and he seemed in no way disturbed."*

It would be difficult indeed to describe all the incidents of this exciting period.

There was another member of the Government whose eagerness to be out of office was unconcealed; this was Lord Althorp.

"He had not come downstairs," says Jeffrey, "and I was led up to his dressing-room, where I found him sitting on a stool in a dark duffle dressing-gown, with his arms bare above the elbows, and his beard half shaved, with an open razor in one hand and a great soap-brush in the other. He gave me the loose finger of his brush hand, and with the usual twinkle of his bright eye and a radiant smile, he said : "You need not be anxious about your Scotch Bills to-night, as I have the pleasure to tell you we are no longer His Majesty's Ministers." †

Lord Althorp's apparent ease of mind arose from his conviction, that the Tories were prepared to take up the Reform Bill, and that they would carry it. The formal dismissal by the King shows a fatal sense of confidence and security.

"Windsor Castle, May 9, 1832.

"It is not without the truest concern that the King acquaints his confidential servants that, after giving due consideration to the Minute of Cabinet which was brought to him yesterday afternoon by Earl Grey and

---

* He had told Mr. Baring that "he should think himself unfit *to crawl on earth* if he did not stand by the King, even at the expense of his own consistency; that he had resolved to carry the Reform Bill, as an inevitable measure, in all its main provisions."

† A day or two later he was seen returning from Covent Garden Market, his carriage filled with flowers and flower-pots,

the Lord Chancellor, and to the consequences of the alternative which it offers for his decision, of being deprived of the benefit of their further services, or of sanctioning the advancement to the Peerage of a sufficient number of persons to insure the success of the Reform Bill in all the principles which they consider essential, His Majesty has come to the painful resolution of accepting their resignations. But His Majesty cannot reconcile it to what he considers to be his duty, and to be the principles which should govern him in the exercise of the prerogative which the constitution of this country has entrusted to him, to consent to so large an addition to the Peerage as that which has been mentioned to him by Earl Grey and the Chancellor to be necessary towards insuring the success of the Reform Bill in the House of Lords.

Lord Grey took his leave in a very pleasing, graceful style :

" For the numerous marks of favour, so far beyond any personal merits which I can claim, which it has been at once my happiness and my pride to receive from your Majesty, I beg to offer to your Majesty my humble but sincere thanks. They have imposed upon me a debt of gratitude which never can be cancelled. More particularly, I feel myself called upon to offer to your Majesty my humble acknowledgments for the promotion of my brother to the See of Hereford ; an act not more valuable for the dignity which it conferred, than from the peculiar graciousness with which it was distinguished."

Lord Grey, on May 10th, also speaks of this " very distressing interview with the King " :

" I never can forget all the kindness and condescension of His Majesty in this conversation. My feelings

were soothed and gratified by the marked expression of
His Majesty's personal regard; but it was painful to see
His Majesty so deeply affected.   Symptoms of no
equivocal nature are already presenting themselves of
the strong excitement in the country.   This, you may
be assured, it will be my endeavour to allay as much as
possible; but I have little reason to hope that any means
I can use will be successful for this purpose.   In the
House of Commons, too, a feeling prevails which we
have no power of controlling.[*]

Such was the attitude of His Majesty towards his
ministers in May, 1832.   They did not dream what an
ill-considered stroke he was about to attempt, and that
they would be " out " but a few days!

[*] The King once said to Lord Verulam : " I frequently argued with
my mother, the late Queen Charlotte, who contended that the King
agreeing to the Catholic Relief Bill after it had passed both Houses
would break his coronation oath.   In this I differed from her; but I
decidedly feel and think that to destroy one branch of the Legislature
for any particular purpose, sanctioned only by the other, and for a
Bill brought forward by one set of men, would be a flagrant violation
of my oath."—" Wellington Correspondence."

CHAPTER V.

WE have now come to the well-known *coup d'état*, when the King restored the Tories, or made his attempt to restore them. There was something dramatic in this desperate effort, and one is inclined to pity the beguiled and deluded King. For, unfortunately, it is but too plain that it was not the result of mere resistance to the dictation of a Ministry that had been for some time working in the King's mind. The chief movers in the plot appear to have been Lord Munster and Lord Howe; but there was a far higher personage engaged, for Lord Howe, the Queen's dismissed chamberlain, wrote in January, 1831, to try to induce the Duke of Wellington to join :

"I am now going to take a great liberty with you ; it is in strict confidence : to show you part of a letter I have just received from the Queen. Of course she does not know that I have submitted her letter to you, and should you think it *right* to send me a few lines which might be shown to her, and of course to the *unfortunate* master, advert only to what I have said, not what I have shown you. . . . God knows whether the King is sincere or not, but is it not frightful to see him acting as he does, while at the same time he detests his agents ?"

A copy of Her Majesty's letter was enclosed :

THE QUEEN TO LORD HOWE.

"Pavilion, 18 January.

"MY LORD,

"I thank you most sincerely for having communicated to me Lady Ely's letter, which I have burnt,
according to your wish, after its perusal. I read it to
the King, who was as much pleased with it as I was.
*His eyes are open, and see the great difficulties in which
he is placed. He sees everything in the right light,* but
I am afraid he is fixed that no other administration
could be formed at present among your friends, and
thinks they are aware of it themselves. How far he is
right or not I cannot pretend to say, for I do not understand these important things ; but I should like to know
what the Duke of Wellington thinks, for he must be a
good judge of this question."

This is surely a significant communication ; and,
when later, at a great crisis, *The Times* (or rather Lord
Brougham) declared, "The Queen has done it all," this
little backstairs plot might be fairly adduced in confirmation.

But, notwithstanding the Queen's doubts, matters
advanced, and by March it was plain they had brought
the King to agree with their plans. For we find the
ex-chamberlain writing in this strain :

"DEAR SIR,

"I have just seen the King, and he has not yet
any answer from Lord Grey, and nothing whatever
passed between him and the King. *Pray, for God's
sake, have Peel ready.*"

Have Peel ready! But, alas! that was to be a political dream. And again:

"Pray, my dear DUKE, DEPEND UPON THE KING. Assure your party, if they will be *staunch*, he will be so."

Which suggests Marshal MacMahon, the Fourtous, etc. The only difficulty was, who was to strike the blow? But the instrument had been found. What more natural than that the name of pliant Lyndhurst should be suggested? And it was no mere coincidence, surely, that just as the King's mind was ripe for action the ex-chancellor should have brought forward and carried his famous motion.

If we were told nowadays that one of the chief justices had rushed to the House and defeated ministers on a Bill which had been read twice in both Houses, and had then gone to the King and set about making a ministry, the cry would have been raised of scandalous indecency—outrage of all public decorum. But if, in addition, it was found that the leader of his party had taken no share in the business, and that he had worked on his own hand, as it were, what conclusions would have been drawn? In the case of Lyndhurst, all through his life suspected of intrigue—the warrantable presumption surely is that he had been prompted by the Court party and by his own ambition. For it is certain that no regular plans had been laid with the Duke or Sir R. Peel. The whole attitude of Lyndhurst through the business was, as usual, suspicious. We find him working in the background, moving the puppets—the few, as it proved, that he could get to work—including the poor Duke, who, almost alone, went loyally through his functions to the end. There is, it must be confessed, one difficulty in the case, viz., how would he have made so terrible a miscalculation, or have entered into an enterprise so certain to fail. I fancy the only explanation could be—though there is little proof of it—that, knowing Peel would refuse, the bait of all power being in his hands was irresistible.

The Duke's account in the House of Lords was that the " King sent for a noble and learned friend of mine, who informed me of His Majesty's intentions, and I considered it my duty to inquire from others, for I was as impressed as His Majesty," etc. Then, Lord Lyndhurst following, said " that, in consequence of his interview with the King, he waited on the Duke." But it is curious to find that with all his candour he made no allusion to his visit to Peel, and consequent rebuff.

" One fine morning, May 9th," says Lord Campbell, " while Lyndhurst was sitting in the Court of Exchequer, listening to the argument on a special demurrer, a letter was delivered to him from Sir Herbert Taylor, requiring his immediate attendance at St. James's Palace. From a King's messenger being the bearer of the letter, the fact was immediately known all over Westminster Hall, and I well remember the sensation excited in the Court of King's Bench by the loud whisper—' The Chief Baron has been sent for.' He immediately unrobed, and in a few minutes he was in the royal presence.

" He first went to Sir Robert Peel, who treated the proposal with scorn. But, to his great delight and surprise, after this rebuff, he found the Duke of Wellington ready to make the attempt.

" Lyndhurst seemed now to have the premiership within his grasp, although it turned out to be a phantom. Instead of trying to clutch it, however, he thought the more discreet course would be to content himself with the resumption of the Great Seal. Therefore, having by appointment gone down to Windsor in the evening of the following day, he explained to the King the Duke of Wellington's willingness to comply with His Majesty's wishes, and tendered the advice that his Grace should immediately be sent for."

Having been with the King, and reached town at night, Lord Lyndhurst wrote to the Duke in this triumphant strain :

"I have just returned from Windsor, and everything is, I think, well. But I must see you for a few moments. Where shall I find you ?"

In half-an-hour the Duke replied, making this curious profession of faith :

"I shall be very much concerned indeed if we cannot at least make an effort to enable the King to shake off the trammels of his tyrannical minister. I am perfectly ready to do whatever His Majesty may command me."

The idea that Lord Lyndhurst could have himself undertaken to form a ministry was absurd ; but the selection of the Duke of Wellington instead of Sir Robert Peel was no less so, as the event proved. Reaction, however, always thinks of a *ministère de poigne.*

"May 10, 1832.

"My dear Duke of Wellington,

"The more I consider the subject of our consultations—and I have considered it much—the more am I satisfied that you must consent to be the minister, or everything will fail. I am confident we can manage the affair, and the situation of the King is such that at all events it *is our duty to try.*"

" Confident we can manage the affair," "you must
be minister or everything will fail." They did not
manage the affair, and everything failed because the
Duke *was* minister. Never was there a prophecy
uttered so damaging for the sagacity of the prophet.
The reserved attitude of Lord Lyndhurst in the whole
affair, and the prognostications of failure which he was
to utter presently, give rise to suspicions, and it certainly
seems likely that a man of such mental power and
sagacity must have foreseen the issue at the very beginning. Another strange thing is that, being "as much
opposed to Reform as ever," he was at the same time
joining the Duke, who had adopted the entire Bill !

Mr. Greville heard from Lord Lyndhurst himself a
full account of the early stage of these transactions.

" Lyndhurst dined here the day before yesterday.
Finding I knew all that had passed about the negotiations for a Tory Goverment in the middle of the Reform
question, he told me his story, which fully corroborates
his account of the duplicity of Peel and the extraordinary conduct of Lyndhurst himself. He said that as
soon as he had left the King he went to the Duke, who
said he must go directly to Peel. Peel refused to join.
The Duke desired him to go back to Peel, and propose
to him to be Prime Minister and manage everything
himself. Peel still declined, on which he went to
Baring.

One who was busy at the Clubs gives a not unro-
mantic sketch of the excitement among the men about
town.

" Sefton," says Mr. Raikes, "was at the opera in
the highest spirits possible ; he came at half-past one
into the supper-room at Crockford's, having most probably driven in the interim to Downing Street, and

I never saw such an alteration. His face was the picture
of despair and vexation.

"*Wednesday, 9th.*—Sefton's face was a true baro-
meter. Still Ministers attended at the levée, and the
King appeared cheerful. Brookes's Club is full of weeping
and gnashing of teeth, so little was the party prepared
for this sudden catastrophe. The funds have not fallen
much, the three per cents. leaving off at eighty-four. In
the evening the King sent for Lord Lyndhurst, and
some violent resolutions were passed at Brookes's, to be
brought forward to-morrow in the Commons. Sefton
told me that he knew the fact early this morning, and
went instantly to communicate it to Talleyrand, who
was thunderstruck at the news, and sent it off by express
to Paris. It must make a great alteration in our foreign
political relations, and be much to the satisfaction of
Holland, Russia, etc.

"*Friday, 11th.*—A great Tory meeting at Apsley
House, when all party schisms were abjured by the ultra
party, and a general reconciliation took place, with a
determination to pull together for the common cause.
I have just seen Adolphus Fitz-Clarence who told me
that he had left the King at two o'clock, who was
in excellent spirits, and said to him on parting, 'I do
not know who are my Ministers; but I am determined
to do that which I feel is right, without consulting
any one.'

"*Saturday, 12th.*—The King came to town this
morning at one o'clock, when he met the Duke at the
Palace, who, after a short interview, kissed hands as
Premier. None of the other appointments are known.
The King, it appears, is in very good spirits. The
first measure to which he has been advised by the
Duke, is not to receive the delegates from the political

union at Birmingham, as an association not authorised by the law.

"*Sunday, 13th.*—There was a great Tory dinner of forty covers at the new club. The Duke in the chair. Many speeches after dinner, which concurred in admitting the necessity of reform. Yesterday, when Lord Foley went to the Palace, to give in his resignation as Captain of the Band of Gentlemen Pensioners, the King said to him, 'I am an old man, and I do not think I shall ever live to see you in place again.'"

The incidents of this change, like a similar one during the last reign, formed a perfect *journée des dupes.* Mr. Greville learned from Arbuthnot, the Duke's faithful friend, all that passed, and the extraordinary intrigue to put the Speaker, Mr. Manners Sutton, at the head of the Government as Premier. A meeting being held at Apsley House, at which the Duke, Lyndhurst, Baring,* Ellenborough, and (I think) Rosslyn or Aberdeen, or both, were present, and to

---

* The mention of this name suggests one of the most remarkable women of this era, Harriet, Lady Ashburton, married to another of the Baring family. This lady is the subject of one of Lord Houghton's graceful "Monographs," and he describes her thus : "She was able," he says, " not only to sustain the social repute of the former generation but to stamp it with a special distinction. I do not know how I can better describe this faculty than as the fullest and freest excessiveness of an intellectual gaiety that presented the most agreeable and amusing pictures in few and varied words, making comedy out of daily life and relieving sound sense and serious observations with imaginative contrasts and delicate sayings." He quotes a few :

"How can I go out (in London), ordering one's carriage and waiting for it, and getting into it, that is not going out ? If I were a shopkeeper's wife I would go out when and how I pleased."

"I always feel a kind of average between myself and any other person I am talking with, so that when I am talking to Spedding I am unutterably foolish."

"I remember when a child telling everybody I was present at

which Sutton came, and held forth for nearly four hours upon the position of their affairs and his coming into office. He talked such incredible nonsense (as I have before related) that when he was gone they all lifted up their hands and with one voice pronounced the impossibility of forming any Government under such a head.

"It was said that this was Mr. Peel's suggestion, who had put Sutton up to this, and desired him to refuse every office except that of Premier. Accordingly, when Lyndhurst went to Sutton, the latter said he would be Prime Minister or nothing, and Lyndhurst had the folly to promise it to him. Thus matters stood when Lady Cowley, who was living at Apsley House, and got hold of what was passing, went and told it to her brother, Lord Salisbury, who lost no time in imparting it to some of the other high Tory Lords, who all agreed that it would not do to have Sutton at the head of the Government, and that the Duke was the only man for them. On Saturday the great dinner at the Conservative Club took place, at which a number of Tories, principally mamma's marriage, and I was whipped for it, but I believed it all the same."

"I am sure you find nine persons out of ten what you at first assume them to be."

This is happily touched. But he has also collected a number of her careless remarks, which denote besides this easy gaiety a surprising power of observation. Here are a few specimens :

"Your notion of a wife is evidently a Strasbourg goose whom you will always find by the fireside when you come home from amusing yourself."

"The most dreadful thing against women is the character of the men that praise them."

"I like men to be men ; you cannot get round them without."

This accomplished woman died in 1857. With Lady Glenbervie and Lady Charlotte Lindsay, Mrs. Grote and Mrs. Carlyle, the race of this type seems to have become extinct.

peers, with the Duke and Peel, were present. A great many speeches were made, all full of enthusiasm for the Duke, and expressing a determination to support *his* Government. Peel was in very ill humour, and said little; the Duke spoke much in honour of Peel, applaud- ing his conduct, and saying that the difference of their positions justified each in his different line. The next day some of the Duke's friends met, and agreed that the unanimous desire for the Duke's being at the head of the Government, which had been expressed at that dinner, together with the unfitness of Sutton, proved the absolute necessity of the Duke's being Premier, and it was resolved that a communication to this effect should be made to Peel. Aberdeen charged himself with it, and went to Peel's house, where Sutton was at the time. Peel came to Aberdeen in a very bad humour, said he saw from what had passed at the dinner that nobody was thought of but the Duke, and he should wash his hands of the whole business; that he had already declined having anything to do with the Government, and to that determination he should adhere. The following Monday the whole thing was at an end.

"I am not sure that I have stated these occurrences exactly as they were told me. There may be errors in the order of the interviews and *pourparlers*, and in the verbal details, but the substance is correct, and may be summed up to this effect: that Peel, full of ambition, but of caution, animated by deep dislike and jealousy of the Duke (which policy induced him to conceal, but which temper betrayed), thought to make Manners Sutton play the part of Addington, while he was to be another Pitt; he fancied that he could gain in political character, by an opposite line of conduct, all that the

Duke would lose ; and he resolved that a Government should be formed, the existence of which should depend upon himself. Manners Sutton was to be his creature ; he would have dictated every measure of Government ; he would have been their protector in the House of Commons ; and, as soon as the fitting moment arrived, he would have dissolved this miserable Ministry and placed himself at the head of affairs. All these deep-laid schemes and constant regard of self form a strong contrast to the simplicity and heartiness of the Duke's conduct, and make the two men appear in a very different light from that in which they did at first." *

On May 13, the Duke writes to the King, " that he has had a long interview with Lord Lyndhurst, the Speaker, and Mr. Baring. The Duke regrets that he cannot report to your Majesty any satisfactory result. He is to see the Speaker again to-morrow. The accept-ance of Mr. Baring appears to depend a good deal upon that of the Speaker."

The King, in reply, "feels satisfied that his Grace is using his best efforts to forward His Majesty's interest."

The Speaker was hesitating. " I must say," he wrote, " with reference to the proposition made by your Grace yesterday, that, if no other arrangement *can* be made, I must give way, though with fear and trembling."

On the day (May 14) that the Speaker made this exhibition, we find Lord Lyndhurst writing to the Duke in this hopeless strain : " I confess I don't like the affair in which I find you engaged to-day. I have a sort of

---

* This suggestion of Mr. Greville's has been scornfully put aside ; but I confess it has always seemed that Peel's behaviour on this occasion was self-seeking and cautious. It is clear he wished to rule alone, and there is nothing improbable in his being willing to see a puppet in office while he might pull the strings. Mr. Greville was likely to have good information.

feeling that it cannot succeed, and the *prose* of this
morning strengthens this feeling.   Will our anti-reform-
ing friends consent to be thus handed over to other
hands ? However, it seems too late to retreat; we must,
therefore, if the offer be accepted, make the best of it.
I incline to think the answer will be favourable.   If it
should be otherwise, we must assemble some dozen of
the best of our young friends in the House of Commons,
and ask them whether they will undertake to fight;
and, if they consent, I think we ought not to give
the affair up."

The Duke was in the same desponding state, but
was determined to go on.   "I confess I did not like all
that passed yesterday; and I had reasons to believe
afterwards that many of our friends will not approve of
the arrangement.   This may be flattery or vanity.   It
is quite clear, however, that I must take steps to
reconcile them to it.   It would not be very easy now to
alter it.*

This gives an idea of the minor difficulties that
attend the formation of a Government.

The Duke followed his counsellor's advice, and
promised to try and gain Mr. Croker.   But here he was
once more repulsed.   It is impossible not to feel
sympathy for the poor simple bemused Duke.

"On Saturday, 12th May," says Mr. Croker, " I

* Meanwhile his adviser was suggesting many plans and persons.
Lord Lowther should not be neglected; "but his pretensions are
high.   Sir J. Beckett—what can you do with him ? Wetherell is a
peculiar character; he will require considerable management. I think
the Duke of Newcastle might assist you.   Wetherell is a most
important card; for if he is not with us, he is sure, I think, to be
against us.   It is, I think, absolutely necessary that Croker should
consent to be a member of the Government. I think, with his assistance, the House of Commons may be managed."

came early into town and called on the Duke.   He said :
' *Well, we are in a fine scrape*, and I really do not see
how we are to get out of it.' . . .   He then told me
that if no one else would, he would himself undertake
the government.   He said he had passed his whole life
in troubles, and was now in troubles again ; but that it
was his duty to stand by the King, and he would do so.
For ' what,' he added ' could I say to those gentlemen
who met here yesterday, and who consented, at my suggestion, to forego all their private feelings and interests
for the great object of preventing a revolution, but that
I would not myself hesitate to undergo all the odium
and all the danger which might attend our attempt ? '
However, when I told him that I had written to urge
Peel, and was about to go to him to entreat him verbally
to undertake the government, his Grace encouraged me
to do so, and authorised me to say to Peel that he was
ready to serve with him, or *under him*, or any way that
he should think best for the common cause.   He then
said : ' I am particularly pleased with the advice you
give Peel, because it leads me to hope that you mean to
act on the same principle yourself, and help me in this
great emergency.'   He spoke doubtingly, as if he knew
that I had expressed a contrary intention, as I had,
indeed, ever since he left office in 1830.   I replied by
begging his Grace to recollect that I had apprised him
verbally, and in writing, soon after we left office, of my
firm resolution never again to enter into it, happen
what might ; that that resolution I had maintained all
along, and by that I must now abide."

His excuse was that, having neither birth nor station,
nor fortune, and nothing but his personal character to
hold by, he put it to the Duke—what would be thought
if he took a well-paid place and was found supporting

Schedule A ?   At Lady Salisbury's he was attacked by
the Tory ladies.

Now, after this piteous account of helplessness, it
was no wonder that Peel was hereafter hardly judged by
his party.   His conduct, if safe, seemed selfish ; but as
we have seen, it is explained by the fact that he had not
been taken into account by the Lyndhursts and other
plotters, and so left them all to shift for themselves.

In these proceedings the position of the King was
mortifying indeed.   Mr. Greville, who seems to have
been animated by some rancorous hostility, gives a
shocking picture of him.

" The joy of the King at what he thought was to be
his deliverance from the Whigs was unbounded.   He
lost no time in putting the Duke of Wellington in possession of everything that had taken place between him
and them upon the subject of Reform, and with regard
to the creation of Peers, admitting that he had consented, but saying he had been subjected to every
species of persecution.   His ignorance, weakness, and
levity put him in a miserable light, and prove him to be
one of the silliest old gentlemen in his dominions ; but I
believe he is mad, for yesterday he gave a great dinner
to the Jockey Club, at which (notwithstanding his cares)
he seemed in excellent spirits ; and after dinner he made
a number of speeches, so ridiculous and nonsensical,
beyond all belief but to those who heard them, rambling
from one subject to another, repeating the same thing
over and over again, and altogether such a mass of confusion, trash, and imbecility as made one laugh and
blush at the same time.

" From the account of the King's levity throughout
these proceedings, I strongly suspect that (if he lives)
he will go mad.   While the Duke and Lyndhurst were

with him, at one of the most critical moments (I forget now at which) he said : 'I have been thinking that something is wanting with regard to Hanover. Duke, you are now my Minister, and I beg you will think of this ; I should like to have a slice of Belgium, which would be a convenient addition to Hanover. Pray remember this,' and then resumed the subject they were upon."

Mr. Stanley, at a meeting of his party, distinguished himself. " He jumped on the table, and in a most stirring and eloquent speech attacked the new Ministers and the Tory aristocracy most unsparingly. It would be hardly fair to record some of the expressions he used in the warmth of the moment, especially as he ended by supporting the course recommended by Lord Althorp. This was adopted by the meeting with some reluctance, as the feelings of the majority were in favour of violent measures.

" The next morning (Monday) Lord Ebrington complained to the Chancellor of the result of the meeting, and persisted in his intention of combining with Mr. Hume to propose a very strong resolution condemnatory of the Duke of Wellington. Several eminent Whigs among the Peers approved of this course. I was assured that Sir Robert Peel, who had up to this time not declared himself, now took the alarm, and positively refused to enter the Ministry. At a great dinner, however, at the Carlton Club, he commended the Duke's conduct in no qualified terms, and urged the party to follow him, wherever he might lead, as the saviour of his country.

" The House filled early on Monday. Such of the new Ministers (expectant) as were present appeared in excellent spirits. Sir Henry Hardinge stepped over to

Lord Althorp before the debate began, and told him that the real difficulties of forming the administration were at an end, and he hoped that Lord Althorp did not disapprove of the Duke's conduct. He seemed too elated to listen to Lord Althorp's cold and unsatisfactory answer, and soon rose to answer Lord Ebrington's question as to the Duke of Wellington's having accepted office on the condition of bringing in a Reform Bill."

Such was the excitement of the times, there could be little doubt the country was on the eve of a revolution. Books were published with directions and illustrations of the pike exercise. Threats of vengeance were used freely at meetings of Ministers, and the people were urged not to pay taxes. It was a strange thing to hear of the Lord Chancellor's brother haranguing a mob to this effect :

"Something has been said about the people not paying taxes, and a resolution to that effect would be highly illegal. People might individually refuse without rendering themselves amenable to law. Now this is an affair easily arranged. If a tax-gatherer calls upon me, and asks me to settle his little bill for taxes, I may say to him in reply, ' I have got a little bill of my own, Sir, which I should like to have settled by the gentlemen down in Westminster who owe it me, and unless that little bill of mine be satisfactorily settled, you must never expect me to settle yours.' Before I conclude, I beg to state to this meeting that my brother the Lord Chancellor is at this moment in better health than ever ; he is in good fighting order, as the sham reformers will will discover to their cost."* (Thunders of applause.)

* There was a well-known tailor, F. Place, of Charing Cross, a good specimen of the shrewd loquacious Radical. This person collected an enormous mass of papers and memoranda relating to these

The whole scheme, however, collapsed from sheer weakness and imbecility. It recalls a similar ludicrous attempt during the early days of the present French Republic, when a certain M. Welche was installed for a day or two.

Mr. Greville describes the *finale :*

" On Monday evening ensued the memorable night in the House of Commons, which everybody agrees was such a scene of violence and excitement as never had been exhibited within those walls. Tavistock told me he had never heard anything at all like it, and to his dying day should not forget it. The House was crammed to suffocation ; every violent sentiment and vituperative expression was received with shouts of approbation, yet the violent speakers were listened to with the greatest attention. The conduct of the Duke of Wellington in taking office *to carry the Bill,* which was not denied, but which his friends feebly attempted to justify, was assailed with the most merciless severity, and (what made the greatest impression) was condemned (though in more measured terms) by moderate men and Tories, such as Inglis and Davies Gilbert. Baring at last proposed that there should be a compromise, and that the ex-Ministers should resume their seats and carry the Bill. This extraordinary proposition was drawn from him by the state of the House, and the impossibility he at once saw of forming a Government, and without any previous concert with the Duke, who, however, entirely approved of what he said. After the debate Baring and Sutton went to Apsley House, and

troubles, all the placards and proclamations, reports of inflammatory speeches, etc., with a view to writing a history of the Political Unions. It appears an extraordinary mass, filling nine large volumes ; but is dreadfully uninteresting and monotonous. Place, however, in his other lucubrations shows himself a shrewd observer. Ministers consulted him, and he was considered a man that knew the mob.

related to the Duke what had taken place, the former saying he would face a thousand devils rather than such a House of Commons. From that moment the whole thing was at an end, and the next morning (Tuesday) the Duke repaired to the King, and told him that he could not form an Administration. This communication, for which the debate of the previous night had prepared everybody, was speedily known, and the joy and triumph of the Whigs, were complete."

From the House of Commons the Duke's faithful friend, Sir H. Hardinge, wrote his impressions of the scene :

"Our difficulties are infinitely increased by the turn the debate has taken. I have pressed Sir R. Peel to see your Grace this night; but, having taken a different line, he objects, unless you express a wish to confer with him. What I fear is, we shall have all the evil of a Reform Bill, with no inconsiderable sacrifice of political character, by attempts to carry a detestable Bill with Peel and *all* his friends neutral, taking credit for the wisdom of their secession, and bringing your Grace's line of action into violent and unfavourable contrast.

"After this night's debate, it is very essential that your Grace should confer with those who have heard what has passed, and are accustomed to form a judgment of the temper of the House."

The reply of the Duke to this sensible warning, supported by the result, offers but one more instance of that dull, hopeless infatuation which can see nothing and learn nothing.

He thus wrote back, at 11 p.m.: "I have just now received your letter, which has surprised me much. I had imagined that the debate had been very favourable in the first instance. I shall be delighted to see Sir R.

Peel or anybody from the House. I confess that I can't see very clearly how speeches or a vote in the House can prevent me from pursuing the course on which I have entered, unless it should be found that the Government be formed for the King in the House of Commons."

This seems rather enigmatical. What was the course on which he had entered and was to pursue, and which was to be independent of the speeches and *votes* even of the House of Commons? We shall know presently what this was, but then came the collapse of the whole plot, and the ignominious surrender of the King, who was obliged to take back his old ministers. But is it too much to say that, while one has some respect for the Duke, who was "left in the lurch," one feels little respect for the crafty man who had led the attack in the House, defeated ministers, and tried hard to supplant them and failed, bungling the matter in the most clumsy fashion. His situation was indeed pitiable if not laughable. He had lost his office—and he had been chancellor for a few days!

While Lord Grey was waiting for the failure, the court party, now grown desperate, was to work the King up to a final act of resistance, who, setting his back against the wall, was to a make a general appeal to the country for aid. Lord Munster and the Duke of Buckingham here again come on the scene. While the letters were passing between the King and Lord Grey, the first-named nobleman was writing to the Duke of Wellington.

"After thirteen hours, since the King's answer last night to Lord Grey, his lordship is *come.* I know not what has passed, but the King repeated to me, five minutes before Lord Grey came in, that *nothing should make him create peers. He is most stout.* For God's

sake be sure, if the King is driven to the wall, of *Peel.*
An appeal to him and his countrymen could not be disregarded. Unless you have Peel, the House of
Commons cannot be managed. The King never will
make peers. In haste, yours ever."

In support of this policy, the Duke of Buckingham,
who was in a state of excitement, addressed no less than
three despatches to the Duke: at noon, at two o'clock,
and at midnight.

At two, he wrote: " I speak from AUTHORITY. *The
King will not make peers.* All depends upon Peel."

Then he asks, " would it be right to prepare Peel for
this appeal to his *allegiance* as a subject ? "

At midnight he wrote, " *The person* has been with
me. . . . I asked whether the King would let the battle
be fought out in the House of Lords, between the
parties, the King engaging not to make peers. The
King, he said, would not make any peers. The King
was pledged very deep indeed upon the other points."

How the unfortunate King was pressed at this
moment may be gathered from what Sir D. Le Marchant
heard—viz., that " during this interval the hopes of the
Tories revived;" and the Queen, who had warmly
espoused their cause, wrote, even after the King had
seen Lord Grey, to an intimate friend, " I do not despair
yet. Lord Dover told me that he had seen the letter."

All these intrigues were suspected, and were with
good reason laid to the account of Lord Munster, who
was at last driven by the many " calumnies " to defend
himself in the House. To us who have just read his
letters, and followed his rather tortuous proceedings, it
seems scarcely a candid one.

" He would take the opportunity of alluding to
certain aspersions which had been cast upon his cha-

racter out of doors. He was at first inclined to consider these calumnies hardly worthy of notice, being convinced that those who knew his character would need no other proof of their falsehood; but as they had been very generally disseminated, he thought, upon consideration, that it would be as well publicly to refute them. It had been stated that he had unhandsomely intrigued against Earl Grey's Government, and endeavoured to undermine that noble lord's Administration. This was a very serious charge; but he would convince their lordships, by a short and simple statement, that it could not, with any justice, be imputed to him. The truth was that, for six months before, and for four-and-twenty hours after the resignation of His Majesty's ministers had been accepted, it was, from certain circumstances, out of his power to act in the manner imputed to him, even if he had been so unworthily inclined."*

* In the papers this comment was made on this lame defence:

" A speech more clearly betraying the embarrassment of him who made it, more palpably evincing the confusion of ideas and reproachful feelings which proceed from a mind ill at ease, could not have been put into your mouth by the imagination of a poet. You say that for six months before the resignation of Earl Grey you were so situated as not to be able to intrigue against the Government. You had better, my lord, have spoken out more clearly, for the benefit of those persons, the great mass of your countrymen, who are unacquainted with the secret history of the Court. You should have told them that Lord Grey had refused you the office of Governor-General of India, that, not satisfied with the efforts made by a high personage for the attainment of this object of your mortified vanity, you had conducted yourself in such a manner as to make your presence at Court extremely undesirable.

" From the moment, my lord, though you voted for the Bill, you were heard in all societies to inveigh in bitter terms against it and the Government, you were again received into the favour and intimacy of certain illustrious dames, and when you had matured yours and their plot, by the success of Lord Lyndhurst's motion, you returned to favour at St. James' with the ease of an expected guest.

Mr. Disraeli's comment on this blindness of the Duke is worth quoting, though found in a novel:

" The future historian of the country will be perplexed to ascertain what was the distinct object which the Duke of Wellington proposed to himself in the political manoeuvres of May, 1832. It was known that the passing of the Reform Bill was a condition absolute with the King; it was unquestionable, that the first general election under the new law must ignominiously expel the Anti-Reform Ministry.

" The Duke of Wellington has ever been the votary of circumstances. He cares little for causes. He watches events rather than seeks to produce them. It is a characteristic of the military mind. Rapid combinations, the result of a quick, vigilant, and comprehensive glance, are generally triumphant in the field ; but in

" Is not all this true, my lord? Who was it that was seen to drive from Belgrave Place to Hyde Park Corner at an early hour, in a close hackney-cabriolet, several mornings together, previously to the memorable division on Lord Lyndhurst's motion? How was the arrival of that cabriolet so easily known to the porter of Apsley House? By what magic did the gates fly open to receive the unwonted visitor without the necessity of the career of the horse being in the least checked? Why were they closed again with such speedy and mysterious precaution?

. " My lord, we have the greatest obligations to your illustrious father, and for his sake we are willing to overlook the errors of his children, when those errors are confined to the impertinences of the Court. But do not forget your maternal origin. Forbear to provoke inquiries, lest we should discover in you rather the manners and the designs of a soubrette than the lofty bearing of a prince. Write bad books, and borrow the unacknowledged assistance of others, as you have done before. Think no more of India. That country cannot be made the plaything of a child. Renounce Court intrigues, in which you alone can injure us; and, remembering that your understanding does not keep pace with your ambition, we shall in future allow you to follow what course in politics you will, without complaint."

civil affairs, where results are not immediate; in diplomacy and in the management of deliberative assemblies where there is much intervening time and many counteracting causes, this velocity of decision, this fitful and precipitate action, are often productive of considerable embarrassment, and sometimes of terrible discomfiture. It is remarkable that men celebrated for military prudence are often found to be headstrong statesmen. In civil life a great general is frequently and strangely the creature of impulse; influenced in his political movements by the last snatch of information."

A letter of the King's to Lord Grey furnishes the *dénouement.* Never was there so humiliating a surrender.

THE KING TO EARL GREY.

"St. James's Palace, May 15, 1832.

"In consequence of what passed last night in the House of Commons, as it has been reported to the King, His Majesty is induced to communicate to Earl Grey his hope and expectation that the difficulties which have arisen may be removed, without resorting to any change of Administration, by passing the Bill with such modifications as may meet the views of those who may still entertain any difference of opinion upon the subject, and as may not be inconsistent with the intentions upon various occasions expressed by Earl Grey to His Majesty.

"An arrangement to this effect would relieve the King from the embarrassment under which he has been placed by the proposal to make so extensive a creation of Peers for the purpose of passing the Reform Bill, [and would be highly satisfactory to His Majesty.

"WILLIAM R."

Here is a piteous, beaten cry, truly humiliating. On which the triumphant Minister took a new and unyielding tone. Lord Grey quietly put aside in his answer all modifications. Things were now changed.

"It is most painful to Earl Grey to press upon your Majesty anything to which he has reason to believe that your Majesty's opinions are adverse, but he is under the necessity of adding, with the unanimous concurrence of his colleagues, that it appears indispensable, if it should be your Majesty's pleasure to continue them in their present offices, that they should have your Majesty's consent to a creation of Peers, if it should be required to give additional strength to your Majesty's Government in the House of Lords."*

* " The King grants permission to Earl Grey, and to his Chancellor Lord Brougham, to create such a number of Peers as will be sufficient to insure the passing of the Reform Bill—first calling Peers' eldest sons.

" WILLIAM R.

" Windsor, May 17, 1832."

CHAPTER VI

THE Cabinet now forwarded their state of the case. Their tone was now quite uncompromising. "There were only two modes of settling the question," they said; "a cessation of the opposition, and a creation of Peers." The former appeared to be an alternative "in which it was impossible to come to any previous understanding or arrangement." The other they were as unwilling to urge him to adopt as they were before, while the hope existed of finding any other way. This seemed enigmatical enough, and amounted to formulating a state of deadlock. But it really pointed to a third course, the one that was actually adopted, viz. while *they* could not arrange for a cessation of the opposition, *the King might.* This was dated May 16th, and on the following day the King took the matter into his own hands, and made an appeal to the Duke of Wellington and other Peers. This was said to have been the suggestion of Sir Herbert Taylor, "which," says Sir D. Le Marchant, "was to his honour, as he was a Tory of the old school, and had always kept up some connection with the party. He said to me at the time, 'I should have opposed the Bill in every stage had I remained in the House of Commons—but I see that it is for the King's interest that it should be carried, and I have done my best to assist the Ministers accordingly.'"

On the seventh he announced this step to the Duke of Wellington, telling him "that all difficulties and obstacles to the arrangement in progress will be removed by a declaration in the House of Lords this day from a sufficient number of Peers, that they have come to the resolution of dropping their former opposition to the Reform Bill. Should your Grace agree to this, as His Majesty hopes you will, he requests you will communicate with Lord Lyndhurst and any other Peers," etc.

The Duke replied coldly and stiffly that, though he had assured the King that he would not attend to the further discussion of the question, "I confess that I don't think that I can declare in the House of Lords what my course will be, as a condition that the Minister should refrain from his recommendation that Peers should be created to carry the Bill, without making myself a party to his proceeding."

The poor King could only protest through his secretary, to Lord Grey: "He believes the intention to relieve His Majesty from the necessity of taking a step which is known to be so odious to him to exist, but unfortunately there is a feeling of soreness and irritation which prevents an intimation being given to that effect, such as would satisfy Earl Grey ; and it is lamentable to reflect that His Majesty's honour, his scruples of conscience, his future peace and comfort, shall be sacrificed to the absence of mere form, and to the disinclination to come to an understanding."

On this, something like recrimination followed, and Sir H. Taylor retorted that he had heard from a Peer, a violent party man, that "several Peers had intended to take an opportunity of declaring their intention of not opposing the Reform Bill in the Committee *and in the subsequent stages, but that your speech was so peremptory and unconciliatory that they abandoned their intention.*"

"The debate, however interesting, left the whole matter in uncertainty; and the next day the old question began again. What was to be done—Peers or no Peers? A Cabinet sat nearly all day, and Lord Grey went once or twice to the King. He, poor man, was at his wits' end, and tried an experiment (not a very constitutional one) of his own by writing to a number of Peers, entreating them to withdraw their opposition to the Bill. These letters were written, I think, before the debate. On Thursday nothing was settled, and at another meeting of the Cabinet a minute was drawn up, agreeing to offer again the same advice to the King. Before this was acted upon, Richmond, who had been absent, arrived, and he prevailed upon his colleagues to cancel it. In the meantime, the Duke of Wellington, Lyndhurst, and other Peers had given the desired assurances to the King, which he communicated to Lord Grey. These were accepted as sufficient securities, and declarations made accordingly in both Houses of Parliament. If the Ministers had again gone to the King with this advice, it is impossible to say how it would have ended, for he had already been obstinate, and might have continued so on this point, and he told Lord Verulam that he thought it would be contrary to his coronation oath to make Peers. Our Princes have strange notions of the obligations imposed by their coronation oath.

"On Thursday, in the House of Commons, Peel made his statement, in which, with great civility and many expressions of esteem and admiration of the Duke, he pronounced as bitter a censure of his conduct, while apparently confining himself to the defence of his own, as it was possible to do, and as such it was taken. I have not the least doubt that he did it *con amore*, and that he is doubly rejoiced to be out of the scrape himself and to leave others in it."

In the House of Lords there was a debate on the subject, in which nothing of the expected complaisance was shown. Mr. Greville recounts the scene, making his usual sagacious summary of events.

In consequence, these overtures were received very coldly, and even hostilely, by Lord Grey. He said: "Nothing could be more unsatisfactory or embarrassing. The Duke and the other hostile Peers had behaved in the House with the utmost violence, and had shown especial virulence;" and the debate (of May 17th) ended without any declaration of the nature Lord Grey looked for.

"This rendered it impossible," he wrote, "for him to say more than that, the communication which he had the honour of receiving from your Majesty on Wednesday last had yet produced no decisive, result, and places him and his colleagues in a situation of extreme embarrassment, which must be the subject of consideration in a Cabinet summoned for to-morrow at twelve, the result of which Earl Grey will have the honour of communicating to your Majesty." To Lord Brougham he wrote that the King's answer was "not pleasant," and would have to be dealt with by the Cabinet. To Sir H. Taylor he wrote privately, in a bitter tone of complaint:

"They got up in a body at the end of Lord Carnarvon's speech, and left the House; which was, I suppose, intended as a secession, but without any declaration of an intention to let the Bill pass, so that they are at liberty to return in force whenever they may see a favourable opportunity for striking a blow.

"This leaves us in a situation of extreme embarrassment; we have no security against their re-appearing in force at any moment; and they are evidently combined, and determined to exert their united efforts to overthrow the Administration if it remains in our hands, whenever they may see an opening for an attack: in short, we remain entirely at their mercy. As the Peers were leaving the House, Lord Strangford said to somebody near him: 'You see Sir H. Taylor's famous letter did no good.'

"In these circumstances I see no resource but our reverting to the Minute which was delivered to the King by the Lord Chancellor and me at Windsor. But this will be the subject of our deliberation in the Cabinet, which is to meet at twelve to-morrow.

"It is evident that a very improper use has been made of the papers communicated to the Duke of Wellington and Lord Lyndhurst by the King. The Duke of Richmond's dissent was openly stated, and there were other allusions to what had passed between the King and his Ministers. The best solution of the difficulty would be the formation of a new Administration; and when our resignation is made a charge against us, I should like to know what is to be said of Sir R. Peel's refusal to take office?"

The allusion in the last paragraph but one, bespeaks Lord Grey's anger at what he considers an unworthy breach of confidence. It was pitiable to find the unhappy King defending himself in this wise:

"His Majesty has learnt with regret, from your lordship's letter, that an improper use has been made of the papers communicated to the Duke of Wellington

and Lord Lyndhurst by His Majesty.   But His Majesty
orders me to observe, upon this point, that he cannot
admit that, circumstanced as he was, he was under
any obligation not to make such communication to those
two Peers as he might consider advisable and necessary.
His Majesty had accepted the resignation of your lordship and your colleagues."

On May 18th, the Cabinet had decided finally that
they must claim the power of making peers or retire,
and Lord Brougham and Lord Grey were deputed to
see the King, and bring him to his knees.   The former
describes the scene :

" On the same afternoon (of the 18th) Lord Grey and
I went to the King.   It was one of the most painful
hours I ever passed in my life, because the King evidently
suffered much, and yet behaved with the greatest
courtesy to us.   It is, however, the only audience I
ever had in which he kept his seat, and did not desire
us to sit down.   After we had urged the matter in the
strongest language it was possible to employ, he said,
' Well, now it must be so, and I consent.'   I think he
added that he retained the same objections to the creation
which he was then agreeing to.   We stated that it might
be necessary to make the creation at any part of the
proceedings, and I added, ' Even on the Bill coming
back from the Commons, as there might be amendments
upon what had been added in the Lords.'   There was a
good deal of conversation upon the probability of the
creation being required.   But he again said he gave his
promise to make such Peers as *both* of us (and he dwelt
upon this) should advise.   We were then about to take
our leave when I said that I hoped His Majesty would
not be offended if I ventured to make an additional
request, ' What ! ' he said, ' are you not satisfied ?   Have

I not done enough?' I said quite the reverse of being
dissatisfied, and we must ever feel deeply grateful for his
great kindness in agreeing to follow our advice. 'Then
what is it,' he said, 'that I am to do more than I have
done?' I said, 'Your Majesty must consider that this
is a most delicate position in which we your servants are
placed, and it would be most satisfactory to us, and
greatly relieve our minds, if you would graciously consent to give us your promise in writing.' He was a
little, and but a little, angry at this and said, 'Do you
doubt my word?' We both said, certainly nothing of
the kind; but it would be more satisfactory for both His
Majesty and us if he would add this to his other great
kindness. I said I was sure Lord Grey would agree
with me—which, on the King looking as if for an
answer, he signified that he did. The King then said
he should comply with the request, and send me a few
lines to-morrow morning. When we came away, Lord
Grey said he was perfectly shocked with what I had
done, and he wondered how I could be so unfeeling
after all that had just passed, and seeing the state
of vexation in which the poor King was. I said you
may rest assured that, before twenty-four hours pass,
you will be fully convinced not only that I was in the
right, but will in all probability find that this written
promise may render the measure of creation unnecessary,
which both of us think an extremity on all accounts to
be avoided. He said ' God grant it may.' "

"The same evening the King wrote in reply to the
minute left with him by Lord Grey and myself, that he
authorised a creation of Peers to such an extent as would
enable Lord Grey to carry the Bill, avoiding as far as
possible any permanent increase to the Peerage, by ' com-
prehending as large a proportion of the eldest sons of

Peers and heirs of childless Peers as can be made available ; and, in the words of the Chancellor, to exhaust the list of eldest sons and collaterals, before resorting to any which should entail permanent addition to the Peerage.'

"Sir Herbert Taylor took upon himself, without any authority from the King, or any communication with us, to let some of the Peers, the most active adversaries of the Bill, know that the King's authority had been given, and was in hands which he was certain would use it. This led to the secession of such a number from all share in the subsequent debates, at least in the divisions, that we carried all the clauses in Committee, and the Bill passed.*

THE KING TO EARL GREY.

"St. James's Palace, May 17, 1832.

"The King transmits to Earl Grey the copy of a communication which has been made by his order to the Duke of Wellington and many other Peers ; and

---

* "Great complaints," goes on Lord Brougham, "were made of Sir H. Taylor for having used the King's name to intimidate the Lords. In truth, he only gave them fair notice of the risk they ran, that every one must believe to be a serious, perhaps an irreparable mischief to the constitution, might be avoided. It is needless to say that Lord Grey and I avowed our responsibility for his act, though entirely ignorant of it, and would not listen to certain of our friends—indeed colleagues—who were disposed meanly to throw the blame upon Taylor. The same persons being strongly prejudiced against him from his long-continued connection with one king after another, had foretold, when we came into office, that we should find him faithful and even friendly on all occasions, possibly on important ones ; but that when any great crisis happened, he then would make an exception. They little knew the man ; and the most important crisis of all —the most unexpected—showed it more strongly than any other."

acquaints him that, in the event of the declaration
being made in the House of Lords which is therein
suggested, Earl Grey is authorised by His Majesty
to state to the House of Lords, that His Majesty has
been pleased to express his desire that Earl Grey and
his colleagues should continue in his Councils.

"WILLIAM R."

"There can be no doubt the whole is a rather
humiliating chapter in politics, and the Reformers above
all should have shrunk from it. No Minister has ever
since ventured on such a proposal. The true constitutional course is of course to let the opposing body act at
their own peril. If they have the country with them,
or likely to come round to this opinion, they will oppose
with safety ; if they have make a mistake in their view,
they will soon retract. The ludicrous part was that the
Reformers' Bill was actually meant to do away with a
similar evil in the House of Commons, when majorities
had been formed by nominated or created members."

But their difficulties were not over. The King, thus
baffled, humiliated, and beaten, was not inclined to be
cordial or even gracious. This had been shown by
grumblings and complaints, during the progress of the
Bill. A new question now arose.

"The King has reason to believe that those who
have dropped their opposition to the Bill, from a feeling
of deference to him, and in order to relieve him from
the painful necessity of creating Peers for the purpose of
passing it, have done considerable violence to their
feelings, and that they are hurt and disappointed that
they have not, by this sacrifice of their opposition,
secured even those modifications which it had been
understood that you would not have felt unwilling

to admit. His Majesty cannot decide how far it may be practicable for your lordship to introduce any on the report, or on the third reading, but he is satisfied that if this were practicable, and were effected, it would tend in the greatest degree to allay irritation, to conciliate many of those to whom I have adverted, and eventually to secure their support to the Government."

Next came the question of giving his assent in person to the Bill; "but this," wrote his secretary, "is a point on which he had determined not to give way; and your lordship will learn from a letter I wrote last night to Lord Brougham, that I had not ventured to submit his letter upon the subject to His Majesty. The expression of his sentiments may appear strong, but yet it is not more so than his occasional remarks warranted."

When the impracticable monarch made his last stand, he in remarkable language expressed his genuine opinions, and betrayed his exasperation against what he had been forced to do.

" He had never attached any value to that popularity which results from the effervescence of the moment—that which is not felt to be due to, and to arise from, a sense of the correct and honourable discharge of duty. He is told that his giving the royal assent in person to the Reform Bill would be agreeable to the people—to those who, within the last fortnight, had so grossly insulted him; and that by this step he would regain the popularity which he is assured he had enjoyed—that he would set himself right again. But he observed, upon this, that he would greatly prefer their continued abuse to the conviction that he had merited it by degrading himself in courting applause which he has learnt to despise."

Reviewing the conduct of the King through the whole transaction, it is not difficult to judge it clearly and fairly. It is impossible to acquit him of a certain shiftiness, for his adhesion and support of Lord Grey was not thorough. He yielded only when he was forced to yield, and he appears to have counted on events and the chapter of accidents to come to his assistance. The moment he saw a chance of success he seized on it, with only the certain result of his own further mortification. Clear also is it that he was prompted and urged on by the secret Court party; and it is but too probable by the Queen, the conduct of her favourite chamberlain being a good index of her own. Later, therefore, when the cry was raised, " *The Queen has done it all!* " this early interference was recollected; and indeed nothing is more probable than that a weak, impulsive monarch should have been pushed into follies by a woman of stronger mind.

At the same time this opens an interesting subject of discussion as to the part the important factors of the Crown and House of Lords should play in resisting changes of the Constitution. There can be little doubt that such opposition, even if fruitless in the end, is not so fruitless, " stupid," or bigoted as it is presumed to be. A measure which is thus contested is likely to be a far better one than one which is suffered to pass unopposed. It acquires greater weight and more dignity and importance, and really represents the general opinion of the country better. All the great measures have been thus dealt with, and the value of his hostility is not not diminished by the violence of individual bigots, auguring ruin and destruction to the Constitution.

Though it is surprising to find a man of the world like the Duke of Wellington, whom we find making a decla-

ration that the day the King set his seal and signature
to the Act the sun of England had set, or words to that
effect.   In Mr. Disraeli's brilliant novel this episode is
described :

"Emboldened by these demonstrations, the House of
Commons met in great force and passed a vote which
struck, without disguise, at all rival powers in the
State ; virtually announced its supremacy ; revealed the
forlorn position of the House of Lords under the new
arrangement ; and seemed to lay for ever the fluttering
phantom of regal prerogative.

"It was on the 9th of May that Lord Lyndhurst was
with the King, and on the 15th all was over.   Nothing
in parliamentary history so humiliating as the funeral
oration delivered that day by the Duke of Wellington
over the old Constitution, that, modelled on the Venetian,
had governed England since the accession of the House
of Hanover.   He described his Sovereign, when his
Grace first repaired to His Majesty, as in a state of the
greatest 'difficulty and distress,' appealing to his never-
failing loyalty to extricate him from his trouble and
vexation.   The Duke of Wellington, representing the
House of Lords, sympathises with the King, and pledges
his utmost efforts for His Majesty's relief.   But after five
days' exertion this man of indomitable will and invincible
fortunes, resigns the task in discomfiture and despair.
From that moment power passed from the House of
Lords to another assembly.   But if the Peers have
ceased to be magnificoes, *may it not also happen that
the sovereign may cease to be a Doge?*"*

* The dream that the sovereign may cease to be a Doge is, after
fifty years' interval, less likely than ever.   One of Mr. Disraeli's
rather romantic speculations has a good deal of truth in it, and there
can be little doubt that it was an expiring struggle of two factors of
the Constitution.

"I have always," says Lord Brougham, " regarded this as the greatest escape I ever made in my public life. Yet there never was any measure on which a powerful party, supported by nearly the whole people, were more unanimously bent than that of a large creation of Peers in 1832. But nothing could be more thoughtless than the view then taken of this important question. The advocates for such a wholesale measure never considered what must happen if the Peers, our partisans, should ever be found at variance with King, Commons, and People; they never foresaw that, in order to defeat such an oligarchy, a new and still larger creation must be required; they never reflected upon the inevitable ruin of the Constitution, by the necessity thus imposed of adding perhaps a hundred to the Lords each time a Ministry was changed. Among all who were the loudest clamourers for a large creation, I have seldom found one who did not admit how wrong he had been, when these objections were plainly stated to him, and these fatal consequences set before his eyes. Since 1832, I have often asked myself the question, whether, if no secession had taken place, and the Peers had persisted in opposing the Bill, we should have had recourse to the perilous creation?

"Above thirty years have rolled over my head since the crisis of 1832. I speak as calmly on this, as I now do upon any political matter whatsoever, and *I cannot answer the question in the affirmative.*

"I *know* that Grey would have more than met me half way in resolving to face that or any risk, rather than expose the Constitution to the imminent hazard of subversion; and I feel assured that the patriotism of our most distinguished political opponents would have helped us to carry a sufficiently large measure of Reform;

not enough to have satisfied those reckless men who were more bent upon the *mode* of obtaining Reform than upon Reform itself, but ample for the requirements and real interests of the country.

"When the Duke of Wellington read my statement to the above effect, two or three years before his death at Walmer, where I always passed a day or two before going to Cannes, he said : " Oh ! then you confess you were playing a game of brag with me ; indeed I always was certain it was a threat, and that you never would have created Peers." To this all I could say was, that we were thoroughly convinced *at the time* of the necessity, and that he himself must have been so satisfied of our resolution to take the step that he would not run the risk of it ; and that if he had not caused, he had at least acquiesced in the secession."

Such was this extraordinary incident, which has been traced with much pains and detail from its inception. It indeed has an unpleasant flavour, as of something in the days of the Stuarts. I think it has been shown clearly that the whole was an organised "cabal," or compromising, on the part of the Court faction, prepared long before. The person most to be blamed was surely the Duke of Wellington, and the person most to be pitied was the unhappy King, who, it is clear, was pressed and goaded by this faction into doing what he thought at least inexpedient. He was heard to say reproachfully: "Why did you lead me into this—why did you not tell me the truth ?" And thus the struggle ended.*

* At this place I may allude—not inappropriately, as this momentous session has closed—to a singular ceremony which heralded the conclusion. For nearly a century the sign and token of the closing session has been the ministerial whitebait dinner at Greenwich, solemnly described every year with a stereotyped minuteness, as though it were some sacred function necessary to the ministerial function. Yet of

Thus the tremendous crisis came to an end. It is strange to find that after all, on our side at least, it was no more than what is vulgarly called " a game of brag," for Lord Brougham, writing long after, declares solemnly that if it came to the point he would have shrunk from the step.

And so the great Reform Bill of 1832 was passed. Having thus followed out the secret history of the measure—its political course having been already dealt with by many competent hands*—I shall now pause, as it were to rest, and turn to a more agreeable topic, namely, the peculiar spirit of English manners, society, and character in these days, which, in the direction of character particularly, offered some striking differences to our own.

late the solemn custom is showing signs of inanition ; the leading ministers begin to absent themselves, the rest seem to hold it as an unfortunate interruption, and perhaps as a nuisance. The world, too, has grown rather tired of going down to Greenwich to eat fish. The origin of the custom, which has really no *raison d'être* discoverable, has been traced to—(it is Mr. Sala, I think, who tells us)—a convivial habit towards the end of the last century indulged in by Sir Robert Preston, M.P. for Dover, of inviting his friend the Right Honourable George Rose—Cobbett's " Old George Rose "—Secretary of the Treasury, to dine with him at his fishing cottage, on the banks of Dagenham Lake, in Essex. Mr. Rose, on one occasion, proposed that a " mutual friend," the Prime Minister, Mr. Pitt, should join in the festivity, and so pleased was " the Pilot who weathered the storm " with his entertainment, that he promised to repeat his visit the following year. On each recurring Trinity Monday it was found that there was an increase in the number of the guests ; and eventually Mr. Pitt proposed that the *venue* of the symposium should be moved to within a more convenient distance from town. Greenwich was fixed upon, and the ministerial dinner became a pic-nic, to which each guest contributed his due quota of the expense. Another absurd ministerial survival may be noted also, being the presentation of bales of fine cloth, sufficient to make several suits of livery, to the various officers of state.

* In Molesworth's " History of England," " History of the Reform Bill," and Roebuck's " Whig Ministry." See also Miss Martineau, Mr. Walpole, Lord Campbell, Lord Brougham, Mr. Greville, on all of whose labours I have drawn abundantly.

CHAPTER VII.

THE closing years of the late King's life had brought about a considerable alteration in the state of society and manners. The complete isolation in which he lived, the existing political questions which were rife, and were also impending, the angry excited state of popular feeling, which found vent in the mobbing of the King and Queen, and in hunting obnoxious Ministers through the streets and sacking their houses, all this checked the pleasant carnival of pleasure and licence which had reigned during the days of the Regency, and made persons of position carefully discreet in their pleasures. But indeed a view of English society, say from 1810 to 1830, offers much that is worthy of study, from the unusual or exceptional elements that chequered its course, and which are not at all likely to recur. People often contrast the present state of social life, its lack of wit, literary tone, etc., with those Eden days, and nothing could be more unfavourable to our time than such a comparison. But it is not difficult to explain, or at least to offer an explanation of this difference, and one that seems to be fairly satisfactory.

We look back fondly and with wonder to the abundance of literary wealth and genius, that was to be found in London, and not only in London but in the best London Society, during the twenty-five years between 1810 and 1835. Though present society affects liberty, equality, and fraternity, it cannot be said that mere literature, or wit, or genius commands an entrance to society, and one could reckon up the numbers of such men—an eminent poet or two, a distinguished painter, and an essayist or so, who are what is called regularly *répandus:* not but that many more would be duly welcomed in the sacred circles, but it probably would be from a love of prestige. Now in this older generation "fashionables" were more cultured, and their *ton* was to relish the letters, wit, and company of cultured *littérateurs.* Hence we find Scott, Rogers, Moore, Campbell, Hook, Hood, the Smiths, etc., all welcomed in the great London saloons. And what a gathering of talent—Byron, Scott, Wordsworth, Coleridge, Shelley, Crabbe, Moore, Rogers, Proctor, Campbell, Tom Sheridan, Canning, Brougham, Jekyll, Frere, the four Smiths (Bobus, Sydney, James, Horace), Hood, Alvanley, Luttrell, Theodore Hook, Monckton Milnes, Mrs. Norton ; but it would take too long to make a complete list. What will be particularly noted is the strong list of wits.*

---

* It may be doubted if there is a single wit in society now comparable to any of these choice spirits. One reason is, no doubt, the lack of opportunity in the abilities of long drinking *sederunts*, and convivial meetings, the shortening of the time of sitting after dinner, etc., and above all the " hurry " in which we live.

One of the last survivors of this school of cultivated story-tellers, and who reflected faithfully the tone and traditions of the time, was

One of the most noted social centres of the time was the well-known and much celebrated Holland House *coterie*. For many years the host, or rather the hostess, used to gather about them at the antique

Mr. Hayward, whose recent demise has impoverished the public stock of harmless pleasure, and made readers of the *Quarterly Review* for the future "poor indeed," and who has been happily described "as a Queen's Counsel without practice, a politician without a seat in the House of Commons, a man of letters, whose compositions never extended beyond the length of an essay, a journalist without a journal, and a critic without specially recognised authority." He was not merely a diner-out, although no man dined out more frequently than he did; he was never called a wit, although he said innumerable clever things. He was a leader of no school, an exponent of no phase of thought, but he unquestionably was consulted by politicians of the first rank, from Lord Palmerston to Mr. Gladstone, and rising orators and men of letters looked anxiously for his good word till the day of his death. As he was the last of the really brilliant and influential pamphleteers, so was he the last of the *raconteurs*. This is said in the face of the excellent anecdotes told by Mr. Grant Duff, and the not less graphic and amusing talk of Mr. Hare. But neither of these admirable talkers has the peculiar method of Mr. Hayward, which consists "in cutting the story down to the bone," as he himself described it. Nothing was more amusing than to hear him enunciate his principles of telling an anecdote. He did not condescend to point out that no story is good which is not pertinent to the matter under discussion, and that therefore no anecdote should be dragged in by the ears. He despised such instruction as elementary, and only deigned to touch on the higher artistic merit. One of his cardinal rules was : "Never explain. Never tell about the place or persons. Always pre-suppose a cultivated audience, and don't insult them by letting them think you know more than they do." His stock of anecdotes is introduced with delightful art into his Reviews, generally finishing some surprising story with, "our correspondent was Lord ——, the hero of the narrative." He could turn "verses of society," and a few privileged friends would be favoured with a sight of a volume of piquant lines on various ladies, beauties, or wits, who figured in society. He died February 3rd, 1884, at a good age.

and picturesque mansion at Kensington, a number of
friends and familiars, more or less witty and learned,
who came to dine or to remain a few days. The
lady of the house seems to have aimed at an imitation of the *coteries* of Madame du Duffanrd and other
French Queens of the Salon. These gatherings have
been celebrated in glowing pages by Talfourd and
Lord Macaulay, and the world outside have looked
back fondly to those delightful feasts of reason as to
something fascinating and that represented the witty
era of letters. Talfourd's retrospect is tinged with
a romantic cast, and his tongue "grows wanton"
with a praise that seems almost too excessive.
He says :

"First, let us invite the reader to assist at a dinner
at Holland House in the height of the London and
Parliamentary season, say a Saturday in June. It is
scarcely seven—for the luxuries of the house are
enhanced by a punctuality in the main object of the
day, which yields to no dilatory guest of whatever
pretension—and you are seated in an oblong room,
rich in old gilding, opposite a deep recess, pierced by
large old windows through which the rich branches of
trees bathed in golden light, just admit the faint outline of the Surrey Hills. Among the guests are some
perhaps of the highest rank, always some of high
political importance, about whom the interest of busy
life gathers, intermixed with others eminent already
in literature or art, or of that dawning promise which
the hostess delights to discover and the host to smile
on. All are assembled for the purpose of enjoyment ;
the anxieties of the minister, the feverish struggles of
the partisan, the silent toils of the artist or critic, are

finished for the week; professional and literary jea-
lousies are hushed ; sickness, decrepitude, and death
are silently voted shadows ; and the brilliant assemblage
is prepared to exercise to the highest degree the extraordinary privilege of mortals to live in the knowledge
of mortality without its consciousness, and to people
the present hour with delights, as if a man lived
and laughed and enjoyed in this world for ever.
Every appliance of physical luxury which the most
delicate art can supply, attends on each ; every faint
wish which luxury creates is anticipated ; the noblest
and most gracious countenance in the world smiles
over the happiness it is diffusing, and redoubles it by
cordial invitations and encouraging words, which set
the humblest stranger guest at perfect ease. As the
dinner merges into the dessert, and the sunset casts
a richer glow on the branches, still, or lightly waving
in the evening light, and on the scene within, the
harmony of all sensations becomes more perfect ; a
delighted and delighting chuckle invites attention to
some jolly sally of the richest intellectual wit reflected
in the faces of all, even to the favourite page in green,
who attends his mistress with duty like that of the
antique world ; the choicest wines are enhanced in
their liberal but temperate use by the vista opened in
Lord Holland's tales of bacchanalian evenings at
Brookes's, with Fox and Sheridan, when potations
deeper and more serious rewarded the Statesman's
toils and shortened his days ; until at length the
serener pleasure of conversation, of the now carelessly
scattered groups, is enjoyed in that old, long, un-
rivalled library in which Addison mused, and wrote,
and drank."

"The conversation at Lord Holland's was wont to mirror the happiest aspects of the living mind; to celebrate the latest discoveries in science; to echo the quarterly decisions of imperial criticism; to reflect the modest glow of young reputations. All was gay, graceful, decisive, as if the pen of Jeffrey could have spoken; or, if it reverted to old times, it rejoiced in those classical associations which are always young. Whatever the subject was, it was always discussed by those best entitled to talk on it; no others had a chance of being heard. This remarkable freedom from *bores* was produced in Lord Holland's by the more direct and more genial influence of the hostess. Perhaps beyond any other hostess, certainly far beyond any host, Lady Holland possessed the task of perceiving, and the power of evoking the various capacities which lurked in every part of the brilliant circles over which she presided, and restrained each to its appropriate sphere and portion of the evening. To enkindle the enthusiasm of an artist on the theme over which he had achieved the most facile mastery; to set loose the heart of the rustic poet, and imbue his speech with the freedom of his native hills; to draw from the adventurous traveller a breathing picture of his most imminent danger; or to embolden the bashful soldier to disclose his own share in the perils and glories of some famous battle-field; to encourage the generous praise of friendship when the speaker and the subject reflected interest on each other; or win from an awkward man of science the secret history of a discovery which had astonished the world; to conduct these brilliant developments to the height of satisfaction, and then to shift the scene by the magic of a word, were among her nightly successes. And if this extra-

ordinary power over the elements of social enjoyment
was sometimes wielded without the entire concealment
of its despotism; if a decisive check sometimes rebuked
a speaker who might intercept the variegated beauty of
Jeffrey's indulgent criticism, or the jest announced and
self-rewarded in Sydney Smith's cordial and triumphant
laugh, the authority was too clearly exerted for the
evening's prosperity, and too manifestly impelled by an
urgent consciousness of the value of these golden hours
which were fleeting within its confines, to sadden the
enforced silence with more than a momentary regret. If
ever her prohibition—clear, abrupt, and decisive—indicated more than a preferable regard for livelier dis-
course, it was when a depreciatory tone was adopted
towards genius, or goodness, or honest endeavour, or
when some friend, personal or intellectual, was mentioned
in slighting phrase. Habituated to a generous partisanship, by strong sympathy with a great political cause,
she carried the fidelity of her devotion to that cause
into her social relations, and was ever the truest and
the fastest of friends.

"Under her auspices, not only all critical, but all
personal talk was tinged with kindness; the strong
interest which she took in the happiness of her friends
shed a peculiar sunniness over the aspects of life presented by the common topics of alliances, and marriages,
and promotions; and there was not a hopeful engagement, or a happy wedding, or a promotion of a friend's
son, or a new intellectual triumph of any youth with
whose name and history she was familiar, but became
an event on which she expected and required congratu-
lation as on a part of her own fortune. Although there
was necessarily a preponderance in her society of the

sentiment of popular progress, which once was cherished almost exclusively by the party to whom Lord Holland was united by sacred ties, no expression of triumph in success, no virulence in sudden disappointment, was ever permitted to wound the most sensitive ears of her Conservative guests. Although the death of the noble master of the venerated mansion closed its portals for ever on the exquisite enjoyments to which they had been so generously expanded, the art of conversation lived a little longer in the smaller circle which Lady Holland still drew almost daily around her; honouring his memory by following his example, and struggling against the perpetual sense of unutterable bereavement, by rendering to literature that honour and those reliefs which English aristocracy has too often denied it; and seeking consolation in making others proud and happy."

We turn now to the more stately and gorgeous periods of Macaulay. "The time is coming when, perhaps, a few old men, the last survivors of our generation, will in vain seek, amidst new streets, and squares, and railway stations, for the site of that dwelling which was in their youth the favourite resort of wits and beauties, of painters and poets, of scholars, philosophers, and statesmen. They will then remember, with strange tenderness, many objects once familiar to them—the avenue and the terrace, the busts and the paintings, the carving, the grotesque gilding, and the enigmatical mottoes. With peculiar fondness, they will recall that venerable chamber, in which all the antique gravity of a college library was so singularly blended with all that female grace and wit could devise to embellish a drawing-room. They will recollect, not unmoved, those shelves loaded with the varied learning

of many lands and many ages ; those portraits in which
were preserved the features of the best and wisest
Englishmen of two generations. They will recollect
how many men who have guided the politics of Europe
—who have moved great assemblies by reason and
eloquence—who have put life into bronze and canvas,
or who have left to posterity things so written as it
shall not willingly let them die—were there mixed with
all that was loveliest and gayest in the society of the
most splendid of capitals. They will remember the
singular character which belonged to that circle, in
which every talent and accomplishment, every art and
science, had its place. They will remember how the
last debate was discussed in one corner, and the
last comedy of Scribe in another ; while Wilkie
gazed with modest admiration on Reynolds' Baretti ;
while Mackintosh turned over Thomas Aquinas to verify
a quotation ; while Talleyrand related his conversations
with Barras at the Luxemburg, or his ride with Lannes
over the field of Austerlitz. They will remember, above
all, the grace—and the kindness, far more admirable
than grace—with which the princely hospitality of that
ancient mansion was dispensed. They will remember
the venerable and benignant countenance, and the
cordial voice of him who bade them welcome. They
will remember that temper which years of pain, of
sickness, of lameness, of confinement, seemed only to
make sweeter and sweeter ; and that frank politeness,
which at once relieved all the embarrassment of the
youngest and most timid writer or artist, who found
himself for the first time among Ambassadors and Earls.
They will remember that constant flow of conversation,
so natural so animated, so various, so rich with observa-

tion and anecdote; that wit which never gave a wound; that exquisite mimicry which ennobled, instead of degrading; that goodness of heart which appeared in every look and accent, and gave additional value to every talent and acquirement. They will remember, too, that he whose name they hold in reverence was not less distinguished by the inflexible uprightness of his political conduct, than by his loving disposition and his winning manners. They will remember that, in the last lines which he traced, he expressed his joy that he had done nothing unworthy of the friend of Fox and Grey; and they will have reason to feel similar joy, if, in looking back on many troubled years, they cannot accuse themselves of having done anything unworthy of men who were distinguished by the friendship of Lord Holland."

In all this it is impossible not to feel that there is exaggeration. It is amazing indeed to turn from this poetical retrospect to the details of this Elysium, furnished by some of the *habitués*, who, in time, appear to have grown heartily tired of the humours and eccentricities of the noble hostess, of the blunt "testiness" of Mr. Allen, of the "page in green," etc., and to have indeed resorted to this place from long-standing habit, as one would go to a club. The host, a martyr to gout, wheeling himself in his chair, rarely attending dinner; the hostess, ordering her guests and dependants with a genuine despotism, squeezing in additional diners to the inconvenience of their neighbours; the quarrels and disputes, the pedantic criticisms, such seem to have been the reality. But let us hear Macaulay to his own family, when speaking unofficially:

"Lady Holland made her appearance. Lord Holland

dined by himself on account of his gout. We sat down
to dinner in a fine long room, the wainscot of which is
rich with gilded coronets, roses, and portcullises. What
however is more to the purpose, there was a most excellent dinner. I have always heard that Holland House
is famous for its good cheer, and certainly the reputation
is not unmerited. After dinner Lord Holland was
wheeled in, and placed very near me. He was extremely
amusing and good-natured. In the drawing-room I had
a long talk with Lady Holland about the antiquities of
the house, and about the purity of the English language,
wherein she thinks herself a critic. I happened, in
speaking about the Reform Bill, to say that I wished
that it had been possible to form a few commercial
constituencies, if the word constituency were admissible.
' I am glad you put that in,' said her ladyship. ' I was
just going to give it you. It is an odious word. Then
there is *talented*, and *influential*, and *gentlemanly*. I
never could break Sheridan of *gentlemanly*, though he
allowed it to be wrong.' We talked about the word
talents and its history. I said that it had first appeared
in theological writing, that it was a metaphor taken from
the parable in the New Testament, and that it had
gradually passed from the vocabulary of divinity into
common use. I challenged her to find it in any classical
writer on general subjects before the Restoration, or even
before the year 1700. I believe that I might safely
have gone down later. She seemed surprised by this
theory, never having, so far as I could judge, heard of
the parable of the talents. I did not tell her, though I
might have done so, that a person who professes to be a
critic in the delicacies of the English language ought to
have the Bible at his fingers' ends.

" She is certainly a woman of considerable talents and

·great literary acquirements. To me she was excessively gracious ; yet there is a haughtiness in her courtesy which, even after all that I had heard of her, surprised me. The centurion did not keep his soldiers in better ·order than she keeps her guests. It is to one ' Go,' and he goeth ; and to another ' Do this,' and it is done. ' Ring the bell, Mr. Macaulay.' ' Lay down that screen, Lord Russell ; you will spoil it.' ' Mr. Allen, take a candle and show Mr. Cradock the picture of Buonaparte.' Lord Holland is, on the other hand, all kindness, simplicity, and vivacity. He talked very well both on politics and on literature. He asked me in a very friendly manner about my father's health, and begged to be remembered to him."

Mr. Greville, another *habitué*, gives a rather ludicrous picture of the life at this house.

" Dined at Holland House the day before yesterday ; Lady Holland is unwell, fancies she must dine at five o'clock, and exerts her power over society by making everybody go out there at that hour, though nothing can be more inconvenient than thus shortening the day, and nothing more tiresome than such lengthening of the evening. Rogers and Luttrell were staying there. The *tableau* of the house is this : Before dinner, Lady Holland affecting illness and almost dissolution, but with a very respectable appetite, and after dinner in high force and vigour ; Lord Holland, with his chalk-stones and unable to walk, lying on his couch in very good spirits and talking away ; Luttrell and Rogers walking about, ever and anon looking despairingly at the clock and making short excursions from the drawing-room ; Allen, surly and disputatious, poring over the newspapers, and replying in monosyllables (generally negative) to whatever is said to him. The grand topic of interest, far exceeding the Belgian or Portuguese questions, was the illness of Lady Holland's page, who has got a tumour in his thigh. This 'little creature,' as Lady Holland calls a great hulking fellow of about twenty, is called 'Edgar,' his real name being Tom or Jack, which he changed on being elevated to his present dignity, as the Popes do when they are elected to the tiara. More rout is made about him than other people are invited to make about their children, and the inmates of Holland House are permitted and compelled to go and sit with and amuse him. Such is the social despotism of this strange house, which presents an odd mixture of luxury and constraint, of enjoyment, physical and intellectual, with an alloy of small *désagréments.* Talleyrand generally comes at ten or eleven o'clock, and stays as long as they will let him. Though everybody who goes there finds something to abuse or ridicule in the mistress of the house, or its ways, all continue to go ; all like it more or less ; and whenever, by the death of either, it shall come to an end, a vacuum will be made in society which nothing will supply. It is the house of all Europe ; the world will suffer by the loss ; and it may with truth be said that it will eclipse the gaiety of nations."

Of course due allowance must be made for the discontent of a man of *ton* forced to dine at five o'clock, and his intolerance of the humours of his hostess ; but we have an instinct that there is a " bottom of truth " in what he says.

The mention of Mr. Rogers recalls the name of one who was intimately connected with all that was social and intellectual. As Sir H. Holland tells us, " he was in many respects the most conspicuous of poets in London society, and this for a period of more than half a century.

Wealthy, unmarried, highly cultivated in all matters of literature and art, his conversation seasoned with anecdote and personal sarcasms uttered in a curious sepulchral voice, he gained and kept a higher place than his poetry alone would have procured for him. He was the arbiter in many of the literary controversies and quarrels of the day. His dinner-table ministered well to this object. In society his most severe sarcasms were often hidden under honeyed phrases ; leaving them obvious to others, while undetected by those whose foibles he assailed. There was foundation for the remark that a note from Rogers generally conveyed some indirect satire on the person to whom it was addressed"—a significant note of character truly, and an elegant refinement of malice.

His "Breakfasts" were *recherché*, and imitated by many, though not with his success. His sarcasms were often in circulation, sometimes evoked by the marriage of a particular friend.*   Like so many of those men who live for society, and society delights, the close of his days was of a disastrous kind—imbecility and isolation. There was even a grotesqueness in his retaining his gifts of telling the old stories in the same strict form.†

That "realistic" view of the hostess of Holland House being a disagreeable personage, whose humours became intolerable, is borne out by Mr. Rogers and Mr. Hayward : "Capricious as her tyranny was, it appeared

---

* As on an elderly man going to marry a girl, he, rubbing his hands : "*Now we shall have our revenge of him !*" Or, on someone telling him of another, all were so glad : "Then all are glad, for his friends are pleased and his enemies delighted."

† Mr. Dickens used often to relate how, having come to cheer him at dinner, the faithful servant, who knew his *répertoire*, would "set him off" with "Tell Mr. Dickens, sir, the story of old Lady Cork." On which the veteran would commence, in a sepulchral tone : "The old Lady Cork was once," etc.

that there was still an *intention* in all she did, which was to maintain her power. She knew how to soothe," he adds, "if she had offended."

"I have," says Sir H. Holland, "the picture still before me of Lord Holland lying tranquilly on his bed when attacked with gout—his admirable sister Miss Fox beside him, reading aloud, as she generally did on these occasions, some one of Miss Austen's novels, of which he was never wearied.

"I cannot attempt a list of the accustomed guests at Holland House during the days of its greatest renown. On the memory of the moment I may name, as those whom I most constantly saw there—Lord Grey, Lord Melbourne, Lord Lansdowne, Lord J. Russell, Lord Durham, Lord Brougham, Lord Palmerston, Lord Carlisle, Lord Althorp, Lord Lauderdale, Tierney, Mackintosh, Horner, Macaulay, Sydney Smith, Hallam, Rogers, Jekyll, Luttrell, Frere, Moore, Charles Ellis, etc. I am noting here a bygone generation, for only one of those I have named is now alive. During the progress of the Reform Bill and the agitations attending it, the Holland House dinners were often a sort of miniature Cabinet, in the persons assembled and the matters discussed.

"It had been often predicted that the society of Holland House would be wholly broken up by Lord Holland's death. It was not so. Though transferred for the most part to the town-house in South Street, and infringed upon by many other deaths, the singular talent of Lady Holland, aided by affection for his memory, kept together the habitual members of this society as long as she herself lived. Her dinners were still amongst the most agreeable in London. I well remember one in October, 1845—the last she ever gave —when Thiers and Lord Palmerston met, as I believe, for the first time, smothering at the table the angry feelings of prior diplomacy.

"I cannot quit the subject of Holland House, without mentioning one who was a member of the family for forty years, and had acquired much influence in it. This was Mr. Allen—familiarly called John Allen—a man of encyclopædic literature, of hard unflinching Whig politics, and a temperament of general scepticism ; yet with sundry warm affections lying underneath. He was cast in a strong Scotch mould both of mind and body—the former nurtured by constant reading and excellent society, the latter pampered by daily luxurious dinners throughout the year. Sitting always at the bottom of the table, before carving had been transferred to the sideboard, he yet mixed largely in the conversation as an expounder of facts, and a sharp commentator on the words and opinions of others. Even Lady Holland, who found pleasure in exciting him, did not escape his angry contradictions and had a certain dim fear of them."

Mr. Rogers' stories about this disagreeable lady are truly characteristic. When she wanted to get rid of a fop, she used to say, "I beg your pardon ; I wish you would sit a little further off ; there is something on your handkerchief which I don't quite like." In another version she had declared that the blacking on his boots was mixed with champagne. And again, when a gentleman, to her annoyance, was standing with his back close to the chimney, she would call out, "Have the goodness, sir, to stir the fire!" Near Tunbridge was a house which no one was allowed to see. She never ceased her exertions till she was allowed to enter, and marched through it with a perfect train after her. Lord Holland would say to Mr. Rogers, as he came out

from a visit, " Well, has she invited you to dinner?"
he having no power to do so.*

Another note of society in these times which most
distinguished it from that of our own day was the now
extinct DUEL, or "affair of honour," as it was called, and
which now seems so far off as an institution that we
scarcely can grasp its significance. It belonged naturally
to an age of license, of "bucks" and "bloods," of box
lobbies and "saloons," and—perhaps most important
factor of all—arose from the gambling at public
tables; for the rage or disappointment of the unlucky
gambler required some such check. How prevalent and
universal was the custom may be conceived from the
fact that Cabinet ministers and prime ministers frequently
settled their disputes with their opponents after this
mode of arbitrament. Nothing is more curious now
than to find, in comedies of forty or fifty years ago, the
duel as a recognised incident.† Now, of course, it could
not be introduced. A rather perplexing question arises

---

* The following was lately offered for sale by public auction :

" Album containing upwards of 120 Letters, Franks, etc., mostly
of the Coterie who rendered this House so celebrated ; amongst the
letters is one from Thackeray to Lady Holland, in which he says, ' I
don't like monthly nurses, do you?' other Letters are from Wm.
Pitt, Jerome Bonaparte, Louis Philippe, Duc de Penthievre, Marshal
Ney, A. Dumas, Victor Hugo, Fouché, Segur, Guizot, E. Landseer,
and J. M. W. Turner; also excellent specimens of Napoleon I.,
George III., William IV., Queen Charlotte, Rogers, William Wordsworth, Rev. Sydney Smith, Mrs. Norton, Lord Chancellor Campbell,
Cottenham, and Brougham ; Premiers Canning, Grey, Palmerston,
Derby, Melbourne, Ripon, Aberdeen, Sidmouth, Russell and Sir
Robert Peel, George Tierney, Shiel, with other Statesmen, Bishops,
and Authors."

Sic transit !

† So late as the publication of "Pickwick," in 1837, we find a
very comic incident founded on the proposed duel between Dr. Slammer
and Mr. Winkle at Chatham.

here—viz., how is it that England of all civilised
countries is the only one in which duelling* is not
tolerated? In Germany, it is sanctioned in the army
by a particular decree of the present venerated Emperor.
In France, Belgium, and America it is the regular
mode of settling a quarrel. In England there is no
pretence made to superior piety or greater sense, neither
is it due to a greater respect for the laws, as these were
in full force when duelling was a custom. It may be
that such a practice would be distasteful to a nation of
business men and traders; while duelling was chiefly
patronised by the upper classes, and the former section
of the community did not obtain its full influence till
the Reform Bill was passed. This may seem rather an
imperfect and halting explanation, but it is the best
that can be suggested for so curious a problem.

Fifty, and perhaps forty, years ago the hour of important ministerial dinner parties was about as late as at
present, viz. eight o'clock, but this was no doubt owing to
the pressure of official business. The average dinner
hour was about seven. King George IV.'s hour was seven.
"Talking" or conversation was then cultivated as a
fine art. During the reign of William IV. there reigned
a didactic tone, which would now be considered *mal
à propos*, and perhaps tedious, and clever men were
admired for displaying their " erudition and information,
giving recondite quotations from the classics, and offering curious historical difficulties for solution." Sometimes
ministers rose hurriedly, as Macaulay describes it, " to
attend a Cabinet Council at ten o'clock." Dinner
parties were then heartily enjoyed, and looked forward

* As is well known, what gave the *coup de grace* to duelling in
England, was the fatal encounter between two brothers-in-law,
Colonels Fawcett and Munro, about forty years ago.

to as an opening for meeting with clever men and
hearing them talk ; and the regular diarists were enabled
to bring away many brilliant remarks and anecdotes,
which the celebrities were expected to give utterance to,
and who accordingly came well prepared. Nowadays
the large dinner party is made part of the social routine
—the guest is but one of a crowd, and chiefly entertains
and is entertained by, his immediate neighbour. Much
of this old social form of enjoyment was owing to the
system of coteries, such as that of Holland House.

Mr. Rush, the American Envoy, describes an
evening party, given in 1823, which offers a pleasant
picture of the gaiety with which a genial, gay minister,
such as Mr. Canning was, could indulge himself. At
the house of Mr. Planta, then an under-secretary, were
assembled various ambassadors and ministers. " Parliament having just risen, Mr. Canning, and his two
colleagues of the Cabinet, Mr. Huskisson and Mr.
Robinson, seemed like birds let out of a cage. There
was much small talk, some of it very sprightly. Ten
o'clock arriving, with little disposition to rise from table,
Mr. Canning proposed that we should play " Twenty
Questions." The game consisted in endeavours to find
out your thoughts by asking twenty questions. It was
agreed that Mr. Canning, assisted by the Chancellor of
the Exchequer, who sat next to him, should put the
questions ; and that I, assisted by Lord Granville, who
sat next to me, should give the answers. First question
(by Mr. Canning) : Does what you have thought of
belong to the animal or vegetable kingdom ?—To
the vegetable.   Second question : Is it manufactured
or unmanufactured ?—Manufactured.   Third : Is it a
solid or a liquid ?—A solid.   Fourth : Is it a thing

entire in itself, or in parts?—Entire. Fifth: Is it for
private use or public?—Public. Sixth: Does it exist
in England, or out of it?—In England. Seventh: Is
it single, or are there others of the same kind?—Single.
Eighth: Is it historical, or only existent at present?—
Both. Ninth: For ornament or use?—Both. Tenth:
Has it any connection with the person of the King?—
No. Eleventh: Is it carried, or does it support itself?—
The former. Twelfth: Does it pass by succession?—
[Neither Lord Granville nor myself being quite certain
on this point, the question was not answered; but, as it
was thought that the very hesitation to answer might
serve to shed light upon the secret, it was agreed that
the question should be counted as one in the progress of
the game]. Thirteenth: Was it used at the coronation?
—Yes. Fourteenth: In the Hall or Abbey?—Probably
in both; certainly in the Hall. Fifteenth: Does it
belong specially to the ceremony of the coronation, or
is it used at other times?—It is used at other times.
Sixteenth: Is it exclusively of a vegetable nature, or is
it not, in some parts, a compound of a vegetable and
a mineral?—Exclusively of a vegetable nature. Seventeenth: What is its shape?—[This question was objected
to as too particular; and the company inclining to think
so, it was withdrawn; but, Mr. Canning saying it would
be hard upon him to count it, as it was withdrawn, the
decision was in his favour on that point, and it was not
counted]. Seventeenth (repeated): Is it decorated or
simple?—[We made a stand against this question also,
as too particular; but the company not inclining to
sustain us this time, I had to answer it, and said that
it was simple]. Eighteenth: Is it used in the ordinary
ceremonial of the House of Commons, or House of

Lords ?—No.   Nineteenth : Is it ever used by either
House ?—No.   Twentieth : Is it generally stationary or
movable ?—Movable.

The whole number of questions being now exhausted,
there was a dead pause.   The interest had gone on
increasing as the game advanced, until, coming to the
last question, it grew to be like neck-and-neck at the
close of a race.   Mr. Canning was evidently under
concern lest he should be foiled, as by the law of the
game he would have been, if he had not now solved the
enigma.   He sat silent for a minute or two ; then, rolling
his rich eye about. and with a countenance a little
anxious, and in an accent by no means over-confident,
he exclaimed : " I think it must be the wand of the
Lord High Steward ! "   And it was—EVEN SO.

" This enlivening game lasted upwards of an hour,
the wine ceasing to go round.   On Mr. Canning's success
—for it was touch-and-go with him—there was a burst
of approbation, we of the diplomatic corps saying that
we must be very careful not to let him ask us too many
questions at the Foreign Office." *

A curious picture of manners.   It is odd to
think of flambeaux, retinues of footmen, etc., at so
recent a period.   Only a few years before, Mr. Rush
noted " running footmen " in the suite of the Spanish
Ambassador.

At a dinner-party at Gloucester Lodge, the conversation became quite literary, and might have been one
in the presence of Dr. Johnson.   " The topic changing,
Swift came on the tapis.   Several of his pieces were
called up, with genuine gusto.   Mr. Canning was on

* I have heard the late Mr. Dickens, at his own house at Gad's
Hill, exhibit his skill at this pleasant exercise of ingenuity, with
delightful aptitude and cleverness.

a sofa, Mr. Planta next to him, I and others in chairs dotted around.

"'Planta,' said Mr. Canning, 'pray hand down the volume containing the voyages, and read the description of the storm in the voyage to Brobdingnag. Seamen say that it is capital; and as true nautically, as Shakespeare always is, when he undertakes to use sea terms.'

"Mr. Planta took down the volume, and read the passage. One sentence in it runs thus: 'It was a very fierce storm, the sea broke strange and dangerous; we hauled off upon the lanniard of the whip-staff, *and helped the man at the helm.*' When he was done, all admired the passage, under this new view and commendation of it, which Mr. Canning had given us. He himself said nothing for a few moments, but sat silent; then, as if in a reverie, he uttered, in a low tone, yet very distinctly, the words, '*and helped the man at the helm! and helped the man at the helm!*' repeating them."

The criticism does not seem very brilliant, or even clear.

At another banquet, we have one of the Royal Dukes learnedly expounding the origin of cards. "Cards being spoken of, His Royal Highness said that the division and numbers of the pack were supposed to have had a connection among the Egyptians (he gave cards that antiquity) with astronomical science. First, the fifty-two composing the pack, answered to the weeks of the year; next, thirteen of a kind agreed with the fourth part of the year, divided into weeks; then again, four different kinds, answered to the four seasons; and, lastly, by counting up from the ace to ten, then counting the knave as eleven, the queen as

twelve, the king as thirteen, you get ninety-one. Four
ninety-ones give you three hundred and sixty-four, the
number of days, according to some calculations, in the
year."

At one of the dinners where ministers were present, it
was related, and apparently accepted by the company, that
two of the servants of the Persian Ambassador having
offended him lately in London, he applied to the British
Government for permission to cut off their heads. On
learning that it could not be granted, he gravely remonstrated. Finding, however, that his hands were
tied up, he told his servants, "it was all one ; they
must consider their heads as being off, for off they would
come when he got them back to Persia !" This may
have been, and was, no doubt, true ; but it could not be
matched by a still stranger relic of barbarism, and which
is yet English.* In November, 1817, Mr. Crabb Robinson

* "The Austrian Ambassador," Mr. Rush was told, "received
ten thousand ducats a year. The Russian got more ; but the Austrian,
besides the above sum from his government, had the same amount
annually allowed him by his father, the elder Prince Esterhazy. The
French Ambassador, he believed, received twelve thousand sterling a
year, with an allowance for occasional entertainments. The Foreign
Secretary of England," he added, " was also allowed for entertainments.
He further stated, that France gave her Ambassador *in London*,
£2000 a year *more* than her Ambassadors at any other Court. Speaking of British Ambassadors abroad, he said, that a service of plate as
a personal gift to them had lately been discontinued. The plate was
now considered as attached to the embassy, and had the public arms
engraved upon it." Mr. Rush in his conversations with various
Ambassadors and official persons, learned other interesting particulars.
The English Under Secretary informed him that "theirs (the British)
had instructions to write, under all ordinary circumstances, a despatch
at least once a fortnight ; but that this was apt to be much exceeded
in point of fact, and that often the number received from them
was very great ; as, for example, from their Ambassador in Paris,
from whom they received, every mail-day—and it recurred twice

witnessed an extraordinary spectacle in a court of law, and which was the last exhibition of the kind in this country.

"I witnessed to-day," he says, "a scene which would have been a reproach to Turkey or the Emperor of Dahomey—a wager of battle in Westminster Hall. Thornton was brought up for trial on an appeal after acquittal for murder. The court was crowded to excess. The declaration, or count, being read to the prisoner, he said : ' Not guilty. And this I am ready to defend with my body.' *At the same time he threw a large glove or gauntlet on the floor of the court.* Though we all expected this plea, yet we all felt astonishment—at least I did—at beholding before our eyes a scene acted which we had read of as one of the disgraceful institutions of our half-civilised ancestors. No one smiled. The

---

a week—from two to three despatches, seldom fewer ; he should think it not improbable, that full three hundred had been received from him during the year just ended. In numbering their despatches, they began afresh with every new year ; and they threw upon the Ambassador the duty of numbering them on the outside also, as well as of endorsing a short abstract of the subject. They thus arrived ready for the files, after being read.

" In answer to inquiries as to the language employed in diplomatic notes in London, he said that this Government was now pushing forward the English language more than at any former period. Sir Henry Wellesley at Madrid, for instance, addressed the Spanish Government in English ; in retaliation of which the Spanish Ambassador in London addressed his notes to Lord Castlereagh in Spanish. The Ambassadors and Ministers of all the other powers, he said, the United States excepted (courteously alluding to the community of the English tongue between us), wrote to Lord Castlereagh in French ; but that the answers were uniformly in English. Formerly, they had been generally in French. It was Lord Grenville who, whilst Secretary for Foreign Affairs, first broke in upon the use of French." In our times diplomatic custom is that each country uses its own language, save in the instance of those having " outlandish " or little known languages.

judges looked embarrassed. Clarke on this began a
very weak speech. He was surprised, 'at this time of
day,' at so obsolete a proceeding; as if the appeal itself
were not as much so. He pointed out the person of
Ashford, the appellant, and thought the court would not
award battle between men of such disproportionate
strength. Time was, however, given him to counter-
plead; and an Act of Parliament abolishing the practice
was passed."

The system of ecclesiastical promotion in those days
was a curious one, and was accepted as a matter of course.
It might be illustrated by many curious instances.
Nothing, indeed, is so remarkable as the change in
the system of appointment to bishoprics and high offices
in the Church. Writing, in "Coningsby," in 1844,
Mr. Disraeli says: "We live in decent times—frigid,

There is an institution known as the "Court Newsman," for which,
it is perhaps little known, the fashionable world is indebted to one of
the late King's confidential agents, who took council with a well-
known character, Townsend, the Bow Street officer. This well-known
character was a personage in these days, and it was the *ton* for everyone of condition to be on familiar terms with "Old Townsend," says
an old reminiscent, "Who does not remember 'Old Townsend,' the
short, dumpy, 'bumptious' Bow Street Officer, in nankeen shorts and
short gaiters to match, with blue and white striped silk hose between;
his blue broadcloth dress-coat buttoned over his portly paunch, which
was always carefully invested in a neat marcella 'vest,' his cranium
closely covered with a flaxen scratch, his flaxen scratch surmounted by
a broad-brimmed drab beaver, his drab beaver surrounded and adorned
with a drab riband and full rosette to correspond, and his right hand
graced with a handsome silver-headed stout Malacca cane? He was
always to be met with for many years at the time and place above
mentioned, sometimes arm-in-arm with the Duke of York, or chatting
familiarly with Lord Sidmouth. In his younger days he had been a
student in shoe-blacking in Newgate; from shoe-blacking he elevated
himself to coal-heaving, from coal-heaving he became a trusty turnkey;
from Newgate he turned Bow Street officer, and principal confidant of

latitudinarian, alarmed, decorous. A priest is scarcely deemed in our days a fit successor to the authors of the Gospels if he be not the editor of a Greek play; and he who follows St. Paul must now at least have been private tutor of some young nobleman who has taken a good degree!"

To be the "private tutor of the young nobleman" is no longer a profession; while, the editing a Greek play, if proffered as a claim for episcopal honours, would now only cause a smile.

But it will be a surprise to find the Duke of Wellington illustrating this system, pressing the singular claims of his brother in a very heated and excited fashion.

This curious and unbecoming dispute arose from the disinclination of Lord Liverpool, in 1826, to promote the Duke's brother to a bishopric, the Premier declining on the ground that the candidate was living separate from his wife.

"Notwithstanding Lord Wellesley's desire that I should

Sir Richard Birnie, Knight; from Bow Street he was advanced to the run of all the royal palaces, and became the intimate of royalty itself from George III. down to William IV., the consulting friend of all the Lord Chancellors, the gratuitous adviser of all Cabinet Ministers.

" He was sent for, consulted as to whether he knew any sensible, decent newspaper writer, who would set down what he was told and no more. The trusty police officer undertook the duty. He selected an elderly police reporter—an old crony of his own—and he was installed in the office and dignity of COURT NEWSMAN. Notices were sent round to all the newspaper offices, that thenceforward circulars— 'Court Circulars'—would be sent round to them from the newly-appointed 'court newsman,' containing the only *authentic* court news; and they were warned against publishing any other. At the same time, all the approaches to the palaces, or any of their appurtenances were strictly tabooed against the incursions of the irregular troops of the press; and the establishment of the 'Court Circular' was complete."

write to you," wrote the Duke, " I had determined that I would not mention it, and I should not have written upon it at all if it was not to call upon your lordship, in common justice to my brother, fairly to inquire whether the insinuations which you have heard, and the suspicions you have entertained, are well founded; because I felt if I wrote at all I must remind you of the following circumstances.

" When you declined to promote my brother to the bench, you told me that you would do everything in your power to improve his situation. I afterwards, at his suggestion, requested your lordship to recommend him for the deanery of St. Paul's, or the deanery of Durham; to which request you replied that those dignities were considered by the Church as on a par with bishoprics, and that the same reasons which prevented your lordship from promoting my brother to the bench must prevent you from recommending him for either of these deaneries. I informed my brother of your decision, and then one of the first arrangements I heard of was the promotion of Dr. Hall, the Dean of Christ Church, to be Dean of Durham! Your lordship offered my brother a living in Yorkshire, which he was under the necessity of declining to accept, as the income of it would not have been sufficient to pay the curate and the expense of taking possession. In the meantime I have scarcely ever approached His Majesty that he has not mentioned to me his anxiety to see my brother provided for in the Church, and he has sent me repeatedly most gracious messages upon the same subject."

After more heated letters, in which the Duke got very angry, and seems hardly to accept scruples of conscience as an excuse, the matter passed from these high moral grounds in a very amusing way, and both parties began recriminating charges of services done and unrequited.

In a letter to Arbuthnot, Lord Liverpool took care to remind the Duke of all he had done already for the family. This was intended as a retort to the "if any man has served you more faithfully," etc., of the Duke.

"I cannot accuse myself of having overlooked the Duke of Wellington's fair pretensions as to his family. At an early period of my Administration I recommended his mother, unsolicited, for a pension, to which I must say, as his mother, she was fully entitled. I afterwards recommended his sister for the same, and I gave his brother-in-law, Cullen Smith, one of the best offices I ever had to dispose of. The chief inducement in these two latter cases was certainly to oblige him. What were Lord Maryborough's claims to office, to Cabinet, and subsequently to a peerage? Certainly not his support of my Administration, for I had no more strenuous opponent till I was firmly established; and he had not to plead for it his connection with Lord Wellesley, for upon the schism between his brother and Perceval he took part with Perceval. I mention these matters for the purpose only of rebutting the allegation that the Duke of Wellington's family have been neglected. I have, in fact, done much more for them than I have for my own.

"I by no means wish you to show this letter. It could answer no good purpose, and my only motive in writing it is to recall to your recollection some circumstances which you may have forgotten."

How painful the whole business was, and what angry passions were roused, will be seen from Arbuthnot's reply to this letter.

"The Duke," he says, "has taken great pains to

know the truth, and his conviction is that his brother is
without taint.   It wounds him, therefore, to the very
soul, that a stigma should be placed upon his brother;
and I might as well endeavour to persuade him not to
perspire when he is heated, as to attempt the calming,
at present, of his galled feelings.   But it is Lord
Wellesley who has done all the harm.   Lord Wellesley
names Gerald to you, but can scarcely be said to have
recommended him.   He anticipates the possibility of
opposition from Goulburn and the Primate, and he
applies a scurrility of language to them which I mentioned to you in conversation, but which I abstain from
writing.   He tells the Duke that you had taken ' a
most lofty tone,' and that in quoting ' Scriptural authority ' you had referred ' to some passage in St. Paul.'
He proceeds to observe that, if ' battle ' with you should
be advisable, there was enough to warrant it.   He
suggests that the Archbishop of Canterbury and the
Bishop of London should be consulted, as they (he had
reason to think) were favourable to Gerald.   And, last
of all, he puts it to the Duke whether the nomination to
the bench might not come direct from the King, as in
the instance of my brother.   ' Gerald might be named
by the King, as Arbuthnot was;' these were Lord
Wellesley's very words."

Archbishop Howley was the last of the old prelates
who lived in high state.   During the season he would
keep open house at Lambeth, some thirty or forty
persons sitting down to dinner every day, and being
entertained sumptuously.

CHAPTER VIII.

An American, who came to England, with excellent introductions—the notorious Mr. N. P. Willis—shows us how English society was likely to strike a foreigner.[*]

Few English people, who were invited to stay with a Duke at his castle, would have the courage of the American, to print a sort of "Our own Correspondent" account of the mode of life, the conversation, etc., which this position as guest permitted them to enjoy. The foreigner, however, holds himself discharged; and, to this feeling, we owe Mr. Willis's too faithful record of all that went on during his visit to Gordon Castle.

"A sudden curve in the road brought the castle into view—a vast stone pile with castellated wings, and in another moment I was at the door, where a dozen lounging and powdered menials were waiting on a party of ladies and gentlemen to their several carriages. It was the moment for the afternoon drive. . . .

"The last phaeton dashed away, and my chaise advanced to the door. A handsome boy, in a kind of page's dress, immediately came to the window, addressed

---

[*] Mr. Willis's travels caused as much amusement as indignation, revealing a sad amount of "snobbery."

me by name, and informed me that his Grace was out deer-shooting, but that my room was prepared, and he was ordered to wait on me. I followed him through a hall lined with statues, deer horns, and armour, and was ushered into a large chamber, looking out on a park, extending with its lawns and woods to the edge of the horizon—a more lovely view never feasted human eye.

"' Who is at the castle ?' I asked, as the boy busied himself in unstrapping my portmanteau. 'Oh, a great many, sir.' He stopped in his occupation and began counting on 'his fingers. 'There's Lord Aberdeen, and Lord Claude Hamilton and Lady Harriette Hamilton— (them's his lordship's two stepchildren, you know, sir) and the Duchess of Richmond, and Lady Sophia Lennox, and Lady Keith, and Lord Mandeville, and Lord Aboyne, and Lord Stormont and Lady Stormont, and Lord Morton and Lady Morton, and Lady Alicia, and—and —and—twenty more, sir.' 'Twenty more lords and ladies ? ' 'No, sir ; that's all the nobility.' 'And you can't remember the names of the others ?' 'No, sir.' He was a proper page ; he could not trouble his memory with the names of commoners. 'And how many sit down to dinner ?' 'Above thirty, sir, besides the Duke and Duchess.'

"Soon after a loud gong sounded through the gallery—the signal to dress ; and I left my musing occupation unwillingly to make my toilet for an appearance in a formidable circle of titled aristocrats, not one of whom I had ever seen ; the Duke himself a stranger to me, except through the kind letter of invitation lying upon the table.

"I was sitting by the fire, imagining forms and faces for the different persons who had been named to me, when there was a knock at the door, and a tall, white-haired gentleman, of noble physiognomy, but singularly cordial address, entered, with the broad red riband of a duke (!) across his breast, and welcomed me most heartily to the castle.

"The gong sounded at the next moment, and, in our way down, he named over his other guests, and prepared me in a measure for the introductions which followed. The drawing-room was crowded like a soirée. The Duchess, a very tall and very handsome woman, with a smile of the most winning sweetness, received me at the door, and I was presented successively to every person present. Dinner was announced immediately; and the difficult question of precedence being sooner settled than I had ever seen it before in so large a party, we passed through files of servants to the dining-room.

"It was a large and very lofty hall, supported at the ends by marble columns, within which was stationed a band of music, playing delightfully. The walls were lined with full-length family pictures, from old knights in armour to the modern dukes in *kilt of the Gordon plaid* (!); and on the sideboards stood services of gold plate, the most gorgeously massive and the most beautiful in workmanship I have ever seen. There were among the vases several large coursing-cups, won by the duke's hounds, of exquisite shape and ornament.

"I fell into my place between a gentleman and a very beautiful woman, of perhaps twenty-two, neither of whose names I remembered, though I had but just been introduced. The Duke probably anticipated as much, and as I took my seat he called out to me, from the top of the table, that I had upon my right Lady ——, 'the most agreeable woman in Scotland.' It was unnecessary to say that she was the most lovely.

"I have been struck everywhere in England with the beauty of the higher classes; and as I looked around me upon the aristocratic company at the table, I thought I had never seen 'Heaven's image double-stamped as man and noble' so unequivocally clear. There were two young men and four or five young ladies of rank, and five or six people of more decided personal attractions could scarcely be found; the style of form and face at the same time being of that cast of superiority which goes by the expressive name of 'thoroughbred.' The calm repose of person and feature, the self-possession under all circumstances, that incapability of surprise or *déréglement*, and that decision about the slightest circumstance, and the apparent certainty that he is acting absolutely *comme il faut*, is equally 'gentleman-like' and Indianlike. You cannot astonish an English gentleman. If a man goes into a fit at his side, or a servant drops a dish upon his shoulder, or he hears that the house is on fire, he sets down his wine-glass with the same deliberation. He has made up his mind what to do in all possible cases, and he does it. He is cold at a first introduction, and may bow stiffly (which he always does) in drinking wine with you, but it is his manner; and he would think an Englishman out of his senses, who should bow down to his very plate and smile as a Frenchman does on a similar occasion. Rather chilled by this, you are a little astonished when the ladies have left the table, and he closes his chair up to you, to receive an invitation to pass a month with him at his country-house, and to discover that at the very moment he bowed so coldly he was thinking how he should contrive to facilitate your plans for getting to him or seeing the country to advantage on the way.

"The band ceased playing when the ladies left the table, the gentlemen closed up, conversation assumed a merrier cast, coffee and *chasse-café* were brought in when the wines began to be circulated more slowly, and at eleven there was a general move to the drawing-room. Cards, tea, and music filled up the time till twelve, and then the ladies took their departure, and the gentlemen sat down to supper. I got to bed somewhere about two o'clock; and thus ended an evening which I had anticipated as stiff and embarrassing, but which is marked in my tablets as one of the most social and kindly I have had the good fortune to record on my travels.

"I arose late on the first morning after my arrival at Gordon Castle, and found the large party already assembled about the breakfast-table. I was struck on entering with the different air of the room. The deep windows, opening out upon the park, had the effect of sombre landscapes in open frames; the troops of liveried servants, the glitter of plate, the music, that had contributed to the splendour of the scene the night before, were gone; the Duke sat laughing at the head of the table, with a newspaper in his hand, dressed in a coarse shooting-jacket and coloured cravat; the Duchess was in a plain morning dress and cap of the simplest character; and the high-born women about the table, whom I had left glittering with jewels and dressed in all the attractions of fashion, appeared with the simplest *coiffure* and a toilet of studied plainness. The ten or twelve noblemen present were engrossed with their letters or newspapers over tea and toast; and in them, perhaps, the transformation was still greater. The *soigné* man of fashion of the night before, faultless in costume and distinguished in his appearance, in the

full force of the term, was enveloped now in a coat of
fustian, with a coarse waistcoat of plaid, a gingham
cravat, and hob-nailed shoes (for shooting), and in place
of the gay hilarity of the supper-table, wore a face of
calm indifference, and ate his breakfast and read the
paper in a rarely broken silence. *I wondered*, as I
looked about me, what would be the impression of
many people in my own country, could they look in
upon that plain party, aware that it was composed of
the proudest nobility and the highest fashion of
England!

"After breakfast the ladies went off unaccompanied
to their walks in the park and other avocations; those
bound for the covers joined the gamekeepers, who were
waiting with their dogs in the leash at the stables;
some paired off to the billiard-room, and I was left with
Lord Aberdeen in the breakfast-room alone. The Tory
ex-minister made a thousand inquiries, with great
apparent interest, about America. When Secretary
for Foreign Affairs in the Wellington Cabinet, he had
known Mr. M'Lane intimately. He said he seldom had
been so impressed with a man's honesty and straight-
forwardness, and never did public business with anyone
with more pleasure. He admired Mr. M'Lane, and
hoped he enjoyed his friendship. He wished he might
return as our minister to England. One such honourable, uncompromising man, *he said*, was worth a score
of *practised diplomatists*. He spoke of Gallatin and
Rush in the same flattering manner, but recurred continually to Mr. M'Lane, of whom he could scarce say
enough. His politics would naturally lead him to
approve of the administration of General Jackson, but
he seemed to admire the President very much as a
man.

"The routine of Gordon Castle was what each one chose to make it. Between breakfast and lunch the ladies were generally invisible, and the gentlemen rode or shot, or played billiards, or kept their rooms. At two o'clock, a dish or two of hot game and a profusion of cold meats were set on the small tables in the dining-room, and everybody came in for a kind of lounging half-meal, which occupied perhaps an hour. Thence all adjourned to the drawing-room, under the windows of which were drawn up carriages of all descriptions, with grooms, outriders, footmen, and saddle-horses for gentlemen and ladies. Parties were then made up for driving or riding, and from a pony-chaise to a phaeton-and-four, there was no class of vehicle which was not at your disposal.

"The number at the dinner-table of Gordon Castle was seldom less than thirty, but the company was continually varied by departures and arrivals. No sensation was made by either one or the other. A travelling-carriage dashed up to the door, was disburdened of its load, and drove round to the stables, and the question was seldom asked, 'Who is arrived?' You were sure to see at dinner—and an addition of half a dozen to the party made no perceptible difference in anything. Leave-takings were managed in the same quiet way. Adieus were made to the Duke and Duchess, and no one else, except he happened to encounter the parting guest upon the staircase, or were more than a common acquaintance. In short, in every way the *gêne* of life seemed weeded out, and if unhappiness or ennui found its way into the castle, it was introduced in the sufferer's own bosom. For me, I gave myself up to enjoyment with an *abandon* I could not resist. With kindness and courtesy in every look, the luxuries and comforts of a regal establishment at my freest disposal ; solitude when I pleased, company when I pleased ; the whole visible horizon fenced in for the enjoyment of a household, of which I was a temporary portion ; and no enemy except time and the gout, I felt as if I had been spirited into some castle of felicity, and had not come by the royal mail coach* at all. The great spell of high life in this country seems to be *repose.* All violent sensations are avoided, as out of taste. In conversation, nothing is so "odd"—(a word, by the way, that in England means everything dis-

* When we consider the headlong railway speed to which we are accustomed, it seems almost impossible to realise the slow progress of the "old coaching days;" and yet it is a fact that the accelerated mail-coach speed of forty or fifty years ago was looked on with pride, as satisfying the utmost aspirations of the reasonable mind. The utmost speed was got that could be attained ; and, indeed, a question arises whether this facility of traffic that we now enjoy has not created an eagerness for movement, and whether the old system was not sufficient for the wants of the community. A single journey then was undertaken seriously, and served instead of a dozen. And, after all, a single journey to Brighton of say seven hours might be shorter and speedier in the end than half-a-dozen of an hour-and-a-half. Keeping this fact before us, that a journey was usually undertaken from necessity, the difference was not so prodigious as might be supposed. The journey from London to Dublin might be accomplished in thirty-eight hours; and to perform the journey in proper state, for two persons, cost over £60. Four nights were spent at inns. The charge for four horses was nigh on £40 ; turnpikes were £5 ; the fare in the steamer was £3 10s. each. Now the whole charge for two persons amounts to about £6. It took Lord Brougham, when a young man, eight days (day and night) to get to Paris from his family seat.

Sir Henry Holland remarked that now every one walked faster, even in London streets, than in the old times, and hurried from country house to country house, staying a much shorter time at each place. Mr. Hayward, who has always something pleasantly *à propos* to relate, tells us that the late General Phipps "made it a rule never to accept an invitation for a less period than would cover the expense of posting at the rate of a day for every ten miles."

agreeable)—as emphasis or startling epithet, or gesture, and in common intercourse nothing so vulgar as any approach to "a scene." The high-bred Englishman studies to express himself in the plainest words that will convey his meaning, and is just as simple and calm in describing the death of his friend, and just as technical, so to speak, as in discussing the weather."

CHAPTER IX

THE extraordinary circumstance of the arrival of the French *emigrés*, who poured into England in enormous numbers during a course of years, and were of all ranks and conditions, formed a social incident of great significance, which really became "a factor," as it is called, in English society. They were a fruitful source of embarrassment to the Government in many ways. The priests were in complete destitution, and had to be supported by private charity with assistance from the State. There were archbishops, princes, and dukes scarcely better off. Many behaved admirably under these trials, showing a fortitude, patience, and energy in surmounting their difficulties that was amazing. Many supported themselves by giving lessons in French, in dancing, music, and other accomplishments, and even in cookery. Nothing was more to the credit of the English than the mode in which they discharged the overwhelming duties thus cast upon them. The aristocracy of the exiles were generously entertained by various noblemen; vast subscriptions were set on foot, chiefly for the clergy; great establishments were hired for them where they might live in common at a fixed allowance. Some, however, contrived to bring with them a small pittance, which they eked out by various contrivances. There were some, however, of a more desperate class, who consented to perform the dangerous *rôle* of spy, and furnish the French Government with news ; a perilous calling, which often ended in summary execution. The Alien Act, too, was put in force, and troublesome awkward characters were summarily driven from the country.

At many noblemen's houses these *emigrés* were hospitably entertained, and the more eminent found homes with the Duke of Buckingham and others. I have mentioned how often these obligations were forgotten ; and we are assured that the noble owner of Stowe advanced large sums, which he was never repaid.

We find Miss Burney, who had married an *emigré*, General D'Arblay, exerting herself humanely to help the unfortunate French. "There were," she says, "no less than 6,000 clergy in England, besides 400 laity in London, and 800 at Jersey." A pittance of eight shillings a week was allowed to each ecclesiastic, which yet required a sum of £7,500 a month, found by generous private subscriptions for a time, when Government took it up, and a grant was given by Parliament. The shifts and straits these poor people were driven to were incredible, and there are the strangest and most piteous stories of their humble, and sometimes successful efforts, to earn a livelihood as dancing masters, musicians, and hair-dressers.

Of the French *coterie* in London, the best known were Prince Talleyrand the Ambassador, Montrond his friend, Pozzo di Borgo, Matuscewitz, a Pole, and Princess Lieven, all witty or *spirituel* persons ; and it speaks much for the English society that so many gay "men about town," addicted to gaming and racing, should have found wit enough to match what their foreign guests brought. It is quite clear that Montrond and even Talleyrand found themselves in a congenial society, and were stimulated to many pleasant sallies.

Prince Talleyrand arrived in London in 1830, as the representative of the Citizen King, and found himself among old friends. He then offered an extraordinary, not to say eccentric, figure, a sort of dilapidated Voltaire, with a malignant sarcasm lurking in his eyes, and, in a sense, deformed. In one of the journals of the day, he is thus introduced as he appeared at the time.

This appeared in the *Morning Post*, and was a curious sketch : " Talleyrand is certainly the most extraordinary being of his kind the world has produced since the creation. Take him in his physical conformation alone, and think of his having outlived so long all the great and good of his time. Talleyrand was born lame, and his limbs are fastened to his trunk by an iron apparatus, on which he strikes ever and anon his gigantic cane, to the great dismay of those who see him for the first time—an awe not diminished by the look of his piercing grey eyes, peering through his shaggy eyebrows, his unearthly face, marked with deep stains, covered partly by his shock of extraordinary hair, partly by his enormous muslin cravat, which supports a large protruding lip drawn over his upper lip, with a cynical expression no painting could render ; add to this apparatus of terror, his dead silence, broken occasionally by the most sepulchral guttural monosyllables. ' Nature,' says he, ' sleeps and recruits herself at every intermission of my pulse.' And, indeed, you see him time after time rise at three o'clock in the morning from the whist table, then return home and often wake up one of his secretaries to keep him company or talk of business. At four he will go to bed, sitting nearly bolt upright in his bed, with innumerable nightcaps on his head to keep it warm, as he said, and feed his intellect with blood ; but, in fact, to prevent his injuring the seat of knowledge if he tumbles on the ground ; and he sits upright from his tendency to apoplexy, which would no doubt seize him if perfectly recumbent. His bed was made with a deep slope in the middle, rising equally at the head and at the feet, his nearest approach to lying down. It was his habit to eat nothing until dinner-time. At this, his only meal during the four-and-twenty hours, his appetite was enormous."

Established in London, this extraordinary figure was regularly found at the "Travellers' Club," playing whist, and Mr. Hayward tells us he did so but indifferently, though he had an advantage in his well-schooled, impassive face. He was at this time nearly eighty years old, having been born in 1754 ; and at the end of his long and shifty career, from not having a *sou* at the date of the Revolution, was now one of the richest men in Europe—the origin of which, Mr. Raikes, who knew him well, tells us, arose out of some plunder (£120,000) from an indemnity paid by Portugal. He had now castles and estates, and lived like a Prince, as he was. He even received a pension from the King of £4000 a year. Many stories were told of his *gourmandise*, which was extravagant. Mr. Raikes, when engaging a cook in Paris for his friend, Lord Willoughby, had several candidates before him who had "served" in Talleyrand's kitchen. These told him how the Prince kept his house. "There were four *chefs*—the *rotisseur*, the *saucier*, the *patissier*, and the *officier*—this latter superintending the dessert, the ices, and the confitures. In all, there were *ten men* regularly employed in producing the Prince's dinner, which was not only exquisite in its kind, but also adapted to his state of health, comprising the essence of everything nutritious in the garb most light and digestible for an infirm stomach. The Prince was always a *great eater*, but only once a day, and generally tasted of every dish, following each mouthful with a sip of wine to humour the palate. The expense of his table was unlimited, his cook had *carte blanche*, and he often remarked, "Why does not he spend more?"

Lord Alvanley was a special friend, and delighted in circulating stories of his wit. One morning, coming to pay him a visit, he was privileged to see the great man at his toilette. He described him as under the hands of two *valets de chambre*, while a third, who was training for the mysteries of the toilette, stood looking on with attention to perfect himself in his future duties. The Prince was in a loose flannel gown, his long locks (for it is no wig) which are rather scanty, as may be supposed, were twisted and *crépus* with the curling-iron, saturated with powder and pomatum, and then with great care arranged into those snowy ringlets which have been so much known and remarked all over Europe.

This acute man of the world's opinion is worth recording, viz., "that his diplomatic talents may have been rather overrated, and that his successful career may chiefly be attributed to a fineness of tact, which enabled him to perceive early the current of the times, and float on its surface." One has an instinct that is a correct view.

A good specimen of his London jests was when someone told him that Chateaubriand complained of growing deaf, on which Talleyrand answered: "He thinks he is deaf because he no longer hears himself

talked of." But a sadly significant one, with a disagreeable flavour, was a little scene repeated by Lady W.
Russell.

"When he was at Valençay with a large party, the
little Pauline came into the drawing-room where they
were assembled, and the Prince said to her : 'Where
were you, little one ?' She answered solemnly : 'I
have been praying to the bon Dieu for you, to make you
pious.' '*Petite bête !*' said the Prince."

Once he was attacked in the House of Lords, when
the Duke of Wellington gallantly stood up to defend
his old friend, paying him many handsome compliments.
Alvanley went to visit the Prince on the following day,
and found him perusing the debates of the preceding
night, and, though much hurt at the attack of Lord L.,
still more affected by the friendly intervention of the
Duke. He expressed his gratitude in the warmest terms,
while the tears ran down his cheeks, and then added :
"J'en suis d'autant plus reconnoissant à M. le Duc,
que c'est le seul homme d'état dans le monde qui ait
jamais dit du bien de moi "—a pleasantly *naïve* confes-
sion, which he would have heartily ridiculed in another.*

He got fatigued, however, by the duties of his
post. Some said he was annoyed at being obstructed
by Lord Palmerston, and went home to France.

In 1838, he was seized with his last illness. There

---

* One of Talleyrand's *mots* at the expense of his "friend," is truly
brutal. Montrond had been subject of late to epileptic fits, one of
which attacked him after dinner at Talleyrand's. While he lay on
the floor in convulsions, scratching the carpet with his hands, his
benign host remarked with a sneer : " C'est qu'il me parait, qu'il veut
absolument descendre." The other, however, could occasionally utter
something amiable, as when Miss Raikes complained of his dealing
rather hardly with her father's new work, he answered : " Vous êtes
le seul ouvrage de votre père que j'aime."

was a ghastly originality in his exit, and in some points
it recalls that of Voltaire.   There was the same natural
eagerness to get him to see and accept his state, even at
three-quarters past the eleventh hour.   He made some
amende to religion.   Like Voltaire, too, he had not long
before been figuring at the Academy.   Great exertions
were made by his family to this end, and, it is said, that
the child whom he had called *petite bête*, at last persuaded
him into a formal recantation.   He was also influenced
on the ground that there would be a scandal.   He fixed
five o'clock in the morning, when Abbè Dupanloup, later
the well-known bishop, arrived, confessed him, and
received his profession of faith.   Then   followed   a
strange scene.   The King and Madame Adelaide arrived
to pay him a visit.   "His state at that moment was
really   extreme,   yet   he   preserved   his   dignity,   and
noticing   that   the   two   physicians   had   not   been
"presented"   he   went   through   that   form,   so   as   to
have all *en règle*."

It is stated that his friend and brother wit, Montrond, tried his best to dissuade him from this step and
ridiculed it.   Mr. Raikes adds an awful truth :   "It was
a perseverance in the dread of public opinion to the last
hour which was fearful.   At the moment when he was
summoned into the presence of his God he seemed more
anxious to avoid the scoffs of the world in case of his
recovery, which was impossible, than to make his peace
with Heaven—before that tribunal where his appearance
must be immediate and inevitable."

At last the moment came.   The wound in his
back, which had spread down his hip, prevented his
lying   down,   or   even   keeping   a   reclining   posture.
"He sat on the side of his bed for the last forty-eight

hours, leaning forwards, and supported by two servants, who were relieved every two hours. In this attitude he was attended to the last by his family and various friends, while the numerous servants in his hotel gathered in the adjacent room. It was in miniature the scene of the death of the old Kings of France. He died in public. The library adjoining the Prince's bedroom, and from which it was only separated by a *portière* or curtain, was constantly filled with servants and dependants. Frequently one of them would draw back the curtain when unobserved, saying to those in attendance: 'Voyons a-t-il signé? Est-il mort?' His voice failed him at twelve o'clock in the day, and at a quarter before four o'clock he expired."

To supply a finishing touch to this sketch, at his funeral the crowd noted with scoffs that the catafalque displayed the family motto, "Rien que Dieu!"

Pozzo di Borgo was yet another foreigner most acceptable in English society. His jests also circulated —as when Lady Holland, exulting in the duration of the Whig Government, notwithstanding the late anticipations of their fall, said to him the other night: "You see, we are still alive." "Yes, madam," he replied, "*les petites santés* always last long." For a vast number of years the Russian Court had found him an admirable administrator, at last making him Ambassador to England, in the room of Prince Lieven. Then foreigners spoke and wrote English better than foreigners of our own day do.

Count Matuscewitz was another of these witty diplomatists. Having been despatched to London in 1830, to aid Prince Lieven, he quite took root here, and adopted all the ways and habits of an Englishman. He

had finally to leave this country, having been appointed
Minister at a foreign Court. How well he wrote English
may be gathered from a letter from Stockholm, addressed
to the hostess of Gore House.

"I should consider it the climax of ingratitude were
I not most anxious and impatient to revisit good old
England, and to find myself once more under the roof
of Gore House, that hospitable roof, under which I am
certain to receive a hearty welcome, and to meet a most
instructive variety of eminent characters, who move
round you as it were by magic, each happy, each
communicative, each contributing his quota to a general
conversation and harmony which, I believe, was never
known to exist amongst them, except at your house."

Another well-known figure was Count Montrond,
the friend or client of Talleyrand, one of those malicious,
heartless men of society who flourished in London during
this reign. From Mr. Gronow, who knew him well, we
shall borrow this incisive description :

"This well-known personage belonged to a good
family; an inveterate gambler, rarely losing. When
very young, at the Court of Marie Antoinette, a certain
Monsieur de Champagne, an officer of the Guards, who
was playing at cards with him, said, 'Monsieur, vous
trichez.' Montrond answered, 'C'est possible; mais
je n'aime pas qu'on me le dise,' and threw the cards in
his face. They fought next morning with swords, and
Montrond was run through the body. He was confined
to his bed for two months, but, when he got well again,
called out Monsieur de Champagne, and, although he
received another wound, succeeded in killing his adversary. This duel set him up in the world as a dangerous
man to meddle with, and saved him from many insults
to which his very suspicious luck at play would have

exposed him. Talleyrand said, *à propos* of this, ' Il vit
sur son mort.' Montrond was thrown into prison
during the Reign of Terror. I knew Montrond well, but
several years later ; he had then no trace of having been
the *charmant garçon* tradition represents him. He was
rather above the middle height, and what the English
novelists call *embonpoint*, and had the appearance of a
vieux bonhomme. He was perfectly bald, had blue
eyes, very small features, and a florid complexion.
There was a peculiar twinkle in his eye, which boded
no good to the victim he had selected for his prey.

" His countenance, as beheld by a casual observer,
bore the stamp of an almost Pickwickian benevolence ;
but, on a closer inspection, there lurked behind this
mask of mild philanthropy the stinging wit of Voltaire,
mingled with the biting sarcasm of Rogers or Sir Philip
Francis. He was not a great talker, nor did he swagger,
speak about himself, or laugh at his own *bons mots.* He
was demure, sleek, sly, and dangerous. He would
receive with a paternal air the silly quizzing of some
feeble jester, but then would come the twinkle of that
little pale blue eye, and then the poor moth or butterfly
was ground to pieces on the wheel of his sharp, sarcastic
wit.

" In the London clubs he went by the name of Old
French, and managed to win very large sums of money
off Lord Sefton (the only specimen I ever saw of a
gigantic hunchback), who, with all his wit and cleverness, lost very largely on all occasions, as well as of the
late Lord Foley, the Duke of York, and many others.
He lived in the best society, both at Paris and in
London, and was on terms, if not of intimacy, at all
events of familiarity, with many of the greatest people
in Europe. In the latter years of his life he resided in

the Place Vendôme, in an apartment now occupied by
Mr. Brooke Greville."

Towards the end of his life he removed to Paris,
and received a pension of £2000 a year from Louis
Philippe for old services. Here he used to see his old
friend Talleyrand.

Though he was constantly on the point of death
from some violent illness, yet he contrived to rally.
"Montrond has had another sort of a fit," wrote a
friend. "I went to see him, and found him very ill
with gout in the stomach. He was very pleasant; but
I really thought him in a bad way. The next day he
dined at the club, and went to the baths at Vichy in
the evening, and is come back, I am told, better than
ever. The old gentleman really seems endowed with a
principle of vitality, which may to him counterbalance
the absence of many others, that shall be nameless.
He seems likely to live as long as his friend M. de
Talleyrand."

The two old *viveurs* seem to watch each other with a
sort of furious and malicious anxiety, that the other
should "go" first. When Montrond was at the point
of death, Talleyrand would come to inquire at the door,
though too feeble to go up to see him. "In the year of
Talleyrand's prosperity Montrond paid him a visit at
Valençay, and a Paris paper, with much delicacy, described him 'dragging with him the infirmities of a
youth prolonged to seventy. Almost blind, racked with
gout, they wheel him about the park, assist him to the
drawing-room, or carry him in to dinner, where he still
continues to utter garrulous sallies to enliven the somewhat *ennuyeux* evenings of the place. It is curious
to find the two old wrecks comforting one another.'"
Montrond was presently to assist—and fancied himself,

no doubt, lucky—at the death-bed of his friend; doing his best, by ridicule and other ways, to hinder his reconcilement with the Church and with decency. It was characteristic that his friend left him nothing out of his enormous fortune.

When Lord Alvanley was going to Venice the next year, 1838, he called on the old *roué* in Paris.

" I was pleased here," he writes, " because I saw our old comrades, Mildmay and Montrond. The first has changed in appearance entirely : the whiskers are suppressed, and a most formidable pair of campaigning moustaches have been successfully cherished. He is grown fat, and, like poor Brummell, has not got beyond 1817 in English affairs—still talks of Macao at Watiers, and asks after —— Montrond is wonderful; apoplexy and gout do their worst, but cannot subdue his spirits and *esprit; he killed us with laughing at his stories about M. de Talleyrand's death, which, though it deeply affected him, has still its ludicrous side; and his legacy of a standing-up desk to write at* did not soften his natural inclination to be a little sarcastic. He said that when the signature to the retractation was signed, a priest declared that it was a miracle, on which he gravely said that he had already known of just such another miracle—that ' when General Gouvins was killed, he, Montrond, with General Latour Maubourg, went to the spot where he lay, and that they asked the only person who had seen the catastrophe how it occurred ; this was a hussar, who replied : " Le boulet l'a frappé, et il n'avoit que juste le temps de me dire, Prenez ma bourse et ma montre ; et il est mort!'" This apologue, as you may suppose, was like a shell thrown into Dino's coterie."

The whole letter, the tone of the person who writes,

the friend making his friends "die with laughing" at
the account of *his* friend's last moments, the legacy of
the "standing-up desk," are touches that would have
pleased Voltaire.

Montrond's own turn came presently. "His death,"
says one account (that of Colonel Gronow), "was a
very wretched one. Left alone, as he lay upon his bed,
between fits of pain and drowsiness, he could see his
fair friend picking from his shelves the choicest
specimens of his old Sèvres china, or other articles
of *virtu*. Shortly before his death he received the
visit of Count Charles de M——, a well-known dandy
of that time, whom he liked to call one of his pupils,
but who, fortunately, only resembled him in two points
—natural wit, and rather extravagant habits. He
turned on the boon companion of his happier days a
glance of hopeless regret, and said : ' My good friend, I
have not got a shilling ; I have no appetite ; I can't
drink ; Desirée's only occupation is to carry off my
best china. " Je vous demande un peu si c'est là
Montrond ? " ' "

This is, however, not the whole. Poor Mr. Raikes,
better informed, describes a more edifying finish. The
Duchess of Broglie, " that good woman," came on the
scene, and was unwearied in trying to turn his thoughts
to the next world. It appears she succeeded, and
Mr. Raikes learned that he died with much edifica-
tion—having received the Sacrament—and perfectly
repentant.

Mr. Raikes, however, who lived in Paris, and is a
better authority than Captain Gronow, ascertained how
this old *viveur* made his exit. He found, to his great
surprise, that the Duc de Broglie had been unceasing in

his efforts to convert him to a sense of religion. "The same effort was made some years ago by that excellent woman, the Duchesse de Broglie, when he was also in a state of extreme danger. She came and prayed by his bedside; but then it was without the slightest effect on his mind, because he felt convinced (as he told me) that he should recover. He has been *administré*, and has confessed three times. The Abbé Petitot is constantly with him; and, during his first interview, said to him : "In your day you have no doubt made many a scoff against religion." "No," said the other, with dignity, "I have always lived among gentlemen." A very happy reply. He desired the crucifix to be placed at his bed's head, and would not suffer it to be removed. Peace to his manes !"

Connected with the Duke of Wellington was another figure at this period remarkable in English social life—the wife of the Russian Ambassador, Princess Lieven. Of this lady but little is known, though evidence of her social power and influence are revealed in the memoirs of Greville, Raikes, etc. The extraordinary feature was, that these two clever persons, representing the Czar at the English Court, instead of concerning themselves with the business of their mission, entered into the struggles of English parties, and did their best to upset ministries. This singular course was the cause of much annoyance and trouble, and seems to have been a factor in several ministerial crises. Madame de Lieven contrived to influence George IV. and his *entourage* a good deal, and the Duke of Wellington and the ministers were often driven to fury by the success of these machinations. The bitterness and even rage of the Duke at finding his measures thwarted by this secret influence may be conceived when we recall his enormous difficulties in managing the King. In August, 1829, his patience gave way :

" I concur in your letter to Lord Heytesbury about Prince and Princess Lieven. They have played an English Party game, instead of doing the business of their sovereign, since I have been in office. I have the best authority for asserting that both have been engaged (as principals) in intrigues to deprive my colleagues and me of power since January, 1828, and that they have misrepresented our conduct and views to their sovereign."

And again :

" I think that our only ground of complaint is that they misrepresent to the Emperor what passes here. A public complaint of their intrigues here is impossible, because, however strong the proofs, they cannot be produced in Court. A private complaint is improper.

" If such complaint should occasion their removal, we shall have to explain ourselves to society at least, and I would prefer to incur not only all the evil which Madame de Lieven can do me, but even all she would wish me, to having to explain my conduct upon any such subject. . . . It is clear to me if we don't complain of the Lievens we must cease to do business with Russia, otherwise than through our minister at St. Petersburg. . . . These tidings show us we cannot trust a secret to the Lievens. . . . That which we must do is not to listen to Lieven, but to answer through Lord Heytesbury."

However, in time, and with the adieu of the Duke

to power, these angry feelings gave way to friendly intercourse. We find the fair *intriguante* consulting the Duke
on politics, and even suggesting a little dinner at their
country place, to which the Duke responded with
alacrity. Four years later, on the eve of their departure
from England, in a conversation with Mr. Greville, she
gave vent to her rage and annoyance; an unfortunate
dispute about sending the late Lord Stratford to
St. Petersburg, which was unacceptable to the Czar,
having led to the recall of M. Lieven. She was in " an
agony" at losing the position in which she had been so long
establishing herself, and it is amusing to find her bitterly
complaining of the treatment she had received in this
country, where she had been accustomed to assume
a position few foreigners have ever taken. Thus she
delivered herself to her friend, as the Duke reports it :

" She fired a tirade against Government ; she vowed
that nobody ever had been treated with such in-
civility as Lieven, ' *des injures, des reproches,*' that
Cobbett, Hunt, and all the blackguards in England could
not use more offensive language ; whatever event was
coming was imputed to Russia—Belgium, Portugal,
Turkey, ' *tout était la Russie et les intrigues de la
Russie;*' that she foresaw they should be driven away from
England. With reference to the war in Asia Minor, she
said the Sultan had applied to the Emperor for assistance,
' *et qu'il l'aurait, et que le Sultan n'avait pas un meilleur
ami que lui,*' that the Egyptians would advance no
farther, and a great deal more of complaint at the in-
justice evinced towards them and on their political
innocence. In the evening I told all this to Mellish of
the Foreign Office, who knows everything about foreign
affairs, and he said it was all a lie ; that Russia had
offered her assistance, which the Sultan had refused, and

she was, in fact, intriguing and making mischief in every
Court in Europe.   George Villiers writes me word that
she has been for months past endeavouring to get up a
war anywhere, and that this Turkish business is more
likely than anything to bring one about.

This lady struck Stockmar as being "of a disagreeable, stiff, proud, and haughty manner. It is true she is full
of talent, plays the pianoforte admirably, speaks English,
French, and German perfectly ; but, then, she is well
aware of it.   Her face is certainly handsome, though too
thin, and the pointed nose, as well as the mouth, which
can be contracted into various folds, show even outwardly the small inclination she has to consider others
as her equals.   *Her neck is like a skeleton's,*" adds the
ungallant German.

This Princess, with Lady Jersey, was one of the
autocrats of Almack's Balls.

Says Mr. Hayward.

"One of the incidents that confirmed the supremacy
of Almack's, was the exclusion of the hero of Waterloo
for coming after the specified hour.   Mr. Ticknor witnessed this incident.   After dining at Lord Downshire's,
he accompanied the ladies to Almack's.   They called on
Lady Mornington on their way, where they met the
Duke.   On his remarking that he thought he should
look in at Almack's by-and-by, his mother exclaimed :
'Ah, Arthur, you had better go in time, for you know
Lady Jersey will make no allowance for you.'   He
neglected the warning ; and a short time after the
Downshire party had entered the room, Mr. Ticknor,
who was standing near Lady Jersey, heard one of the
attendants say to her : 'Lady Jersey, the Duke of
Wellington is at the door and desires to be admitted.'
'What o'clock is it ?' she asked.   'Seven minutes after

eleven, your ladyship.' She paused a moment, and then said with emphasis and distinctness : ' Give my compliments—give Lady Jersey's compliments to the Duke of Wellington, and say she is very glad that the first enforcement of the rule of exclusion is such, that hereafter no one can complain of its application. He cannot be admitted.' This was in 1819. Another traditional story is that, about the same time, the Duchess of Northumberland was refused a ticket on the ground that, although a woman of rank, she was not a woman of fashion. The fact is, she was refused for not submitting to the preliminary of an introduction to the patronesses ; their rule being that no one could be admitted who was not on the visiting-list of one of them."

The secret of the influence of this extraordinary lady seems to explain the merciless despotism she exercised in society.* Sir H. Holland tells us :

" She wielded power both in Russian diplomacy, and as a patroness of the Almack's balls, then the leading fashion or folly of the day. Even as a physician I was often witness of the effects of this dominating passion, having seen more than one case defying medicine, cured

* Lady C. Campbell gives a specimen of this grand lady's behaviour : " One evening, after her Excellency had herself executed on the pianoforte a most brilliant and scientific piece of music, she pressed Lady G—— to play in her turn. The latter, whose musical powers were far superior in point of feeling and expression, though less *bruyante* than that of the Russian, complied with her request ; but the Princess Lieven paid no attention to the music, and impertinently turned away as if in scorn ; yet her want of good breeding on this and many similar occasions was overlooked, and the Russian Princess continued to daunt the ladies of the English aristocracy ; and finally, when recalled from the British Court, all the *élite* of female society united in presenting her with a valuable tribute of their respect and remembrance."

by a ticket for Almack's opportunely obtained. I knew the Princess Lieven more intimately after her life had been embittered, first by the French Revolution of 1848, and afterwards by the Crimean war—both of which events infringed deeply on the antecedents of her career. Like so many others who outlive a high position in the world, she felt strongly, and expressed to me frequently, the change thus attaching to her life."

But there is yet another phase of English Society to be considered, and which will be found interesting.

CHAPTER X.

SOME forty or fifty years ago there was in fashionable Parisian society a decided English element which, though small, exercised an influence that seemed out of proportion to its size. On the other hand, as we have seen, there existed a French element in English society represented by such important names as Talleyrand, his friend Montrond, the Princess Lieven, and D'Orsay, but whose influence on English manners was comparatively unimportant. It would almost seem that the same English spirit, which assimilated to itself these lively French guests, had travelled with its sons to Paris, there to produce the same effect. This may have been owing to the difference of national character. The qualities of *aplomb* and reserve, with the advantages that follow, naturally excite the envy, or at least imitation, of those possessing the more ornamental gifts of society ; while the man of *aplomb* and reserve would be inclined to look down, as frivolous, on those less solidly endowed. The truth is, English fashion has always, since the French Revolution, been followed in Paris, either in matters of sport, bearing, and even dress. At the present time every Frenchman of *ton* and fashion has his clothes made ·in London, *chez Poole,* or by some other artist of note, while English horses, dogs, harness, and coachmen, English clubs, and English beer are in universal favour. This English taste began to set in shortly after the peace, in 1815, when Louis XVIII., who had learnt the language and habits during his residence in England, and, liking both, naturally encouraged the new mode.

The true reason, perhaps, was to be found in the relation which was brought about by emigration during the French Revolution. The *crème de la crème* of the French nobility—and never was the *crème* in so pitiful a way—found its way to London where they were cordially welcomed by their brethren. The intimacy that then arose was cemented by marriages, and some of the more distinguished young men received commissions in the English army. The old Duke of Castries married a young Irish girl of no fortune, the Polignacs and Macdonalds became allied ; Count Walewski married a daughter of Lady Sandwich's. The Grammont family once more found itself in England and was welcomed at Devonshire House where one of the daughters captivated the heir of the Tankervilles, while the other, who had married Sebastiani later, had an opportunity of returning hospitality as French Ambassadress in London. Nor must the once popular and attractive Flahaut be forgotten, whose marriage with an English heiress of wealth as well as rank—Miss Mercer, later Baroness Keith— together with rank and influence in his own country ensured him a brilliant career.

But it was not until the opening of the reign of Louis Philippe that the English element became conspicuous in French society. The titled English would repair thither for the season, and it reads strangely to hear of the Duke of Sutherland arriving with six carriages and thirty servants, and of "Lord and Lady Barbara Ponsonby" taking the Hotel Crillon. Then, too, we hear of many an Englishman of fashion whose resources had been crippled by gambling, finding it convenient to commence afresh in Paris, where his previous costly training as "a dandy" stood him in good stead. Conspicuous among these were Gronow, and Raikes, Ball Hughes, who had fixed himself in a pretty house at Enghien, Standish, one of the "fast men" of the Regency, who had married a connection of Mdme. de Genlis, Berkeley Craven, who had also married a Frenchwoman, and who shot himself on learning that Bay Middleton had won the Derby.

Where there were so many Englishmen, it might be expected that so national an institution as "the club" would not be wanting; and it might appear to be owing to this influence that the smallest town in France is furnished with a "*cercle*" of some description. It should be added, however, that this favour is owing to the opportunities afforded for gambling, rather than for sociality. But the large Paris clubs—"the aristocratic Jockey," the great and little "*cercles*"—came into existence under English patronage. It was in such places that the fashionable Briton established his influence, and found his most servile imitators.

It is impossible to think of the English colony in Paris without recalling one family, whose proceedings seemed to excite notice from their prodigality and eccentricity. This was the Hertford family and its various members. The Parisian Lord Hertford— Thackeray's "Lord Steyne"; well-known for his pictures and the nickname of "Bagatelle," and the doer of many doings — was the son of a more original person still, Lord Yarmouth, the friend of the Regent, and known as " Red Herrings," from the colour of his whiskers, etc.*

" Lord Hertford," Mr. Labouchere tells us, " who died in 1870, cut off his successor with the comparatively small settled estates, because the Seymour family had always refused to recognise his brother, Lord Henry Seymour, and thereby cast a serious reflection on Maria, Lady Hertford. If the late Lord Hertford had died in the lifetime of his younger brother (who, of course, was his heir), it was understood to be the intention of the Seymours to try the question of Lord Henry's legitimacy; but a great scandal was averted by his dying many years before his elder brother. Lord Hertford was well aware of the hitch, and in consequence of it he had made a will, which was settled by the most eminent counsel of the day, in which he bequeathed his vast estates in the north of Ireland to Lord Henry, who himself possessed a very large fortune. Their mother, Lady Hertford, who died in 1856, was the daughter of the Marchesa Fagniani. " Old Q." left £150,000 and three valuable houses to " Mie Mie," as she was called, and he made her husband his residuary legatee, which meant the best part of a million. Selwyn left her £33,000. It was an odd history altogether."

When Lord Hertford died, his executors had to put his valet in prison on a charge of embezzlement,

* One of the oddities of the time was this exercise of wit upon personal peculiarities. There was some point in this *sobriquet*, connected, as it was with the article of commerce in the place from which he derived his title. There was " Poodle " Byng, so called from his flowing hair; Kangaroo Cooke, from a strange walk; " Pea Green " Haynes; " Dog " Jennings; " Frog " somebody else; in short, the system of *nicknames*—always a poor form of jesting, but which, it is curious, obtained always in most societies.

just as he was about to leave England in a new carriage, and with a service of plate that he had bought, value 2000 guineas. The depredations were found to be enormous.

Lord Henry Seymour, a pleasant writer tells us, first President, whether of the French Jockey Club, or of its Comité des Courses, was born in 1805, and died at Paris, the place also of his birth, in 1859. He is said never to have been in England in his life. He would drive about with four horses, postilions, outriders, and bugle-horns; would sit at the window of the famous *Vendanges de Bourgogne*, with other *viveurs*, to see the *descente de la Courtille* in the early morning after "Mardi Gras," and would scatter among the maskers a *friture d'or*. His curious testamentary writings amounted to a little over a score between 1855 and 1859, while he left a handsome bequest of £72,000 to be divided between the "hospices" of Paris and London. There were few, if any, mourners, beyond four or five members of the French Jockey Club at his funeral; his intimate friends were probably few; and his fun was certainly of a questionable sort. His last moments, it is said, were much soothed by the ingenious device he had hit upon for making the loss of him felt by his servants. He left not a penny to any one of them, expressly that they might miss him. But it is just possible that he believed himself to have been plundered by them in his lifetime; that he had submitted to it for the sake of peace and quietness; and that his apparent want of generosity was merely his playful way of showing that he had not been so blind as they supposed. At any rate, he left annuities and exemption from all saddle work to four or five favourite horses.

"Lord Henry Seymour may be said to have encou-

raged horse-racing both by example and by precept—by
personal performance, and by proxy in the form of a
professional jockey—almost from the cradle. He imported Royal Oak, sire of Slane, from England; and,
more than that, he imported—to take the charge of his
training stables—the renowned Thomas Carter, who was
for many years the *doyen* of French trainers. It was
Carter who introduced Tom Jennings and Henry
Jennings, *par nobile fratrum* and *par nobile* of trainers,
and, strange as it may appear for one so long and so
intimately associated with the Turf, he left behind him
a reputation for honesty and integrity above all things
when he died, but a year or two ago, in 1879, full of
years and honours, and was followed to his grave by the
whole Anglo-French population of Chantilly."

His taste was indeed but one shape of arrogance,
as he was glad to show that there were other things
besides rank and money in which he could excel; and
when neither his judgment, his rank, or his money
together could ensure him success, he grew pettish.
Thus he piqued himself on driving faster horses than
anyone in the Bois, and it was one of the traditional
but probably exaggerated legends of the boulevards, that
he had expended vast sums in securing horses with a
view to out-trot some mysterious stranger who contrived
to keep in advance of him. On one occasion he was
bold enough to " cut in " in front of the King's carriage,
which brought down an' order from the Court to quit
France at once. This, however, he contrived to have
revoked.

These acts furnished wonder and amusement to
Paris for many years. It must be allowed that the odd
estimate of English character which prevailed so long in
Paris was pardonable enough, considering the specimens

that were thus presented to a society too mercurial or indifferent to take the trouble of making fine distinctions. And, from this point of view, the Lord Allcash of Scribe, with other stage milords, could not be considered a very gross exaggeration. Even the persistent renunciation of his country—it was said that he had never set foot in London—by a man of rank and enormous wealth, seemed in itself a singular eccentricity ; and it could not be readily accounted for, save on the theory of its being national.

One of his dependants, a man of small means, and who was fond of horses, though an indifferent rider, he insisted should ride out with him. But it was noticed that his lordship's friend was invariably mounted on some vicious animal ; any horse in the stable noted for temper being allotted to the unlucky equestrian. He was so often put in peril of his life that he was at last obliged to forego the honour of riding with his friend. But even more disagreeable were his tricks at the expense of those who were in a lower class, and whom the sense of his own dignity ought to have taught him to spare. When the fencing-master had exchanged his clothes for the professional dress, he would secretly cover them with a peculiar powder, known as "*poudre à gratter*"—scratching powder— and enjoy the tortures of the victim. Another trick, which he repeated often under various forms, was that of putting jalap into chocolate or coffee.

These stories are reported by M. de Villemessant, who, like other Frenchmen acquainted with the English lord, speak with a sort of horror of his sardonic and cynical tastes. Allowance must be made for professional exaggeration, especially in the case of the editor of such a paper as the *Figaro*. One cannot, therefore, guarantee their truth. But there is a coherence in these specimens of character. "You my friends?" he would say sneeringly to those who so styled themselves; "get along! You come here because it amuses you and it suits you." The same thought occurred to him in reference to his servants. There were two or three who had grown grey in his service—a favourite body-servant; a trusty English groom, named Briggs; and, above all, a poor broken-down gentleman of good blood, actually an Italian marquis, who for years had occupied a position of genteel dependence about him, looking after his guns and other arms, serving out the precious cigars, and making some "particular" eau-de-cologne, for which he had a receipt. His "master" affected to treat him with great favour, though he was never weary of rallying him on his titles and good blood. But in his case, as in that of the old servants, the idea no doubt occurred to him: "These fellows think themselves quite secure—count on large legacies as their right. This is the secret of their long stay in my service. They begin to look on it as their right." Then came the notion of punishing them for this assumed offence. And accordingly, in the disposal of his vast fortune, not a halfpenny was left to the broken-down marquis or to any of the old servants. His heirs, however, generously allotted them a pension of sixty pounds a year each. So with his charities, as he would have called them, which were often splendid, but which he carried off as caprices or bits of sensation. He was once at a fair seen to give a remarkably handsome but wicked-looking bandit or gipsy of sixteen twenty pounds, and when asked if that was not a piece of cruel kindness to the boy, replied coolly "that it would give him a taste for money; and that when it was spent he would probably go and murder someone to get more." It may again be doubted if this be true, and it is but fair to say that his more thoughtful friends looked upon such speeches as mere pieces of pleasantry, with which he tried to get rid of the artificial character of the benevolent and charitable, which he felt to be irksome and unsuited to him. At Boulogne he was made the hero of a somewhat sensational scene, which rather belongs to the Chatelet or Porte St. Martin Theatre. In a great storm some sailors were seen clinging to the shrouds of their shipwrecked vessel, and through the tempest his voice was heard offering, now ten thousand francs to save each life, now twenty-five thousand, and finally, when the number was reduced to two, one hundred thousand. It is certain, however, that he presented the town with a lifeboat and house all complete. Yet it is not surprising to learn that he was, for a man of such a fortune, stingy. At play he would only risk a few twenty-franc pieces : and once, when he had gone beyond his usual amount, and lost a few thousand francs, he was so piqued that he declared he had been cheated. This compliment he paid to his own club. Neither do his hospitalities appear to have been of a large or substantial kind. There was a particular emphasis laid on his cigars, of which he was an admirable judge, and of which stores of the choicest brands were sent to him. With these he took as much pains as other men would with their wine. He treated them scientifically. Vast oaken cases were laid out in thousands of leaden cells, one for each. Before its admission into the collection he himself personally examined every cigar, rejecting such as seemed to be at all inferior. After lying by for some months, a fresh examination and final selection was made ; the rejected ones, still of the choicest kind, were disposed of to friends, or to some favoured tobacconist. His life was that of a sybarite—the day being laid out with a view to elegant pleasure. Yet this rich and haughty seigneur was solitary ; as was said of Garrick, "He had friends, but no friend." It is stated that his chief enjoyment was looking down from his windows at the crowd turning into the Café de Paris underneath.

It was noted what exceeding caution and care for his person were displayed in every one of his proceedings. Fond as he was of boxing, he would not box unless in the padded armour of the school, requiring that his adversary should wear the gloves, though he himself did not. When he was almost a boy, his favourite sport was to give a hackney-coachman a couple of louis, seize the reins, and drive in the most disorderly manner down some narrow street, upsetting barrows, and all but running over someone ; and then, when a hue and cry had been raised and pursuit was growing warm, he would slip down and escape, leaving the driver to bear the consequences.

It is surprising that he should have been endured so long, and it is unfavourable to the character of the French noblemen and gentlemen with whom he associated that they should have put up with such a patron, whose patronage was, besides, unprofitable. Gradually, however, his behaviour, which had long tried their patience, became at last too outrageous to be endured. A cruel incident, which he treated as a matter of course, furnished a good excuse for exhibiting an indignation which had long been felt, and he was gradually "dropped" by his "friends."

The "little circle" held its meetings at the Café de

Paris, which was, in fact, the lower storey of his hotel. It was a pleasant club, including about a hundred members, most of whose names were well known. Among them were those of Roger de Beauvoir, Ball Hughes, Prince Belgioso, Lord Bury, Major Frazer, Captain Gronow, Alfred de Musset, St. Cyran, Count Horace de Viel Castel, and Lord Henry Seymour. A severe system of blackballing was established, one in six excluding. Alexandre, the proprietor of the café, was the caterer. Whist was played for pretty high points.

It was here that Lord Henry Seymour presented himself one morning after the scandal just alluded to, and found a chilling welcome. He rested his hand on the billiard-cushion, when one of the players, we are told, deliberately aimed the ball at his fingers. When the English lord angrily declared that he was awkward, the other answered that he had done it on purpose. On which he quitted the room without saying a word. This insult is told by M. de Villemessant, as though it were an heroic, instead of being a childish and boyish action. Certainly no English gentleman, wishing to reprobate the conduct of a person whom he had known, would take so absurd a mode of showing his resentment. M. de Villemessant does not see that such an exhibition of womanish spite quite justified Lord Henry Seymour in withdrawing from the club. But he determined to punish the members still more, by destroying their club. He sent word to the proprietor of the café that he must give his fashionable patrons notice to quit, unless he wished to receive notice to quit himself. Furious at having thus to sacrifice his best customers, the owner of the café complained loudly of the harsh dilemma in which he was placed. And the members, at once taking

a hostile tone, sent the noble landlord word that if he
persisted, he would have to reckon with them. It is
stated that on this threat he gave way. Such a depth
of meanness seems improbable, especially as we find him
later carrying out his ejectment, and driving the club to
the corner of the Boulevard de la Chaussée d'Antin.
Having lost its *locale*, the club soon languished, and
before long died out.

It was stated that as he opened his pile of morning
despatches, his trained intelligence soon construed the
first delicate approach to an application for aid, and he
would at once throw the letter into the fire without
reading further. He used to give out that he had been
so systematically and almost invariably deceived, that
he had determined to indemnify himself by declining to
give charity at all. It must be said that his acquaintances credited him with too much logic to accept this
excuse, and set his lack of charity down to a less re-
putable and more selfish cause.

This strange being died in the year 1859.

Nor was the family without its share of wit and
power of ready repartee. Thus, at the club in Paris,
some comments, not of a very flattering nature, passed
on the son of an English nobleman who had just
returned to England. One of the speakers, a younger
son of the Duc de ———, thoughtlessly observed to
Yarmouth, who was present : "J'ai toujours remarqué
du reste que les aînés des grandes familles en Angleterre
avaient plus de suffisance que de mérite." Yarmouth
replied : "C'est vrai : ils sont à peu près comme les
cadets ici."

There were other characters in the family, less noted
but quite as eccentric, such as Lord W. Seymour, who
died in 1837, aged seventy seven, brother to the first

Marquis of Hertford. He was a very eccentric character, and led a wandering life—travelling over the country on foot, in the dress of a sailor; living at wretched inns at little expense, with this peculiarity, that he always had during the night several candles burning in his room.

In 1835 there was alive one of these Anglo-French noblemen, the old Duke of Grammont, about eighty years old, having seen the strangest vicissitudes. He was captain of the Guards to Louis XVI., which situation, being venal, like all other places about the Court in those days, he purchased for 500,000 francs. This sum was lost to his family. He had shown Mr. Raikes where he rode down the great stone staircase near the orangeries in the garden at Versailles, at the head of his regiment, when the mob came from Paris to assail the king and queen at the commencement of the Revolution. He has been a steady adherent of the Bourbons; he followed them into banishment wherever they could find a refuge, and returned with them at the Restoration.

This family was much in England, and had English connections. One served in the Guards, while the Duchess of Grammont was a sister of the famous Count D'Orsay. The beautiful "Corisande" de Grammont, who married Lord Tankerville, was to furnish Mr. Disraeli with a heroine's name. The Chabots and De Jarnacs also settled in this country, and married into English families of distinction.

CHAPTER XI

RETURNING now to English ground it will be found interesting to enumerate a few special specimens of popular characters, who certainly increase the reader's harmless pleasure. We have now unhappily no noblemen whose witty or lively sayings are quoted like Lord Alvanley's, no enterprising lady of fashion that can be named with Lady Cork or Lady Holland.

Lord Alvanley presents one of those figures which are familiar enough to most readers, but of whom little is known beyond a few *bons mots*. Diary-keepers like Mr. Raikes and Mr. Greville are fond of recording what "Alvanley said," and how "Alvanley came into Brookes's." He certainly had a pleasant wit, and though not taking any active part in politics, he associated so much with political men, he was consulted, his opinions were quoted by them and found useful.

He was the son of "Pepper Arden," a law officer and judge of reputation.* He became a gay, easy-

* Upon one occasion a Frenchman, accompanied by his interpreter, entered one of our law courts, when Sir Pepper, with a stentorian voice, and in a great rage, was haranguing the jury. The Frenchman inquired what the lawyer's name was. The interpreter

going man of pleasure, a distinguished gourmand, and seems to have had the art of attaching his friends.

"I much doubt," says Mr. Raikes, "whether the year 1789 did not produce the greatest wit of modern times, in the person of William, Lord Alvanley. After receiving a very excellent and careful education, Alvanley entered the Coldstream Guards at an early age, and served with distinction at Copenhagen and in the Peninsula; but being in possession of a large fortune, he left the army, gave himself up entirely to the pursuit of pleasure, and became one of the principal dandies of the day. Not only was Alvanley considered the wittiest man of his day in England, but, during his residence in France, and tours through Russia and other countries, he was universally admitted to possess, not only great wit and humour, but *l'esprit Français* in its highest perfection ; and no greater compliment could be paid him by foreigners than this. He was one of the rare examples (particularly rare in the days of the dandies, who were generally sour and spiteful) of a man combining brilliant wit and repartee with the most perfect good-nature. His manner, above all, was irresistible, and the slight lisp, which might have been considered as a blemish, only added piquancy and zest to his sayings. He resided in Park Street, St. James's, and his dinners there and at Melton were considered to be the best in England. He never invited more than eight people, and insisted upon having the somewhat expensive luxury of an apricot tart on the sideboard the whole year round.

translated literally Sir Pepper's name from English into French, and designed him as " Le Chevalier Poivre Ardent." " Parbleu ! il est très bien nommé," replied the Frenchman.

When Sir G. Elliot became Lord Minto, it was suggested that the title might be Pepper-Minto.

'This, with a neck of venison, a small turbot, and lobster sauce,' he said 'was a dinner for an Emperor.'

"Alvanley was a good speaker; and having made some allusion to O'Connell in rather strong terms in the House of Lords, the latter very coarsely and unjustly denounced him, in a speech he made in the House of Commons, as ' *a bloated buffoon.*'"

His was the well-known reply to the coachman's, "It's a great deal for only having taken your lordship to Wimbledon."

"No, my good man," said Alvanley; "I give it you, not for taking me, but for bringing me back."

This, however, has been given to the Duke of Sussex.

"Everybody knows the story of Gunter, the pastry-cook. He was mounted on a runaway horse with the King's hounds, and excused himself for riding against Alvanley, by saying, 'Oh, my lord, I can't hold him; he's so hot!' 'Ice him, Gunter; ice him!' was the rejoinder.

"He always read in bed, and when he wanted to go to sleep, he either extinguished his candle by throwing it on the floor in the middle of the room, and taking a shot at it with the pillow, or else quietly placed it, when still lighted, under the bolster. At Badminton, and other country houses, his habits in this respect were so well known, that a servant was ordered to sit up in the passage to keep watch over him.

"His creditors having become at last very clamorous, that able and astute man of the world, Mr. Charles Greville, had undertaken to settle those of Alvanley. After going through every item of the debts, matters looked more promising than Mr. Greville expected, and he took his leave. In the morning he received a note from Alvanley, to say that he had quite forgotten to take into account a debt of fifty-five thousand pounds.

"In his latter years Lord Alvanley was a martyr to the gout, but preserved his wit and good humour to the last. He died in 1849."

In 1841 he was on his travels, having visited Italy and the East. His letters from that country were written at great length, and showed much observation, wit, and sense. One, to his friend Raikes, from Naples, written in 1839, is charming for its placid gaiety and feeling, to say nothing of the style :

"DEAR RAIKES,

"In the hotbed of politics and civil war in which you are living, it will be tranquillity to you to receive a letter from the headquarters of *far niente*, of political apathy, macaroni, tarantella, and sunshine. I have got to think that looking out of the window at the sea, snuffing up the afternoon breeze, driving up and down the Corso at night, and then supping lightly on fish and Lacryma Christi, is the perfection of existence ; and when a souvenir of more brilliant amusements, more exciting pleasures, and younger and happier days, flashes across my memory, I only ·heave a little quiet sigh, drink another glass of Lacryma, and relapse back into the vacancy of thought from which it had momentarily roused me.

"News comes here so late that it has lost its freshness ; and absence, that foe to friendship as well as love, has operated on all my friends in England, so that the only letters I get are a few on business, which I am grown too much of a Neapolitan even to open ! My thoughts, however, will revert to those whom I have

loved and lived with ; and, in spite of my philosophy, I
find myself longing to see or hear of them.   I therefore
fire this shot at you, to tell you that I am alive, and to
summon you to give me a like assurance.

"You saw in the papers that I was to be married.
No such luck has befallen me.   The person mentioned is
a charming woman, young enough to be my daughter ;
and, as I saw a good deal of her, the newspapers, who
pursue us English wherever we go, popped in an article
which might have made it unpleasant for her and
myself, had we not had too much good sense to
mind it.

"This place is intended for elderly gentlemen, who
wish to go easily down the inclined plane of life.   Pleasing but quiet society, plenty of gaiety out of doors for
the eye, and very good cheer in the house for the appetite, and perfect liberty to do what you like without
being questioned.   The people of the world here are
glad to see you if you come to them, and don't care if
you don't.   All this, and an air perfumed with orange-
flowers, makes existence glide away imperceptibly and
easily.

"Why should you not put on your travelling cap,
get into the *malle poste*, run down to Marseilles in three
days, and come by Geneva, Livourne, etc., here in five
more ?   I will receive you with open house and arms, and
we will rail at the world together, talk of the past as
perfection, and the present as deteriorated, after the
fashion of elderly beaux, and then turn to and enjoy
ourselves over a bottle, and our past conquests and
pleasures.   Do this, my dear Tom, I beg of you ; if you
will not, write me a letter of excuse.'

These sketches of character at Rome are amusing.
The man that could write in this gay agreeable style

to another professional *viveur*, must have had many
remarkable gifts to redeem his follies. " I am *tellement
morfondu* in this dullest of holes, that I have not energy
enough left for anything. We should have expired of
ennui had it not been for the presence of the Duc
de Bordeaux (which disunited society as much as the
Guelphs and Ghibelines of old), and now we have lost
him ! The said Prince is fat, fair, but not forty, he
might have passed for the prototype of Pickwick's fat
boy, did he go to sleep ; but he is, on the contrary,
très éveillé, with a laughing eye, agreeable smile, and
singularly good manners. His figure threatens the
Dixhuit, but he walks and rides with dignity, and,
preceded by halberdiers down St. Peter's on Christmas
Day, would not have made Louis the Fourteenth
ashamed of him ! He was here six weeks, and I have
not heard of one foolish thing said or done by him.
Latour Maubourg, with or without orders, tried to stifle
him, and have him ejected. The Pope took his cue
from Austria, and received him in demi-royalty—
details I will spare you, as I understand them not.
Maubourg then quarrels with Russia and Bavaria,
because they had been present at parties given in his
honour. The consequence is, Master Spauer no longer
walks on Pincio with Master Maubourg, though, the
Bavarian *bonne* remarked to the Parisian, they were too
young to talk politics ! "

Another of the men of that day, with an established reputation for wit, excites astonishment, for
little has come down to us of his humour. This
was Mr. Joseph Jekyll, whose pleasantry secured the
friendship and patronage of the Regent, who extorted
for him from Lord Eldon a lucrative place by a most
original expedient—coming betimes, forcing his way

into his bedroom, and refusing to leave till his
request was granted. This was no mere jest. He
belonged to the Theodore Hook and Charles Greville
coterie. A pleasantry of his has often been repeated
concerning old Lady Cork, who, he declared, was like
a shuttlecock, "*all cork and feathers.*" A delightful
letter of his to Lady Blessington gives an agreeable
impression of the man :

"Romsey, September 19, 1833.

" How kind and considerate to launch a letter from
the prettiest *main possible* in the world, and relieve
the monotony of a château by 'quips and cranks' as
interesting as the 'wreathed smiles' I enjoy in Seamore
Place. Yet I have as many *agrémens* here as content
me : a good library, total uncontrol, and daily gratitude
to William Rufus for the drives he left me in the New
Forest. Thanks for the royal talk ; we had at the bar
a learned person, whose legs and arms were so long
as to afford him the title of *Frog Morgan*. In the
course of an argument he spoke of our natural enemies, the French ; and Erskine, in reply, complimented
him on an expression so personally appropriate. We
breathe here an Imperial atmosphere—one Queen sailed
away, and the embryo of another reigns in the Isle of
Wight, who endures royal salutes from a yacht club
every half-hour. The French Admiral, Mackau, squalled
horribly at Cherbourg, when he found himself invaded
by a squadron of *Cowes*. They have swamped the
pretty town of Southampton with a new *pier*, though
they had Lord Ashton, an old Irish *peer*, residing there,
whom they might have repaired for the purpose.
Sydney Smith was asked what penalty the Court of

Aldermen could inflict on Don—Key, for bringing them
into contempt by his late escapade ? He said : 'Melted
butter with his turbot for a twelvemonth, instead of
lobster sauce.' I was asked gravely if Quinine was
invented by Doctor Quin ? In poor Galt's Autobiography, I find a scene at your *soirée* between Grey and
Canning—and I find in Byron's attack on Southey,
great fulmination against your correspondent, Landor.
No matter who deserts London—for with such imaginative powers you are never alone—and I am sure, often
by no means so solitary as you wish—though I suppose
even the Bores have ceased to infest ⸺ House. I left
you among thieves, as the Levite did of old the stranger,
and had no hope that Bow Street would play the
Samaritan. I am a fatal visitor to Dowager Peeresses,
for while I was lunching with Lady Ellenborough, a
rogue descended her area for silver forks. A toady of
old Lady Cork, whom she half maintains, complained to
me of her treatment. 'I have,' she said, ' a very long
chin, and the barbarous Countess often shakes me by
it.' It seemed without remedy, as neither the paroxysm
nor chin could be shortened."

This specimen of letter-writing suggests the lively
Kirkpatrick Sharpe, to whom scarcely sufficient credit
has been given for his wit. He has left some sketches
of London society, in letters to friends, unsurpassed
for their animation and brilliancy. One might lament
that more have not been collected of this clever being,
who left a deep impression on his contemporaries.
When he first came on town he wrote in this vivacious
strain. But all the men about town wrote well, and
seem to have cultivated letter-writing as a fine art.

"London, Wednesday.

" DEAR——,

"Nothing but smothering heat, and parties that melt one into inanity. To go into the streets is to endure the fiery ordeal (which none of us here at present can well abide) ; and to venture into an evening assembly is to tumble into a kettle of boiling sprats. For my part, I have endured every culinary effect of fire mentioned by Hannah Glasse, and all the newer processes of steam besides. I am in the condition of that poor princess in the "Arabian Nights," who fought so fatally with the genius about the transformation of a monkey (my concerns are full as apish). Thank heaven, however, I am not in love! That alone saves me from utter conflagration ; for, indeed, dear——, I cannot 'join the multitude to do evil,' in finding Lady Elizabeth B——, and Miss Rumbold, and twenty more, so very, very charming. But I am firmly resolved not to say one word about the disasters at Carlton House ; though I saw one miserable person brought out upon a board, and many gentlewomen worse attired than Eve in her primitive simplicity. You must have heard all these horrors long ago ; so I shall begin with Lady Mary L. Crawford's ball, most magnanimously given in the Argyll Street rooms to all her friends, or rather her enemies—as even by her own account of the matter, she is at deadly feud with the whole world. I could admire nothing at the entertainment—not even herself. Fancy her attired in draperies of muslin covered with gold spots the size of a sixpence ! When she reclined under that frippery canvas bower at the end of the ballroom, she looked exactly like an ill-favoured picture of Danaë in the shower of gold. To crown the whole,

Skeffington,* with rouge on his cheeks and ultramarine
on his nose, handed her to supper! 'Sure such a pair!'

"I was one of the happy few at H——'s ball, given in
Burlington House, a house I had been long anxious to
see, as it is rendered classical by the pen of Pope and
the pencil of Hogarth. It is in a woeful condition, and,
as I hear, to be pulled down. The company was very
genteel (I can't get a less vulgar word to express the
sort of things) and very dull; but all the ladies were
vastly refreshed with an inscription chalked upon the
floor, which each applied to herself. Within a wreath
of laurel, like burdock, fastened with fifty crooked true-
love knots, were the mysterious words '*Pour elle*.'
Indeed, my dear——, the words written on the wall,
which we read of in the Bible, could not have produced
a greater sensation. First, there was such a flocking
to the centre of the room—such a whispering—such a
'Dear, I should like to see it!'—'Pray, Lady Louisa, let
me see it!'—'Goodness! whom can it mean?'—and then
a triumphant retreat; smiles upon every lip, exultation
in every eye. It was quite amusing afterwards to ask
any lady who the '*elle*' could be—the downcast look of
affected humility, then the little sigh of half-surfeited
vanity, and then the stare of confident triumph, crowned
with 'How should I know?' were delightful. After all,
the true *elle* is said to be Lady E. B——, for whom a
friend of mine is at present very sick, and carving her
name upon every tree he finds in the country. We had
much waltzing and quadrilling, the last of which is certainly very abominable. I am not prude enough to be

---

* "Mr. Skeffington is still alive, the very wreck of a beau; he is
to be seen sometimes like a fly half dead and stupefied, which has
outlived the summer." Thus Lady C. Campbell.

offended with waltzing, in which I can see no other harm
than that it disorders the stomach, and sometimes makes
people look very ridiculous ; but after all, moralists,
with the Duchess of Gordon at their head, who never
had a moral in her life, exclaim dreadfully against it.
Nay, I am told that these magical wheelings have already
roused poor Lord Dartmouth from his grave to suppress
them.   Alas ! after all, people set about it as gravely as
a company of dervishes, and seem to be paying adoration
to Pluto rather than to Cupid.   But the quadrilles I can
by no means endure ; for till ladies and gentlemen have
joints at their ancles, which is impossible, it is worse than
impudent to make such exhibitions, more particularly in
a place where there are public ballets every Tuesday
and Saturday.   When people dance to be looked at,
they surely should dance to perfection.   Even the Duchess
of Bedford, who is the Angiolini of the group, would
make an indifferent figurante at the Opera : and the
principal male dancer, Mr. North, *reminds one of a
gibbeted malefactor, moved to and fro by the winds, but
from no personal exertion.*"

A singular figure that flits about English society in
these days is that of Mr. Ward.   We would know more
of him than we do, and yet the little we know seems
scarcely to warrant the reputation he enjoyed—that of
a wit and clever man, and finally a conspicuous oddity.
He was the son of Lord Dudley, then only a baron.
His son was well off, was in Parliament, was sought
as a lively, witty man, with such a name for dry sarcasm
that he could dress or behave generally much as he
pleased.   An intimate friend of his was Dr. Copleston,
afterwards a bishop, with whom he kept up a diligent
correspondence, spreading over many years.   These
letters, amounting to nearly a hundred, are of a sober,

didactic character, and are amusingly opposed to the notion of a man of wit. But their real interest is in marking the stages of a hypochondriacal temperament, commencing in fits of low spirits without any apparent cause—he was rich and in good health—and passing gradually to the final stage of mania. As these papers were published with the sanction of his friends, there can be no impropriety in dwelling a little on this unfortunate business. "When setting out on a journey," he writes in 1822, "I lingered on for upwards of five weeks. Of the delay, I have had abundant cause to repent. For the last week I laboured under such a fit of anxiety, nervousness, irresolution, and despondency, attended by a derangement of the stomach, as made life quite loathsome to me. I ascribe this misfortune to two causes—to my having allowed some unpleasant circumstances to dwell too constantly upon my thoughts, and to staying in Italy after the hot weather had set in, for experience has at last convinced me that great heat, though agreeable, is highly pernicious to me."

This was the first symptom. He returned to London, and there was plunged into the most gloomy state.

"This attack has been coming on for some time. If I had been better aware of its nature, I might have guarded against its approach; as it is, I am quite under the dominion of very tormenting feelings. It is in vain that my reason tells me that the view I take of any unpleasant circumstances in my situation is exaggerated. Anxiety—regret for the past—apprehensive uneasiness as to my future life, have seized upon me as their prey. I dread solitude, for society I am unfit, and every error of which I have been guilty in life stands constantly before my eyes. I am ashamed

of what I feel when I recollect how much prosperity
I still enjoy: but it seems as if I had been suddenly
transplanted into some horrible region beyond the
bounds of reason or of comfort.   Now and then I
enjoy a few hours' respite, but this is my general
condition.   It is a dismal contrast, for you well remember that I was naturally gay and cheerful.   Pray
let me see you after Dr. Maton's, not so much out
of kindness to a friend as out of compassion to an
unhappy fellow-creature.   My situation is truly horrible.
I know not what is to become of me.   My feeble body
cannot long resist the violent agitation of my mind.
Sleep has in a great measure forsaken me.   It was
that alone which hitherto sustained me and enabled
me to go through the day.   I am weary without being
able to repose."   His friends asked him to visit them,
and he would promise to go ; but as the day fixed drew
near, it hung before him like a pall, and he would
at last forego his intention, through something like
horror.

"Saturday was a very bad day.   I dined out,
unluckily for me, since I was so nervous and distressed
that upon my arrival at the house of my host I was
hardly able to walk into the room.   To-day I am more
composed.   W. R., a fellow-sufferer, is coming to dine
with me, and his gloom, which hangs upon him almost
as heavily as it does upon me, does not prevent him
being a very agreeable companion.   This has been one
of my very worst days."

"After spending a few days with me at Oxford,"
says Dr. Coplestone, "during which there were many
variations, occasional gleams of hope succeeded by gloom
and nervous agitation, then calmness, and then a return
of horrible paroxysms, he resolved to go either to Buxton

or to London, but was long undetermined which. He left my house with post-horses for the London Road, promising to write after his journey's end. The next letter, however, was dated from Buxton." After many of these miserable alternatives, Mr. Canning in September, 1822, proposed to him to become under-secretary. This offer threw him into a fresh state of misery. He could not make up his mind. He besieged everyone for advice. "The last word is not yet said, and perhaps it may not be in time for the post. In any case I should be an object of compassion—to you I may speak thus undisguisedly—for a long time to come. I see no escape. Do what I may my character must be lowered and my feelings wounded." He declined it in the end, but not to find peace. Lady C. Campbell affected to have known the reason of this singular depression. "No one," she said, "either for his own sake, or alas! more probably, for his brilliant position in life —was ever more courted by the fair sex, in despite of a very plain exterior and coarseness of manner. He was accounted one of the most agreable and seductive of men. The beautiful Mrs. B—— was one of those reported to have been not insensible to his attentions. Her melancholy death was, it is said, the actual cause of finally confirming his mental derangement; and when he gave a ball at the desire of another lady, who enjoyed his favour, he sat apart in a room by himself, and on her remonstrating with him for so doing, he said: 'Ah, she for whom I should have liked to have given it, is cold in her grave.' It is curious that most of those persons associated with Lord Ward had a melancholy fate. The Princess, at whose board he was so often the merriest and most amusing of her guests, was a victim to her own folly, and the persecution of an unjust husband.

Mrs. B——, the woman for whom his attachment was the most sincere and lasting, died of an agonising malady; and the last beauty at whose shrine he bent the knee, was taken away in the midst of her youth and the height of her worldly renown and prosperity." But it is in his more amusing eccentricities that he is most familiar to the public, and it seems most extraordinary that a man of such oddity should have been entrusted with high offices of State. It was noted that he had two voices, one "a squeak," the other a deep, and a pleasant man said it was like Lord Dudley talking with Ward. Nothing was more strange than to listen to him debating aloud as if with himself whether he should accept some proposal made, as when one said he would turn back and walk a little way with him, and he was heard to mutter: "I think I can endure him for ten minutes." "Lord Dudley," says Mr. Moore, "it is well known, has a trick of rehearsing over to himself, in an undertone, the good things he is about to *débiter* to the company, so that the person who sits next to him has generally the advantage of his wit before any of the rest of the party. The other day, having a number of the foreign ministers and their wives to dine with him, he was debating with himself whether he ought not to follow the Continental fashion of leaving the room with the ladies after dinner. Having settled the matter, he muttered forth, in his usual soliloquising tone: 'I think we must go out altogether.' 'Good God! you don't say so!' exclaimed Lady ——, who was sitting next him, and who is well known to be the most anxious and sensitive of the Lady Whigs, with respect to the continuance of the present Ministry in power. 'Going out altogether' might well alarm her. A man not very remarkable for agreeableness once proposed to walk from the House of Commons to the Travellers' Rest with Lord Dudley, who, discussing the proposal mentally (as he thought) with himself, said audibly : 'I don't think it will bore me very much to let him walk with me that distance.' On another occasion, when he gave somebody a seat in his carriage from some country-house, he was overheard by his companion, after a fit of thought and silence, saying to himself : 'Now, shall I ask this man to dine with me when we arrive in town ?' It is said that the fellow-traveller, not pretending to hear him, muttered out in the same sort of tone : 'Now, if Lord Dudley should ask me to dinner, shall I accept his invitation ?'"

Another more ludicrous instance of his official behaviour was this : On some misunderstanding taking place between the Russian and the French Governments —the object of the English ministry being to mediate between these two Powers—Lord Dudley had to forward private despatches to both Governments of great importance, it being essential that neither should know what was going on in the case of the other. The absent-minded Foreign Secretary put each into the wrong envelope and despatched them. It may be conceived what confusion and alarm was caused, and hurried explanations were despatched accounting for the mistake. But the French Ambassador merely replied, with a knowing air, that he was too *fin* to be taken in by Lord Dudley's ingenious device.

A happy specimen of his wit was his retort to a German lady at Vienna, who had somewhat rudely complained of the bad French spoken by " you English," in London. " True, madame," he said, " we have not enjoyed the advantage of having had the French twice in our capital."

This recalls a retort about as good made by an English lady to the Duc de Broglie, when Ambassador in England, who said, with equally lax manners, that he now found they were right in thinking the English a nation of shopkeepers. "Perhaps so," was her reply; "just as we always thought you were a nation of soldiers."

When Mr. Ward became Lord Dudley and Foreign Secretary in 1827, the strain of office only developed his oddities. He enjoyed these honours but for a short time. Lord Palmerston describes a curious scene, Lord Goderich's ministry being in the agonies of dissolution, when he and Lord Dudley and Huskisson walked home together and debated whether they should "hold on."

After his retirement his curious mania, and various oddities increased to an extravagant degree, and were the talk of the town, which, however, soon came to accept them as it does all kinds of oddity. He would go to dinner parties and sit without uttering a word excepting to himself. During some brief "flashes of silence," Mr. Raikes tells of a friend of his whom he describes as good-natured and a very good-looking man, not overflowing with intellect. "It was at a time when poor Dudley's mind was on the wane, when his caustic humour would still find vent through the cloud which was gradually overshadowing his masterly intellect. He was sitting in his room, unheeding those around him, and soliloquising aloud, as was so often his custom. His favourite Newfoundland dog was at his side, who seemed to engross the whole of his attention. At length, patting his head, he exclaimed: 'Fido mio, they say dogs have no souls. Humph! And still they say —— has a soul!'" Upon one occasion Dudley

found Allen at White's about seven o'clock, and asked
him to dinner. On his arrival in Park Lane, he found
it was a *tête-à-tête* with the host. When in the evening
he was asked how the dinner went off, Allen said:
"Lord Dudley spoke a little to his servant, and a great
deal to his dog, but said nothing."

In this state, too, he would invite large companies
to dinner, who, stranger still, would accept his invitations; though when they came he would not address
them. Mr. Moore, who loved cheerfulness and gaiety,
complained mournfully of these festivities as damping
and depressing. For the host would sit the whole time
in a sort of stupor, or converse with himself, or have a
volume of Hume open before him which he would read
through his dinner. This was the beginning of the end.
A short time afterwards, in 1832, it was known that
Sir Henry Halford had directed that he should be put
under restraint, and on the 6th of March, 1833, this
brilliant but eccentric man expired. He was only fifty-
two. A relation of his, the Rev. Mr. Ward, succeeded
to the title with four thousand pounds a year only, while
eighty thousand pounds a year passed to his son.*

One saying of his is quoted and is highly characteristic. He declared "that the quality of *the melted
butter* was almost significant of the moral character of
one's host." Let this be his epitaph.

The pleasant epigram is well known:

> Ward has no heart, they say;
> But I deny it.
> He has a heart, and gets his
> Speeches by it.

---

* There is a letter of his to Sir E. Codrington on the eve of
Navarino, written in his official capacity, and which is refreshingly
opposed to all stiff traditions.

This was supposed to be by Byron, but really was manufactured by Rogers, with some little assistance from Richard Sharp. Byron also contributed an "epigram" in reference to Ward's being "re-whigged." Before he could be "re-whigged" he said he must be "rewarded." Someone asked Mr. Rogers had he seen our Ward's last review? "*Our* Ward?" he growled; "you may keep him all to yourself."

It is curious to think that little over forty years ago there was flourishing an animated old lady, giving "Sunday parties" in New Burlington Street, who could tell stories about Dr. Johnson, whom she had met in society some sixty years before. This remarkable woman retained her ardour for company and the enjoyments of life to the last, and competed with Lady Morgan and Lydia White for her share of such "lions" as might be roaring or stalking about town.

Mr. Luttrell, the wit, likened her to a shuttlecock, because she was all "cork and feathers," an indifferent conceit; while others speculated on her vast age in somewhat unfeeling fashion. The late Mr. Croker, who had a morbid penchant for convicting women of suppression on this point—in them a not unpardonable failing—made some investigations into the question of her age, *à propos* of a dinner to which she had invited him. In 1835 he wrote: "The Hon. Mary Monckton, born April, 1746. Lodge's Peerage dates her birth 1737; but this is a mistake, for an elder sister of the same name, now in her eighty-ninth year, Lady Cork, still entertains and enjoys society with extraordinary health, spirits, and vivacity." In July, 1836, he puts down that "she wrote to me the following lively note: 'I would rather be a hundred, because you and many other agreeable people would come to me as a wonder.

The fact is, I am only verging on ninety. I wish the business of the nation may not prevent your giving me the pleasure of your company at dinner on Wednesday the 3rd, at a quarter before eight. It is in vain, I suppose, to expect you at my tea-drinking on Friday, the 5th, or in the evening of the 3rd, in the event of your not being able to dine with me on that day.'" This pleasantly turned invitation—so amazing for its freshness and even grace—suggests to the critic that there is only "one mark of anility" in the whole, viz., that she did not remember he was out of Parliament and out of office at the time ; a fact not of so much importance after all, and which younger folk might not have kept in mind. "I found," he says, "by the Register of St. James's parish, that she had understated her age by one year."

Of her proceedings in the pursuit of lions, and her art in collecting and making them perform, some very diverting stories are told. She took a great fancy to Mr. Thomas Moore, then in the zenith of popularity ; and one evening took it into her head to gratify her guests with some passages of dramatic reading. "Mr. Moore was the medium selected for this 'flow of soul,' upon which it seemed the lady had set her heart, but against which it proved he had set his face : he was exceedingly sorry — was particularly engaged — had besides a very bad cold—a terribly obstinate hoarseness ; and declared all this with an exceedingly 'good-evening' expression of countenance. Her ladyship was puzzled how to act, until 'Monk' Lewis came to her relief ; and in a short time she made her appearance with a large Burgundy pitch-plaister, with which she followed the wandering melodist about the room, who in his endeavours to evade his well-meaning pursuer and her formidable recipe, was at length fairly hemmed into a corner."

More droll, however, was the following incident, contrived by the same agreeable farceur. The vivacious countess determined to have a charitable lottery, combined with some shape of entertainment, and consulted her friend on it. "Under his direction the whole affair was managed. As it was arranged that everybody was to win something, Lewis took care that the prizes should be of a nature that would create the most ludicrous perplexity to their owners. Gentlemen were seen in every direction, running about with teapots in their hands, or trays under their arms, endeavouring to find some sly corner in which to deposit their prizes; while young ladies were sinking beneath the weight, or the shame, of carrying a coal-scuttle or a flat-iron. Guinea-pigs, birds in cages, punch-bowls, watchmen's rattles, and Dutch ovens, were perplexing their fortunate, or, as perhaps they considered themselves, unfortunate proprietors; and Lady Cork's raffle was long remembered by those who were present as a scene of laughter and confusion." Long after, when Mrs. Gore, the novelist, then in the height of her popularity, brought out "The Dowager," the character was instantly recognised as a portrait of Lady Cork, whose death had just taken place. Mrs. Gore thus wrote to her friend Lady Morgan: "You are very kind to like my new book. Till you praised it, I was in despair. It sells, and I was convinced of its utter worthlessness; for surely nothing can equal the degradation of the public taste in such matters! The subject and title were of Bentley's choosing; and my part distinctly was to avoid hooking 'M.C.O.' into the book. In certain mannerisms The Dowager may resemble her; but not in essentials.

She was better or worse." What an amiable disclaimer!
Lady Morgan's comment in a diary on the poor old
lady's death, which took place in 1840, is that she died
" full of bitterness and good dinners." The truth was
there could be little respect for the exhibition of this
craze for society at such an advanced age. It was
curious that there should have been three old ladies with
the same mania—Lady Cork, Lady Morgan, and Lydia
White. One of the most graceful of Sir Joshua's portraits
represents the former in a dreamy, pastoral attitude,
seated in a garden half stooping forward, her arm
reclining on a pedestal beside her, a dog at her feet. A
few days before her death, Mr. Redding met her at
dinner, when he noticed that she was well able to ascend
from the dining-room like other ladies, leaning on a
friend's arm. " She invited to her house men of all
creeds and parties, because their opinions had nothing
to do in sharing her hospitalities. The peculiar circumstances attending her marriage were well known, at least
in contemporary life. It would be unfair to judge her
by the last score or two of years that she lived. My
impression is that she had at no time superior mental
attainments to other ladies in the circles of fashion,
where youth and vivacity never fail to be attractive.
She had some eccentricities, and I am inclined to think
she was not of an amiable disposition, because she did
not disguise her distaste of children, and this is a
good criterion for judging of female character. To
more advanced youth she was a torment in employing
it for her various purposes. There were two sweet girls
in their 'teens,' whose visits to town were few and far
between, and had, therefore, little time for sight-seeing.
She would drive to them in their lodgings of a fore-
noon, with a list of names, and occupy them with

writing her notes of invitation until dinner time, knowing perfectly well how they were situated. I advised
that they should not be 'at home,' for the exaction was
unjustifiable. Sydney Smith admirably developed her
character under another head, when he made a species
of allegory of her conduct, illustrative of that of the
bishops towards the deans and chapters. His friend,
Lady Cork, told him she was so deeply moved at his
charity sermon, that she 'borrowed' a sovereign of
someone going out of church and put it into the plate.
All the world knew her propensity for carrying off anything upon which she chanced to lay her hands. 'Don't
leave those things about so, my dear, or I shall steal
them,' was, perhaps, said for her. She called one
morning on Rogers the poet, and found he had gone
out, when she carried off most of the best flowers upon
which he was choice. The poet of the epigrammatic
month could not forgive her for a good while, and the
distance lasted nearly a whole year, when she wrote
to him, that they were both very old, that he ought to
forget and forgive, and closed her note with an invitation to dinner the next day. Rogers wrote her that
he 'would come, dine, sup, and breakfast with her,' and
thus their quarrel, which at their age Lady Cork called
ridiculous, was made up."

A very vivacious letter of hers was written to Lady
Morgan from Tunbridge :

"It is actually nine months since I received a letter
from dear Lady Morgan. 1 immediately conceived a
letter of thanks, but never had it in my power to bring
it to light. Lucina is not at hand, nor any other friendly
assistant. The bantling with bright thoughts is quite
decayed, and I remain your stupid old eighty-six, without a second idea. I should not venture to intrude

upon you to-day, but that I really am anxious to be
regaled with one of your pretty greetings. Tommy
Moore told me my macaw had spoke both witty and
clever. Bulwer, &c., &c., said the same, and that they
would send it to me. I have never seen it. When can
I hear of it? Answer this, and tell me, when you come
to England. I don't wish it till April, when I promise
you constant, pleasant *réunions*. I am more *chez moi*,
and go out less than ever. I collect pleasant people,
and like this last act of the play as well as any part of
my life. I am in good health, and have many kind
friends, among whom I trust you'll allow me to set you
down in the first class.

"For I am, very truly,

"Your faithful and obliged servant,

"M. C. O.

"A true Whig."

Let us now look back sixty years to the "Blue
Stocking" days, when Boswell sets before us a picture
of himself and this lady with some of his happiest
touches.

"Johnson was prevailed with to come sometimes
into these circles, and did not think himself too grave
even for the lively Miss Monckton (now Countess of Cork),
who used to have the finest bit of blue at the house of
her mother, Lady Galway. Her vivacity enchanted the
sage, and they used to talk together with all imaginable
ease. A singular instance happened one evening, when
she insisted that some of Sterne's writings were very
pathetic. Johnson bluntly denied it. 'I am sure,' said
she, 'they have affected me.' 'Why,' said Johnson,
smiling and rolling himself about, 'that is because,
dearest, you're a dunce.' When she, some time after-

wards, mentioned this to him, he said, with equal truth and politeness: 'Madam, if I had thought so, I certainly should not have said it.'

"Another evening Johnson's kind indulgence towards me had a pretty difficult trial. I had dined at the Duke of Montrose's with a very agreeable party; and his Grace, according to his usual custom, had circulated the bottle very freely. Lord Graham and I went together to Miss Monckton's, where I certainly was in extraordinary spirits, and above all fear or awe. In the midst of a great number of persons of the first rank, amongst whom I recollect, with confusion, a noble lady of the most stately decorum, I placed myself next to Johnson, and, thinking myself now fully his match, talked to him in a loud and boisterous manner, desirous to let the company know how I could contend with Ajax. I particularly remember pressing him upon the value of the pleasures of the imagination, and, as an illustration of my argument asking him: 'What, sir, supposing I were to fancy that the —— (naming the most charming duchess in His Majesty's dominion) were in love with me, should I not be very happy?' My friend, with much address, evaded my interrogatories, and kept me as quiet as possible; but it may easily be conceived how he must have felt. However, when a few days afterwards I waited upon him and made an apology, he behaved with the most friendly gentleness."

At this extreme old age she was full of vivacity and ardour, and learnt lines to the last. A pleasant, farcical, and quite characteristic scene, is thus described by one of her "friends": "She gave a dinner to twenty special guests the other day. Her last intrigue '*aux choux et aux raves*' was driving a hard bargain with the Tyrolese to sing at her party. She picked them up in the Regent's

Park, and brought them down to thirty shillings, which she was heard wishing to beat down to eight, when she stood with them where she thought there was no one to listen; but they held out for the thirty shillings. At the Duke of St. Alban's, where there were all the opera people, she said: 'Duke, now couldn't you send me the pack for my evening?' 'Certainly,' said he, and they were sent, with a grand pianoforte. When they came to her, Lady Cork got frightened, and said: 'Je suis une pauvre veuve, je ne saurais payer de tels talens, mais vous verrez la meilleure société, la Duchesse de St. Albans, etc., etc." The Primo Amoroso bowed, and acknowledged the honour; but intimated that the Duchess always paid them. Lady Cork went to the Duke and accused him of taking a word at random, *tout de bon*.

" The Duchess, overhearing, came forward in a rage, and scolded the little Duke like a naughty schoolboy. The angry Duchess took all upon herself. Lady Cork was very angry."

Another extraordinary old lady of fashion was Lady Salisbury, who perished by a sad and peculiar accident. A conflagration broke out at Hatfield House, which narrowly escaped being burned to the ground; but it was found impossible to rescue the Dowager Marchioness, who, wishing to write her letters before going to bed, had lit three candles, and by some accident had set herself on fire. " She was one of the beauties of her day, and famed for her equestrian exploits. Till a late period in life she constantly hunted with the Hatfield hounds, in a sky-blue habit with black velvet collar, and a jockey cap, the uniform of the hunt; riding as hard and clearing the fences with as much ardour as any sportsman in the field."

" Her Sunday parties and suppers in Arlington Street continued for near half a century to attract all the most distinguished society in London, with this peculiarity, that no cards of invitation were sent out. It was always 'come to me on Sunday,' to those whom she met in the preceding week, and all the young aspirants were anxious to attract her notice for the summons."

Connecting her with the ancient borough of that name, Lady Salisbury latterly went by the *sobriquet* of Old Sarum, with this exception, that she to the last bid defiance to reform.

"She was the last remnant of what may be called the old school in England, and of that particular *clique* composed of the Duchess of Devonshire, Duchess of Rutland, Ladies Sefton, Cowper, Melbourne, etc., etc., who for many years gave the *ton* to society in London. She was an amiable, good-natured person, with the high-bred manners of a *grande dame*, remarkable for her fine figure, but very short-sighted, which perhaps might have occasioned this dreadful catastrophe. Lady Salisbury scrupulously adhered to the state of former days; she always went to Court in a sedan-chair with splendid liveries, she drove out in a low pheaton with four black ponies in the park, and at night her carriage was known by the flambeaux of the footmen. But the last sad pageant is denied her; not a vestige of her body has been found to claim the rights of a funeral, at least according to the latest accounts."

Another extraordinary being was Lydia White, who also to an advanced age received company, though lying gasping on a sofa, all swelled, and a terrible spectacle. She was the "Tory virgin," as one of her guests describes her. The records of fashion are stored with such painful examples.

"I remember a story of the Duchess of Richmond," says Mr. Raikes, "long ago which, at the time, was often repeated. She went one Sunday with her daughter to the Chapel Royal at St. James's, but being late they could find no places. After looking about some time, and seeing the case was hopeless, she said to her daughter : 'Come away, Louisa ; at any rate we have done the *civil* thing.' This was completely the idea of the *card-leaving* dowager of her day."

A figure was now (1820) met with in society—aged and eccentric, which offered the most singular and melancholy instance of reversal of character and talents. This was Lord Erskine, the great and intrepid advocate, the brilliant orator and accomplished man, the friend of the Regent, now strangely metamorphosed into something that suggests his odd countryman, Lord Monboddo. He had long been out of favour at Court—an old-fashioned survival, laughed at, and scarcely respected. Mr. Rush met him at some fête.

"This distinguished peer," he says, "indulges in eccentricities in conversation. 'England,' said he, 'is a blackguard country.' 'A great country,' I rejoined. 'Yes,' said he, 'a great blackguard country : a boxing, fighting country, and don't you call that blackguard ?' I said that he jumped to his conclusions faster than I could follow. 'Ay,' said he, 'you are accredited to the King ; but, for all that, the King has been constantly fighting with Providence ; Providence gave him high endowments, with a fine person, and had been trying to make him the head of a great and glorious people ; but the King had been for ever battling it with him, and at the end of about the thirteenth round, with the advantage of good bottle-holders, he had now fairly beaten Providence off the ground.'"

CHAPTER XII.

THE "Reviewer" at this time was a typical personage in society, and foremost of these was Mr. Croker, a remarkable man in his way, who deserves some notice here. He came to London as an "Irish adventurer," in the more becoming sense of the term. Born in 1780, and brought up in Ireland, he first showed his abilities by an amusing little volume in verse, the well-known "Familiar Epistles on the Irish Stage," written in imitation of the "Rosciad," in which the Dublin actors were vivaciously sketched, praised, and satirised. He had previously, however, tried his pen in London, but soon found that politics were the true road to fortune. He succeeded in getting into Parliament in 1807, where his vigorous style and readiness for fray soon attracted attention. His long quarrel with Macaulay, not to the credit of the great essayist, lasted from 1831 for more than twenty years. But it is in his connection with the "Quarterly Review," from its foundation in 1809 for over forty years, that his career is interesting. His devotion to the journal was extraordinary; and it is evident from the perusal of his always recognisable articles that his heart was in the business. The extraordinary number of these

papers, the ardent eager style in which they were
written, show that he was prompted by each subject
to a deliverance, just as a popular speaker in the House
of Commons is prompted to a sudden reply. But the
angry, hostile, and too often malicious tone of these
papers shows that his passion, rather than a calm
judicial temper, was what imparted to them this spirit.
It is impossible at the same time not to admire the
amount of general knowledge displayed in the particular instance : and the vigorous fashion in which
he exposed follies and contradictions ; but, at the same
time, there was often much unfairness shown in strain-
ing the sense to make a point. Thus, in a fierce attack
upon Sir N. Wraxall's book we find this extraordinary perversion. He represented the writer as having described
King Joseph of Portugal as "*a drunken old Moor.*"
In vain the Baronet pleaded that his words were, "in
his cheeks he had a high scorbutic humour, attributed
commonly to excesses of wine, though it might partly
arise from violent exercise, constantly taken under a
rising sun. His face, indeed, was nearly as dusky as
that of a Moor." The "Reviewer" returned to the
charge, declaring that he had said the King had "a face
carbuncled by hard drinking."

The person he hunted down and exposed with the
most effective logic and rancour was "Bonaparte,"
together with the Wardens, O'Mearas and other apo-
logists. It is amusing to read the violence of his language to the ogre, who is dealt with as a sort of bravo.
At one point, on alluding to an escape from assassina-
tion—he says *tout bonnement*, that it was a pity the
attempt had not been successful. His advocates were
branded as liars and knaves, and certainly more amusing
reading could not be found than his gibbeting of Ber-

trand, Montholon, and others, who are shown up as a gang of unscrupulous adventurers, which, perhaps, they were.

But in the case of a few persons—notably ladies—the reviewer shows his fury in a way that seems extraordinary. His morbid views as to ladies' ages, and the vast trouble he went to, searching registers for evidence to convict them of untruth, caused much amusement at the time. His ungenerous attacks on Lady Morgan are, perhaps, unexampled as a display of critical rancour. When the lady published her "France," in the two great quartos then fashionable, he fell on her like some wild animal in the Zoological Gardens on a piece of raw meat at feeding time. "One merit, however," he begins, "the title has—it is appropriate to the volume which it introduces, for to falsehood it adds the other qualities of the work—vagueness, bombast, and affectation." On her making an allusion in the introduction to her recent marriage, which, in truth, has made her happy, Mr. Croker says, "she does well to speak thus modestly of the former part of her position—of the latter, she may be as positive as she pleases. Happiness is a relative term, or, as it is more correctly explained by Slender to his cousin Shallow, *thereafter as it may be.*"

After some further preliminaries, calling her "the elegant Lady Morgan, a mere bookseller's drudge," he goes seriously to work :

"Our charges (to omit minor faults) fall readily under the heads of Bad Taste—Bombast and Nonsense—Blunders—Ignorance of the French Language and Manners—General Ignorance—Jacobinism—Falsehood—Licentiousness, and Impiety. We undertake, as we have said, to prove them from Lady Morgan's own mouth. BAD TASTE.—The work is composed in the most confused manner, and written in the worst style—if it be

not an abuse of language to call that a *style* which is
merely a jargon. There is neither order in the subjects
nor connection between the parts. It is a huge aggre-
gation of disjointed sentences, so jumbled together, that
we seriously assert that no injury will be done to the
volume by beginning with the last chapter and reading
backwards to the first, and yet it has all the affectation
of order : it is divided into *parts.*

" *We*, indeed, have been obliged to labour through
these tomes, because our duty imposes that task upon
us ; but we have not heard of any voluntary reader who
has been able to contend against the narcotic influence
of *her prating, prosing, and plagiarism,* and get through
even the first volume." What must have been the gall
and blackness of the man's heart that could pen such
abuse ? And what could have been the cause of such
hostility ? In her Memoirs it is stated that he was a
sort of devoted admirer of the lady's, when he was in
Dublin, and a rather obsequious letter of his is given.
Yet, in his article, he declares that he did not know her !

That this animosity was a sort of mania, or perhaps
the subject so quickened and stimulated his peculiar
style of writing, that he could not resist giving the
unfortunate authoress " a smashing blow," *passim,* as
it were, in other articles on other subjects. And the
persons who alluded to her with anything like favour
were certain to receive about the same treatment.

Another lady cruelly mauled by him was Miss
Burney, whose last work offered but too tempting
openings. Another was Lady Charlotte Bury, whose
vivacious "Diary of the Times of George IV.," full of
piquant incidents, traits of manners, and "characteristical"
letters, was dismissed as " a catchpenny," untruthful and
worthless. Now, it is extraordinary to what an extent

the innumerable books of memoirs since published support all that is set out in it, though it was so impugned at the time. The same rehabilitation is being gradually extended to Sir N. Wraxall's curious volumes, so lately reprinted with new notes by an enterprising publisher. Moore's "Diary" was similarly assailed, blows being also aimed at Lord Russell, the editor, and when the latter retorted, it is characteristic to find the veteran reviewer grown suddenly indignant at the attack and addressing bitter remonstrances. All these lucubrations were set out and emphasised by a series of arts now fallen out of use, and unknown to the present race of reviewers; a copious use of italics, in combination with capitals of various degrees and sizes, which lent a curious "bill poster" air, and certainly doubled the effect of his points. The last expiring effort of the veteran was his counter-thrust to Macaulay—a review of his history in return for the review of Croker's "Boswell," and which was held to have been a weak effort.

Croker was, however, a conspicuous figure in other directions; a well-known secretary to the Admiralty, the friend of King George IV., who used to call him "Croko," and who favoured him with many confidences, among others assuring him that "there was not a particle of truth in that story of his marriage to Mrs. Fitzherbert." His great work, the editing of Boswell, is truly a monument, and will always be in demand. He could be witty at times, as a little epigram of his on Dr. Coplestone's editing "Lord Dudley's remains :"

> Than the first martyr's, Dudley's fate
>   Still harder must be owned;
> Stephen was only stoned to death,
>   Ward has been Coplestoned.

His widow not long since died in Hampton Court Palace.

Anyone that has followed Croker's course, and read his reviews, letters, etc., must own that the elaborate sketch, in "Coningsby," of Mr. Rigby, besides being a masterly figure in itself, is copied with great fidelity, and delineated with much *finesse.* For nothing is so difficult to describe as the more delicate points of character.

"What was," asks Mr. Disraeli, "this man, confided in by everybody, trusted by none ? His counsels were not deep, his expedients were not felicitous; he had no feeling, and he could create no sympathy. It is that, in most of the transactions of life, there is some portion which no one cares to accomplish, and which everybody wishes to be achieved. This was always the portion of Mr. Rigby. In the eye of the world he had constantly the appearance of being mixed up with high dealings, and negotiations and arrangements of fine management, whereas in truth, notwithstanding his splendid livery and the airs he gave himself in the servants' hall, his real business in life had ever been, to do the dirty work.

" Mr. Rigby had been shut up much at his villa of late. He was concocting, you could not term it composing, an article, a ' very slashing article,' which was to prove that the penny postage must be the destruction of the aristocracy. It was a grand subject, treated in his highest style. It was full of passages in italics, little words in great capitals, and almost drew tears. The statistical details also were highly interesting and novel. There never was a fellow for giving a good hearty kick to the people like Rigby. Himself sprung from the dregs of the populace, this was disinterested. What could be more patriotic and magnanimous than his Jeremiads over the fall of the Montmorencis and the

Crillons, or the possible catastrophe of the Percys and the Manners'! The truth of all this hullaballoo was that Rigby had a sly pension."

Ungracious as was this political character, it must be said that, in his quarrel with Macaulay, which arose out of the Reform Bill debate, the latter has always seemed to have behaved with a pettiness and spite unworthy of himself.

One of the happiest stories of this reviewer is his little discussion at a dinner with the Duke of Wellington, in which he flatly contradicted the Duke on some point connected with the Battle of Waterloo. The conversation turning on percussion caps, this contradictory person again took the opposite view, when the Duke good-humouredly said to him: "My dear Croker, I can yield to your superior information on most points, and you may perhaps know a great deal more of what passed at Waterloo than myself, but as a sportsman, I will maintain my point about the percussion caps." A friend once said to Lord Wellesley at the castle: "I have had a very melancholy letter from Croker this morning." "Ay!" said Lord Wellesley, "written, I suppose, in a strain of the most sanguine despondency."

Mr. Croker's retiring from politics was a disinterested act, as he was always sure of a seat. But he was ever gloomy, and, on the loss of his son, withdrew from politics.*

---

* A much more fortunate reviewer was the well-known Gifford. During the time that he was editor of *The Quarterly Review*, Mr. Murray paid him £900 a year. He received annually, as one of the comptrollers of the Lottery Office, £600; he had a salary of £300 as paymaster of the band of Gentlemen Pensioners; £200 a year as clerk of the Estreats in the Court of Exchequer; and, in addition to all these sums, he enjoyed a pension of, we believe, £400 per annum from Lord Grosvenor.

Mr. Rush went on a visit to one of the most interesting survivals of this time, Mr. Coke, or "Coke of Norfolk,"* as he was invariably called. His long life, his political course, his intimacy with Fox and other Whig leaders, his patriotism and principle, and his pleasant eccentricity together with his vast intellect, employed in the best fashion for the good of his country, all combined to make him a most interesting figure. The minister was greatly struck with the vast scale on which an English squire of this kind lived. He was in the habit of inviting large companies of his friends to Holkham, his well-known country place, for festivities of sheep-shearing, etc., which were celebrated on a magnificent style. The gala lasted for three days, and

---

* Coke, of Norfolk, was twice married, marrying for the second time when he was seventy; after which he had a numerous family. One of his children was, indeed, born when he was seventy-six. He died in 1842, at the age of ninety, and could have carried back his memory of events to very remote times, owing to his being connected with so many persons remarkable for their talents and position. These elements are necessary to form the links with the past, which are always so interesting, when we reach back some extraordinary distance by the aid of two or three persons—" stepping-stones" they have been termed. The veteran, Mr. S. C. Hall, was the friend of a man whose father fought at the Battle of the Boyne. He knew a Sir Francis Macnaghten, who was born in 1765, when this father was eighty-four years old. At this moment Lady Rolle lives and flourishes, and it is curious to think that her husband, Lord Rolle, entered the House of Commons at the same time as Mr. Pitt—close on a hundred years ago. Another of these "stepping-stones" is not less curious. Lord Brougham's grandfather was born in Queen Anne's reign, and had conversed with a person who was alive one hundred and eighty years ago, and who might have heard a relative, who lived to one hundred and six years, speak of Queen Elizabeth. Mr. Planché, one of the most kindly veterans of his age, used often to tell pleasantly, to the astonishment of his audience, how he recollected the illuminations at the Peace of 1802; but it turned out he was held up as a child in his nurse's arms.

he entertained about fifty guests in his house; but at dinner some six hundred guests sat down. His house was filled with pictures, and statues, and a fine library; and all was supported on an income of £60,000 a year. The annual consumption of beer in the establishment, as his steward told Mr. Rush, amounted to the value of £3,000.

In such an age of pleasure and self-indulgence, dining became a sort of fine art, and the time and money devoted to the indulgence of the palate was extraordinary. Mr. Hayward, in a well-known essay, has collected many particulars on this subject, which he treats with a seriousness worthy of it.* He mentions

* In his pleasant way he tells us how the " gin punch" of the " Garrick " was composed :

"Pour half-a-pint of gin on the outer peel of a lemon, then a little lemon-juice, sugar, a glass of maraschino, about a pint-and-a-quarter of water, and two bottles of iced soda-water. The result will be three pints of the punch in question. The gin punch made at the Garrick Club is one of the best things we know, and we gladly take this opportunity of assigning the honour of the invention to the rightful patentee, Mr. Stephen Price, an American gentleman, well known in the theatrical circles and on the turf. His title has been much disputed ; but Mr. Thomas Hill, the celebrated 'tercentenarian' of a popular song, who was present at Mr. Hook's first introduction to the beverage, has set the matter at rest by a brief narration of the circumstances. One hot afternoon, in July last, the inimitable author of 'Sayings and Doings' (what a book might be made of his own!) strolled into the Garrick in that equivocal state of thirstiness which it requires something more than common to quench. On describing the sensation, he was recommended to make trial of the punch, and a jug was compounded immediately under the personal inspection of Mr. Price. A second followed—a third, with the accompaniment of some chops—a fourth—a fifth—a sixth—at the expiration of which Mr. Hook went away to keep a dinner engagement at Lord Canterbury's. He always eats little, on this occasion he ate less, and Mr. Horace Twiss inquired, in a fitting tone of anxiety, if he were ill. 'Not exactly,' was the reply; 'but my stomach won't bear trifling with, and I was tempted to take a biscuit and a glass of sherry about three.'"

how this and that duke imported or reared rare birds, for their own special eating; what famous dinners* were given at the " Clarendon "—now long swept away.

" It may not be deemed beside the purpose to state that Prince Talleyrand is extremely fond of the birds —ruffs and reeves—his regular allowance during the season being two a day. They are dressed like woodcocks. Dunstable larks should properly be eaten in Dunstable; but Lord Sefton has imported them in tin boxes (in a state requiring merely to be warmed before the fire), with considerable success. Larks are best in January. The largest pheasant ever known of late years was sent, a short time since (by Fisher), to Lord William Bentinck, at Paris. It weighed four pounds wanting an ounce. A cock of the woods, weighing very nearly ten pounds, was sent, a few weeks since, to Lord Balcarras, by Fisher, of Duke Street, St. James's, confessedly the best poulterer in London. *He enjoys the unlimited confidence of Lord Sefton, which is one of the highest compliments that can be paid to any man directly or indirectly connected with gastronomy.*"

Much of this ardour for "good eating" was no doubt owing to the scarcity of good French cookery, the plain "boiled and roast" of old English fare being the general entertainment. Now, good cookery is

---

* Lord Campbell put by the *menu* of a dinner given by him in 1820—a solid meal enough:

First Course.—Cod's Head and Shoulders, Potatoes, Boiled Rice, Mulligatawny Soup. *Second Course.*—Vegetables, Boiled Turkey and Celery Sauce, Pigs' Feet and Ears, Tongue, Fricandeau, Saddle of Mutton, four roast Woodcocks, Wildfowl, and four Sweets. Burgundy, Champagne, White and Rosy Hermitage, Red and White Contabille, Port, Madeira, Sauterne.

The time was half-past six o'clock; they drank hardly till one; then coffee, tea, and liqueurs. They broke up between two and three o'clock.

so diffused, that this taste for gormandising is scarcely noticed.*

Among other pleasant vices, gambling was one of the most popular, there being a special recognised club in St. James's Street — the notorious "Crockford's," later the "Wellington" restaurant, now the Devonshire Club—devoted to that ruinous pastime. Here whole fortunes were lost.

There are some old novels, curious as pictures of the manners of the time, in which living characters were introduced under fictitious names, and for which there were "keys" in circulation. There were "Almack's"—in which ladies of fashion were introduced— "Crockford's," "D'Horsay," † and "A Week at Long's." Even Mr. Disraeli adopted this system, and his Earl of Monmouth, in "Coningsby," is a sketch of Lord Hertford, as his Rigby is of Croker. It is a curious thing that Mr. Croker, in real life, filled the same office to his patron

---

* The growth in this sort of enjoyment may be shown by the increase in the consumption of champagne. In the reign of William IV. not half a million bottles were imported annually; now, five million bottles are taken, of which one firm alone supplies a million !

† A copy was thus lately advertised : "'D'Horsay, or the Follies of the Day,' by a Man of Fashion (John Mills), 1844. 8vo, with portrait, vignette, and ten clever plates by 'George Standfast,' in the original cloth, uncut. £2 2s. An extraordinary and truthful *exposé* of the fast life of fashionable London thirty years ago. Anecdotes concerning the adventures of 'Count D'Horsay, the Marquis of Hereford, the Earl of Chesterlane, Mr. Pelham, General Peel, Lord George Bedtick, Mr. George Bobbins, auctioneer, Earl of Raspberry Hill,' Lord Beaconsfield, Lord Huntingtower, the Countess of Blessington, and other well-known personages are depicted with piquancy. The original owner of this copy has written in the names. The plates contain portraits of D'Orsay, Fanny Ellsler, Lord Chesterfield, Mr. George Payne, the Countess of Blessington, etc. The present copy contains the chapter describing the closing scene of the life of the 'Marquis of Hereford,' which is often wanting."

as Rigby did in the novel. This fashion he adopted even so lately as the days of " Lothair." As a contrast to our day, when constant publicity is in vogue, this is significant; for a picture at the Academy was labelled " Portrait of a Lady," and nowadays keys to a novel circulated mysteriously would be disdained.

It was early in this reign that some new clubs were formed in London, which have since become far more important institutions than the older and more famous ones ; while " Brookes's," " Boodle's," and " White's," have now completely lost their political complexion. It was determined to form a new Tory Club. Lord Kensington's House, in Carlton Gardens, was taken, and the Duke of Wellington took particular interest in the scheme. They hired the Duke of Escar's cook from Paris, who had the reputation of having killed his master by his rich dish of sausages. Mr. Croker's name is connected with the foundation of the Athenæum Club, who, Mr. Crabb Robinson says, was " one of the most active of the founders of the Athenæum Club, one of the trustees of the House, a permanent member of the committee, and, according to common report, the officious manager and despot, ruling the club at his will. I had been told in the morning (during the year 1829) that the committee had meant to have a neat portico of four columns —the one actually erected—but that Croker had arbitrarily changed the plan, and the foundations were then digging for a portico of two columns, not at all becoming so broad a space as the front occupies." A curious scene followed. Mr. Robinson indignantly denounced this piece of Vandalism, when Mr. Croker, in reply, said he was under a great mistake—that there never was any intention to have any other portico than the one now preparing. The other retorted that " individual men might be deterred by his opposition, but I knew," raising my voice, " that there were other designs, for I had seen them." Then Mr. Croker requested me, as an act of politeness, to abstain from a motion which would be an affront to the committee. This roused me, and I said that if any other gentleman would say he thought my motion an affront, I would not make it ; but I meant otherwise. There was then a cry of " Move, move," and a very large number of hands were held up for the motion. So it passed by acclamation. I was thanked by the architect, and everybody was pleased with what I had done.

The year 1831 saw the foundation of that interesting club, " the Garrick," " projected, principally by Mr. Francis Mills and Mr. Henry Broadwood, with the avowed object of supporting the drama. The scheme was warmly taken up, a committee formed, and a house in King Street, Covent Garden, known as " Probert's Hotel," was secured. On the 15th of February, 1832, the opening was inaugurated by a dinner, H.R.H. the Duke of Sussex, who had signified his pleasure to be patron of the club, taking the chair, supported by the Earl of Mulgrave, afterwards Marquis of Normanby (president), the Marquis of Clanricarde, the Marquis of Worcester, the Earl of Chesterfield, Viscount Castlereagh, Lord Adolphus Fitz-Clarence, and others, whilst the general company included the majority of the principal dramatists and actors then living. James Smith, Poole, and Charles Mathews the elder, were original members. The Rev. Richard Harris Barham (Tom Ingoldsby), Theodore Hook, Thackeray, Charles Dickens, and a host of memorable names were gradually added to the list."

In the short space of twenty years was witnessed some remarkable changes in London in the direction of locomotion, and which helped the town wayfarer almost as much as steam did the traveller in the country. Up to the year 1823, the traditional hackney-coach, and more odious hackney-coachman, were one of the troubles of the cockney—the wet straw of the former, with its execrable horses, and the insolence, extortion, and low pace of the latter, forming one of the bitter trials of the play-goer or party-goer. A benefactor, of the name of Davies, appeared in this year of happy memory, 1823, who started "twelve cabs," which stood near Portman Square. These were clearly the undeveloped "hansom," only the driver sat beside his fare, separated by a partition. It was a sort of covered gig, with a third seat on the right, and the reader will find an excellent sketch of the vehicle in an early number of "Pickwick," where is portrayed the memorable dispute of the driver with his amiable "fare." The next blessing we owe to the French, viz., the "omnibus," which appeared in London in 1829,* introduced by one Shillibeer. It was made

* When Mr. C. Robinson was at Paris in 1828, his attention was drawn to a novelty—a number of long *diligences* inscribed, "Entreprise générale pour des omnibus." "And on my return, in October, I made frequent use of them, paying five sous for a *course*. I remarked then, that so rapid is the spread of all substantial comforts, that they would certainly be introduced in London before Christmas, as in fact they were." They plied from various inns, such as "The Old Bell," in Holborn, and took clerks and others to the suburbs. Finally it was resolved by an ingenious coach-builder, viz., Robinson, in 1839, to devise a small, handy, one-horse carriage, which should hold two or three or even four, and which has in truth revolutionised the principle of carriage-building, abolished the old heavy system of "chariots," coaches, etc. This was creditably named, in compliment to a fallen statesman, the Brougham.

at first to hold twenty inside, and none outside, and was drawn by three horses.

Such is a review of social life, and its characters and peculiarities, in the days of William IV. It might be infinitely extended, but enough has been said to give a satisfactory outline of men and manners in those days.*

---

* In 1837, 126 millions of letters, newspapers, etc., passed through the Post, of these 7 millions were franks. These were carried by 54 mail coaches, whose rate of speed was something over 10 miles an hour. London to Holyhead—261 miles—was covered in 27 hours. Sedan chairs had almost entirely disappeared, though some lingered till the year 1850. The first postage stamp was issued in 1840, but the question was being agitated eagerly during the last years of the King's reign.

CHAPTER XIII

His Majesty was now helped to recover, during the disastrous interval after his fall, by various interviews with Tory lords, who craved audiences, and who encouraged him with stout words. Lords Howe, Camden, and others thus comforted him ; and, to encourage the Duke, they sent him reports of what they had done.

Lord Camden met the King in the month of December, 1832, when His Majesty asked curiously about the Duke and Sir R. Peel: "Had they met during the summer, or lately ? Was there any feeling of *hostility?*" When assured there was not, he said, "I have heard it was as I have mentioned. The Duke was not pleased when there was an attempt to form a new Government, nor was I." Having heard since that Peel and Wellington had met, Lord Camden told the King, who said he was very glad to hear it : "You understand me as speaking confidentially to you. It is right I should know, in the present alarming state of the country, the condition of men's minds and parties." Then he said, "As to the resignation of ———, time ought to have been given to the ultra-Tories." He quoted a saying of the late Duke of Queensberry, that the King and Treasury could always carry a Government through. The impression left was, that there was a decided wish to place himself in other hands at the proper time.

In October, Lord Camden had an audience, or several
audiences, one of at least four hours. "There was not
a marriage or an inheritance, of the present or former
time, that he did not remember. He seemed anxious
about the county elections, because, now that nomination
boroughs were gone, which he most sincerely lamented,
the best chance was that good men should represent
counties. He avoided politics as an unpleasant subject
—not unnaturally.

Again, in December, the same nobleman was favoured
with another audience, at the Pavilion.

We have before met with that pleasant correspondent
of the Duke of Wellington, Sir H. Cooke, who seems to
have been a shrewd observer and a lively satirist; but
we are hardly prepared to find him so venturesome as
to think of ridiculing his sovereign to his face, which
he did in an interview to which His Majesty invited
him. The follies of the King during the passing of the
Reform Bill had been extended to other subjects, such
as the relations of the country to France. In this
direction he had been exhibiting some extraordinary
antics, which had created much amusement, especially
from his affecting to have a particular knowledge of the
country, of which he was in reality profoundly ignorant.
Sir Henry wrote an account of his visit :

"The King, to my surprise, sent for me, and commenced a protracted interview by saying that it had
come to his knowledge that I had spoken of the French,
and the French army, in a manner that excited much
interest in his mind ; for he had urged the same opinions,
and wished I would candidly say what I had seen, and
what I dispassionately felt. On which," this *farceur* says,
" he accepted the invitation in the same grave spirit ; and,
assuming the character of a French General, proceeded
to give a view of French politics, the King listening

with solemn admiration. Sometimes he expanded, and rose to the height of burlesque, as he dwelt in inflated language on the prospects of the French. For," he said, " on no other ground could I have hazarded such *thrusts* at His Majesty.

" ' The French—however divided, however prostrate —are of opinion that your Majesty's countenance *is a tower of strength ;* and the reflecting part of the nation consider that your Majesty's amity counteracts principles sufficiently revolutionary to ensure the support of the Jacobin party. We may laugh to scorn the efforts of Europe, so long as England *marche de concert* with us. Let us,' I continued, as speaking for a French general, ' but gain time for a defensive war on revolutionary, or rather, Republican principles— namely, terror and equality—and the nation will acclaim the majority.' I must do His Majesty the justice to say I experienced no interruption ; neither did he say one syllable, excepting that he had urged the same opinions more than once. I had the talk all to myself. I interspersed my tirade with observations upon dress, worsted epaulettes, and crimson overalls. Finally, His Majesty said with great simplicity and kindness : ' You think France in a very weak and critical state, prostrate, and ready to cut all others' throat for Henri V.' I replied : ' I should say, formerly His Majesty was in great ignorance of the state of France, and of Europe generally, and that he is taught to believe his alliance with France will ensure permanent tranquillity.' Upon leaving his presence, he was pleased to say I had given him some valuable information."*

* Sir H. Cooke gave, however, a more serious and less burlesque account of his interview to other friends. "Cooke," said he, "was much surprised yesterday morning by a message from the King to come to the palace. On entering the ante-chamber at St. James's he met Lords

This scene was not evidence of much respect for His
Majesty, and gives a good idea of the jocular tone
assumed about his proceedings.

Grey and Palmerston, who showed evident surprise at seeing him
there. Palmerston recognised him as usual, but Lord Grey took not
the slightest notice of him. When introduced, the King prefaced by
saying that, as he was just returned from the Continent, he wished to
have his opinion of the state of feeling and of the army in France ;
on which Cooke told him his frank opinion. He said that France was
in a most prostrate state ; that she might be said to exist only by
the countenance of this country ; that her army as to numbers was
grossly exaggerated, and chiefly composed of raw recruits ; that, as it
now seemed ascertained that Gérard's army was to march into Belgium
on the 15th instant (which circumstance he assumed on purpose to
sound the King, who did not in the least contradict it), his firm
opinion was, that they would shortly be exterminated by the climate
and the campaign, particularly if the Dutch could prolong their
resistance. Here the King interrupted him in a very animated way,
by saying : 'I have always maintained that this would be the case.'
Which was proof at once how much he differs from his Cabinet. He
next questioned him about the South of France, the Carlist party, the
National Guards at Paris, and of public opinion on the Continent ;
to all which he gave the answers that may be supposed to His Majesty.
With respect to the latter question he did say, that throughout the
Continent the general opinion was, that the admission of French
troops into Belgium was a most unpopular proceeding. He took good
care, during the whole interview, never to glance at the present proceedings as of our Government, but as of France, and many times
did the King's countenance change when it struck him how irresistibly
the remarks applied equally to both. The King then said : 'I understand that —— is a great rogue ; that he has appropriated to himself
large sums that were voted for the organisation of the army ; and that
he will be impeached by the Opposition on the opening of the
Chambers." But when Cooke mentioned the remark of a French
general to him : 'Donnez nous encore six mois d'une guerre défensive,
alors, pourvû que nous n'ayons pas à faire avec Wellington, nous
aurons une armée à reconquérir tous les hauts faits de la première
révolution,' the King seemed rather confused at the mention of the
Duke's name. In the evening Cooke dined with us, and gave me
some more particulars of this rather singular interview. On entering
the King's closet, Sir H. Taylor, who introduced him, said : 'I
beseech you not to enter into any political discussions with him !'
How all conspire to keep the poor man in the dark !"

The rage and anger of the defeated faction may be conceived. We find the Duke still interchanging such encouragements as he could light upon with the congenial Howe. " Can there be any Government," the former asks, " in this empire after this revolution is completed ? Time may do much for us ; the eyes of our Sovereign *may at last be opened.*" To which Lord Howe replies : " If it had pleased God to send us the Reform Bill through the medium of a Bonaparte, or some other such clever scoundrel, I should be almost inclined to kiss the rod ; but to be ruined by such a set of imbeciles as these is enough to break one's heart. Anything that an honest man can do to injure this, I will with pleasure do, as a sacred duty, but in this case I fear we have not grounds for acting. You may do much for us—*i.e.*, in the late fashion." This " opening the eyes " of His Majesty was of little use if they were to be shut again the next moment. Lord Howe then reported the indifferent result of his efforts in this direction. " It is evident that his anxiety for a change of Government is rather increased of late. He cannot even yet get rid of the idea that the House of Lords are now what they were and ought to be, *but for his own folly*—a body powerful enough to assert their own independence, and assist him by turning out his ministers." In a conversation of an hour and a half this prudent councillor endeavoured to open his eyes. The King said : " Is it not odd that they never mention the vacant see of Waterford ?" I said it was reported in town that they intended to suppress or greatly alter any vacant see. At this he seemed astonished and doubted what I said. I think he likes the addresses now sending up, and said he didn't in the least wonder that the people of this country disliked a war against so good an

ally, and added : " The day of reckoning must come ere
long for the ministers." Is not his infatuation quite
unaccountable, if he really thinks this, and yields every
point one after the other? Presently arose the question
of the restoration of the officials dismissed for voting
against the Bill. Lord Howe* was offered his place
about the Queen, but as the offer was clogged with
certain conditions, he must remain " neutral."

In this momentous question we find the ex-chamberlain consulting the Duke at every stage, and determined
to make it useful in annoying ministers. Their letters
are useful, as showing the spirit of intrigue, and how
eager the Court party was to work the Duke up into
action, by the agency of the Queen.

" I am certain," wrote Lord Howe in August, 1832,
"you will not leave me, and, I may venture to add, *Her
Majesty in the lurch.*" " I decline," he adds, " to send my
answer to the Queen, desiring her not to deliver it until
she had seen yours. The Queen did not wish me to make
any alteration, and delivered *my* epistle, which caused
great *anger in Sir Herbert's mind,* the King expressing
himself very *kindly* respecting it. . . . The Queen has
requested me to say she never can forget the kindness you have shown her, on this and former occasions.
No words can express her gratitude to one who has been
so truly her friend."

The Duke, moreover, in his answer prayed his acknowledgments to His Majesty: " I don't trouble her

---

* " Lady Howe," says Mr. Greville, " begged her husband to show
me the correspondence between him and Sir Herbert Taylor about the
Chamberlainship. It is long and confused; Taylor's first letter, in
my opinion, is very impertinent, for it reads him a pretty severe
lecture about his behaviour when he held the office before. Howe
is a foolish man."

much with paying my court. *It is better. I can be of more use to her by refraining from doing so.*"

In September Lord Howe wrote to the Duke, in terms which reveal, as plainly as words can, the plans of the Court party :

" The astute Secretary and his master, Lord Grey, are in a towering passion at my insolence. I shall say nothing, remain quiet, *and hope to God I may yet be the humble means of getting rid of this curse and his faction.* A more unfit man, with good intentions, never filled an important station. Should *better days* come, I am satisfied a man, intimately connected with the Government, if not an extra Secretary of State, ought to fill the situation, when the principal is unable, as now, to commit his meaning to writing."

This letter of Sir H. Taylor's was certainly a severe reproof, pointing out to him that, by his behaviour, he had suggested the idea that the Queen was taking part against the King and the Government, and had thus placed her in a false position with the public. A curious tone to take, considering the gossip that was in circulation. But notwithstanding there was much protocoling and debating on this tremendous business the Chamberlain firmly refused to resume his office, as his terms were not granted. The Duke wrote :

"November 6, 1832.

" You did quite right to decline to accept. I wish that I could say that I have any prospect of change, and of relief for the King and his family, and his subjects, from the miserable position in which we are placed. I see none. The great mistake was made in April, 1831. We shall suffer before we get out of the scrape into which the King has brought himself. Yet it was then said of His Majesty, ' He is up to the mark !' "

It is really amazing to follow the persistent intrigues of these indiscreet persons. Lord Howe goes on to propose that the Duke should send his letters to *him* for the Queen :

"The Queen wants much to know whether you think she may venture to hold out against appointing my successor ? I suppose you could not write to her yourself ? If you do, if you send it under cover to me, I can forward it to her. Such is her wish." The Duke was sensible enough to decline to adopt this mode of correspondence, but advised that the Queen should continue to complain that she had not been treated with respect, and should decline to appoint a Chamberlain.

But the ramifications of this Court intrigue extended in all directions. A good instance of the violence of the factions on both sides was given by the Sefton incident.

"Previous to the late dinner which the King gave to the Jockey Club, Lord Sefton, who was indignant at the resignation of his friends the ministers, and most clamorous at what he called the duplicity of the King, in a fit of pique and vexation erased his name from the list of members, and sent an excuse to the dinner as no longer belonging to the Club. The King, who was not then aware of his motive, graciously requested that he would come as his friend. He never went. Circumstances soon took a different turn. Lord Grey resumed office, and Lord Sefton's animosity subsided. The Queen gave a ball on Friday night, where the whole Sefton family made their appearance, and His Majesty, who was then better informed, turned his back openly on his lordship. *Dans ces entrefaites* Lord Molyneux had attended a public meeting at Liverpool, where he made a speech, and, actuated by his father's feelings, alluded very bitterly to the conduct of both the King

and Queen. He afterwards came to town, and appeared
with his family at the ball. On the following day the
King commanded Mr. W. Ashley, as vice-chamberlain to
the Queen, to write to Lord Molyneux, and request he
would not appear at Court again."

Later on we have the sequel :

" At the conclusion of Ascot races, Lord Lichfield,
Master of the Buckhounds, as usual gave a dinner on
Saturday to the royal party at his house at Fern Hill.
When the list of guests was submitted to the King's
approval, he particularly commanded that Lord Sefton
should not be invited. Lady Lichfield made some
attempt to interest the Queen, by saying that, if this
had any reference to the conduct of Lord Sefton with
the Jockey Club, she believed that it had been much
misrepresented. The Queen coldly replied, that she
hoped it was so, and made no further comment."

Lord Sefton was a man about town, who had a
certain influence and authority, for which, "Sefton
said," was occasionally quoted. But it was curious
that he should also have quarrelled with the late King.
He appears to have had a biting tongue, which he did
not restrain.*

---

* Mr. Greville records some pleasant stories of this lively *farceur*
—his "chaffing" Lord Brougham, on his appointment as Chancellor.
When they were leaving the dining-room, his seizing a poker, and
carrying it before him as a mace ; his ridicule on a so-called friend,
Cornelius, at the brewery dinner, his vowing he "never saw a man
so put down in his life as Brougham was by Cornelius." His spirits
were unbounded. He was deformed in person.

CHAPTER XIV.

In this year some excitement was caused by the sudden death of a person in whose life many were interested, that of Mr. Greenwood, the well-known banker and agent, who was a friend of the Royal Family. His pleasant speech at a dinner was often recalled, when on the Duke of York proposing his health, with many compliments, as the gentleman "who so kindly took care of our money," the subject of the toast said "it was rather His Royal Highness and others that generally took care of his money." He was at the Pavilion, spending the evening with the King and Queen, being then eighty-five years old.

"I had been playing at whist with him," wrote Sir H. Taylor, "and towards eleven o'clock he complained of headache, and we advised him quit the hot room and go into the gallery. He walked out alone (as we were afraid of fussing him by accompanying him), and very steadily, but I followed him, and found him sitting in the gallery. He told me he felt unwell, and would go to his room—got up, moved one step, said he feared he should not reach his room, and fell back on my arm senseless, and with a rattle in his throat. Lord Erroll appearing at the door at this moment, I begged him to call Mr. Davis the surgeon, who came immediately and loosened his neckcloth, which seemed to relieve him a little, though he continued senseless ; and Mr. Davies said he feared death was approaching.   There was a large party, and I waited until they had left the house, and then broke the sad event to the King, who was greatly shocked and affected, as he was very partial to poor Greenwood.   I sent a messenger to Mr. Charles Hammersley last night, and I expect him every moment."

Next came the question of calling the new Parliament, and dissolving the old one.   Nothing could have been more logical or fitter than this step.   The passage of the Reform Bill had condemned the existing House of Commons, whose dealing with any measure of importance would be idle and valueless, as not representing the proper feeling of the country.   But here the King again showed himself obstructive.   In November, when he assented to the measure, "he appeared," says the Chancellor, " very much out of humour.   This first showed itself when I asked him to let me present the new Solicitor-General (Campbell) for knighthood, which I had always followed the practice of having performed in the closet. ' Let him wait,' was the answer.   I afterwards said he was anxious to go to Dudley for re-election, and not to have any extraordinary difficulty arising from the approaching general election.   ' What general election ? Let him wait till after the levée.'   I saw there was something wrong.   I hastened the Council.   He made no objection ; looked sulky ; asked me if it was quite necessary ; received for answer, 'absolutely, Sir ;' and we dissolved and returned the great, Liberal, and Reformed Parliament—the last of the kind we are ever likely to see."

Lord Campbell, the new knight thus spoken of, describes in a dramatic way the scene that followed :

"I found Lord Grey, Brougham, and several other Ministers,* standing round the King in his closet. They all seemed, at first, to be in a state of great excitement. His Majesty then put a few unmeaning questions to me, without attending to my answers, and we *subjects* all withdrew."

He afterwards fully explained to me that they had just had a most stormy interview with the King, who had been more obstinate and wrong-headed than they had ever found him ; that they had tried with all sincerity and respect to explain to him that, although he might have withheld his assent from the Reform Bill, now that it had, with his concurrence, become law, a dissolution was inevitable, as the existing Parliament stood condemned and sentenced, and the people were entitled to the exercise of their new franchises. " No !" he declared, "he could see no necessity for that."

This being a sort of legal question, the argument on the side of the ministers was left almost entirely to the Chancellor, who tried to show that the Reform Bill, in its spirit, really enacted an immediate dissolution, and who assured His Majesty that, if not fairly acted upon, instead of being, as His Majesty had in the conclusion of his speech from the throne prayed that it might be— "fruitful in promoting the security of the State, and the contentment and welfare of the people "—it might lead to rebellion and civil war. Still the King was not convinced, " when Lord Grey, in a low, respectful, but solemn tone, informed His Majesty that his present servants, after due deliberation, were unanimously of

* It will be seen, as was indeed natural, that Lord Grey and the other ministers had their share in influencing him.

opinion that the reassembling of the present Parliament would be an unconstitutional and most inexpedient step, for which they could not be responsible, and therefore that they must immediately, with all humility, resign their offices into His Majesty's hands. 'Well,' said the King, 'I yield, but, my Lords and Gentlemen, remember it is against my opinion and my wishes.'"

I do not propose to deal on the course of politics in the reign, save only where the King took a prominent part. I pass by, therefore, the next two years, until we come to the embarrassments of 1834, which led to Lord Grey's retirement. It is worth while noting with what wonderful perseverance His Majesty, undeterred by his late failure, watched every opening which might furnish an opportunity for getting rid of his ministers.

The position of the ministry during the few months before this final retirement was even worse than that of the Duke of Wellington's in 1830, before his final *congé*. As Lord Londonderry wrote : "And one can hardly imagine how any Minister can remain in office and suffer two such indignities as have been heaped upon him (Lord Grey) by his colleagues. Brougham's exhibition on the Pluralities and Residence Bill (of which Grey knew absolutely nothing); and Lieven being recalled on Tuesday by letters to Palmerston, which Grey knew nothing of till Tuesday. In addition, however, to all this, the difficulties in the Commons are so great that their warmest partisans admit they are at a loss what course to take ; and my good uncle, Lord C., tells me he *knows* Althorp is only looking for an opportunity to cut and run. All looks in extreme confusion. Still my own feeling is, things will tide on." *

* It has been often noted into what sudden odium the Reformers fell within a very short period. "Mark my words," said Lord Grey

The share of Lord Brougham in this change has been ridiculed by Lord Campbell and others; but it is certain that by an adroit device and bold, sudden action, the Chancellor succeeded in keeping his friends in their places. For, it must be considered, the Lords Grey and Althorp, who, with himself, were the leading spirits of the ministry, had determined to retire. In the natural order, "the Government was out." So the King and the Opposition considered it to be. His plan was to announce that it was ready to go on, and could go on. His first step was to impress this on His Majesty.

"On Grey's resignation I went to the King, and assured him that I believed I could persuade Althorp to retract his resignation, and that I hoped Grey would return also, as we all most anxiously desired his continuance; and all must be aware how severe a blow on the Government his retirement would inflict. His Majesty seemed puzzled, and repeated his former assertion of some weeks before, that while Grey and I remained together he was firm in our support. He expressed great doubt of our being able to go on, and left on my mind the very distinct impression that he was disposed to accept *all* our resignations, and try a Tory Government."

It seems scarcely credible that he could have

to the veteran Sidmouth, "within two years we shall have been unpopular, for having brought forward the most aristocratic measure ever proposed in Parliament." They even suffered repeated defeats on minor questions. "Report says," Lord Eldon writes, "*some* of the Ministers, when they were beaten in a vote a few nights ago, offered their resignations, and that their master said: 'No; if any go, all shall go.' All remained. There is a report, believed by some (I know not what to make of it), that there are movements towards forming a Coalition Ministry of Whigs and Tories."

thought that Lord Grey would return ; but the King was so far beguiled as to entertain the idea, provided a coalition with the Tories could be managed, and in this view he accepted Lord Melbourne as first minister.

The King, indeed, he says, was " panting for a Tory Ministry, and loathing one which was ever on the point of breaking and leaving him in the position of all others to kings the most hateful and even alarming, that of being left for a time without a government, and so feeling all responsibility thrown on themselves." He therefore hoped they would break up and leave him.

" A new Conservative Government," says Lord Campbell, " would certainly then have been formed, but for the extraordinary promptitude, vigour, and daring, exhibited by Brougham. He contrived to see all the other members of the Cabinet privately and separately, and he persuaded them that there was no occasion for them to retire ; that if Althorp would come back they could get on without Grey ; that Althorp would come back for the public good if his original wish for the mitigation of the Coercion Bill were now complied with; that they ought not to send in their resignations, and that the King—while the House of Commons, elected in the fervour of reform, still subsisted—could not force them out, to bring in the boroughmongers. They all agreed to ' stand by their guns.' " Brougham has often told me that at this time he had himself the offer of being Prime Minister, but that he positively declined it, and named Melbourne. I strongly suspect that this only appeared to him in a dream, and that the story is now believed by him only because it has been so often narrated by him. But certain it is that, either without any such offer to Brougham, or after it was rejected, the

offer was made to Melbourne, and that he, despising all
pretended modesty, at once agreed to become Prime
Minister.

But the Lord Chancellor, by declining to go, and
further proposing to call in Lord Melbourne to take
Lord Grey's place, destroyed his chance. His answer,
through Sir H. Taylor, was to this effect, and it may be
imagined with what a relish he told them, "that it was
not his wish or his intention to have called for that
resignation any more than for that of Lord Grey or any
other member of the Administration; but that it was
impossible for him to view the circumstances under which
the Administration was placed by the resignations which
had been tendered to him, and which he considered
himself under the necessity of accepting, as involving
anything short of its dissolution. *It has, in His
Majesty's opinion, fallen to pieces;* and that event has
been produced, not by any irresistible or overbearing
opposition to the measures of the Government, but by
the operation of internal causes, against the wearing
effects of which, the high character and influence and
the irreproachable conduct of Lord Grey, and the un-
qualified and undeviating support which the Government
over which his lordship so ably presides received from
His Majesty, have proved unavailing."

"Under this impression and this view, which have
not been removed, His Majesty felt it to be his duty
not to delay taking such steps as appeared to him best
calculated to extricate himself, and the country over
which he has been called to rule, from the difficulties in
which both are placed; and the instructions with which
His Majesty has thought fit to entrust Lord Melbourne,
resulted from a conviction on his mind that the safety
of the country, its dearest interests, and the maintenance

of the blessings which it has so long enjoyed under its present admirable constitution and valuable institutions, would be best promoted by a union of the most respectable and influential individuals of those parties which have shown any solicitude for the preservation of those advantages, and from the hope that, with the aid and the support of these, His Majesty might be able to check the designs of lawless agitators and the progress of violent changes."

He adds, in conclusion, that he was most anxious to obtain the Lord Chancellor's "concurrence" in his views. Indeed, the whole tone of the communication leaves the idea that Brougham was officially tendering suggestions, and anxious to have it supposed by the public that he was directing the changes. His account of the affair is exquisitely self-complaisant; and, it must be said, more than supports the sarcastic view given by his friend, Lord Campbell.

It is evident too, from the conclusion of the King's letter, that His Majesty hoped for the Chancellor's support in the coalition scheme; and some compliments were lavished, in the hope of bringing him to adopt his view: "His Majesty estimates too highly your lordship's talents, the extraordinary resources of your mind, and your indefatigable zeal in the pursuit of all that you undertake, and in the discharge of most arduous and important duties—he is too well assured of your lordship's solicitude for the welfare of this great country, and too sensible of the value of your influence on the public and in society—not to feel most anxious to obtain your concurrence in views which, as a patriot and a faithful servant of the Crown, you cannot but approve."

In a publication of Lord Brougham, printed in the year 1838, he gives this account of this ministerial crisis: "This unreasonable feeling of disappointment, and the unhappy necessity which existed for the Coercion Bill in Ireland, had excited a clamour against the Government of Lord Grey; and when that justly esteemed individual quitted office, the King had undoubtedly resolved to take advantage of this clamour, and would have at once changed his ministers, had they given him an opening, by hesitating whether or not they should continue to hold the Government, after Lord Grey's secession. The declaration, *first communicated by the Chancellor* in private to His Majesty, and then on the same day made by him in the House of Lords, that the ministers were quite willing to remain, disconcerted all such designs; and the King could not take the step he so much wished until Lord Spencer's death in the following November gave, or seemed to give, a kind of ground (or rather a hollow pretext) for accomplishing the same purpose. This was the very worst step, as it was the most inconsiderate, and proved for his own comfort the most fatal that this excellent monarch ever took; and he had been beforehand warned distinctly of the inevitable consequences, but he disregarded the warning."

The King, when offering the succession to Lord Melbourne, appears to have gone much farther in his proposal of a coalition than Lord Brougham was aware of. For the former he actually invited "to enter into communication with the leading individuals of parties, and to endeavour at this crisis to prevail upon them to afford their aid and co-operation, towards the formation of an administration upon an enlarged basis, combining the services of the most able and efficient members of each, and your Majesty further desires that Viscount Melbourne will communicate with the Duke of Wellington, with Sir Robert Peel, with Mr. Stanley, and with others of their respective parties, as well as with those who have hitherto acted with himself and have otherwise supported the administration, and that he will endeavour to bring them together, and to establish a community of purpose." "Your Majesty is graciously pleased to add, that 'you do not disguise from yourself the difficulty of the task which your Majesty is desirous of imposing on Viscount Melbourne, nor the objections which Viscount Melbourne may possibly feel to take an active part in the endeavour to carry it into effect, but your Majesty trusts Viscount Melbourne will not refuse to become your confidential agent upon this critical occasion.' "*

But Lord Melbourne, in a calm, pleasant, and even sarcastic tone, put the proposal aside on the simple ground "that the distinguished individuals enumerated by His Majesty had all and each of them expressed, not only general want of confidence in His Majesty's Government, but the strongest objections, founded upon principle, to measures of great importance, either introduced into Parliament, or adopted by virtue of your Majesty's prerogative."

Mr. Torrens states the same belief that the "distinguished individuals" in question really expected to be joined with Melbourne in the King's councils, and that it was on this ground that the late Home Secretary had been chosen. This, it will be seen, shows that the Chancellor had little to do with the selection of Prime Minister. An odd proceeding—but which is intelligible—followed. Lord Melbourne was directed by His Majesty to send copies of this reply to each of "the distinguished individuals;" of course, to prove that the fault of this in-

* "Lord Melbourne's Letters."—"Life," ii. 6.

justice did not lie with His Majesty. This, only that the King was known to have peculiar modes of thought and action—feminine almost—would have appeared a slight. Lord Melbourne said simply that "he had been directed by His Majesty to send this document, for the purpose of putting your Grace and those gentlemen in possession of His Majesty's feelings and opinions upon the present position of public affairs. The tenor and substance of my letter to His Majesty renders it almost unnecessary for me to add, that I wrote this communication solely in obedience to His Majesty's commands."

The Duke acknowledged the communication in a reserved fashion, and, after begging his Lordship to convey to His Majesty his grateful acknowledgments for his most gracious consideration, added: "I do not understand that it is His Majesty's wish or intention that I should make any observations upon the paper sent to me by your Lordship."

In this there is a curious likeness to the "pettish" mode in which his late royal brother used to indemnify himself for the misfortune of having to accept a ministry which he disliked.

THE KING TO SIR R. PEEL.

"Windsor Castle, July 14, 1834.

"The King received yesterday, from Viscount Melbourne, the letter which Sir Robert Peel addressed to His Majesty, in consequence of the communication which he had desired Viscount Melbourne to make to him.

"His Majesty cannot forbear assuring Sir Robert Peel of his sense of the manner in which he has met this communication, and of the terms in which he has adverted to the feeling and the motives which have influenced His Majesty's consent upon this occasion. It is satisfactory to him to know that these are justly understood and appreciated in so respectable a quarter; and, although he cannot help regretting the failure of his purpose, His Majesty is bound to admit that the opinions which have been so forcibly stated by Sir Robert Peel, and by others, of its impracticability, have appeared to him conclusive.

" WILLIAM R."

Sir R. Peel, in a note on this correspondence, declares that he and the Duke all through acted in concert, showing each other their letters. " We had no wish to be invited to take office, but were resolved, if invited, not to decline."

CHAPTER XV

On the day that Lord Melbourne had been sent for by the King, July 9, the Chancellor was exhibiting his gifts as a *farceur* in the House of Lords. After an almost pathetic farewell to office, uttered by Lord Grey, the Chancellor declared solemnly that the ministry must not go. "Of all men who ever held office, the present Ministry would be the most without excuse if they could think of leaving the service of their King and country, unless through an unavoidable necessity. This has ever been my opinion since I came into office; it is my opinion to the present hour; and I feel that I should not discharge my duty if, at all sacrifice of my comfort —at all abandonment of my own ease—at the destruction, if so it may be, of my own peace of mind, I do not stand by that gracious monarch and that country, whose cordial support I have received during the three years and a half I have had the honour to hold the Great Seal. After having said this, need I add that *I have not tendered my resignation.*" (Loud laughter in the House below the bar and on the steps of the throne.) Irritated by which "hilarity" he went on: "Do your lordships, or do any who listen to me, think that there is anything peculiarly merry or amusing in being a Minister at the present conjuncture? If they do, I invite them to take a part in the reconstruction of the Government. But they know better. If they are not aware of the annoyance which must attend such a situation—I am ; and I will tell these noble and laughing lords, that such is my feeling with respect to office, that nothing but a sense of imperative duty could have kept me in office one hour after the resignation of my noble friend."

But on the following day, the strange Duke of Buckingham declared that they might think they had buried Lord Grey, but that "the noble Earl's spirit would arise and interpret the festivities of the learned Lord on the Woolsack, when he may attempt to drink, with pottle-deep potations, to the health and prosperity of the new Administration."

To which the Chancellor retorted: "The noble Duke who has just addressed the House must be conversant with the dialect adopted in some alehouse, with which I am unacquainted. I have been in the habit of meeting the noble Duke elsewhere, but I have never had the honour of seeing him at the alehouse, where the noble Duke must have been so often in order to have picked up the terms of his slang dictionary."

Cries of "Order" resounded from all sides, and a scene followed, which, for the dignity of the House and the credit of all concerned, says Lord Campbell, "I wish to be forgotten." It is difficult here to award the palm of indecorousness.

The next step was to try to bring back Lord Althorp, and this the Chancellor attempted. On the 9th, the day into which so much had been crowded, the pushing Chancellor addressed him a sort of rebuking letter, in which his own sense of all-in-all responsibility is amply revealed.

"July 9, 1834.

"My dear Althorp,

"I enclose a copy of my letter to the King. I stated the same thing in my place. Your step of resigning has, I fear, sealed the fate of this country. Rather than be plagued by two or three speeches addressed to a House of Commons which has more confidence in you than ever, you have done your best to dissolve the only Government the country will bear, and I hear that Abercromby and Rice are afraid to remain. I regard them, next to you, as the cause of all the mischief which may ensue; they, too, are resolved to fly from their posts, and deliver us over to the Tories and the mob, in succession, because they don't like being badgered. I shall do all I can to ward off the calamity; but how can I, if everyone in the House of Commons is afraid to keep his ground? At least, I am resolved that the country shall see whom it has to thank for whatever is to happen. I really must say, I look upon all of you as answerable, and most deeply answerable, for the event. One thing of course you must make up your minds to. As you and your companions in desertion will most probably prevent a Liberal Government from being made, you are of course prepared to give your cordial support to a Tory one. Surely, you don't mean we should have no Government?

"Yours ever,
"H. B."

Lord Althorp retorted in plain language:

"I admit," he wrote next day, "that I am answerable as the proximate cause of the dissolution of the Administration, but the situation in which I was placed was not by any act of my own. I wish you would look a little at the share you have taken in the business. Without communication with one of your colleagues — with the view, I know, of facilitating business in Parliament—you desired Littleton to write to Lord Wellesley, and you wrote to him yourself, to press him to express an opinion that the three first clauses of the Bill might be omitted. . . . He had said, he did not want the Court-Martial Clauses; we properly omitted them. He then said, he could go on without these three clauses, and I think we ought to have omitted them also; but you, having originally produced the difficulty, by writing to Lord Wellesley, gave your decision directly against what you had advised Lord Wellesley to do. The consequence of all this was, that I got placed in a position which rendered it impossible for me to go on." *

* What led to Lord Grey's resignation, was the well-known imbroglio about Mr. Littleton—the Irish Secretary's indiscreet revelations, under the seal of secrecy, to Mr. O'Connell. He had been assured that certain Coercion Clauses would not be in the Government Bill, but the Government changed its intention, and O'Connell considered himself as betrayed. Lord Althorp was the person who had advised him to make this communication; and there is no doubt he ought to have enforced the measure being carried, or else should have retired. The Secretary, however, was made the scapegoat.

It is amusing to read Lord Brougham's allusions to this charge in his "Autobiography:" " The mischief-makers attempted to get up a case against me, founded upon a letter I had written to Lord Wellesley. A letter was in fact written about this period, but it was of a purely private nature, and could not at any time have exercised the smallest influence on his mind. How should it? It was a letter about some verses of Lord Wellesley's, and about other gossip, too private to be here quoted. But the sentence I have referred to was as follows: 'You have done yourself much credit, in my opinion, in recommending the giving up the Court-martial Clauses in the Bill. If things were in such a state as to justify you in recommending the omission of the unconstitutional clauses about meetings also, you would be on a pinnacle.' That was the exact sentence."

After this, it was not likely that the Chancellor could claim to have brought back Lord Althorp. The unusual homage of an address of regret, and of assurance of support, signed by over two hundred members, joined with the entreaties of Lord Grey, and the refusal of Lord Melbourne to " go on without him," induced this esteemed and unselfish man to yield; and when he was assured that the obnoxious clauses which had caused his resignation should be withdrawn, he had no reasonable excuse for refusing.*

The King, according to the Chancellor, was indignant at being thus *joué*—particularly angry at his Chancellor's behaviour. He was seriously annoyed at the suggested address to Lord Althorp, of which he takes an odd view.

" My dear Lord,

" I do not delay acknowledging the receipt of your lordship's letters of this day, which I have had the honour of submitting to the King, who was very glad to learn from them that he had misconceived your expression of a disposition in certain members of the House of Commons to urge upon Lord Althorp their desire that he should resume the situation in the Government, into a desire or an intention to force a

---

* Lord Essex wrote in rapturous terms to Lord Spencer: " What an angel is your son ! He has saved his King and his country, by sacrificing all his own feelings for the public good, and he must reap the reward such conduct deserves from a generous people ! Lady Grey said to me yesterday morning, ' Of all the persons now to be admired in this world, is Lord Althorp ; never was anything like it !' This is general feeling. The Tories are frantic."

The late Lord Belper, seeing him walking to the House, remarked to a friend, " I see the Government are still in," giving as his reason, " because Lord Althorp looks so unhappy."

Minister upon His Majesty; and that their language could not be construed into disregard of the most constitutional views of the royal prerogative, which His Majesty considers it due to the interests of the State, as well as to his own honour, that he should jealously guard.

"The King is quite willing to admit your lordship's construction of his rights, and he does not doubt your doing justice to the principle on which he asserts them.

"It is also satisfactory to His Majesty to be assured by your lordship and by others that there is a friendly feeling in many, even popular, quarters towards himself, and a disposition to consider the difficulties in which he is placed, and to give him credit for an honest desire to consult the peace and the welfare of the country. His Majesty would be glad, however, to know that there is allied to those sentiments a more conciliatory feeling towards the aristocracy, of which he considers the existence, and the maintenance with unimpaired influence, to be clearly connected with that of the monarchy, and essential to the character and credit of the country.

"His Majesty rejoices to gather, from your lordship's expression on the subject, that you approve of his not abandoning the attempt to effect a union of parties until it fail; and although he has ceased to entertain much hope of success, he will not regret having made the trial. Mr. Stanley's answer to Lord Melbourne appears to him, as it does to you, extremely creditable to him; and His Majesty has learnt with sincere pleasure that he has so well redeemed, by his letter to Lord Grey, the error he committed in attacking so violently his late colleagues and friends in his speech on Friday week last.

"I have the honour to be, with my best regards my dear lord, your lordship's most obedient and faithful friend,

*
                                        " H. TAYLOR.

"P.S.—I have this moment received and communicated to the King your lordship's third letter, of this date ; and not wishing to detain your messenger until after dinner, I have only time to say that His Majesty gives you full credit for the zealous motive which produced your communication to Lord Rosslyn (of whom His Majesty entertains, as you do, a very high opinion), and that he must derive satisfaction from anything that may offer a hope of reconciling jarring feelings and views."

But this sort of sharp practice in politics, though for the moment, brought on him the serious inconvenience of the royal enmity. After his fashion, he boasted that "this speech decided the affair, for the Commons and the country rallied round me ; and anything we chose was voted by the one and backed by the other. But the King never forgave it. I pardon him—the measure was a strong one, but it was necessary. The letter to himself prevented him from dismissing us, except at the peril of being opposed in and out of Parliament. My speech prevented any relaxation of support in Parliament. If I had deferred it, even for twenty-four hours, I should have given him time for intriguing with other parties, and accomplishing his favourite object of turning us off and taking in the Tories. Both steps were necessary, but that could not well make either step agreeable to him. He yielded a sudden compliance, wrote me a letter that he accepted

Melbourne for minister, and never more smiled on me while he lived."

He was to enjoy this triumph but a few months, and when his party again returned to office he was harshly and ignominiously excluded for ever by general consent. Here the dislike of the King was no doubt a factor in this ostracism, or at least was found convenient. The new arrangement, however cleverly and ingeniously contrived, could have no permanence. As was happily said, the ministry had been "decapitated," how could the lifeless trunk simulate life and motion?

CHAPTER XVI

THE extraordinary and fantastic freaks of this high official that followed have been recorded by his friend, Lord Campbell, with a malicious but certainly diverting power; how he wore his cocked hat and robes before a committee, patronised the Prime Minister, and spoke of him as "Lamb," and behaved with extraordinary unceremoniousness to the King.

"Nothing," says Lord Campbell, "could excuse the unceremonious and dictatorial tone which he now assumed in the royal presence—making the Lords of the Bedchamber stare—and evidently exciting surprise and disgust in the mind of the King. Entertaining stories were circulated of deliberations in the Cabinet, in which he denounced the *hallucinations* of his colleagues in very unmeasured terms."

But a singular incident connected with *The Times* reads strangely: "One morning the Chancellor, in his Court at Lincoln's-Inn-Fields, was seen by a prying clerk to tear up a letter and throw the pieces carelessly away. The man carefully gathered the fragments, took them home and pasted them together, when the following communication from one of the members was revealed :

"DEAR BROUGHAM,

"What I want to see you about is *The Times*, whether we are to make war on it or come to terms.— Yours ever, ALTHORP."

"Come to terms," and this from noble and virtuous Althorp ! It was a most awkward disclosure, and the result was that instead of the ministry "declaring war" on *The Times*, that journal at once opened a pitiless and brutal series of attacks on the luckless Chancellor, in one of which it declared that "Lord Melbourne would soon find him out, as the honest men of the community were an overmatch for the knaves." He was pronounced to be mad, and "under a morbid excitement seldom evinced by those of His Majesty's subjects who are suffered to remain masters of their own actions." His strange restlessness and vanity suggested, indeed, the greediness of Bottom the weaver, who, when the parts were being cast, wished to engross every one to his own share. The same longing to attract the attention of the public by every little function has been seen in our times in the case of a certain eminent politician.

But he was now longing to appear on a provincial stage, and the occasion was furnished by a banquet which the Scotch Liberals were about to offer to Lord Grey in Edinburgh. On such occasions, and especially in the case of this veteran and popular public servant, it was to be expected that all would be eager to pay a tribute to the central figure, and that the most ordinary delicacy would require that no one should interpose between the public and the person it was about to honour. Not so thought the irrepressible Brougham, who determined to engross a substantial share of homage or at least attention. It is difficult to give a full idea of the fussy interference which distinguished him in this matter.

He first attempted to get himself appointed chairman.* As his *friend* says, " the ruling passion operated on him, and he was resolved to show that he had more popularity in Edinburgh than the supposed father of the Reform Bill, and, in common phrase, *to take the wind out of Lord Grey's sails.*" The antics he indulged in on his road to that city were long the talk of Glasgow. "At Rothiemurchus, then the residence of the Dowager Duchess of Bedford, he found a large party of English ladies, with whom he romped so familiarly, that to be revenged on him they stole the Great Seal. At last he was in such real distress about it that the ladies took compassion upon him, assured him it was in the drawing-room, and that he might find it blindfolded, one of them assisting him by playing loud on the piano when he approached it. He was blindfolded accordingly, and by the hints which the piano gave him, he, in due time, dragged the bauble from a tea-chest. This was very harmless sport ; but unfortunately exaggerated accounts of it were sent to a lady-in-waiting at Windsor Castle, who, in relating them to the royal circle there, did much mischief."

"When he received the freedom of the city of Inverness he made a singular speech, in which, after the indiscretions, he complimented the King, saying that,

* This is the way he contrived it. "He first asked me to preside," he wrote to Lord Grey ; "but, as I told them, a Scotch grandee would be better than the Duke of Hamilton." At the same time he told him, "*if they preferred me I cheerfully would.*" They preferred the Duke.

'to find he lived in the hearts of his subjects afforded him pure and unmixed satisfaction, and will, I am confident, be so received by His Majesty when I tell him (as I will do by to-night's post) of such a gratifying manifestation.'" He sent for an old boon companion, one Macpherson, to "The Caledonian Arms," and was there found drinking toddy. He ordered a glass for his friend while he went to a side table and indited to His Majesty "the fatal missive which was soon to prove the chief instrument of his downfall." These extraordinary proceedings excited universal ridicule and anger. Lord Durham, whom he had helped to exclude from office, attacked him in a speech, saying that "Lord Melbourne was incapable of treachery or intrigue." The King declared to people around him that he must be out of his mind. Of this remarkable progress Lord Campbell gives this amusing account:

"I never was so much astonished as when I heard that Brougham was to sit down at table with them there, and to pass the night under the same roof. He was very late in appearing, and we had all been assembled in the drawing-room expecting him. My heart beat violently as often as any noise arose that might indicate his approach. At last a servant opened the door and announced 'the Lord Chancellor.' I must say that his demeanour was noble and grand. Without any approach to presumption or vulgar familiarity, in an easy, frank, natural manner, he laid hold of the hand of Lord Grey, who, though stiff and stately, could not draw it back or refuse to acknowledge his salutation. He then most respectfully, but without betraying any consciousness of there being any misunderstanding between them, paid his court to Lady Grey, and actually engaged her in conversation, beginning with some complimentary expressions about the festival to be celebrated on the morrow. The two daughters, the Ladies Grey, long avoided him by every manœuvre they could resort to, but, before the evening was over, he had got them both to talk to him about the place where they were to be stationed next day so that they might best see and hear their papa. In his conversation he seemed anxiously desirous that the festival should be devoted exclusively to the honour of Lord Grey, and should be so conducted as most to gratify the feelings of all connected with him.

"Next day, however, at the public dinner, his object evidently was to make himself the most conspicuous object—improving the opportunity to glorify himself and to assail his opponents. In responding to the toast of 'His Majesty's Ministers,' which was received with much applause, he began with the praise of his Royal Correspondent:

"'I owe this expression from you, not by any means so much to any personal deserts of my own, as to the accidental circumstance, but to me most honourable, of having the pride and gratification to serve that great and gracious Prince who lives in the hearts of his people, and who for all the services he has rendered his country, and for his honest, straightforward and undeviating patronage of the best rights and interests of that country, has well earned the unparalleled praise bestowed on him so justly and without any exaggeration by your noble chairman, "that none of his predecessors ever more richly deserve the affections and gratitude of his subjects."'"

"He next alluded to 'the irreparable loss which His Majesty's ministers had lately sustained in the chief, to whose great services this most splendid and unparalleled

national testimonial had been so appropriately given.'
Then he came to the more agreeable topic of *himself*,
when he really grew sincere, earnest, eloquent, and
impressive.

" ' My fellow-citizens of Edinburgh, after having been
four years a minister, *these hands are clean*. In taking
office, and holding it, and retaining it, I have sacrificed
no feeling of a public nature ; I have deserted no friend ;
I have forfeited no pledge ; I have done no job ; I have
promoted no unworthy man to the best of my knowledge ; I have stood in the way of no man's fair pretensions to promotion ; I have not abused my patronage ;
I have not abused the ear of my master ; and I have
not deserted the people.' "

This venomous and piquant sketch is scarcely warranted by the facts, for we find the Chancellor, on the
very eve of the expedition and after it, receiving the
most cordial letters from Lord Grey.*

Reading the numerous extraordinary *escapades*, as
they might be called, of Lord Brougham, the *paillasse*
antics in which he indulged, one is inclined to speculate
whether there was not something like derangement of
mind at work ; thus, with that scene during his
speech on the Reform Bill in the House of Lords, when
he knelt, "moving his lips" as in prayer, with other
absurd exhibitions. Notice, however, has not been taken

---

* Thus, on August 24th : "I cannot be otherwise than highly
gratified by your thinking me worthy to have your speech dedicated
to me." "The only way with newspaper attacks is, as the Irish say,
'to keep never minding.'" And after the banquet, on September 15th,
he wrote to him : "Into the other matters of your letter I will not
now enter, further than to express to you how very sensible I am of
all its kindness to me, and to repeat to you that *I never for one
moment believed* that you had entered into any intrigue, and least of
all with Althorp, to remove me from office."

of a strange letter preserved among the Duke of Wellington's papers, and written when he was holding the office
of Chamberlain.   It is addressed to an old obscure
friend, and is written in the deepest despondency :

"For myself personally I care not.   *I mean to make
an attempt to get rid of my peerage the moment I quit the
Great Seal. I pant to be back in the House of Commons.*
. . . I protest to you, as an old and valued friend, that
no situation would better suit my taste and habits and
time of life, than to enjoy what for twenty years I have
been panting for, namely, my entire liberty, and the
uncontrolled power of doing what I like, in letters, in
science (my first love).

"I look to trying what can save this country ; and
therefore, while I have no exclusive feelings, I should
heartily prefer the burdens and one thousand discomforts
of my present position to seeing the Government broken
up, and feeling myself restored to that great weight
which I lost when I took the shadow of office."

The passage that has been italicised seems utter
incoherence and a mad dream, since, in serious moments,
he must have known there was no mode of "getting rid
of his peerage, and re-entering the House of Commons."
It is curious that, not many months before, this idea of
his being unsettled in mind had struck one of his
colleagues.*

* The following appeared in the *Examiner*, entitled, "Letter from
a Gentleman who travels for a large Establishment to One of his
Employers, Mr. William King :

"Dear Sir, the account here forwarded,
    Of favours since the 4th,
Presents a very handsome stroke
    Of business in the North.

"Peel," writes Lord Ellenborough, "thinks Brougham really rather mad, and would not be surprised to hear he was confined. Last year he was melancholy, and his friends and *he himself* feared he might commit suicide. Now he is in an excited state." Mr. Greville mentions others who held the same idea.

> Our firm's new style don't take at all,
> So thought the prudent thing
> Would be to cultivate the old
> Established name of King.

> " If any friend attention shows,
> And asks me out to dine,
> When company my health propose,
> In toddy or in wine,
> My heart's eternal gratitude
> About their ears I ding,
> With, ' Be assur'd I'll mention this
> Next post to Mr. King !'

> "I met with Grey the other day,
> Who, since he left the firm,
> Has travell'd on his own account,
> And done, I fear, some harm ;
> So thought it right, where'er he went,
> To whisper round the ring,
> ' Perhaps you don't know *how* he lost
> The confidence of King.'"

It had been remarked " that the demeanour of Earl Grey and the Chancellor towards each other, at the late dinner at Edinburgh, was of such a kind as warranted the conclusion that no very cordial feeling existed between them."

CHAPTER XVII

But, after these imaginary triumphs, ruin and downfall were at hand; and who would have supposed, before a year was out, that this man was to be on the verge of losing his reason from mortification; that from that hour, to the end of an unusually long life, he was destined never to know the sweets of office again, and to be tabooed and ostracised by all Governments. So sudden a political judgment has rarely overtaken a man of his position, and could only be matched by the ruin which overtook a Chancellor of our own times, whose bearing was more arrogant.

In November there died an old and respected nobleman, long retired from public life; and here again an apparently trifling incident was productive, beyond precedent, of the most momentous results. Unconnected with politics and government, his death instantly overthrew the Ministry. This was Earl Spencer, father of Lord Althorp, who had to leave the Lower House, and seized on the opportunity to retire from politics. In any case a more serious difficulty was the filling of his place in the House of Commons. It was recollected with what difficulty he had been induced to join the Government, and the anxiety of the Cabinet was shown in a letter addressed to him only the day after his father's death, when Lord Melbourne almost implored him to do nothing hastily :

"I have not forgotten your letter to me, when the recent Government was formed, with respect to your conduct in case of that event occurring which has now taken place. I say nothing at present except that I trust that you will not come to any hasty, unalterable determination ; particularly in the frame of mind which is produced by such scenes as those which you have been recently contemplating. I hope also that you will not suffer yourself to be influenced by any indiscreet communications which you may receive from any other quarter. I do not know of any such, but I think them not improbable.

"Believe me,
"My dear Althorp."

All that follows forms one of the dramatic scenes in the rather dull programme of politics, and we shall now present a complete view of all the transactions of this curious episode.

The first step taken by Lord Melbourne, who is admitted to have acted indiscreetly, was to write to the King on November 12th. He reminded him that the Government had been mainly formed upon the personal weight and influence possessed by Lord Althorp, which was now lost to them. He himself would never abandon the King, but he entreated that no personal consideration for him would prevent His Majesty taking any measures that seemed good to him, or seeking other advice.* Such a piece of abnegation was exactly what

* The Duke of Wellington was given a copy of this private and confidential document—an odd proceeding—by the King, which was sent to Sir Robert Peel in Rome.

would be desired by a person of the King's disposition, who instead of treating it with magnanimity, accepted it literally as giving him liberty of action. In conclusion, he asked for a private interview at Brighton.

This took place on November 13th, and the King himself gives the following account of what took place between them (" Stockmar," i., 327.)

"Nothing material occurred until His Majesty received from Lord Melbourne an account of the critical state of the late Earl Spencer.

"The correspondence which ensued, until November 14th inclusive, is also in the hands of Sir Robert Peel, and will show Lord Melbourne's *immediate* apprehension of the difficulty and embarrassment under which the Government would be placed by the death of Earl Spencer, and the removal of Lord Althorp* to the House of Lords, as well as His Majesty's concurrence in the feeling so strongly expressed.

"The King's first conclusion was that Lord Melbourne (who had, as well as Lord Grey, attached, after the secession of Mr. Stanley, a paramount importance to Lord Althorp's services in the House of Commons) would resign, whenever the contemplated event should take place; but in the next letter, as far as His Majesty recollects (for he has not reserved any copies), Lord Melbourne stated a hope that Lord Althorp might be prevailed upon to continue in the Administration, although a member of the House of Lords, and His Majesty's answer did not give any opinion that this would facilitate the arrangement to be made. In fact, His Majesty did not contemplate the possibility of Lord Melbourne's submitting any that would prove satisfactory; and, when he intimated his

---

* Earl Spencer's son, who now became Earl Spencer.

intention of coming to Brighton, His Majesty had persuaded himself that he was coming to tender his resignation, and had made up his mind to accept it.

"Lord Melbourne came to the King on November 13th, and the conversation between them was free, unreserved, and dispassionate. The only arrangement which his lordship brought forward, as he stated, with the concurrent opinion and advice of all his colleagues and those most competent to suggest any opinion with respect to the feelings of the House of Commons, was that Lord John Russell should succeed Lord Althorp as leader. His Majesty objected strongly to Lord John Russell; he stated, without reserve, his opinion that he had not the abilities nor the influence which qualified him for the task, and observed that he would make a wretched figure when opposed by Sir Robert Peel and Mr. Stanley.

"Lord Melbourne thought the King laid more stress than was justifiable upon the necessity of being a good speaker, or ready debater; these being advantages which Lord Althorp did not possess, while he exercised an extraordinary influence in the House of Commons. He did not mean to say that Lord John Russell, or any other member of the Government, could in this respect effectually replace Lord Althorp, but he did not allow that there was any reason to apprehend that the business of the Government might not be carried on satisfactorily.

"The King objected equally, if not more, to Mr. Abercrombie,* whose name appeared to have been also suggested to Lord Melbourne, as had Sir John Hobhouse's, and Lord Melbourne did not seem to think

* Mr. Abercrombie was afterwards Speaker of the House of Commons. He was created Lord Dunfermline in 1839.

either eligible, any more than Mr. Spring Rice, whose name His Majesty stated he expected to have been proposed to him.

"Lord Melbourne therefore persisted in urging preferably the nomination of Lord John Russell. But His Majesty had further objections. He considered Lord John Russell to have pledged himself to certain encroachments upon the Church, which His Majesty had made up his mind, and expressed his determination to resist (and Lord Melbourne could not deny that he had done so, as had others of his colleagues, especially as to the results of the commission of inquiry into the state of the Irish Church) ; and His Majesty did not disguise his apprehension that, whenever that question should be brought forward, his opposition to the measure which might be suggested would produce 'a serious difference between him and his Government ; nor that this apprehension had been increased by communications from Lord Duncannon, who, before he went to Ireland and on his return, had, at two audiences, suggested the propriety of suspending the *non-cure* parishes,* and had increased His Majesty's alarm with respect to the projected encroachment and constitution of the Established Church.

"Nor did His Majesty conceal from Lord Melbourne that the injudicious and extravagant conduct of Lord Brougham had tended to shake his confidence in the course which might be pursued by the administration, of which he formed so prominent and so active a feature, and in its consistency.

"Lord Melbourne did not appear surprised that the King should have a strong feeling with respect to the measures which might be proposed, as arising out of

---

* There were, in Ireland, benefices without any cure of souls.

the pledges of Lord John Russell and some of his colleagues; but observed that, with respect to those measures, or the results of the commission of inquiry, His Majesty had not pledged himself, and therefore would be at full liberty to refuse his assent to any measure submitted to him. He added that he (Lord Melbourne) had not pledged or committed himself. His lordship admitted indeed that one or two of his colleagues had a strong feeling upon the Church question, which might induce them to go to the full length of His Majesty's objection; and His Majesty thinks that he named Lord Lansdowne and Mr. Spring Rice, and that he stated that the introduction of the measures supposed to be contemplated by Lord John Russell and some of his colleagues would probably occasion their resignation. But His Majesty may very possibly have misunderstood him. Be this as it may, Lord Lansdowne had very distinctly stated to the King, at the period of the secession of Mr. Stanley and of those who retired with him, that he concurred most decidedly in their feelings on the Church question; and that the earnest solicitation of Lord Grey and his declaration that he would resign if Lord Lansdowne withdrew himself, had alone induced him to continue a member of the Administration.

"But Lord Melbourne did not upon this occasion state, nor had he at any former period stated to the King, that differences of opinion prevailed in the Cabinet which might produce its dissolution before the meeting of Parliament, or when measures might be proposed upon which they should not agree; nor did he express any doubt of his ability to carry on the Government, with the aid of those who had been admitted or might be admitted to His Majesty's councils.

"It was observed to Lord Melbourne that His

Majesty had always been told by Lord Grey that the removal of Lord Althorp from the House of Commons after the loss of Mr. Stanley would be, of itself, a sufficient reason for breaking up his Administration; and that Lord Melbourne had laid the same stress upon the retention of Lord Althorp's services in the House of Commons, when he succeeded Lord Grey. The opinion of the supporters of the Government to the same effect had been unequivocally manifested by their address to Lord Althorp. His Majesty, therefore, was not prepared for the removal of those difficulties; and the impression on his mind, produced partly by these previous circumstances and partly by his own view of the resources of the Government in the House of Commons, was, that they could not carry on the business satisfactorily; and, at any rate, that to carry it on they must count and depend upon the support of those whose views, especially with respect to the Church, were at variance with the King's, and must eventually, and probably soon after Parliament met, lead to a serious difference.

"That His Majesty had the highest confidence in Lord Melbourne and in some of his colleagues, and that he believed them to be *Conservative* in principle and purpose—opposed to the designs which he deprecated; but that he had not the same confidence in others of his colleagues—he dreaded their principles; and under these circumstances he could not but apprehend putting off the evil day, especially as he felt that any accession of strength must be sought in the ranks of those who would urge and advocate *extreme* measures, and would therefore hasten rather than avert the crisis.

"The question was not brought to issue on the 13th, and it was agreed that His Majesty should give his full consideration to what Lord Melbourne had submitted and should see him again on the following morning.

"The King was sensible of the frank and unreserved manner in which Lord Melbourne had discussed the whole subject, and had replied to the various questions he had put to him ; but his lordship had failed in convincing him that any arrangement could be made which would enable him to carry on the Government satisfactorily, or which could prevent the early dissolution of the Administration at a period more inconvenient than the present, and more pregnant with exciting causes."

At the conclusion of this conversation, the King said cheerily, "Now, let us go to dinner;" and according to current accounts, a pleasant evening followed, during which, it was rather maliciously said, the Premier fancied that his agreeable social powers had exerted a useful influence on the King. But next morning there was a disagreeable surprise in store for him. His Majesty thus relates what took place :

"Under these circumstances, and considering also that if he delayed coming to a decision the opportunity of dissolving the Parliament during its prorogation (if it should be deemed advisable) would be lost, His Majesty at once made up his mind to communicate to Lord Melbourne, on the following morning, his regret that circumstances did not, in his opinion, justify his sanctioning the arrangement he had proposed, or the continued existence of an Administration so situated ; and this intimation was reduced to writing to prevent any misconception, and in order that His Majesty might relieve himself from the embarrassment of the verbal opening of a painful communication.

"The King saw Lord Melbourne again on the following morning (November 14), and gave him the note, which it is unnecessary to transcribe here, as Sir Robert Peel possesses a copy of it.

" Lord Melbourne, in the handsomest manner, and from feelings of devotion and attachment to which His Majesty is anxious to do the fullest justice, suggested a partial alteration, which, without changing the general sense, divested this communication of all that could give offence to any individual; and it will appear that the declared and ostensible ground of His Majesty's decision was his conviction that the general weight and consideration of the Government had been so much diminished in the House of Commons, and with the country at large, as to render it impossible that they should continue to conduct the public affairs with advantage."*

Lord Melbourne, who was later to be accused of having devised the ejection of his party from office, was reduced to some ingenious special pleading to give a fitting turn to his advice to the King. His correspondence with the King on the subject was not made public, though it was shown to several persons, and it seems to support unpopular views. In his letter of November 12,† he reminds His Majesty that the Government was mainly founded upon the personal weight and influence possessed by Earl Spencer. He (Lord Melbourne) was ready to go on, and " will never

---

* The version of the story in circulation was that, during the dinner, His Majesty had shown much good-humour and marks of favour to the Minister, who had been thus led to form the happiest auguries; when, on rising from the table, His Majesty said : "By the way, as to the Government, can't go on. You are all out, and here is a letter to the Duke of Wellington, which I will get you to deliver." Virtually, indeed, something of the kind occurred.

In the " Peel Memoirs."

abandon His Majesty, but entreats that no personal consideration for him will prevent His Majesty from taking any necessary steps for seeking any other advice.

"The King, after the very confidential conversation with Lord Melbourne on the state of the country, in consequence of the removal of Viscount Althorp to the House of Peers, and in therefore becoming Earl Spencer, thinks it right to inform Lord Melbourne that His Majesty conceives that the general weight and condition of the present Government is so much diminished in the House of Commons, and with the country at large, as to render it impossible that they should continue to conduct the public affairs in the Commons, particularly when it is considered that the King's confidential servants cannot derive any support from the House of Lords, which can balance the wand of success in the Commons. His Majesty, therefore, under this view and the appreciation of the eulogiums, which the King has expressed to Lord Melbourne verbally, does not think it would be acting fairly or honourably by his lordship to call upon the Viscount for the continuance of his services in a position of which the tenure appears to the King so precarious. His Majesty need hardly repeat the assurance, so often conveyed to Lord Melbourne, of the high sense the King entertains of his lordship's valuable services and character.

"WILLIAM R.

"Pavilion, Brighton, November 14th, 1834."

It will be seen that Lord Althorp's adhesion would have made no difference in deciding the question. Mr. M'Cullagh Torrens relates what next occurred:

" As he passed through the adjoining room he could
not refrain from saying to Sir Herbert Taylor, by whose
aid he knew that the written form of his dismissal had
been prepared, ' Your old master would not have done
this.' The private secretary was embarrassed, as he well
might be, what to reply; and in his confusion said he
had just concluded a letter to Sir Henry Wheatley,
which his master thought it of the utmost importance
to have delivered that night. Would his lordship object
to allowing his servant, on reaching town, to leave it at
St. James's Palace? It was impossible not to divine
that the missive which the perplexed amanuensis had
just sealed contained a summons to the Duke. The
ludicrous aspect of the affair was irresistible; and
Melbourne, with a grim smile, undertook to play the
part of first mute at his own funeral."

This letter, which is only found in the Duke of
Buckingham's papers, is the one alluded to by Mr.
Greville as a sort of explanatory circular addressed by
the Duke to certain Tory Peers. He assured Mr.
Greville " that he had papers and letters in confirmation
of every word of it, viz. minutes of Lord Melbourne's
conversation with the King," etc. That we may have
all *pièces justificatives* before us, I subjoin this account
also :

" Lord Melbourne had written to the King and
descanted on the great difficulty in which the Government was placed in consequence of Lord Spencer's
death, and had intimated that the measures which he
should find it necessary to propose to him would produce a difference of opinion in the Cabinet—in point of
fact that it was, to say the least, probable that Rice and
Lansdowne would retire. When he went down to
Brighton, and they talked it over, Lord Melbourne put

it to His Majesty whether, under existing circumstances, he would go on, placing himself in their hands, or whether he would dispense with their services, only recommending that if he resolved not to endeavour to go on with this Government (with such modifications as circumstances demanded) he would declare such resolution as speedily as possible. The Duke says he did not actually tender his or their resignations, did not throw up the Government, but *very near it*. The King suggested the difficulty of his situation, and Melbourne told him 'he had better send for the Duke of Wellington, and depend upon it he would get him out of it.' 'In fact,' said the Duke, 'Melbourne told him I should do just what I did.' Accordingly the King did send for the Duke, and it is true that Melbourne offered to be the bearer of His Majesty's letter. When some question was asked about the messenger, Melbourne said: 'No messenger will go so quick as I shall; you had better give it to me.' The Duke said that no man could have acted more like a gentleman and a man of honour than Melbourne did, and that his opinion of him was greatly raised."*

* Mr. Henry Reeve, commenting on this statement, says the portion referring to Lord Melbourne requesting the King "to place himself in the hands of his ministers, or dispense with their services," etc., has certainly not been confirmed by the subsequent publication of papers, or by the narrative of the King himself. It is very extraordinary that the Duke of Wellington should have been led to believe it; but this is only another proof of the extreme difficulty of arriving at an exact knowledge of what passes in conversation between two persons, even when both of them are acting in perfect good faith. But it is evident Lord Melbourne put the matter so delicately, and with such fine shadings of expression, as to escape the ruder comprehension of the King. It was natural that he should assume that Lord Melbourne's liberal mode of putting the situation should be equivalent to a resignation.

There is yet another account—the King's—given to Lord Canterbury, then Mr. Manners Sutton, and by him to Mr. Raikes :

"Lord Canterbury gave me a long account at dinner of the communications which he had with the King, as Speaker in 1834, on the subject of the conflagration of the Houses of Parliament, which were afterwards maliciously interpreted by the other party into secret machinations to effect the overthrow of the Whig Cabinet, which took place shortly afterwards. The King then said: 'Such being the case, my lord, how far do you feel competent to carry on the trust confided to you?' Melbourne's reply was far from confident. 'They must see how matters would turn; they must try their strength; and, if the case became desperate, there would be no other alternative but a resignation.' The King then said: 'If you yourself look upon the prospect as so doubtful, would it not be better at once to make up your mind, and break up the Government? Melbourne, who at the time really felt anxious for retirement, from a sense of his own incompetence without the aid of Althorp in the Commons, readily assented to the proposal. Upon which the King observed, that he really was unprepared for this crisis, and hardly knew himself to whom he should apply to form a new Administration. Lord Melbourne then without any hesitation remarked, that there was one individual whose services he doubted not would be at the command of His Majesty, and that was the Duke of Wellington. 'Do you then approve,' said the King, 'of my writing to him?' Melbourne replied in the affirmative; and moreover added, 'As I shall probably travel to London quicker than any ordinary messenger, I will myself take charge of the letter.'"

Anyone that considers the whole transaction apart from the various pretexts used, etc., will see that it was the dread of the Cabinet becoming more advanced and radical, owing to the introduction of Lord John Russell, that caused the King to take the step he did.[*]

Returning to town Lord Melbourne met Lord Palmerston at Downing Street, where later the Chancellor, coming from Holland House, called in to learn that all was right. To his consternation he was informed, under seal of secrecy until the Cabinet appointed for the morrow had met, of all that had occurred. Next morning everyone read in *The Times*:

" We have no authority for the important statement which follows, but we have every reason to believe that it is perfectly true. We give it, without any comment or explanation, in the very words of the communication which reached us at a late hour last night : ' The King has taken the opportunity of Lord Spencer's death to turn out the Ministry, and there is every reason to believe the Duke of Wellington has been sent for. The Queen has done it all." [†]

---

[*] This was the Duke of Wellington's view, as reported by Mr. Greville: " He says that it is evident that Melbourne despaired of being able to carry on the Government, and that the gist of the King's objection was the nomination of Lord John Russell to lead the Government in the House of Commons, which His Majesty said he could not agree to, because he had already declared his sentiments with regard to the Church, and his resoultion of supporting it, to the bishops, and on other occasions; and that Lord John Russell had signalised himself in the House of Commons by his destructive opinions with regard to the Establishment."

[†] Mr. McCullagh Torrens states that Lord Brougham " communicated the startling intelligence to *The Times*," but this seems unlikely when we consider the gross attack made on him a day or two later by that journal, and its declaration that it had " no authority " for the statement.

This charge against the Queen was, in this instance at least, unjust. It was shown, as Lord Campbell states, that she knew nothing of the matter till the day after Lord Melbourne had been dismissed. It will have been seen that the King was but following his own inclinations and convictions, and that he was only carrying out what he had been obliged to postpone at the formation of the last Government.

The luckless ministers, from feeling that their position was a mistifying one, were inclined to think that the Premier had played his cards badly. And no doubt some of the daring shown by Lord Brougham on the last occasion might have had effect on this. He had been too amiable and had not asserted the constitutional right due to the situation. The Chancellor's (Lord Brougham) letter was characteristic.

"Saturday.

"MY DEAR ALTHORP,

"What you and I thought, and all men of sound minds thought, quite impossible, is come to pass, and because—and only because—you are removed from the House of Commons, the King *turns us all out!*—a thing never before done—and without waiting for the House of Commons to express its distust in John Russell or in us. So that Wellington has not now to come in because we have broken up and left the country without a Government, but he comes in because he expects the House of Commons and the country prefer the Tories to us ! It seems incredible, but he will be goaded on by his hungry creatures to try this desperate experiment, which means two dissolutions if it fails, and a Radical Government.

"*Your* case is now clear ; but you will violate every

duty to your friends and the country if you think of anything like withdrawing from politics. *Your duty* is to stand by the country, and your retiring would enable the Tories to misgovern us again, much more than all else.

"I have written to the King to throw all the consequences on him and relieve myself.

"Yours ever,

"H. B."

The Times laid all the disgrace to his account.

"There could not, indeed," said *The Times*, "be a more revolting spectacle than for the highest law officer of the empire to be travelling about like a quack doctor through the provinces, puffing himself and his little nostrums, and committing and degrading the Government of which he had the honour to be a member. His Majesty could not but be indignant at such conduct. And it is a fact, notwithstanding all the fulsome adulation heaped on his ' gracious master ' at Inverness, Aberdeen, Edinburgh, and elsewhere, that the peripatetic keeper of the King's conscience has not once been admitted since his return from his travels to the honour of an interview with royalty, either at Windsor or Brighton."

Again :

" It is in general admitted that the downfall of the Government is referable in a great measure to the unbecoming conduct of Lord Brougham as Chancellor."

He was indeed in such a fury at his fall, and by various speeches of the King which were reported to him (" he never wished to see his ugly face again "), that he is said to have sent back the Great Seal in a bag by a messenger !

CHAPTER XVIII.

MEANWHILE the Duke of Wellington had left his country seat and hurried to Brighton on the afternoon of the 15th. "The King," says Mr. Torrens, who enjoyed the advantage of many conversations with the old Lord Lansdowne on the subject, " told him no one had as yet been made aware of what he had done the previous day ; and it is said that when the names of the guests who were to dine that evening were presented by the lord-in-waiting to Queen Adelaide, she expressed surprise that the list included his Grace, of whose arrival she was not aware. He represented at the outset the impossibility of any Tory combination which would afford the prospect of carrying on the Government unless Sir Robert Peel was at its head ; and the Liberal majority in the Commons being two to one, he did not see how even with that advantage success could attend the experiment. For his own part he was willing to occupy any position that might be considered expedient, but he was endeavouring to dissuade His Majesty from proceeding further in a change of hands so unprepared, when Sir Herbert Taylor entered the room, and apologised for calling his royal master's attention to the paragraph in *The Times* that morning, which stated that ' the Queen had done it all.' The anger which these long-remembered words excited may be readily conceived. 'There, Duke, you see how I am insulted and betrayed; nobody in London but Melbourne knew last night what had taken place here, nor of my sending for you; will your Grace compel me to take back people who have treated me in this way?'"

The Duke on this agreed to take office. The King, after some discussion, asked him to form a Government; but he replied that he should choose a minister in the House of Commons. His Majesty answered that he would not have hesitated to do so had Peel been in England; but that as he was abroad, and it was necessary to act immediately, he had sent for him. The Duke then agreed to assume temporarily the office of the absent Premier.

But a confidential letter of the Duke of Wellington's, addressed to a friend, gives a full, clear, and authentic account of the King's behaviour in this transaction :

THE DUKE OF WELLINGTON TO THE DUKE OF BUCKINGHAM.

"London, Nov. 21, 1834.

"MY DEAR DUKE,

"I am anxious that you should have a knowledge of the circumstances which have led to the late changes in H.M.'s Government, of its present state, and of the part which I have taken in what has occurred.

"The death of the late Earl Spencer, which removed Lord Althorp from the House of Commons, from the management of the Government business in that assembly, and from the office of Chancellor of the Exchequer, occasioned the greatest difficulty and embarrassment. His personal influence and weight in the House of Commons was the main foundation of the strength of the late Government, and upon his removal it was necessary for the King and his Ministers to consider whether fresh arrangements should be made, to enable H.M.'s late servants to conduct the affairs of the country, or whether it was advisable for his Majesty to adopt any other course.

"The arrangements in contemplation must have had reference, not only to men, but to measures. The King felt the strongest objections to some of the latter, of the details of which H.M. had been informed by conversation with his Ministers, particularly to some relating to the Church of England in Ireland.

"H.M. had besides had reason to believe that he did not object more strongly to the measures in contemplation, than [to] certain of the noblemen and gentlemen composing the Cabinet. He had reason to expect, therefore, that the measures proposed, which were to enable his Ministers to conduct his affairs, would have had the effect of inducing those members of the Government to retire, probably at a more critical moment than exists at present.

"The King might likewise have been exposed to the necessity of taking into his councils men to whom neither H.M. nor the public could give their confidence. Under these circumstances, the King thought proper to send for me, and to desire me to form a Government for him.

"I pointed out to H.M. the great difficulties of the task, particularly in the House of Commons, resulting from the late changes, and I earnestly recommended that H.M. should choose a Minister in the House of Commons, and that Sir Robert Peel should be the person.

"The King would have adopted that course if Sir Robert Peel had been in England, but H.M. said that as he was absent, and it was necessary to act immediately, he had sent for me.

" I submitted to H.M. that I was ready to do anything for his service ; that it was unreasonable to expect that Sir Robert Peel would undertake to conduct the measures of an Administration, of which the arrangements should have been formed by another person ; and that such a course would be equally injurious to Sir Robert and to H.M's service ; that, under these circumstances, I recommended to H.M. that he should appoint me First Lord of the Treasury, and Secretary of State for the Home Department, which offices I would hold till Sir Robert Peel should return home, when he might submit to H.M. such arrangements as he might think proper ; that Lord Lyndhurst might hold the Great Seal temporarily, by commission or otherwise, as might be expedient ; and that no other arrangement should be made not absolutely necessary for the conduct of the public business.

" H.M. was pleased to attend to my recommendation. Sir Robert Peel has been sent for, and may be expected in the end of the first week of December, and at that period, I conclude that he will form the arrangements necessary for the conduct of the affairs of the country.
" Believe me, etc."

A letter written from Berlin, by the Duke of Cumberland, who, whatever were his other defects, was an ardent partisan, is not without interest.

" One *thing*," he writes, " is perfectly clear, that if the Conservatives were surprised at the breaking up of the late Government, *they* themselves were *not less* so ; and, in fact, on the 14th they felt certain that H.M. would sanction the proposal which Lord M. had gone down to Brighton to propose, namely, that Lord John Russell was to succeed Lord Althorp as the Chancellor of the Exchequer, and consequently leader of the House of Commons; for precaution's sake, however, *two* other names were carried down, which, I believe, were Spring Rice—whether Mr. Littleton or Abercrombie was the third, I cannot precisely make out.

"Upon this, H.M. is said to have inquired into the state of the parties in the Cabinet, and as to *what* proposals they meant to lay before Parliament respecting the Irish Church and the corporate bodies; the reply was of a nature that alarmed him, and he instantly resolved to get rid of such dangerous Ministers.

"The appearance of the D. of W. at the Pavilion was a complete surprise to all the inmates, as not a living soul there had had the slightest idea of *his* having been sent for."

The Duke of Wellington mentioned also that Lord Brougham was in such a state of excitement that he refused to put the Great Seal to the commission for proroguing Parliament; and when the old ministers were sent for to give up their seals, it was noticed that "they were sulky enough." "The King," the Duke adds, "had expected it, and had desired me to have Members of Council in attendance, in readiness. They were called in that night to be sworn." To such a height had passions been inflamed.

The next thing was to recall Sir Robert—known to be in Italy—who had left England, he tells us, on October 14th, with Lady Peel and his daughter Julia, afterwards Lady Villiers, having had no communication with the Duke of Wellington, or others, as to the prospects of the party, and no concert with the King.

Letters were prepared, and a messenger was sent off post-haste, all which curiously recalls the crisis, King George III.'s illness, when emissaries were despatched in pursuit of Fox, also travelling in Italy.

" Hudson, then," says Mr. Torrens, in an interesting passage, "a young man, having been one of the royal pages, and afterwards assistant to Sir Herbert Taylor, for whom he always entertained sincere regard for the priceless services rendered to the King, in 1831 and 1832. When the Whig Ministry were dismissed, Sir H. Taylor asked Hudson if he would like to go abroad. He said ' Yes.' ' Then you must start to-morrow morning in search of Sir R. Peel, and take him a letter from the King, and one from the Duke of Wellington.' He came to town to make inquiries about Peel, but could find no direction at his house. It was Sunday evening, and he had no money for his journey. He went to the Keeper of the Privy Purse, who told him he had nothing like £500, which Hudson said would be necessary; but through an old clerk at Herries' Bank he got that sum, and set off for Paris. The news had preceded him, and he could get no information from Lord Granville, or anyone at the Embassy, as to the whereabouts of Sir Robert. It was supposed he was still in Italy, but that was all. By dint of driving hard and paying freely, he got to Rome on the ninth day, which was considered then great speed. On reaching Peel's hotel, he found that he was at a ball at Torlonia's. He left the letter with Lady Peel, and returned for the answer later. When he was shown in, Sir Robert stood behind a large table covered with papers, bowed formally, asked what day he had left England, and what hour he had reached Rome ; and then observed drily : ' I think you might have made the journey in a day less, by taking another route.' Hudson bit his lip with chagrin at this ungracious reception, but, taking the despatches in reply, set out forthwith for England. At Paris he was very differently received ; but, hurrying on to Boulogne, he had the vexation to see the mail packet steaming out of the harbour. Some fishermen undertook, for a large sum, to take him across in a small boat. The weather was fine; but when close to Dover a panic seized them; they said they would be taken prisoners if they ventured to land in England, and no expostulations or bribes could induce them to proceed. Luckily, Hudson was enabled to make signals to a vessel in the offing, which took him on board and landed him at Dover. On reaching London he went straight to Apsley House and left his letter for the Duke, who immediately forwarded its contents to Windsor. The messenger was so tired that he went to his rooms at St. James's and was soon asleep. The first person of the household whom he saw told him he had got into a devil of a scrape by omitting to present the letter for the King on the previous night. He hastened to do so; and on entering the anteroom met an old servant, who said to him, ' I did not think you were so green as to *come* with the letter, after making the mistake you have done.' He took the hint, and leaving Sir Robert's reply, made his way back to town. For nearly a month he did not venture to present himself to His Majesty, who was highly displeased with him. But he was then advised to wait upon the King, and after some manifestations of ill-humour he was forgiven, and told he might keep the balance of £70 he had unspent out of the £500 he started with. And this was the upshot of his first journey to Italy in the affairs of which he was destined in later life to play so conspicuous a part."

This was the "hurried Hudson" so pleasantly described by Mr. Disraeli, no doubt adopting Canning's playful alliteration of, " the revered and ruptured Ogden." He, later, became the better known Sir James Hudson, Minister to Italy.

CHAPTER XIX.

"On Tuesday, November 25th," says Sir Robert Peel, "I was returning from a ball at the Duchess of Torlonia's when a letter was given to me at the Hôtel de l'Europe. I was about to leave for Naples on the next day, or the day after."

He sat down at once and wrote his answer to the letters received. These ran as follows :

SIR H. TAYLOR TO SIR ROBERT PEEL.

"Brighton, Nov. 15.

" My dear Sir Robert,

"The King has ordered me to introduce to you Mr. Hudson, who is the bearer of His Majesty's and the Duke of Wellington's letters to you. He is resident Gentleman Usher to the Queen, and has always been employed confidentially by the King, who has the highest opinion of him, which he well merits. I may add that he is deservedly a general favourite in this circle."

THE KING TO SIR R. PEEL.

" Pavilion, Brighton, Nov. 15.

"The King having had a most satisfactory and confidential conversation with the Duke of Wellington, on the formation of a new Government, calls on Sir

Robert Peel to return without loss of time to England, and put himself at the head of the Administration of the country.

"In the meantime, His Majesty has appointed the Duke of Wellington First Lord of the Treasury and Secretary for the Home Department, in order to hold the Government till the return of Sir Robert Peel. It will likewise be necessary to put the Great Seal in commission, and the King has named Lord Lyndhurst the First Commissioner.   " WILLIAM R."

Sir Robert's answer, written at eleven P.M., was simply to the effect that he would "proceed on his journey to England without a moment's delay." "By dint of considerable exertion" they got ready and started at three o'clock the next day. Travelling almost night and day (that is, for eight nights out of the twelve), they reached Dover on the evening of December 8, and arrived in London on the next day.

Other letters from the Duke reached him later, one of which contained this curious reflection : "You will observe that the King's case is not quite one of his ministers quitting him. I think that it might have been such an one, if His Majesty had not been so ready to seize upon the first notion of difficulties resulting from Lord Spencer's death. Lord —— swears that they are turned out. . . . All delighted—particularly Melbourne—to be released."

SIR ROBERT PEEL TO MR. CROKER.

" MY DEAR CROKER,   " Whitehall, December 9, 1834.

"Though I have only been one night in bed since I left Lyons, and have found anything but repose since my arrival here this morning, I must write you one line, to certify to you for myself, that I am here. Lady Peel and Julia travelled with me as far as Dover; travelling by night over precipices and snow eight nights out of twelve. I shall be very glad to see you. It will be a relief to me from the harassing cares that await me.

"Ever affectionately yours,

"ROBERT PEEL."

Such was this extraordinary and almost unprecedented change; perhaps one of the most unconstitutional and high-handed ever attempted by an English sovereign. A ministry, having a majority, was dismissed, solely because it was distasteful to the King; the pretext being, that a member of it —not the Premier—had been removed from the House of Commons. The King later defended himself in this fashion : *

"His Majesty might possibly have brought Lord Melbourne and his colleagues into greater difficulty, by subjecting the appointment of Lord John Russell to a declaration of his views and intentions, to which the unanimous assent of his colleagues should be attached ; or he might have made his disapprobation of the course pursued by Lord Brougham the chief ground of his objection, and have required from Lord Melbourne that he should be removed from his councils. But His Majesty had no desire to place Lord Melbourne in difficulty, or to embarrass him by the nature of his proceedings. He preferred to meet him on the frank and honest terms on which his lordship had ever shown his disposition to deal with His Majesty ; and he is satisfied that he has adopted on this occasion the plain and simple course which

* " Stockmar," *ante.*

becomes him, and which best entitles him to the confidence of his subjects in general, and now particularly
to the confidence of those * who have so handsomely
and kindly met his recent appeal to their valuable
support and services. He flatters himself that he has
established another, not immaterial, claim to their confidence, in the absence of all attempt, during every
period of the preceding Administrations, at communications with them, direct or indirect, which could afford
the slightest cause of jealousy or suspicion to those
who formed those Administrations, notwithstanding
the serious difficulty and doubt in which His Majesty
was at times placed ; and his present Ministers are well
aware that this reserve was maintained to the very
last moment, and that when he came to the final
determination, on November 14, there had been no
communication *of any sort* from which he could learn
their sentiments, or their means of relieving him from
the difficulty in which he had felt it his duty to place
himself.

"The King does not, indeed, deny that, while taking
this step, he entertained sanguine expectations, amounting
almost to conviction, that he would find in those of
a kindred feeling, the aid and support which he felt
to be so essential and important towards enabling him
to *hold his own,* to uphold the ancient and sacred institutions of the country ; and experience the co-operation
and support of those who had shown and declared
that they felt, as His Majesty did, that it had become
imperiously necessary to endeavour to stem the torrent of encroachment, and to prevent useful and
judicious reforms from being converted into engines
of destruction.

* The Tories.

"But it must be obvious from all that has passed, and from His Majesty's statement of it, that the decision to which he came and the judgment which produced it were caused more by the circumstances under his *immediate* consideration, and by the dread of danger and embarrassment which might result from indecision and delay, than by any calculation of the nature and extent of the support he might obtain ; and therefore that they could not be biassed, either by the unreasonable expectation of unquestionable success, or by dread of ultimate failure and disappointment.

"His Majesty did not, in taking his resolution, place out of view the possibility of an arduous struggle, nor did he commit himself without having made up his mind firmly to persevere in a course, adopted on what he considers firm principle, and suggested by a deep sense of sacred and moral obligations. His Majesty trusts that, with the help of God, he shall be able steadily to pursue that course to a successful issue, without endangering the existence of the monarchy or the peace of the country."

Lord Palmerston, in a memorandum, dated November 15th, 1834, after giving much the same account of Lord Melbourne's interview with the King, thus admirably analyzes the situation, and forecasts the results :

"The Government, therefore, have not resigned, but are dismissed ; and they are dismissed not in consequence of having proposed any measure of which the King disapproved, and which they nevertheless would not give up, but because it is thought they are not strong enough in the Commons to carry on the business of the country, and their places are to be filled by men who are notoriously weak and unpopular in the Lower House, however strong they may be in the Upper one.

"*It is impossible not to conclude that this is a pre-concerted measure*, and therefore it may be taken for granted that the Duke of Wellington is prepared at once to undertake the task of forming a Government. Peel is abroad, but it is not likely that he should have gone, without a previous understanding, one way or the other, with the Duke, as to what he would do, if such a crisis were to arise.

"I lament this event, because I can see nothing but mischief arising out of it; and all merely to gratify the ambition of the Duke of Wellington, and the prejudices or sordid feelings of his followers. Either Parliament will be dissolved or it will not. If not, the Opposition will be most virulent and powerful, and the Government will soon be beaten; and, in the meantime, Whigs and Radicals will be jumbled together, and the former will be led on by party passion to identify themselves too much with the latter. Besides, a dissolution will be always considered as hanging over our heads, and men will be making violent speeches and giving extravagant pledges to curry favour with their constituents with a view to the next election. If, on the other hand, an immediate dissolution takes place, there will be no limit to the fury of opposite factions. The Tories may win fifty or sixty votes, which will still leave them in a minority; and the majority will consist of men who have pledged themselves on the hustings, chin-deep, for triennial Parliaments, ballot, and universal suffrage; and a fine state we shall then be in, with a House of Commons that will follow no Ministers who will not propose measures of this extravagant kind."

That the policy was as short-sighted as it was high-handed, was proved by the short, temporary reign of the new ministry, called that of "the hundred days."

Any one who studies the history of the Opposition during the preceding ministry must see that there was sufficient and certain grounds of failure there indicated, and which made ministerial success hopeless. There were then as now "opportunists"—wise folk who saw with truth, that a Tory ministry could not *stand*, and that a wiser policy would be to control the existing ministry. The fact of Peel, after all his cautious reticence in opposition, and hesitation in joining the Duke, being betrayed into taking up this perilous and short-lived term of office, is a significant comment on the policy of those whom Archbishop Whateley has styled "rashly cautious men."

Mr. Greville, as usual, gives a lively sketch of the rival ministries—incoming and outgoing—meeting at the Council:

"It was amusing to watch them as they passed through the camp of their enemies, and to see their different greetings and bows; all interchanged some slight civility except Brougham, who stalked through looking as black as thunder and took no notice of anybody. Then the Duke, and all the Privy Councillors were summoned. After greeting them all, and desiring them to sit down, His Majesty began a speech nearly as follows: 'Having thought proper to make a change in my Government, at the present moment I have directed a new commission to be issued for executing the office of Lord High Treasurer, at the head of which I have placed the Duke of Wellington, and his Grace has kissed hands accordingly upon that appointment. As by the Constitution of this country the King can do no wrong, but those persons are responsible for his acts in whom he places his confidence—as I do in the lords now present—it is necessary to place the Seals of the Secretary of State for the Home Department in those hands in which I can best confide, and I have therefore thought proper to confer that office likewise on his Grace, who will be sworn in accordingly.' Here the Duke came round, and, after much fumbling for his spectacles, took the oath of Secretary of State. The King then resumed : ' It is likewise necessary for me to dispose of the Seals of the other two Secretaries of State, and I therefore place them likewise for the present in the same hands, as he is already First Lord of the Treasury and Secretary of State for the Home Office.' "

" An amusing story was circulated that the King had written to the Duke about something—no matter what, but I believe some appointment—and added *à propos de bottes*, " His Majesty begs to call the attention of the Duke to the *theoretical* state of Persia." The Duke replied that he was aware of the importance of Persia, but submitted that it was a matter which did not *press* for the moment."

With a somewhat theatrical air the Duke of Wellington carried out his *rôle* of administering all the offices of State. Mr. Greville says it caused much " merriment " to see him thus roving about from the Home Office to the Treasury, asking to see the latest despatches. Complaint, however, was made of the unceremonious and somewhat uncourteous mode in which, without previous notice, he entered into the vacant offices, taking actual possession, without any of the usual preliminary civilities to the old occupants.

These things were significant. He told his friends that both he and the King were fully aware of the

importance of the step that his Majesty had taken—
that this was, in fact, the Conservatives' last cast—and
" —and that he (the King) is resolved neither to flinch
nor falter, but having embarked with them, to nail his
flag to the mast and put forth all the constitutional
authority of the Crown in support of the Government
he is about to form."

There was much truth in this, for the cast was
desperate, and suggests Marshal MacMahon's last at-
attempt. In fact it proved to be the last chance that
came to the *old* Tories.

"The Duke is bored to death with the King, who
thinks it necessary to be giving advice and opinions
upon different matters, always to the last degree ridiculous and absurd. He is just now mightily indignant
at Lord Napier's affair at Canton, and wants to go to
war with China. He writes in this strain to the Duke,
who is obliged to write long answers, very respectfully
telling him what an old fool he is. Another crotchet of
his is to buy the Island of St. Bartholomew (which
belongs to Denmark, and which the Danes want to sell)
for fear the Russians should buy it, as he is very jealous
of Russia. The Duke told him that it would cost
£70,000 or £80,000, for which they must go to Parliament. He thinks his present Ministers do not treat
him well, inasmuch as they do not tell him enough.
The last, it seems, constantly fed him with scraps of
information which he twaddled over, and probably
talked nonsense about; but it is difficult to imagine
anything more irksome for a Government beset with
difficulties like this, than to have to discuss the various
details of their measures with a silly bustling old fellow,
who can by no possibility comprehend the scope and
bearing of anything."

One of the most extraordinary Tory ideas of the new Government was that of gaining over *The Times*, by treaty. It will be recollected how, when the Tory Government was falling in 1830, it had contemplated subsidising the press; but the present step was more formal. The Duke and Lord Lyndhurst prepared a sort of memorandum of the terms, and Mr. Greville was employed as negotiator. Mr. Barnes held out for some time, but, at a dinner at Lord Lyndhurst's, the whole was ratified!

A pitiable instance of political miscalculation was speedily shown, by the answer of the constituencies to the dissolution. Parliament being dissolved, a new House was returned favourable to the Liberals. On the meeting of the House, the late Lord Carlisle, then Lord Morpeth, moved an amendment to the Address, to the effect that His Majesty's Commons could not but lament that the progress of Reform should have been interrupted and endangered, by the dissolution of a Parliament earnestly intent upon the vigorous prosecution of measures to which the wishes of the people were most anxiously and justly directed. This was actually carried in the new House by a majority of seven!

The King's answer reflected his personal feelings more truly than such things usually do:

"I thank you sincerely for the assurances which you have given me, in this loyal and dutiful address, of your disposition to co-operate with me in the improvement, with a view to the maintenance, of our institutions in Church and State. I learn with regret that you do not concur with me as to the policy of the appeal which I have recently made to the sense of my people. I never have exercised, and I never will exercise, any of the prerogatives which I hold, excepting for the single purpose of promoting the great end for which they are entrusted to me—the public good; and I confidently trust that no measure conducive to the general interests will be endangered or interrupted in its progress, by the opportunity which I have afforded to my faithful and loyal subjects of expressing their opinions through the choice of their representatives in Parliament."

After a significant defeat on the election of Speaker, on April 8th, the Government was defeated on a resolution referring to the Irish Church. To the King's mortification he found himself exactly where he was only a few months before, with the additional humiliation of having to ask the services of the men he had so unceremoniously dismissed. On the morning of April 9th, he sent for Lord Grey and, by his advice, summoned Lords Lansdowne and Melbourne, with whom he had a consultation. He was for his old Utopian plan of a union of moderate men from both sides. It was once more shown to him that the radical difference of principle rendered such impossible.

The year after the Reform Bill, the Duke of Wellington, who seems to have been sunk hopelessly in the most antiquated of Tory doctrines, enunciated this opinion in a letter to a friend:

"The truth is, that all government in this country is impossible under existing circumstances. I don't care whether it is called monarchy, oligarchy, aristocracy, democracy, or what they please, the Government of the country, the protection of the lives, privileges, and properties of its subjects, and the regulation of the thousand matters which require regulation in our advanced and artificial state of society, are impracticable as long as *such a deliberative assembly exists as the House of Commons, with all the powers and privileges which it has amassed in the course of the last two hundred years.*"

Lord Broughton explains the steps of the formation of the Melbourne Government. " On the day that Sir R. Peel resigned, viz., Wednesday, April 8th, the King did not send for any one ; but on the following day he merely consulted Lord Grey as to whom he should send for. He, the latter, recommended Lords Lansdowne and Melbourne. When they came with Lord Grey, on the Friday, the King did not make any proposals to them, but suggested a coalition, which they, in decided terms, said was wholly out of the question. On Saturday the King saw Lord Melbourne alone, and gave him a commission to form a Government. On consulting his friends, various difficulties were started. It was not until Sunday afternoon that he finally agreed and sent for Lord John Russell, who had been married only the day before, and found his honeymoon thus rudely interrupted. On the Monday His Majesty began, as usual, to make some difficulties about the household and the creation of Peers, but he gave way, and all went on smoothly. But on Wednesday came a letter of his, six pages long, about O'Connell and Hume, and, above all, about the spoliation of the Church, to which his Majesty protested he could not consent. Lord Melbourne had to write a very short and decisive answer, and immediately went to St. James's. He told His Majesty that " he would not submit to have anyone excluded, but there was no intention of employing either O'Connell or Hume." He also told the King he must do one of three things : First, act on the late resolution of the House of Commons with a new Cabinet ; Second, oppose the resolution, recall the old Cabinet, and go on with the present Parliament; Third, dissolve the Parliament. The King said it would be madness to dissolve now, and seemed satisfied." But, shortly after Lord Melbourne left the palace, there came another letter from him, full of scruples about the Coronation Oath, proposing that the judges should be consulted; this was strongly objected to, but, as usual, the King gave way. Next, and as a last. resource, he proposed that they should ask the advice of Lord Lyndhurst on the point; to which Lord Melbourne rather contemptuously replied that he would not do so, but that there was no objection to His Majesty doing so if he was inclined. The King did so, and Lord Lyndhurst declined to give any advice. All these *tracasseries*—the account of which is given at length by Lord Broughton in his diary—show that His Majesty was incurable, and that he still was led by every shifting influence of the *camarilla*. It will be noted how unceremonious the Whig ministers had grown, from the consciousness of their power, and the helplessness of their sovereign.

On Saturday, April 11th, he finally made up his mind to intrust the Government to Lord Melbourne, who, on the same evening, received from him the following letter :

THE KING TO VISCOUNT MELBOURNE.

" Gloucester House, April 11, 1835.

" The King returns approved, to the Viscount Melbourne, the letter he has this instant received at Gloucester House, signed by five of the Cabinet Ministers who formed the administration under Lord Grey.

" The King requests the Viscount to make known to

Lord Grey His Majesty's anxious wish to see the Earl
at the head of the Government, and to recall to the
recollection of Lord Grey the serious regret of His
Majesty at being deprived of the able services of the
Earl, and consequently the satisfaction the King must
feel at the return of the Earl to the head of His Majesty's
confidential servants.

"The King trusts to see Lord Grey to-morrow, to
repeat these sentiments to his Lordship, and to arrange
the Earl's acceptance of First Lordship of the Treasury.

"(Signed)   WM. R."

Now was to occur that dramatic incident—which had
almost a grim air of tragedy for the person concerned—
the proscription of Lord Brougham. The turbulent,
self-seeking, intriguing, vain man, was at last overtaken
by the most signal and mortifying chastisement. Neither
the King nor his late colleagues could endure the thought
of having him. "Although he would be dangerous as
an enemy," said Lord Melbourne, "he would be certain
destruction as a friend." But, now he was to be passed
over, who would even venture to tell him?

"Melbourne," says Mr. McCullagh Torrens, "with
characteristic pluck resolved to be the bearer of his
own message, and to take upon his own head the responsibility of the unexpected blow. Late in the
evening he called at Berkeley Square, and, in an interview which lasted more than two hours, sought to
mitigate the pain he was obliged to inflict, and to soothe
the irritation which he too well knew was likely to prove
dangerous. When he said he was not in a position to
offer the Great Seal to anybody, Brougham at a glance
divined what was coming, and said that had he come to
offer it to him he would not have accepted it. Equally

adroit, Melbourne rejoined that he was not at all surprised to hear him say so. It was for a time a contest of finesse, in which the ex-Chancellor strove to hide his mortification in profuse compassion for the crippled and helpless condition in which his friend would find himself at the head of a feeble Ministry ; while the new Premier appealed to the magnanimity of his ostracised colleague to maintain a dignified and generous attitude, which would enable him to effect much public good. Brougham was hard to be convinced that someone else was not about to have the Great Seal; but when assured that it was in contemplation to put it in commission for some time, he grew more tractable, and began to think that, after all, his interest was to be sacrificed only for a season to appease the ill-humour of the Court.* Before the end of the interview he was half disposed to forgive Melbourne for the sake of the enjoyment of patronising and protecting him, even as Pitt befriended Addington. So readily did this vanity strike root and grow, that during the rest of the session he was irrepressible in assiduous care of what he chose to call a Ministry of transition."

* Lord Campbell gives another account : " They told him that from his proceedings in Scotland during the last autumn having been misrepresented to the King, His Majesty had contracted a strong, although groundless, prejudice against him, which would gradually wear away—that, according to a French phrase, *si vous avez un Roi, il faut un peu le ménager*—you must not fly in his face ; if you insult him the people may take part with him against you. Therefore, to give a little time for things to run smooth, the Great Seal would be put in commission. When I was told of this, and that the Commissioners were to be Shadwell, the Vice-Chancellor, Pepys, the Master of the Rolls, and Bosanquet, a Common Law Judge, all of them having more business in their own courts than they could dispose of, I earnestly and honestly remonstrated, foreseeing that the plan could not possibly work well, and that the interests of justice would be sacrificed by it to party expedience. But Brougham was duped, and acquiesced."

This exclusion, says Mr. Hayward, in his article on
Lords Lyndhurst and Brougham, was put upon the
King; but there were other reasons. "More than one
act of treachery had been brought home to him. We
can vouch for one. When the jointure of Queen
Adelaide was discussed in Lord Grey's Cabinet, Mr.
Charles Grant stood alone in objecting that £100,000 a
year was too much. The day following, at a Court or a
Drawing-room reception of some sort, he perceived a
marked difference in the Queen's manner towards him.
When "the Queen had done it all" came out, Her
Majesty revealed the fact that the positive information
of what passed in the Cabinet touching her fortune had
reached her the same evening from the Lord Chancellor.
Our authority for this story is Lord Glenelg (then Mr.
C. Grant)."

"No means were used," says Lord Campbell, "to
break the intelligence to Brougham. He first learned
from the public newspapers that Sir Charles Pepys was
Chancellor under the title of Lord Cottenham. In
my opinion, Brougham was atrociously ill-used on this
occasion. Considering his distinguished reputation, considering what he had done for the Liberal cause, considering his relations with the Melbourne Government,
I incline to think that at every risk they ought to have
taken him back into the Cabinet, however difficult it
might have been to make conditions or stipulations with
him as to his future conduct and demeanour. But sure I
am that in the manner in which they finally threw him off
they showed disingenuousness, cowardice, and ingratitude.
I have myself heard him say, with tears in his eyes:
'If Melbourne had treated me openly and kindly, he
might have done what he liked with the Great Seal, and

we might have ever remained friends. The pretence about the King's dislike I found to be utterly false. William may have been angry at the moment, and perhaps justly, for things I had said and done; but in April, 1835, when he was obliged to dismiss his Tory Ministers, he did not care a button what individuals succeeded; and I was not a bit more disagreeable to him than Melbourne himself.' "

Thus beguiled, he lent an unofficial support to his friends, and looked forward confidently to the season which should bring the fulfilment of his wishes. But another blow was in store for this unfortunate man. Clamours began to arise as to the state of business in the Court of Chancery, which the Cabinet could not disregard. It was determined to appoint a Chancellor, and, on this occasion, without a word to Lord Brougham, the Solicitor-General, Pepys, was named.

It was not surprising that it was said his reason had given way. For more than forty years—the length to which his later life was almost prolonged—his restless soul had to comfort itself with the presidency of local associations and extra official speechings.

There were some other troubled and troubling spirits who were no less odious to His Majesty. One of these was the Earl of Durham, Lord Grey's son-in-law. He desired to be Foreign Secretary, but Lord Palmerston's claims were superior, and he was consoled with the embassy to St. Petersburgh. Another claim, no less embarrassing, was that of O'Connell, whom, it was rumoured, was to be Attorney-General for Ireland.

All this is remarkable, as being the last serious struggle, and last defeat, of an English sovereign in conflict with his Parliament. So mortifying, so painful was the incident in its consequences that the King may be said never to have recovered it, and showed by his dejection and pettish sallies how the iron had entered his soul.   He found comfort in drawing up a sort of vindication of himself in these awkward transactions, which we shall give in the next chapter.

CHAPTER XX.

THIS singular—or at least exceptional—step was taken by the King in 1835, when, no doubt stung by the hostile comments on his proceedings during the four years of his reign, he drew up a vindication of himself, which he placed in the hands of Sir Robert Peel. Portions of it have been already given ; the rest is now subjoined : *

"*A Statement of His Majesty's General Proceedings, and of the Principles by which he was guided from the period of his Accession, 1830, to that of the recent Change in the Administration, January, 14, 1835.*

"As it is impossible that the circumstances attending the recent change of Administration should not lead to discussion in both Houses of Parliament, in which reference would unavoidably be made to the course pursued by the King at periods when he was placed under the necessity of taking council more or less of himself, and of trusting his own judgment with respect to the decisions it became his duty to adopt, His Majesty thinks it may be useful to Sir Robert Peel and

* It was first published in " Baron Stockmar's Memoirs."

his colleagues to receive from himself a statement of his general proceedings, and of the principles by which he was guided, and that this statement should embrace the prominent features of those proceedings from the period of His Majesty's accession, in June, 1830, to that of the recent change in the Administration ; the circumstances connected with the last event being alone given in any detail.

"Upon the King's accession His Majesty, without any hesitation, determined to maintain in the administration of the affairs of the country those who had been the confidential servants of his late brother, those whose political principles and measures had continued to be, as far as a necessary and well-judged deference to public feeling, and to the important object of maintaining the peace of the country would allow, such as had been approved by his late father.

"To the Government so constituted the King gave his full and undeviating support, and during the short period of its further existence nothing was done, or required by His Majesty which could produce difficulty or embarrassment to it.

"In November of that year (1830) Sir Henry Parnell brought forward a motion, which was resisted by the Government as being an attack on the prerogative of the Crown, but which nevertheless received the support of a considerable number of Members of the House of Commons, who had become hostile to the Government in consequence of its concessions to the Roman Catholics, and who were distinguished by the appellation of ultra-Tories. The result of this junction with the Opposition, and of the majority thus obtained by the latter in the House of Commons upon so important a question, was the immediate resignation of the Duke of Wellington and his colleagues, and the unanimous opinion that His Majesty had no other alternative than to resort to the opposite party for the means of forming an Administration ; to which was added the advice of his Lord Chancellor that he should address himself at once to Earl Grey. In concurrence with this advice His Majesty sent for Lord Grey, who agreed to take upon himself the trust proposed to him, upon a clear understanding that he should be at liberty to introduce at once the measure so long contemplated and advocated by him and his party of an extensive reform of Parliament, and that in the prosecution of his plan, to effect it, he should receive the King's countenance and support. This condition had been anticipated by His Majesty and by his late advisers, and no objection could be made by him to the introduction of a measure to which Earl Grey had pledged his character and political consistency.

" Earl Grey and his colleagues lost no time in preparing the Bills for the reform in the representation in the United Kingdom, and His Majesty sanctioned the introduction of them to Parliament, after some correspondence, into the character of which it is unnecessary that he should enter, as it was placed in the hands of the Duke of Wellington and Lord Lyndhurst, in May, 1832. After some discussion, the House of Commons passed the proposed Bill by a majority of eight only, and His Majesty was, in consequence, advised by Earl Grey, and his other confidential servants, to dissolve Parliament.

" The King is aware that it has been remarked that he had inconsiderately and improperly neglected the opportunity which was afforded him at this period of *emancipating* himself from the thraldom of a party

which had introduced, and was pursuing, measures of
excessive and dangerous reform by refusing to dissolve
the Parliament; and he does not deny that such a
refusal would have been equivalent to the dismissal of
Earl Grey and his colleagues from his Council. But
supposing that this course could then have been adopted
with due regard to the peace and the tranquillity of the
country, in which the cry of reform had been so
generally and so extensively raised, His Majesty was
then satisfied, as he now continues to be, that he could
not have adopted it without seriously compromising his
own character as a sovereign and a gentleman, inasmuch
as it would have exposed him to the just imputation
that, although he had, in the moment of difficulty,
appealed to Lord Grey for his aid and services; and,
although these had been given upon the understanding
that His Majesty would admit the introduction and
support him in the prosecution of a great public
measure, to which his character was pledged, His
Majesty had not scrupled to desert and sacrifice him at
the hour of trial, when the moment arrived which should
offer the proof whether the compact had been made
on the part of His Majesty with the honest intention
of observing it. It is very possible that by the dismissal
of his Ministers at that period, and the consequent
exclusion of the Reform Bill, as it had been introduced,
measures less objectionable might have been proposed;
but His Majesty very much doubts whether the country
was then in a temper which would have enabled the
Administration succeeding that of Lord Grey to maintain its ground long enough, to give effect to any great
measure, and whether any other course than that which
His Majesty pursued would not have led to changes of
Administration, rapidly succeeding each other, and to

the destruction in every quarter of that confidence in
the fair and honourable dealings of the sovereign which,
in His Majesty's opinion, does and ought to constitute
the best safeguard of the monarchy.

"Therefore, whether right or wrong in policy, His
Majesty's decision was made upon a principle which he
feels to have been correct ; and such being his feeling,
he could not, if he had not acted upon it, have relied
with the same confidence on the aid and support of
others whenever he might have occasion to resort to
them.

"To proceed, the discussion on the Reform Bill was
resumed in the new Parliament, and prosecuted in a
manner and under circumstances to which it would be
foreign to the object of this paper to revert, until the
apprehension of a defeat in the House of Lords induced
Lord Grey, at the earnest solicitation of *some* of his
colleagues, and ultimately with their *unanimous* consent,
to submit to the King that an addition should be made
to the Peerage ; to which, as at first limited, His Majesty
agreed, after considerable hesitation and objection. But,
to obviate so odious an expedient, as well as the risk of
a collision between the two Houses, which was equally
the subject of serious apprehension, communications
were admitted and encouraged by His Majesty with a
view to some compromise, and to such modifications of
certain clauses as should render the Bill more palatable
to the majority of its opponents in the House of Lords.

"These failed, and the failure having had the effect
of increasing the violence of the Opposition, rather than
allaying it, Lord Grey and his colleagues brought forward a proposition for an increase of the Peerage which
appeared to His Majesty so unreasonably extensive, so
injurious to the character of that branch of the Legisla-

ture, and so degrading in its effects to the aristocracy of
the country, that he refused to acquiesce in it.

"The result of this decision was, as might be expected, the resignation of Lord Grey and his colleagues
in May, 1832; and His Majesty sent for Lord Lyndhurst,
who had been his High Chancellor, and requested him
to communicate with the Duke of Wellington and others
who might be disposed to come to his assistance and to
attempt to form an Administration.

"The appeal was nobly met by his Grace; but, after
some ineffectual attempts to accomplish the purpose,
the Duke of Wellington and Lord Lyndhurst stated
to His Majesty that their endeavours had become
hopeless, and advised His Majesty to resort again to
Earl Grey, and to make the best terms he could with
him with respect to the peerage question, if his Lordship should consent to return to the direction of his
Councils.

"Fortunately, the interval had been short; nothing
had occurred to occasion angry feeling; His Majesty
experienced no difficulty in prevailing upon Lord
Grey to resume the Administration, and he is bound
to do that nobleman the justice to say that neither
then, nor at any subsequent period, did he show the
least disposition to take advantage of the position in
which His Majesty had placed himself towards him and
his party, by the unsuccessful attempt to change the
Government, and to defeat the measure for which they
had contended.

"But the natural and unavoidable result of this
return to Lord Grey was the abandonment of His
Majesty's objections to the increase of the peerage,
providing it could not be obviated by prevailing upon
the opponents of the Reform Bill to drop their oppo-

sition to it, and, sensible as His Majesty had become of any attempt to obtain sufficient or efficient support in the opposite party; apprehensive as he was of a collision between the two Houses, if the Lords should persist in the opposition; and anxious as he had ever been to prevent what he viewed as the degradation of that body, His Majesty did take some steps[*] towards inducing them to abandon their opposition, which had the desired effect; although many, who did not fairly estimate the difficulties of his situation, questioned the propriety of His Majesty's proceedings on this occasion.[†]

"The King is aware that another step, taken by him at a subsequent period, became the subject of animadversions. He alludes to the letter which he addressed to the Archbishop of Canterbury, in deprecation of the course pursued by the ecclesiastical members of the House of Lords; and, with a view to prevail upon them

---

[*] The King caused his private secretary, Sir Herbert Taylor, to address the following circular letter to a number of Tory peers:

"St. James's Palace, May 17, 1832.
"My dear Lord,

"I am honoured with His Majesty's commands to acquaint your lordship that all difficulties to the arrangement in progress will be obviated by a declaration in the House to-night from a sufficient number of peers, that, in consequence of the present state of affairs, they have come to the resolution of dropping their further opposition to the Reform Bill, so that it may pass without delay, and, as nearly as possible, in its present shape.

"I have the honour, etc.
"Herbert Taylor."

This letter had the effect of inducing about 100 Opposition peers to absent themselves during the remaining discussions.

[†] Cf. May, "Const. Hist.,' vol. i. pp. 119, 120.

to abstain from taking so prominent and so warm a part
in general discussion, as might increase the disinclination
and the prejudice, which had been already excited and
magnified against them.

"The King does not deny that, in endeavouring to
moderate the inconsiderate zeal of some of the high
dignitaries of the Church, he sought to extricate himself
and his Government from difficulty; but he is justified
in taking credit to himself also for an anxious desire to
screen those respectable individuals from the increasing
effect of hostile feelings and the popular clamour of
which they were becoming the objects, at a period when
the Established Church was threatened with encroachment, and when it appeared to him desirable to conciliate,
as well as to resist.

"The King will pass on to the period of the secession,
in May last,* of Mr. Stanley, the Duke of Richmond,
Lord Ripon, and Sir James Graham from the Government, whereby its efficiency and consistency were so
much shaken that Lord Grey would readily have resigned his situation; and if His Majesty had wished to
avail himself of that opportunity of dissolving the
Administration, he might have taken advantage of the
opening afforded him by his Lordship. But, after the
failure on a former occasion, His Majesty naturally
felt the necessity of extreme caution in all his proceedings. He felt, also, that Lord Grey and some of
his colleagues had established strong claims to his
regard and confidence and gratitude, by the manner
in which they had acted towards him at that period,

---

* On May 27, 1834, Mr. Ward, in the House of Commons, proposed a resolution in favour of the reduction of the temporalities of
the Established Church in Ireland. This led to the secession of the
four ministers named in the text.—*Hansard*, vol. xxiii., p. 1396.

and since they had returned to his Councils; and it was, therefore, with perfect sincerity that he urged Lord Grey to retain his situation and to endeavour to make an arrangement for supplying the vacancies which had arisen.

"Events succeeded which produced the resignation of Earl Grey,* and as these are before the public, and His Majesty had no concern whatever in producing them, and could not have prevented them, we need not dwell upon them.

"It occurred to him that advantage might be taken of this state of affairs to effect an union of parties, of which the object should be Conservative, and this became the subject of communications to Lord Melbourne, and through him to the Duke of Wellington, Sir Robert Peel, and Mr. Stanley.

"The result proved that His Majesty was mistaken in his expectations, and it disappointed hopes which he had long cherished. He was aware that impressions prevailed in some quarters that this opportunity might have been taken of effecting a change in his Councils; but he could not satisfy himself that this could be then attempted with such a prospect of success as would justify the risk and secure him against the consequences of a failure; and, after fully weighing every contingency, he determined to entrust to Viscount Melbourne, whom he had employed in the communications, the reconstruction of the Administration.

"As the whole correspondence which passed on this occasion (in July last) is in the hands of Sir Robert Peel, it is quite unnecessary that His Majesty should enter into any particulars. But he cannot help calling the attention of Sir Robert Peel, and that of those of

* In July, 1834,

his colleagues to whom he may communicate this paper, to the candid manner in which he exposed to Lord Melbourne, in his memorandum of last July, the grounds upon which he adopted the alternative and stated his predilection for Conservative measures, and for those who advocated them, and endeavoured to guard himself against further encroachments, and against the introduction to his Council of individuals on whose principles he could not rely as he could on those of Lord Melbourne and some of his tried colleagues.

" In the review of the policy observed with respect to France, there is one point which His Majesty cannot pass without notice—namely, his earnest and unceasing endeavours to prevail upon his Government, and more especially upon the individual entrusted with the administration of its Foreign Affairs, to check the disposition which had been shown by the French Government to tolerate, if not to countenance and encourage, a system of propagandism tending to disturb and agitate the neighbouring States; and His Majesty cannot say that he was satisfied with the attention given to this point, and with the inclination shown by the French Government to drop so mischievous a system. The course of events has, however, produced the result to which His Majesty's remonstrances had been unavailingly directed—Louis Philippe having discovered that his own security is deeply concerned in checking the general progress of the mischief.

" His Majesty has at all times felt solicitous to maintain the most friendly relations with Austria and Prussia; and, taking all circumstances into consideration, he is bound to give credit to the late Administration for its inclination to pursue a course which should be in accordance with His Majesty's wishes. He is sensible, indeed, that too great a disposition was manifested on some occasions to interfere in the internal arrangements and regulations of other States ; and this disposition may possibly be attributed to a predilection for Liberal institutions and constitutional innovations, which it might be considered advisable or necessary to manifest in deference to popular opinion and support.

" This remark applies more particularly to interferences with respect to the internal affairs of the German Confederation, which was more than once the subject of objection on the part of His Majesty ; but, in saying this, he is bound to add that he concurred with his Government in considering that, as a party to the Treaty of Vienna of 1815, and a guarantee of its stipulation with respect to the general establishment and constitution of the German Confederacy, England had a right to participation in the discussion of certain general questions from which Austria and Prussia sought to exclude her.

" In all that related to the affairs of the Italian States, and of Switzerland, His Majesty considers his late Government to have acted with great prudence and caution ; and he is sensible that there have been periods, when any departure from that course might have brought very imflammable matter to an explosion.

" With respect to the contest in Portugal, of which the issue was so long doubtful, His Majesty does not deny that he concurred decidedly with his Government in the policy and propriety of supporting the cause of its present Queen ; not indeed from any predilection for her late father, Don Pedro, or from any desire to encourage the introduction of a constitutional form of Government, which he was sensible

that the great mass of the Portuguese nation rejected,
but because he considered the continued sovereignty of
Don Miguel the greatest evil of the two, and that
which threatened the greatest mischief to British
interests. The result of this contest, and the prospects
which are now opened, will, His Majesty trusts,
realise his hopes that peace and prosperity may
gradually be restored to that long distracted and
impoverished country; and that the re-establishment
of a predominant British influence may tend to its
future advantage and security.

"The King has uniformly approved of the policy
adopted by his late Gavernment with regard to the
affairs of Spain, and, above all, of its abstaining from
intervention, and of using its influence with France
towards producing a similar line of conduct. But
His Majesty does not think that sufficient attention
has been paid to his *early* suggestion, that the
Spanish Government should be urged and advised
to endeavour to conciliate the provinces which are
the seat of a destructive and murderous civil war,
by offering to confirm to them their ancient rights
and privileges, the attachment to which His Majesty
believes to influence them in a much greater degree
than does affection for the cause or person of Don
Carlos.

" It remains only for the King to notice the conduct
which has been pursued with respect to Russia, and
there is no branch of the foreign policy of this country
which he has watched with greater solicitude, none
which in its results has given him less satisfaction,
especially as far as it embraces the affairs of the
Levant.

" The Porte had been so much crippled in her naval

resources by the unfortunate combination against her of England, France, and Russia, and by the 'untoward' action of Navarino, and subsequently in a more general sense, by the war with Russia, which was terminated by the peace of Adrianople; both had entailed such a sacrifice of territory and loss of revenue, as to have left the Sultan in a state ill calculated to cope with his rebellious subjects in various quarters; and more especially with the Pasha of Egypt, who had been preparing to take extensive advantage of the situation to which his sovereign might be reduced.

"These circumstances, added to the disordered state of Greece, and the occupation of Algiers and other points on the coast of Barbary, by the French, had induced the King repeatedly to press upon his Government the importance of strengthening materially the naval force in the Mediterranean, and in the Archipelago; and he urged this yet more earnestly when he learnt the rapid strides of Mehemet Ali, and the alarm they had excited at Constantinople. This was done some time previously to the first mission of Namic Pasha to England; and there is every reason to presume that the presence of four or five sail of the line in the Mediterranean at that period, and their appearance off Alexandria, would have effectually checked the designs and the progress of Mehemet Ali, and relieved the Sultan from the necessity of making a very unwilling appeal to the dangerous protection of his powerful and ambitious neighbour.

"His Majesty believes those composing his Government to have been more or less alive to the importance of being prepared in due time for the course and the possible event of the contest between the Sultan and Mehemet Ali, and willing to act upon His Majesty's suggestion ; but withheld by the apprehension of not experiencing, with a view to any foreign object, that support from the House of Commons which would insure the necessary supplies, and by the fear of bringing forward any measure which might deprive them of the goodwill of those who were continually urging economy and reductions, to the exclusion of all other considerations.

"Thus the opportune moment of preserving or recovering our long-established influence in the councils of the Porte was lost, and it was transferred to a power which, after having so materially contributed to lower the resources of the Porte, was watching for any and every opportunity of turning her exhausted state to its own advantage.

"The progress of Mehemet Ali was arrested, and although the interposition of England and France was not without effect upon this occasion, as acknowledged by Mehemet Ali, the actual pressure of a Russian fleet and army obtained at Constantinople, as might be expected, the whole credit for this event. Russia did not neglect to avail herself of the influence thus acquired ; and one of the first fruits of her protectorship was the conclusion of the Treaty of the 8th July, 1833, obviously extorted with a view to secure to herself advantages of navigation from which other powers should be excluded.

"Against this treaty England and France protested, they declared that they should consider the treaty as 'non avenu.' The Cabinet of St. Petersburg replied that it should consider the protest 'non avenu,' and afterwards assumed that the question had then been brought to a satisfactory close.

"France, which was less interested in the question,

appears to have dropped it, while England has, through her Minister at Constantinople, called for explanations, which, under the influence of Russia, have been evaded.

"In the meantime a British squadron has been assembled, and has for a considerable period maintained, in the neighbourhood of the Dardanelles, a station which may fairly be presumed to have produced a more conciliatory tone at St. Petersburg, and greater caution in its measures, though no abandonment of designs which may be carried on by safe means when the more open attack is felt to be exposed to direct opposition. The King dwelt upon these circumstances, as he is anxious to state to his present Government his conviction arising out of them, and often expressed to his late Government that, notwithstanding all her professions of moderation and disinterestedness with regard to the Porte, Russia had never abandoned and will never lose sight of her ambitious projects in that quarter, and that, notwithstanding the veil which she endeavours to cast over her proceedings, they may be easily traced to be at variance with her professions. Of this a proof may be found in her recent opposition to the projected establishment of a steam communication with India, by the Euphrates, which, if it could be carried into effect without the contingent apprehension of interruption from the actual condition of the country which it must traverse, would doubtless tend to the essential benefit of *all* concerned in it.

"Russia has indeed recently concurred with England and France in preventing the renewal of hostilities between the Sultan and Mehemet Ali; and this might be construed into a desire to consult the welfare of the Porte, and to relieve herself from necessity of again hastening to its protection, if there were not reason to

suspect that she apprehended the pressure of a British
squadron, might prove as efficacious as the dreaded
approach of a Russian army in checking the operations
of Mehemet Ali, and that the merit of protecting the
Sultan from insult might be transferred from herself to
England.

"His Majesty is indeed satisfied that the maintenance of an adequate British naval force in the
Mediterranean will tend more than any apprehension
of Russian interference to keep Mehemet Ali in check;
and although he is persuaded that the Porte cannot
recover the power while so great a portion of her
territory and resources remain under the control and
at the disposal of this ambitious vassal. His Majesty
fears also that the result of this struggle between
them would exhaust the resources of both, to the
ultimate advantage of Russia, which, on the other hand
if left at liberty to take its own independent course,
would encourage such renewal of it in the hope of
its affording a plea and opportunity of again inter-
fering, and for a more permanent occupation of
Constantinople.

"If these remarks be well grounded, the King conceives that he is justified in attaching so much importance to the continuance of the squadron in the
Mediterranean, as offering the best security against the
further encroachments of Mehemit Ali and against the
eventual designs of Russia.

"It is possible indeed that circumstances may arise
which may favour the application of a British naval
force to the emancipation of the Porte from the
difficulty and embarrassment in which it is kept by the
usurpation of Mehemet Ali; and His Majesty cannot
but feel persuaded that whenever this can be accom-

plished by British intervention, it will be the most severe blow that Russian policy can receive.

" WILLIAM R.

"Pavilion, Brighton, January 14, 1835."

One day the King had a number of military and naval officers, with the officials belonging to their respective departments. "The land forces were ranged on one side of the table, and the sailors on the other. His Majesty gave several toasts with appropriate speeches by way of preface. That of the evening was : 'The health of the two services,' whose valour and devotion he loudly extolled. They should never forget that it was their peculiar good fortune to serve a country where men of all ranks, from the highest to the lowest were eligible to command. ' Here, on my right,' said the King with especial emphasis, ' is my noble friend descended from a line of ancestry as ancient as my own ; and here on my left is my gallant friend, a rear-admiral sprung from the very dregs of the people.' On another day the banquet was given to prelates and clerical dignitaries of various degrees. The toasts were appropriately ecclesiastical. That of the Church was prefaced by its temporal head, with an account of his own change of opinions : ' When I was a young man, as well as I can remember I believed in nothing but pleasure and folly ; nothing at all. But when I went to sea, got into a gale, and saw the wonders of the mighty deep, then I believed ; and I have been a sincere Christian ever since.' "

There were other ebullitions of a no less singular character.

" For some time William IV. persisted in omitting the members of the Cabinet from his invitations to

dinner; and, except the officers of his household, no one
holding political office partook of his hospitality. His
favourite guests were those who were most distinguished
for their adverse zeal. Greville himself, intensely Conservative, calls him a true King of the Tories, and
believed he was only waiting an opportunity to get rid of
the Liberals. Many stories are told of the caprices and
oddities of his manner at this time."

Then came a strange, vehement burst about the
militia—a hobby of His Majesty's—to say nothing of
another curious scene, on the petition of Admiral
Sartorius,* praying to be restored to his rank. When this
was read, the King, after repeating the usual form of
words, added : "And must be granted. As Captain
Napier was restored, so must this gentleman be, for
there was this difference between their cases ; Admiral
Napier knew he was doing wrong, which Admiral
Sartorious was not aware of." Lord Minto said : "I
believe, sir, there was not so much difference between
the two cases as your Majesty imagines, for Admiral
Sartorius——" Then followed something which I could
not catch ; but the King did, for he said, with considerable asperity : "Unless your lordship is quite sure of
that, I must beg leave to say that I differ from you, and
do not believe it to be so ; but since you have expressed
your belief that it is so, I desire you will furnish me
with proofs of it immediately. The next time I see you,
you will be prepared with proofs of what you say, for
unless I see them I shall not believe one word of it."
Minto made no reply to this extraordinary sortie, and
the rest looked at each other in silence.

"But Melbourne knew better," says Mr. Torrens,

---

* Admiral Sartorius still lives (January, 1884). He is the oldest
Admiral of the Navy, having reached his 94th year.

"the waywardness and weakness of the aged Prince. He suggested therefore without comment that the petition of Sartorius should be referred to the Admiralty to report upon, and this being the last business of the day the Council thereupon broke up. When they reassembled on the 5th of October, the report being favourable, the gallant officer was restored. Melbourne took care to be present; the First Lord of the Admiralty did not attend; and by that time the fretful mood of valetudinarian Majesty had passed away."

The King, in the most mortifying situation that could be conceived, had to put the best face he could on the situation. It was curious that this was the third humiliating situation of the kind in which a sovereign had found himself within six years. George IV. having to take back a dismissed ministry once, and the present sovereign twice, in each case owing to the blind miscalculations of the Tory party.

Mr. Greville heard that, "notwithstanding the good face which the King contrives to put upon the matter in his communications with his hated new-old ministers and masters, he is really very miserable; and the Duchess of Gloucester, to whom he unbosoms himself more than to anybody, told Lady Georgiana Bathurst that with her he was in the most pitiable state of distress, constantly in tears, and saying that 'he felt his crown tottering on his head.'"

The daily life of His Majesty at this time was thus described by one of his sons to Mr. Greville:

"He sleeps in the same room with the Queen; at a quarter before eight every morning his *valet de chambre* knocks at the door, and at ten minutes before eight exactly he gets out of bed, puts on a flannel dressing-gown and trousers, and walks into his dressing-room. He is long at his ablutions, and takes up an hour and a half in dressing. At half-past nine he breakfasts with the Queen, the ladies, and any of his family; he eats a couple of fingers and drinks a dish of coffee. After breakfast he reads *The Times* and *Morning Post*, commenting aloud on what he reads in very plain terms, and sometimes they hear, 'That's a damned lie,' or some such remark, without knowing to what it applies. After breakfast he devotes himself with Sir Herbert Taylor to business till two, when he lunches (two cutlets and two glasses of sherry) ; then he goes out for a drive till dinner-time ; at dinner he drinks a bottle of sherry —no other wine—and eats moderately ; he goes to bed soon after eleven. He is in dreadfully low spirits, and cannot rally at all ; the only interval of pleasure which he has lately had was during the Devonshire election, when he was delighted at John Russell's defeat. He abhors all his Ministers, even those whom he used rather to like formerly, but hates Lord John the most of all. When Adolphus told him that a dinner ought to be given for the Ascot races, he said : ' You know I cannot give a dinner; I cannot give any dinners without inviting the Ministers, and I would rather see the devil than any one of them in my house.' I asked him how he was with them in his inevitable official relations. He said that he had as little to do with them as he could, and bowed them out, when he gave any of them audiences, as fast as possible. He is peculiarly disgusted with Errol, for whom he has done so much, and who has behaved so ungratefully to him ; but it is a good trait of him that he said ' he hoped the world would not accuse Errol of ingratitude.' "

The scenes at the Privy Council, swearing in of new officials, etc., always gave an opening for speechings ;

and on such occasions he would exhibit his disgust
and detestation of the ministry he was obliged to receive.
An extraordinary scene was that of the appointment of
Sir C. Grey.

" After Sir Charles Grey was sworn, the King said to
him, ' Stand up,' and up he stood. He then addressed
him with great fluency and energy nearly in these words :
' Sir Charles Grey, you are about to proceed upon one of
the most important missions which ever left this country,
and, from your judgment, ability, and experience, I
have no doubt that you will acquit yourself to my entire
satisfaction. I desire you, however, to bear in mind
that the colony to which you are about to proceed has
not, like other British colonies, been peopled from the
mother country—that it is not an original possession of
the Crown, but that it was obtained *by the sword.* You
will take care to assert those undoubted prerogatives
which the Crown there possesses, and which I am determined to enforce and maintain ; and I charge you by
the oath which you have just taken strenuously to assert
those prerogatives, *of which persons who ought to have
known better have dared even in my presence to deny the
existence.'* His speech was something longer than this,
but the last words almost precisely the same. The
silence was profound, and I was amused at the astonishment depicted on the faces of the Ministers. I asked
Lord Lansdowne and Lord Holland who it was that he
alluded to. Neither knew, but the former said he
thought it might be Ellice, and that the King referred to
something Ellice had said to him when he was Minister.
Somebody said they thought it was Spring Rice ; but that
could not be when Rice was sitting at the table. I have
heard many specimens of his eloquence, but never anything like this. After this he had to give Durham an

audience on his embassy, which must have been very
agreeable to him, as he hates him and the Duchess of
Kent, whose *magnus Apollo* Durham is."

THE KING TO LORD MELBOURNE.

"June, 1835.

" It is impossible that the King should view or
describe, otherwise than as an important measure, that
which, in principle and substance, sets out by the repeal of all Acts, charters, grants, and letters patent, now
in force relating to certain boroughs. The information
offered to the King on this head is as yet imperfect,
inasmuch as the schedules to which reference is made are
not annexed to the Bill transmitted ; but enough has
been submitted to him to show that the whole spirit
of the Bill, its principle and provisions, affect rather
seriously the royal prerogative, and are calculated to
lessen the authority and influence of the Crown."

He then pointed out the abuses :

" It appears evident to the King that the ill blood
which will arise at one contest will not have subsided
before the canvassing will begin in anticipation of the
next ensuing election.

CHAPTER XXI.

A PARTICULAR subject of irritation with His Majesty were the progresses which the Duchess of Kent used to make, with her charge, through various parts of the kingdom. The perpetual salutes annoyed him, and he ordered them not to pay such compliments. The ministers thought it would be more delicate to suggest to her that she herself should decline these honours. The Duchess refused this act of abnegation, and insisted on her rights. Mr. Greville learned " that Conroy (who is a ridiculous fellow, a compound of 'Great Hussey' and the Chamberlain of the Princess of Navarre) had said, 'that, as Her Royal Highness's *confidential adviser*, he could not recommend her to give way on this point.' As she declined to accede to the proposals, nothing remained but to alter the regulations, and accordingly, yesterday, by an Order in Council, the King changed them, and from this time the Royal Standard is only to be saluted when the King or the Queen is on board."

Mr. Greville is so jaundiced where his prejudices are concerned that, in such instances, every particular takes some odium. There was probably more of farce in all these scenes; and the humour of the King passed away quickly. It is impossible not to smile when we read

2 A

of what occurred the day after a scene, when the
Queen was not ready for dinner.   When dinner was
announced, and he was waiting, he asked, "Where's the
Queen?"   They told him she was waiting for the
Duchess of Kent, when he said, loud enough for every-
body to hear, "That woman is a nuisance."

This is a well-known scene, described in Mr.
Greville's liveliest fashion, which may be repeated here,
as showing the unpleasant state of feeling which existed
between the Court and the party of the Duchess.   In
August, 1836, the King had invited the Duchess to
repair to Windsor.   She declined the invitation, as she
wished to keep her own at Claremont, but offered to
attend to his a little later.   This irritated him exceedingly.   His anger was inflamed by finding that she had
taken possession of some rooms at Kensington Palace,
seventeen in number, which he had refused to her
already.

"This put the King in a fury ; he made, however, no
reply, and on the 20th he was in town to prorogue
Parliament, having desired that they would not wait
dinner for him at Windsor.   After the prorogation he
went to Kensington Palace, to look about it ; when he
got there he found that the Duchess of Kent had appropriated to her own use a suite of apartments, seventeen
in number, for which she had applied last year, and
which he had refused to let her have.   This increased
his ill-humour ; already excessive.   When he arrived
at Windsor, and went into the drawing-room (at
about ten o'clock at night), where the whole party
was assembled, he went up to the Princess Victoria,
took hold of both her hands, and expressed his pleasure
at seeing her there, and his regret at not seeing her
oftener.   He then turned to the Duchess and made her

a low bow, almost immediately after which he said that
'a most unwarrantable liberty had been taken with one
of his palaces; that he had just come from Kensington,
where he found apartments had been taken possession of
not only without his consent, but contrary to his commands, and that he neither understood nor would endure
conduct so disrespectful to him.' This was said loudly,
publicly, and in a tone of serious displeasure. It was,
however, only the muttering of the storm which was to
break the next day. Adolphus Fitz-Clarence went into
his room on Sunday morning, and found him in a state
of great excitement. It was his birthday, and though
the celebration was what was called private, there were
a hundred people at dinner, either belonging to the
Court or from the neighbourhood. The Duchess of Kent
sat on one side of the King, and one of his sisters on the
other, the Princess Victoria opposite. Adolphus Fitz-
Clarence sat two or three from the Duchess, and heard
every word of what passed. After dinner, by the
Queen's desire, 'His Majesty's health, and long life to
him' was given, and as soon as it was drunk he made a
very long speech, in the course of which he poured forth
the following extraordinary and *foudroyante* tirade: 'I
trust in God that my life may be spared for nine months
longer, after which period, in the event of my death, no
Regency would take place. I should then have the
satisfaction of leaving the royal authority to the personal
exercise of that young lady (pointing to the Princess),
the heiress presumptive of the Crown, and not in the
hands of a person now near me, who is surrounded by
evil advisers, and who is herself incompetent to act with
propriety in the station in which she would be placed.
I have no hesitation in saying that I have been insulted
—grossly and continually insulted—by that person, but

I am determined to endure no longer a course of behaviour so disrespectful to me. Amongst many other things I have particularly to complain of the manner in which that young lady has been kept away from my Court ; she has been repeatedly kept from my drawing-rooms, at which she ought always to have been present, but I am fully resolved that this shall not happen again. I would have her know that I am King, and I am determined to make my authority respected, and for the future I shall insist and command that the Princess do upon all occasions appear at my Court, as it is her duty to do.' He terminated his speech by an allusion to the Princess and her future reign in a tone of paternal interest and affection, which was excellent in its way.

"This awful philippic (with a great deal more which I forget) was uttered with a loud voice and excited manner. The Queen looked in deep distress, the Princess burst into tears, and the whole company were aghast. The Duchess of Kent said not a word. Immediately after, they rose and retired, and a terrible scene ensued ; the Duchess announced her immediate departure and ordered her carriage, but a sort of reconciliation was patched up, and she was prevailed upon to stay till the next day."

All this had been complicated by dissensions existing between her mother and the Royal Family. His son, Lord Adolphus Fitz-Clarence, gave Mr. Greville an account of the late Kensington quarrel : "The King wrote a letter to the Princess offering her £10,000 a year (not out of his privy purse), which he proposed should be at her own disposal and independent of her mother. He sent this letter by Lord Conyngham with orders to deliver it into the Princess's own hands. Conyngham accordingly went to Kensington (where

Conroy received him) and asked to be admitted to the Princess. Conroy asked by what authority. He said by His Majesty's orders. Conroy went away, and shortly after Conyngham was ushered into the presence of the Duchess and Princess, when he said that he had waited on Her Royal Highness by the King's commands, to present to her a letter with which he had been charged by his Majesty. The Duchess put out her hand to take it, when he said he begged Her Royal Highness's pardon, but he was expressly commanded by the King to deliver the letter into the Princess's own hands. Her mother then drew back, and the Princess took the letter, when Conyngham made his bow and retired. Victoria wrote to the King, thanking him and accepting his offer. He then sent to say that it was his wish to name the person who should receive this money for her, and he proposed to name Stephenson. Then began the dispute. The Duchess of Kent objected to the arrangement, and she put forth her claim, which was that she should have £6,000 of the money and the Princess £4,000. How the matter had ended Adolphus did not know when I saw him. It never was settled."

Meanwhile, the behaviour of His Majesty to his ministers, still continued to be of the kind by which the Regent often indemnified himself, when a Cabinet, that was distasteful to him, had been forced on him. Mr. McCullagh Torrens relates some extraordinary and undignified scenes that took place in the Royal Council Chamber.

"Towards Lord Melbourne individually he was not ungracious or unkind, but towards other members of the Cabinet his words were full of heat, and his demeanour sometimes almost hostile. The militia had, he said, been too long neglected. He thought it would be an excellent measure to embody them. He said, "he thought those who objected to preparations on the ground of cost were penny wise and pound foolish. He heard that Russia had one hundred thousand men ready for embarkation in the Baltic; he did not know how his lordship felt, but he owned they made him shake in his shoes."* The subject frequently recurred, and was calculated to cause uneasiness in those to whom such language was addressed. Melbourne, who knew him long and well, said it was temper, not political purpose; and he pointed to the military estimates of Peel, three months before, which were less in the number of men asked for, than for twenty years preceding. His Majesty seldom, if ever, indulged in these ebullitions when alone with Melbourne or Palmerston.

Lord Gosford, a man of excellent character and judgment, had been named Governor of Canada; and no objection had been raised to his appointment. At a meeting of the Cabinet, on the 11th of July, Lord Melbourne addressed his colleagues: "Gentlemen, you may as well know how you stand," and then proceeded to read a memorandum of a conversation after the review the day before, between Lord Gosford and the King. His Majesty said: "Mind what you are about in Canada. By —— I will never consent to alienate the Crown lands, nor to make the Council elective. Mind me, my lord, the Cabinet is not my Cabinet; they had better take care, or, by ——, I will have them impeached. You are a gentleman, I believe, I have no fear of you; but take care what you do." The ministers present stared at one another, but agreed that it was better to take no notice of what had occurred, and see if

* Hobhouse, vol. iii. p. 142, June 26th.

the excitement would pass away. The same day he gave excellent advice to M. Dedel, the Dutch Minister, bidding him let the King of Holland know that he was ignorant of his true position, and that Belgium was lost irrevocably. Hobhouse owns that though he was uniformly treated with kindness and consideration in audience on the affairs of his department, he shared at times the doubts of others whether incivilities that appeared gratuitous and unseemly were not prompted in some degree by a hope that they might provoke resignations and lead thereby to a break up of the Government. Lord Frederick Fitz-Clarence, who saw with concern from day to day all that was going on, told him that his father had much to bear, being beset by the Duke of Cumberland and the Duchess of Gloucester by day, and by the Queen at night. "It seemed clear to me that if we continued in office it would be entirely owing to the good sense and good manners of our chief, who knew how to deal with his master, as well as with his colleagues, and never, that I saw, made a mistake in regard to either. I must add, that when a stand was to be made on anything considered to be a vital principle of his Government he was as firm as a rock."

Lord Gosford was advised to take no notice of what had passed, and abide by his instructions, which would be specific and clear. When these were first submitted for approval, His Majesty broke out violently against the use of certain words, saying : "No, my lord ; I will not have that word ; strike out 'conciliatory'; strike out 'liberal.'" And then he added : "You cannot wonder at my making these difficulties with a ministry that has been forced upon me." However, as Glenelg went on reading, His Majesty got more calm. He approved of what was said about the Legislative Council and the territorial revenues.

In short, he approved of the instructions generally on that day, and also on the following Monday; but when Glenelg went into the Closet two days after, he was very sulky and indeed rude; and objected to some things to which he had previously consented. Melbourne was told by Glenelg how he had been treated, and when he went in, the King said he hoped he had not been uncivil to Lord Glenelg, on which the First Minister made only a stiff bow. The King took the reproof most becomingly; for, when Glenelg went in a second time, His Majesty was exceedingly kind to him, and said he "approved of every word of the instructions," and remarked that he was not like William III., who often signed what he did not approve. He would not do that, he was not disposed to infringe on the liberty of any of his subjects, but he must preserve his own prerogative. The storm being over, the afternoon proved more serene. At the Council all was sunshine; and though the Chief Justice Denman being detained at Guildhall, kept the King waiting a long while, he received his apologies when he came very kindly, asked where he lived, and invited him to Windsor, adding, when he had gone through the Recorders' Report, "I hope you won't hang me, my Lord."

This outburst could not be passed over, and Lord Glenelg, the party who was thus glanced at, felt constrained to take the matter up. Lord Melbourne almost reproached the King, and said it was impossible to carry on the Government if such things occurred. His Majesty said that he was greatly irritated, and had acted under strong feelings in consequence of what Glenelg had said to him. Melbourne rejoined: "Your Majesty must have mistaken Lord Glenelg."

"Not at all," said the King; and he then went into a dispute they had had about the old constitution of Canada—I forget what, but something the King asserted, which Glenelg contradicted. He repaired to the Colonial Office, and told Stephen, who informed him that the King was right and he was wrong. This was awkward; however, it ended in the King's making a sort of apology. Such was the substance, and, in great part, the very words, of His Majesty's harangue. We looked at one another. Lord Melbourne was very black and very haughty; I thought he would have broken out. He preserved, however, his self-control, and thereby escaped the mischief and scandal of an altercation which, once begun, must have ended either in a humiliating retractation on the part of the King, or in a second attempt within twelve months to get rid of an Administration having the confidence of the House of Commons. The Speaker was another object of his intentional rudeness, the King affecting not to see him at the Drawing Room, and treating his predecessor with studious politeness. At the Levee, Lord Torrington was reading out the names, and read : " So-and-so, *Deputy-Governor.*" "Deputy-Governor ! " said the King; "Deputy-Governor of what?" " I cannot tell your Majesty," replied Torrington, "as it is not upon the card." "Hold your tongue, sir," said the King; "you had better go home and learn to read;" and shortly after, when some bishop presented an address against (I believe) the Irish Tithe Bill, and the King was going as usual to hand over the papers to the lord in waiting, he stopped and said to Lord Torrington, who advanced to take them : " No, Lord Torrington ; these are not fit documents to be entrusted to your keeping." His habitual state of excitement will probably bring on, sooner or later, the malady of his family. Torrington was a young man in a difficult position, or he ought to have resigned instantly and as publicly as the insult was offered.

"His fear and anger knew no bounds: 'Lord Grey would never have done this, and would never sanction it. Melbourne was too flexible—too easy; but he would put in writing without delay the terms on which alone he would appoint the new ministers.' On Wednesday morning came a letter of six pages, about O'Connell and Hume; and, above all, about the appropriation of Church revenues, to which His Majesty protested he would not consent. Melbourne wrote a short and very decisive answer, and subsequently went to St. James's. He told His Majesty that he would not submit to have anyone excluded, but that there was no intention of employing either Hume or O'Connell." By adroit management this claim was put aside. By these eccentricities were the later years of this well-meaning, good-natured, but perverse monarch distinguished.

His Majesty had become possessed with the idea "that it was indispensable to the safety of the realm to resuscitate the militia. Upon various occasions he had sought to impress this view upon his ministers, without evoking any other than the sort of deferential acquiescence which practically implied nothing. His Majesty was led to believe that his patriotic suggestions were merely trifled with; and when his assent was asked in Council to the proposal for the further reduction of the militia staff, he was much excited, and exclaimed with great vehemence:

"Nothing should induce me to assent to this, but for two reasons; one is that I do not wish to expose those colonels who have deserted their duty and done

so much to injure this constitutional force ; the other
is that I am resolved the system shall be put upon a
better footing next session of Parliament. My lords,
I am an old man—older than any of your lordships
—I therefore know more than any of you. In 1756,
George II. had, as I have now, what was called a
Whig Ministry ; that Ministry originated a Militia
Bill, to form a constitutional defence of the kingdom.
George II. had not the advantages which his successors
possessed. He opposed the Bill, and he was seconded
by certain persons in different counties, some from
one motive, some from another, perhaps subserviency ;
but his ministers wisely persevered and carried their
measure ; since which time, this great force has been
kept up as it ought to be, and shall be, in spite of
agitators in Ireland and agitators in England ; for,
my lords, I dread to think what might be the consequences if Russia were to attack us unprepared. I say
I never will consent to the destruction of this force,
and early in the next session of Parliament, whoever
may be, and whoever are, ministers, I will have the
militia restored to a proper state. I say this, not only
before my confidential advisers, but before others
(Charles Greville and two or three others of the
household), because I wish to have my sentiments
known."

But now this worthy and well-meaning sovereign was
to close his short reign, and in May of this year the
symptoms of his last illness began. It is curious that
his latest important act was one of gracious kindness to
the young Princess who was to succeed him so soon.
She was now just of age, and the King, in his illness,

had prayed that he might live to celebrate the event. Of this last illness there is extant a full and minute narrative, which shows that the King made a very dignified, and even edifying passage from this life. In this he resembled his brother, the Duke of York, an account of whose last illness has been given in another work.*

"RECOLLECTIONS OF THE LAST DAYS OF KING WILLIAM IV."

"The following narrative of the rapid progress of his late Majesty's final, fatal illness, and the pious resignation of the King during that solemn period, cannot fail to be read with deep interest. The initials that follow, and the place whence the 'Recollections' are dated, sufficiently demonstrate that the most full confidence may be placed in them." The writer then proceeds:

"Though a slight decline of strength had been perceptible to the immediate attendants of our lamented King at the commencement of the year, yet it was not till the month of May that the state of His Majesty's health excited any serious apprehensions. On the 17th of that month His Majesty held a levee, but, on his return to Windsor Castle, showed great signs of debility

---

* The author's "Life of George IV." A history of the King's illness was published shortly after his death, in a little volume. "On Wednesday," says Mr. Greville, "it was announced for the first time that the King was alarmingly ill, on Thursday the account was no better, and in the course of Wednesday and Thursday his immediate dissolution appeared so probable that I concerted with Errol that I should send to the Castle at nine o'clock on Thursday evening for the last report, that I might know whether to go to London directly or not."

and exhaustion, and oppression of breathing, in consequence of which he had considerable difficulty in ascend-
ing the staircase, and, when he had reached the corridor,
was under the necessity of resting on the nearest sofa.

"Though the King had experienced very considerable oppression during the night, yet His Majesty
appeared refreshed, and was considered better the next
morning, Thursday, May 18th, and was not prevented
from going to St. James's to hold a drawing-room, which
had been appointed for that day. On these occasions,
the last on which His Majesty appeared in public, he
sat down; but this deviation from his usual practice did
not excite so much alarm as the traces of sickness
visible in his countenance. His debility, however, notwithstanding the exertions of the day, on reaching
Windsor Castle, was not so great on this as on the
preceding evening, and a slight improvement the following morning revived the hopes and spirits of His
Majesty's anxious friends.

"This day, Friday, was the anniversary of the battle
of La Hogue, and by command of His Majesty, several
officers of distinction resident in the neighbourhood,
together with the field-officers of the garrison, had been
invited to dinner. In the course of the evening, the
King detailed, with great minuteness, the causes, the
progress, and consequences of the different naval wars
in which this country had been engaged, during the last
and present century, and gave, perhaps, greater proof on
that than on any occasion, of the extraordinary accuracy
of his memory, and of his intimate acquaintance with
English history. His Majesty's voice, with the exception
of one or two moments of oppression of breathing, was
very strong and clear, but no one present could fail to
entertain apprehensions as to the effects of this exertion.

" The next day, Saturday, May 20th, His Majesty continued to suffer from the same distressing symptoms. At breakfast and luncheon, his appetite, which had been gradually declining, altogether failed, and, at the latter meal, he fell back in his chair with a sensation of faintness, to which several persons alluded with strong expressions of alarm.   His Majesty, on leaving the white drawing-room, sat down in the corridor, evidently feeble and exhausted.   He did not leave the Castle this afternoon.   At dinner His Majesty was affected by a similar seizure, and, to prevent increasing faintness, the Duchess of Gloucester, who was seated next to him, bathed his forehead and temples with eau-de-cologne. His Majesty rallied in the evening, but it was not till ten o'clock that he consented, in compliance with the Qoeen's request, to abandon his intention of going to St. James's the following morning, to be present at the re-opening of the Chapel Royal.

" The King retired to bed at his usual hour of eleven, labouring under manifest indisposition.   This was the last time His Majesty appeared in the drawing-room.   The next morning, increasing indisposition confined him to his private apartments, which he never quitted during the continuance of his fatal malady.

" The state of His Majesty's health now excited much and well-founded alarm.   Sir H. Halford and Dr. Chambers were sent for; but as the latter had no ostensible situation in the royal household, it was thought advisable, in order to avoid causing any unnecessary alarm to the King, to introduce him to His Majesty as the medical attendant of the Queen, who had at this time but very imperfectly recovered from a long and dangerous illness, on the ground that he wished to make a report of Her Majesty's health.   Dr.

Chambers was most graciously received by the King, who did not hesitate to avail himself of his advice in his own case. The arrival, however, of Dr. Chambers at the Castle was so late, that this interview did not take place till the following morning.

"It were needless to trace minutely the progress of the King's disease, the fluctuating nature of which produced constant alternations of hope and fear. On Monday, May 22, and the following morning, the King gave audiences to Lord Melbourne, Lord Hill, Lord Glenelg, and other ministers; but the unfavourable impression produced by the King's appearance on all who were admitted to his presence, served but to extend the alarm now generally entertained. The next two days were passed uncomfortably, from the effects of this fatigue; but on Saturday, May 27th, His Majesty felt sufficiently strong to hold a Council, and subsequently to give audience to all the Cabinet Ministers and officers of state, by whom it was attended. That the King's debility had already made very rapid and alarming progress, may be inferred from the fact that he had already lost the power of walking, and that it was now necessary for his medical attendant, Dr. Davies, to whom alone the King would entrust that duty, to wheel His Majesty in an easy chair into the Council-room.

"The King had looked forward with pleasure to the assembling of a large party, whom he had invited to Windsor Castle, to be present at the Eton regatta, on June 5th, and at Ascot races, which immediately followed.

"In the afternoon of this day an unfavourable change in the King's state was evident to his attendants With. his usual benevolent feeling, however, he still, for the sake of others, took an interest in those amusements in which he could not personally participate. Every order issued by the King bore evidence of his very kind consideration, even in the most minute particulars, for the comfort and convenience of his guests, and of the Eton boys, whose pleasure he was always anxious to promote.

" Influenced by a similar feeling, so predominant in His Majesty's character, and so remarkably exemplified in the closing year of his life, the King expressed his special desire that the Queen should attend the races at Ascot—preferring rather to dispense with the great comfort of Her Majesty's society, than that the public should experience any disappointment from the absence of the Royal Family.

" However little in accordance with the painful state of her own anxious feelings such a scene might be, the Queen did not hesitate to acquiesce in His Majesty's wishes. Her Majesty, therefore, drove to the course, but returned at the end of two hours to Windsor Castle, to resume her almost unceasing attendance on the King, and to find, alas ! even in that brief interval His Majesty had undergone much and unexpected suffering.

" The next morning, Wednesday, June 7th, Sir H. Halford and Dr. Chambers found the King weaker, but cordials supplied temporary strength and power to take nourishment, which supported him during the day. Nevertheless, the greatest gloom, and even the most melancholy forebodings, pervaded the party assembled in the Castle, which were distressingly manifested, as it will doubtless with pain be remembered, by all who were present at dinner on that day in St. George's Hall.

" For some time previously, the King's medical attendants indulged the sanguine hope that His Majesty might derive considerable benefit from change of air. Many circumstances had conspired to prevent an earlier proposal of any plan which had reference to this object; but with the concurrence of the physicians, Sir Herbert Taylor submitted this day to His Majesty their wish that he should remove for a few weeks to Brighton, where, with the advantage of the sea air, he would enjoy every comfort requisite in his present situation.

"The King did not, as it was feared, express any disapprobation at the suggestion—on the contrary, he assented with pleasure to the arrangement, and expressed his hope that he might soon regain sufficient strength to undertake the journey. Preparations were accordingly made by His Majesty's command at the Pavilion. The kindness of the King's disposition was displayed even in the selection of the persons whom he appointed to attend him.

"The state of His Majesty's health next morning (rendered worse by a sleepless night) was such as to damp any hope that might have been entertained with regard to the removal to Brighton. Increased difficulty of breathing, stoppage of the circulation, with the necessary consequences of coldness of the extremities and swelling of the legs, were among the symptoms which could not fail to excite the fear that the King's situation had now become one of extreme danger. Under these circumstances the party staying in the Castle dispersed this morning, Thursday, June 8th, in obedience to the Queen's wishes; and while grief and despondency reigned within the palace, the same feelings were quickly propagated among an affectionate and loyal people, by the unexpected absence of the royal *cortège* from Ascot.

"Contrary to expectation, the King passed a tranquil night. He was easier the next morning, but appeared very languid and feeble while transacting business with Sir Herbert Taylor, and his signatures to official papers were made with difficulty. His Majesty now, for the first time, consented that a bulletin should be issued, to allay, if possible, the anxiety which the public had long manifested.

"In the afternoon of this day His Majesty experienced great and instantaneous relief from medicines which produced very copious expectoration. The amendment was so decided and evident as to inspire the hope that it might be more than temporary, and His Majesty was certainly enabled to pass the ensuing day without any distressing oppression of breathing. For this alleviation of the pains, as well as for the more tranquil rest which he enjoyed during two successive nights, the gratitude to the Almighty felt and expressed by His Majesty was truly edifying. He was frequently heard to give utterance to these sentiments, with eyes raised to heaven, in the most sincere and unaffected terms. His patience and cheerfulness had at all times excited the astonishment and admiration of all who had an opportunity of witnessing them. No murmur ever escaped his lips, and often, in moments of the greatest suffering (which was subsequently proved to have far exceeded what his physicians had reason to suspect) he testified his grateful sense of the care and attention of all who approached him, and his regret that he should be the cause of imposing on them the duty of so much painful attendance.

"At no period, from the commencement of his attack, had His Majesty been insensible to his critical state ; but when he alluded to the subject, it was evident that any anxiety which he felt arose less from personal apprehension than from solicitude for the country, and from a contemplation of the embarrassment into which

it might possibly be thrown by his early dissolution.
It was to such reflections as these that His Majesty gave
expression on the morning of the 16th, when he observed to the Queen : 'I have had some quiet sleep ;
come and pray with me, and thank the Almighty for
it.' Her Majesty had joined in this act of heartfelt
devotion, and when the King had ceased, said : 'And
shall I not pray to the Almighty that you may have a
good day ?' To which His Majesty replied : 'Oh,
do ! I wish I could live ten years, for the sake of the
country. I feel it my duty to keep well as long as I
can.'

"On the morning of Sunday, the 11th, grateful for
the refreshing rest which he had enjoyed, His Majesty's
mind was impressed with the most pure devotional
feelings. Seeing Lady Mary Fox occupied with a book,
he inquired what she was reading, and being told that
it was a prayer-book, his countenance beamed with
pleasure, but he said nothing. After a considerable
lapse of time, the Queen asked whether it would be
agreeable to him if she read the prayers to him. His
Majesty answered : 'Oh, yes ! I should like it very
much ; but it will fatigue you.' He then desired to be
informed who preached that morning in the chapel of
the Castle ; and when Lady Mary had ascertained, and
told him that it was Mr. Wood who preached, he
directed that he might be sent for.

" When Mr. Wood entered the room, the King said :
'I will thank you, my dear sir, to read all the prayers
till you come to the prayer for the Church Militant.'
By which words His Majesty intended to include the
Communion Service, and all the other parts of the Liturgy
used in the celebration of public worship.

" It was equally an affecting and instructive lesson

to observe the devout humility of His Majesty, fervently
dwelling, as could be perceived from his manner and
the intonation of his voice on every passage, which
bore even the most remote application to his own
circumstances. His mind seemed quite absorbed in the
duty in which he was engaged, and to rise for a time
superior to his bodily infirmities; for during the whole
service his attention was undisturbed, and he experienced
none of those fits of coughing and oppression, which
for some time past had formed an almost uninterrupted
characteristic of his complaint. As Mr. Wood withdrew, His Majesty graciously expressed his thanks, and
afterwards said to the Queen : ' It has been a great
comfort to me.' Nor was this a transitory feeling. To
this pure and scriptural source of spiritual consolation
His Majesty recurred with unfeigned gratitude ; and on
each day of the ensuing week did Lord Augustus
Fitz-Clarence receive the King's commands to read to
him the prayers, either of the morning or evening
service. On one of these occasions, when His Majesty
was much reduced and exhausted, the Queen, fearful
of causing any fatigue to him, inquired hesitatingly,
whether, unwell as he was, he should still like to have
the prayers read to him ? He replied, ' Oh, yes ! beyond
everything.' Though very languid and disposed to
sleep from the effects of medicine, His Majesty repeated
all the prayers. The fatal progress of the King's complaint was very visible during the three following days,
June 12th, 13th, and 14th. Nevertheless, on Tuesday,
the 13th, His Majesty gave audience to his Hanoverian
Minister, Baron Ompteda, whom, contrary to the suggestions of his attendants, he had specially summoned
on business connected with that kingdom, in the welfare
of which he had never ceased to feel a truly paternal

interest. On Wednesday, the 14th, His Majesty received a visit from the Duke of Cumberland.

" The King's attention to his religious duties, and the great comfort which was inspired by their performance, have already been referred to. It will, therefore, create no surprise that His Majesty joyfully assented to the Queen's suggestion, that he should receive the Sacrament, or that he at once named the Archbishop of Canterbury as the person whom he wished to administer that holy rite. Sunday was the day fixed by the King for the discharge of this solemn duty; and a message was accordingly sent to his Grace, desiring his presence at Windsor Castle on the ensuing Saturday.

" The two intervening days were a period of great suffering to the King, whose illness more than once in that interval assumed the most alarming form, and in the evening of Friday excited apprehensions of His Majesty's immediate dissolution. The next morning, however, the King felt easier, and the most urgent symptoms had disappeared. In the usual course of business with Sir H. Taylor, he signed two public documents, though not without difficulty; but on every subject which was brought before him, His Majesty's power of perception was quick and accurate, and he anticipated with pleasure and thankfulness the approaching sacred duty of the morrow.

" On the morning of Sunday, the 18th, though His Majesty's mental energies remained vigorous and unimpaired, a greater degree of bodily weakness was perceptible. He raised himself in his chair with greater difficulty than the day before, and required more aid and support in every movement. The expression of his countenance, however, was perhaps more satisfactory. He transacted business with Sir H. Taylor, and affixed

his signature to four documents—the remission of a court-
martial, two appointments of colonial judges, and a free
pardon to a condemned criminal. This was His Majesty's
last act of sovereignty. Increasing debility prevented
the repetition of a similar exertion ; and thus, in the
closing scene of his life, was beautifully and practically
exemplified, by an act of mercy, that spirit of benevolence and forgiveness which shone with such peculiar
lustre in His Majesty's character, and was so strongly
reflected in the uniform tenor of his reign.

"It had been arranged, as has been already remarked,
that the King should on this day receive the Sacrament
from the hands of the Archbishop of Canterbury ; and
when Sir Herbert left the room, it appeared to the Queen
that the most favourable time had arrived. The physicians, however, suggested to Her Majesty the expediency
of deferring the ceremony till the King should have in
some degree recovered from his fatigue ; but His Majesty
had already experienced the blessed consolations of religion, and removed the doubts which his anxious attendants were entertaining, by eagerly desiring the Queen to
send for the Archbishop, seeming, as it were, anxious to
ratify the discharge of his earthly, by the performance of
his spiritual duties. His Grace promptly attended, attired
in his robes, and at a quarter to eleven administered the
Sacrament to His Majesty and the Queen ; Lady Mary
Fox communicating at the same time. The King was
very calm and collected—his faculties were quite clear,
and he paid the greatest attention to the service, following it in the prayer-book which lay on the table
before him. His voice, indeed, failed, but his humble
demeanour and uplifted eyes gave expression to the
feelings of devotion and of gratitude to the Almighty,
which his faltering lips refused to utter.

"The performance of this act of religion, and this public attestation of his communion with that Church, for the welfare and prosperity of which he had more than once during his illness ejaculated short but fervent prayers, was the source of great and manifest comfort to His Majesty.

"Though the shorter form had been adopted by the Archbishop, His Majesty was, nevertheless, rather exhausted by the duration and solemnity of the ceremony; but as his Grace retired, the King said, with that peculiar kindness of manner by which he was so much distinguished, and at the same time gently waving his hand and inclining his head, 'God bless you—a thousand, thousand thanks!' There cannot be more certain evidence of the inward strength and satisfaction which the King derived from this office of religion, than, that in spite of great physical exertion, His Majesty, after the lapse of an hour, again requested the attendance of the Archbishop, who, in compliance with the wishes of the Queen, read the prayers for the Evening Service, with the happiest effect on the King's spirits. This being done, the Archbishop, naturally fearing the consequences of so much mental exertion on His Majesty's debilitated frame, was about to retire, when the King motioned to him to sit down at the table, on the opposite side of which he himself was seated. His Majesty was too weak to hold any conversation, but his spirits seemed soothed and comforted by the presence of the Archbishop, on whose venerable and benign countenance His Majesty's eye reposed with real pleasure.

"The King at this interview stretched his hand across the table, and taking that of the Archbishop, pressed it fervently, saying, in a tone of voice which was audible only to the Queen, who was seated near

His Majesty, 'I am sure the Archbishop is one of those persons who pray for me.' The afternoon of this day witnessed a still further diminution of His Majesty's strength, but in proportion to the decay of his bodily power was the increase of his spiritual hope and consolation. At nine o'clock in the evening the Archbishop was again summoned by His Majesty's desire. The King was now still less able to converse than on the last occasion; but his Grace remained more than three-quarters of an hour, supplying by his presence the same comfort to the King, and receiving from His Majesty the same silent, though expressive, proof of his satisfaction and gratitude. At length, on the suggestion of the Queen, that it was already late, and the Archbishop might become fatigued, the King immediately signified his assent that he should retire; and crossing his hands upon his breast, and inclining his head, said, as his Grace left the room : 'God bless thee, dear, excellent, worthy man—a thousand, thousand thanks.'

" The whole course of His Majesty's illness affords abundant proof not only of his composure, his patience, and his resignation, but that even when under the pressure of great pain and suffering, his mind, far from being absorbed with the sad circumstances of his own situation, was often dwelling on subjects connected either with the affairs of the country, or with the comfort and convenience of individuals.

" His Majesty rose this morning with the recollection that this was the anniversary of the Battle of Waterloo. As early as half-past eight he alluded to the circumstance, and said to Dr. Chambers : 'Let me but live over this memorable day—I shall never live to see another sunset.' Dr. Chambers said : 'I hope your

Majesty may live to see many.' To which His Majesty replied in a phrase which he commonly employed, but the peculiar force of which those only who had the honour of being frequently admitted into His Majesty's society, can fully appreciate—'Oh ! that is quite another thing.'*

"A splendid entertainment, as is well known, has been always given on this day, by the Duke of Wellington, to the officers engaged in that glorious action, and since his accession to the throne, His Majesty had himself honoured it with his presence.

"Under the present circumstances, the Duke, naturally feeling unwilling to promote any scene of festivity, had sent Mr. Greville to request the King's commands, or at least to ascertain the wishes and opinion of the Queen. Previous to the flag, annually presented by his Grace, being deposited in the guard-chamber, it had been brought to His Majesty, who, laying his hand upon it, and touching the eagle, said, 'I am glad to see it. Tell the Duke of Wellington that I desire his dinner may take place to-morrow : I hope it will be an agreeable one.' In the course of the night, the Queen observed to His Majesty, that the Archbishop had only been invited to stay till the following day—that his Grace wished to be honoured with his commands—and that he had expressed himself not only willing but anxious to stay as long as his services could be either acceptable or useful to him. The King immediately said, 'Yes ; tell him to stay. It will be the greatest blessing of God to hear that beautiful service read by him once more ;' alluding to the Liturgy of the Church of England, from the frequent use of the

* It was usually employed by His Majesty to express his dissent or incredulity with regard to any subject under discussion.

prayers of which His Majesty had been so much comforted and supported in his illness..

"*Monday, June* 19.—Though His Majesty passed a tolerably tranquil night, yet no corresponding effect was produced upon his health. Decaying nature could no longer be recruited by the ordinary sources of strength and sustenance. His Majesty, however, rose at seven, for he had at no time during his illness been confined to his bed, and had even, for some weeks, anticipated by an hour his usual time of rising. There was much in the King's language and manner this morning which bespoke his sense of approaching death. On awaking, he observed to the Queen, ' I shall get up once more to do the business of the country ,' and when being wheeled in his chair from his bed-room to his dressing-room, he turned round, and looking with a benign and gracious smile on the Queen's attendants, who were standing in tears near the door, said, ' God bless you !' and waved his hand.

"At nine o'clock, by desire of the Queen, who was naturally anxious that the hope so fervently expressed by the King on the preceding night might be gratified as soon as possible, the Archbishop entered the King's room, and was received as at all other times, with the significant tokens of joy and thankfulness, which his Grace's presence never failed to call forth.

"On this occasion the Archbishop read the Service for the Visitation of the Sick. The King was seated, as usual, in his easy chair; the Queen affectionately kneeling by his side, making the responses, and assisting him to turn over the leaves of the large prayer-book which was placed before him. His Majesty's demeanour was characterised by the most genuine spirit of devotion. Though unable to join audibly in the responses which occur in the service, yet when the Archbishop had rehearsed the articles of our Creed, His Majesty, in the fulness of his faith, and labouring to collect all the energies of sinking nature, enunciated with distinct and solemn emphasis the words, 'All this I steadfastly believe.'

"During the whole service His Majesty retained hold of the Queen's hand, and in the absence of physical strength to give utterance to his feelings, signified, by his fervent pressure of it, not only his humble acquiescence in the doctrines of our holy faith, but his grateful acknowledgment of those promises of grace and succour, which so many passages of this affecting portion of the Liturgy hold out to the dying Christian, and the belief of which His Majesty so thankfully appreciated in this his hour of need.

"With the other hand, His Majesty frequently covered his eyes and pressed his brow, as if to concentrate all his powers of devotion, and to restrain the warmed emotions of his heart, which were so painfully excited by the distress of those who surrounded him. His Majesty did not allow the Archbishop to without the usual significant expression of his gratitude, 'A thousand, thousand thanks.'

"It was when the Archbishop pronounced the solemn and truly affecting form of blessing, contained in the 'Service for the Visitation of the Sick,' that the Queen, for the first time in His Majesty's apartment, was overpowered by the weight of affliction.

"The King observed her emotion, and said, in a tone of kind encouragement, 'Bear up, bear up.'

"At the conclusion of the prayers, His Majesty saw all his children ; and as they successively knelt to kiss the hand, gave them his blessing in the most affectionate terms, suitable to the character and circumstances of each. They had all manifested the most truly filial affection to His Majesty during his illness; but on Lady Mary Fox, the eldest of His Majesty's surviving daughters, had chiefly devolved the painful, yet consolatory duty of assisting the Queen in her attendance on the King.

"The extreme caution of His Majesty, and his anxiety to avoid causing any pain or alarm to the Queen, was very remarkable. He never alluded in distinct terms to death, in Her Majesty's presence. It was about this period of the day that he tenderly besought Her Majesty not to make herself uneasy about him; but that he was already anticipating his speedy dissolution was evident from his expressions to several of his relatives. Even at this advanced stage of his disease, and under circumstances of the most distressing debility, the King had never wholly intermitted his attention to public business. In accordance with his usual habits, he had this morning frequently desired to be told when the clock struck half-past ten, about which time His Majesty uniformly gave audience to Sir Herbert Taylor. At eleven, when Sir Herbert was summoned, the King said, 'Give me your hand. Now get the things ready.' On Sir Herbert saying that he had no papers to-day, His Majesty appeared surprised, till Sir Herbert added, 'It is Monday, Sire; there is no post, and no boxes are come;' when he replied, 'Ah, true—I had forgot.' The Queen then named Sir Henry Wheatly, who had entered the apartment. The King regarded him with a gracious look, and extended his hand to him, as he did also to Dr. Davies, evidently influenced by the same motive which had prompted a similar action to Sir Herbert Taylor—a last acknowledgment of their faithful services. His Majesty then passed several hours in a state of not uneasy slumber; the Queen almost uninterruptedly kneeling by his side, and gently chafing his hand, from which assurance of her presence His Majesty derived the greatest comfort.

"During this afternoon, to such an extremity of weakness was the King reduced, that he scarcely opened his eyes, save to raise them in prayer to heaven, with a look expressive of the most perfect resignation. Once or twice indeed this feeling found expression in the words, 'Thy will be done!' and on one occasion he was heard to utter the] words, 'The Church—the Church!' and the name of the Archbishop.

"It was about nine o'clock in the evening of this day that the Archbishop visited the King for the last time.

"His Majesty's state altogether incapacitated him from joining in any act or exercise of devotion; but, as at each preceding interview, his Grace's presence proved a source of joy and consolation to the dying monarch, who strove in vain to convey any audible acknowledgements of the blessings which he sensibly enjoyed; but when, on leaving the room, the Archbishop said, 'My best prayers are offered up for your Majesty,' the King replied, with slow and feeble yet distinct utterance, 'Believe me, I am a religious man.'

"After this exertion His Majesty gently moved his hand in token of his last farewell, and the Archbishop withdrew.

"As the night advanced, a more rapid diminution of His Majesty's vital powers was perceptible.

"His weakness now rendered it impracticable to remove him into his usual bed-room, and a bed was accordingly prepared in the royal closet, which communicates

with the apartment in which His Majesty had passed
the last ten days of his life.   At half-past ten the King
was seized with a fainting fit, the effects of which were
mistaken by many for the stroke of death.   However,
His Majesty gradually, though imperfectly revived, and
was then removed into his bed.

"From this time his voice was not heard, except to
pronounce the name of his valet.   In less than an hour
His Majesty expired, without a struggle and without a
groan, the Queen kneeling at the bedside, and still
affectionately holding his hand, the comfortable warmth
of which rendered her unwilling to believe the reality of
the sad event.

"Thus expired, in the seventy-third year of his age,
in firm reliance on the merits of his Redeemer, King
William the Fourth, a just and upright king, a forgiving
enemy, a sincere friend, and a most gracious and indulgent master.

                                                "J. R. W.

"Bushey House, July 14th, 1877."

In both Houses all statesmen united in warm praises
of the late King's character.   Lord Melbourne referred
to "a loss which had deprived the nation of a monarch
always anxious for the interest and welfare of his subjects; which had deprived him of a most gracious master,
and the world of a man—I would say one of the best of
men—a monarch of the strictest integrity that it had
ever pleased Divine Providence to place over these
realms."

Sir Robert Peel added: "He did believe it was the
universal feeling of the country that the reins of
government were never committed to the hands of one
who bore himself as a sovereign with more affability

and yet with more true dignity—to one who was more
compassionate for the sufferings of others, or to one
whose nature was more utterly free from all selfishness.
He did not believe that in the most exalted or the most
humble station there could be found a man who felt
more pleasure in witnessing and promoting the happiness
of others."

While, later, the Archbishop of Canterbury stated :
" It was not many days since I attended on His Late
Majesty, during the few last days of his life, and truly
it was an edifying sight to witness the patience with
which he endured sufferings the most oppressive ; his
thankfulness to the Almighty for any alleviation under
the most painful disorders ; his sense of every attention
paid him ; his absence of all expressions of impatience ;
his attention to the discharge of every public duty to
the utmost of his power ; his attention to every paper
that was brought to him ; the serious state of his mind,
and his devotion to his religious duties preparatory to
his departure for that happy world where he hoped that
he had been called.   Three different times," added the
prelate, " was I summoned to his presence the day before
his dissolution.   He received the Sacrament first ; on
my second summons I read the Church service to him ;
and the third time I appeared, the oppression under
which he laboured prevented him from joining outwardly
in the service, though he appeared sensible of the consolations which I read to him out of our religious service.
For three weeks prior to his dissolution, the Queen sat
by his bedside, performing for him every office which a
sick man could require, and depriving herself of all
manner of rest and refection.   She underwent labours
which I thought no ordinary woman could endure.
No language can do justice to her meekness and calmness."

Miss Wynne, the "lady of quality," writing at the time, makes the following comparison :

'How strange it is that, in thinking of a departed sovereign, one can from the bottom of the heart pray, '*May my latter end be like his.*' Who that can look back some years—say to the period when we saw the Duke of Clarence at Stowe, where he was certainly endured only as an appendage of the Prince of Wales— who would have thought that he would have died more loved, more lamented, than either of his predecessors on the throne ? Least of all, who could have thought he would have died the death of a good Christian, deriving comfort and hope from religion, and every alleviation which the most devoted conjugal affection could shed over him. Even his sins seem to have poured from their foul source pure streams of comfort in the attention and affection of his children. The Queen is said to have complained that in the last days, after he well knew his situation, she never was left alone with him. The public, edified by every detail which comes to light, can feel but one regret, which is, that the Princess Victoria was not summoned to receive his blessing.

"It is very interesting to compare the appearance of the town now, with that which it wore after the death of George IV. ; *then* few, very few, thought it necessary to assume the mask of grief ; *now* one feeling seems to actuate the nation ! Party is forgotten, and all mourn, if not so deeply, quite as unanimously, as they did for Princess Charlotte. After a few days of short unsatisfactory bulletins, a prayer for the King was ordered, and sent with pitiful economy by the twopenny post, so that, though the prayer appeared in every newspaper of Saturday evening, it was received by hardly any of the London clergy in time for morning service on Sunday.

In our chapel, prayers were desired for *Our Sovereign Lord the King, lying dangerously ill;* and these introduced in the Litany just as they would have been for the poorest of his subjects! To me this simple ancient form was far more impressive than the *fancy* prayer, though it was a good one of its sort."

Such is the life of this worthy, honest, rough, and somewhat eccentric Prince, who had many virtues, and was, on the whole, a kindly, good-natured, and respectable sovereign. Something of what was good in his nature he owed to his service in the navy, while, for many of his failings, the bad example of members of his family were perhaps accountable. Unlike his eldest brother, he was true to his friends. He will always be remembered as the last sovereign of England who attempted to take his part in the old time-honoured system of government by *"King, Lords, and Commons,"* which has since given place to that of government by " Lords and Commons," and which, ere long, will give place to that of government by the last of these factors. Before he died, he was somewhat roughly taught the lesson that "the King reigns but does not govern." *

* Queen Adelaide survived till December 2nd, 1849. We have already given the list of his illegitimate children, but it is not so generally known that by Queen Adelaide he had two daughters, Charlotte Augusta, born and dying in 1819, and Elizabeth Georgine, born in December, 1820, and who lived but three months.

INDEX.

THE END.

CHARLES DICKENS AND EVANS, CRYSTAL PALACE PRESS.

TINSLEY BROTHERS' PUBLICATIONS.